Starfall

Starfall

The Starlight Trilogy
Book Two

Lauren Jade Case

ISBN Kindle: 978-1-9168887-3-9
ISBN Paperback: 978-1-9168887-2-2

Cover design: Artwork by Amira Naval,
type work by Enchanted Ink Publishing
Book interior: Evenstar Books

First print, 2025

This is for those who don't know who they are yet.
You will find and know your truth, and you will be fearless.

Other Books by
LAUREN JADE CASE

THE STARLIGHT TRILOGY:

Starlight

Starfall

THE ABNORMAL SPIES SERIES:

Bearer of Masks

Treasurer of Skulls

Content Warning

My intent with this book and this story is never to harm and I don't want to risk someone's health by not disclosing that which may cause such things. While some triggers may appear in one chapter, in one line, in large or small quantities, I never want or mean to hurt another person. And while warnings aren't required, I don't want to compromise anyone with anything. Below is a list of what the following book does contain and so now please be aware that these things are present in the story of STARFALL to some degree.

This book contains the following content warnings:
Adult language
Injuries/ injury detail
Blood/ Gore
Torture
Violence
Pregnancy/birth
Anxiety
Depression
Possession
Scenes of a sexual nature
Death/Loss of a sibling or parent
Suicide
Imprisonment
Kidnap

Pronunciation Guide

I've always loved seeing little pronunciation guides in books I've read, especially if there are difficult names or places to learn throughout them. This is my version. Obviously, as these books go on, you will come across more and more Monster types, so the list will keep expanding, but for now:

Welcome to **STARFALL MONSTER PRONUNCIATIONS 101.**

Scorpio – Scor-Pee-Oh

Calefaction – Kale-fack-shun

Jij – Jih-j

Kifflegger – K-iff-leg-er

Poena – P-oh-nah

Mitter – Mih-ter

Shadow – Shah-doh

Siltapolia — Sil-tah-poh-lee-ah

Geminis – Gem-in-ih-s

Snask – Snah-ss-k

Wiska – Whiss-kah

Chimera – Kie-meer-rah

Chiksaaz – Sh-ik-sar-z

Maddner – Mad-ner

1

Drowning in an Hourglass

THE BABY SCORPIO SLID FROM THE BLADE, turning to ash that blew off in the wind before it even hit the floor.

Natalia wiped her weapon on the wall. It'd been an easy kill, not one requiring skill or training. She did it without taking her eyes off what she'd come to see.

The last pane of glass slid into place. Weeks prior the windows had been blown out and the store wrecked completely. Threads of Shadows had stumbled around the place, searching for Natalia to steal her, who'd cowered in a corner instead of facing the threat head on.

Natalia stood across the street now, watching, her face hidden behind her hair. With no breeze, nothing revealed her. She was alone in a sea of people and refused to be seen. Venderly's residents passed by care-free. They hadn't seen the Monster.

June had started with a flurry of thunderstorms but they were mostly gone now. Just like the mess of *Katherine's Koffee and Kakes.*

Natalia had watched the progress of refurbishment all month, but always from afar. Every time new glass was put in, new furniture was brought through the doors, she was relieved. Just because she'd not been inside, it didn't mean she'd stopped caring about the café or its owner.

But she could never get closer. Bile rose in her throat at the prospect.

She turned away.

"Natalia!"

She stopped, raised her head, and turned back around. There, in the middle of the otherwise quiet road, stood Katherine.

The woman wore no smile and no lipstick. Seeing her without her two most notable things was like a thorn in Natalia's palm - it stung. Her black skin and dark hair, inches longer than before, shone under the sun. She looked *good.*

But this woman was on a march.

Natalia backed away until her back pushed into another shop's wall. She put her hands out beside her, spreading her fingers over the brick. The instinct to defend herself rose throughout her chilling body. Not that she thought Katherine would attack her.

She was wrong.

Puddle water from the road sprung up and spluttered into Natalia's face. She gasped and shook her head, then scraped her drenched hair back from her face.

"What the fuck was that for?" she half-yelled, more annoyed at herself for sticking around to be hit than the attack itself.

Katherine ignored the question, replying with one of her own. "Did you think I couldn't see you?" She didn't come too close. "I've seen you *every* day. You keep running off though, and this time I wasn't going to let you flee."

Natalia felt the water slide down her cheeks. "I shouldn't be here."

"Really?" Katherine folded her arms with an accusatory glare. "Then why do you keep coming?"

Up close, Natalia could see the flour that coated one of Katherine's cheeks and she battled with herself over reaching out and wiping it off. In the end, the need to stay back won.

Katherine waved her hands and the water droplets rose off Natalia's skin. They hung in the air and eventually returned to the puddle they'd been pulled from. Sometimes it was easy to forget Katherine was a water nymph and not Human.

The few Humans that continued to pass were as oblivious to them as before.

Natalia gulped, her heart pounding like a drum. "I had to see." Her voice came out no louder than a whisper.

"You should come inside," Katherine offered. "It's cleaner in there too."

Natalia kept her mouth firmly closed. Katherine studied her, putting her on some silent trial. But Natalia didn't want to be a specimen under a microscope.

"It's had a complete revamp," Katherine added.

Natalia attempted to smile but it felt too forced. "What colours?"

"Grey and mustard, like we'd planned before. I just had an excuse to finally do it."

An excuse because of me.

Natalia hadn't forgotten. How could she? The only reason the café had been broken was because of her. The only reason it needed redecorating was because of her. She'd ruined her work place. Worse, she'd ruined several *people*. And not once had she gone to them.

What would I even say?

Apologies covered nothing. How could she show her face to them? Surely they'd tear it off. Or kill her in cold blood. She deserved it.

The best thing, for everyone – so no one would become the murdered or the murderer – was to stay clear, to avoid them. And that's what she'd done. For the last month and a half. Her only release was a single walk every day, coming to see the café's progress and maybe a trip to the local store.

"Maybe your holiday will end soon?" Katherine suggested as she moved aside for a woman and her buggy to pass. "And you'll *have* to return."

"I don't think that would—"

"Just, think about it."

The look on Katherine's face said that the topic wasn't up for debate. The twinkle in her eye said that her heart went out to Natalia, and Natalia felt worse for it. There was no blame but Natalia felt she *should* be blamed. That Monster that day had come for *her*.

Halfway back towards her café, Katherine called over her shoulder. "I'm not sorry about the water! I just wanted to talk to you." A playful smile drew onto her lips and she left as easily as she'd come, though with more of a spring in her step.

The water had indeed frozen Natalia, giving Katherine what she wanted in the process. Now she was free again, Natalia wanted to run through the crowd. However, she walked away, head down, as if she hadn't stopped at all.

Something swooped overhead, and Natalia looked up again. She had no idea how long she'd walked for, but she was surrounded by stacks of brightly coloured metal containers. Cranes worked in the background, as did people, their shouts ringing over clanging metal. Water gently lapped the edges of the dock area nearby. She tried to swallow the thick lump in her throat but it wouldn't go away.

She was at the shipping docks.

The last time she'd been here, it had been empty and she'd needed saving.

She twisted round stacks of crates like they were a maze, trying to get to the centre.

And then stopped.

Though it looked like the ground had been scrubbed, remnants of blood remained. The concrete stained a rusty-red. Stained by a man who had tried to save her because she'd been helpless and trapped. Because she'd been wanted.

She hadn't thought about it since the incident. *Am I still wanted?* There had been no indication that she was. No Monster had tried coming for her again – only the "normal Monsters" remained, like the baby Scorpio earlier – and yet she couldn't help but feel the danger was only just beginning.

There would be another storm.

Finding no comfort and only pain, Natalia moved away. Her feet carried her until the memory had been subdued, replaced with that of salt water.

She slipped out of her sandals and dipped her toes into the sea. The cool waves touched her feet and before she knew it she was in up to her ankles. Many other people were doing the same but they likely had different reasons.

Natalia's eyes were drawn out to the faraway distance. A flash of light caught the surface of the water and for a moment she thought she caught sight of a silver fin. Her heart quickened.

She's not here. There's no silver fin!

Natalia didn't know where Peri was, or even how she was. Worse still, she didn't want to think about the baby. She hoped they were ok – she wasn't ashamed to admit to praying to the Seven Gods of Creatures to make it so – but she knew that if something had gone wrong, it was her fault.

However, there was nothing, which she took as a positive sign. No news seemed like good news. She assumed that if something *had* gone wrong, she would've heard something by now.

But that didn't stop her worrying, still fearing the worst.

Her feet padded through the water with little resistance, her sandals swinging in her grip. She kept her eyes focused forwards without looking at anything specific. No one bothered her. Why would they bother a quiet girl on a summer's day?

This time, she knew where she was headed.

A week or so ago, she'd heard about a collapsed part of the

cliffside. There'd been no gossip or real news on why it'd fallen but Natalia suspected Monsters. If there'd been a fight, it could've weakened the previously strong area.

No one stopped her from disappearing round the side.

The cliff had collapsed from the inside. The fallen parts were broken and spread across the sand, reaching for the sea. What remained now made an arch above her head. Finding no reason not to, she dipped beneath it. The sensation of walking under what had once been a full cliff gave her the same feeling walking under a ladder did – a weird panic that bubbled up from her stomach.

On the other side, Natalia peered up. Opal House loomed above. It was as if the cliff had purposely broken knowing she'd follow its pieces here. This beach had otherwise been basically private, only a rickety wooden ladder led up the cliffside towards the House. Was the world tormenting her? Or had the cliff broken to block her path?

With tears stinging her eyes and streaking down her face, she quivered. She couldn't hide from herself, no matter how much she'd tried.

When the tears dried, she shuffled away. Clearly no one was home in the house above the sea. Not that she wanted them to find her there anyway. She couldn't face them. Every minute an hourglass was filling with sand, counting the moment from *that* incident to now, counting her pain in grains. And she was being suffocated beneath it all.

In the last month, she hadn't even seen Noah. Except once. But Natalia had abandoned him early, sneaking off without a goodbye. Noah was supposed to be her best friend and he was keeping to that unsaid promise despite her pulling away.

Guilt weighed her down with no constraint. She wanted to rectify it, not just with Noah, but didn't know how or where to start.

Would anyone let her?

No. Not after what I've done.

The general store was quiet. Natalia didn't pick up a basket on her way in. She had one thing on her mind and beelined for the wine aisle. She knew now that Creature's didn't get drunk as easily as Humans, especially Fairies – they had their own drinks like Lemonspark – but that wouldn't stop her.

The aisle was clear, bar one person. Natalia seized. She took a gasping breath and managed to force herself to back away round the corner.

Natalia willed herself to become invisible – a very rare occurring Fairy ability she'd learnt about – but knew she wasn't shifting. She watched helplessly as Alex Darby came wandering towards her, whistling. Her curly hair was tied up into a lopsided bun and her self-cut fringe appeared to be growing out. Her brown skin had a suntouched glow.

Alex didn't once look in her direction.

Natalia breathed in slowly and then, to her horror, remembered Alex could hear *anything*. The girl held her breath but Alex was already turning, tantalisingly slow. She sniffed the air and Natalia tucked further round her corner until she lost sight of the Werewolf. Her heart thudded louder and louder.

Let this end. Let her walk away.

Clutching her chest, Natalia peered round the corner and Alex was indeed walking away.

Stealing her chance, Natalia ran down the wine section, grabbed what she wanted and sprinted for the checkouts, picking snacks in a hurried frenzy along the way. The cashier gave her an odd look and Natalia wiped her face and paid before he could ask if she was alright.

The whole way home, she kept peering over her shoulder. The main thrum of people had disappeared from the streets but that meant nothing. If Alex had sensed her, the girl would've chased her down.

Diving for her front door the second she saw it, Natalia slammed it shut behind her and rested her head against the frame.

For several seconds she counted her sharp intakes of breath. Then, she walked away, leaving behind what had happened outside. This house was her safe space. She didn't need to bring anything negative inside with her.

Her dad was in the kitchen. Something was bubbling on the oven-top but he wasn't tending to it. Instead he leaned next to it, arms folded, one leg crossed over the other. His eyes, lined with wrinkles, found her across the room.

"How was your walk?" he asked.

From the first moment she'd been going on them, her dad had known about it. He'd been surprised at first. But she'd explained that it was her way of getting out without doing much. She didn't like being stuck at home, but it was for the best. A walk a day was a compromise between the depressing monotony she'd enforced and the life that was out of reach now.

"I went for some supplies," she said, placing the bag on the table.

"Is that all? Did you go and see Katherine?"

Since the first time Natalia hadn't shown up for work, her dad had tried to convince her to talk to Katherine. But cutting people out had been easier than explaining her weaknesses. Katherine *had* graciously given her time off without being asked to allow it and hadn't even tried contacting her - Natalia suspected her dad and Katherine talked secretly - until today.

Natalia stared at her father. The roots of his hair were greying. He'd grown out a grey beard and moustache in the last couple of weeks too which suited him. Under the kitchen yellow lights, his stare was dark, eyes emerald in colour.

"I saw her," Natalia said.

"And?" he pressed. "What did she say?"

Natalia looked out the window. "She told me to think about coming back."

He huffed and shifted his legs over. "And are you going to think about it?"

She turned back to find concern written in his expression. *Beats me,* was what she wanted to say. Honestly though, she didn't know if she *was* going to think about it. Katherine was willing to take her back, despite the damage she'd caused, but that didn't mean she should return. The possibility of it all happening again was greater than before, especially if whoever wanted her was still roaming around. They'd be more desperate this time, more dangerous.

Deciding to forgo answering, she asked, "What's for tea?"

Her dad sighed. "Vegetable stew," he answered, moving from the counter to stir the contents of the saucepan. "With dumplings."

"It's summer?" Natalia said in question.

Her dad laughed; a noisy yet welcomed sound – it sent Natalia's mouth twitching into a ghost of a smile. "Would it be better if we ate outside?" he suggested. "Would it make it more summery?"

Natalia nodded and pulled down two glasses an overhead cupboard. She fought with the top of the wine before it twisted open, then poured it into the glasses.

She watched her father labour over the food. Stew was one of her favourites and she *knew* he was making it for her. He knew what she'd been through, he'd been told, but not the extent of how hard it'd hit her. To him, this was just another thing he did for her to make sure she had all she could. To her, it was much more than that.

Her eyes welled with tears and she turned away to get them under control.

To get away, she set the table outside. The garden itself needed work – the weeds pulling and the grass seeding and watering – but it was a pretty place to eat in summer. Branches from the neighbours' cherry blossom tree hung over the fence to create shade for part of the small enclosure; though the pink flowers had dried and were gone now they were in the summer months. Birds flew in and out of the space, usually dipping in for their bath and diving off again towards the cliff and sea beyond.

Dinner came and went with little chatter. Her dad either waited for her to comment or had decided on his own conversation that wouldn't evoke reaction - like his job. By the end, they were stuffed and slumped in their chairs, sipping at their second glass of wine each; she could only afford the treat now her Creature salary was being paid out.

"I spoke to Sarah today."

Natalia was thankful for the overprotective grip she had on her glass. She lowered it to the table, hand shaking, and pushed it away.

Her father didn't notice the displacement in her emotions. He faced the garden, glass to his lips. "They haven't heard from you," he continued.

"Oh?" She made it sound like a surprise.

He swivelled and his glare landed on her; she wondered if his eyes could see the layers underneath her fake shock. "Natalia." His voice was low, solemn. "Sarah said they haven't seen or spoken to you in about a *month.*"

Natalia was sure her face was cracking. "She did?"

"Yes and you know they did. You haven't seen or spoken to them, have you?" Natalia remained silent, which she was sure that gave her away more. He shrank as he sighed. "You barely leave the house anymore."

"I get some fresh air outside in this garden every day," she argued meekly.

"A walk every so often isn't much!"

Natalia reached for her glass again, downed the contents, and slammed it on the table. She had loved the Darby's. *Still* loved them. They'd supported her when she could barely stand. They'd shown her the path through life. They'd had her back the whole way.

And all she'd done was bring them closer to ruin.

"The baby's fine."

Natalia choked on air. "*What?*"

Her dad's features softened. His eyes seemed to plead with her, trying to communicate the need to go and see them. Or to simply reach out, one hand at a time.

"When I spoke to Sarah, she said the baby is fine. Healthier than ever."

Blinking, Natalia tried to control her welling eyes. Her cheeks heated, and she fanned her face like it was just the sun affecting her. "Good. That sounds good."

"Peri's at about five or six months now. But..." His voice turned sad. "Apparently, no amount of magic could reattach her arm."

"Oh." Her voice shook and she dared not say another word.

Natalia forced the images of limp arms that'd sprung to mind away. Whenever she closed her eyes, it was all she could see: Peri and Archie being trapped by a Calefaction, Jasper being manipulated inside out by a Shadow, Kiva and her parents. And then there was the scariest part: the hooded figure being unaffected by her blade and even using it themselves.

"Peri's adjusting," her father reassured her, not seeing how her mind had strayed. "Archie's fine too. Sarah and James are sorting things out. Alex has a broken wrist and ribs." Natalia couldn't remember seeing a cast when she'd spotted the girl, but it'd just been a passing glance. "And Jasper's a little cut up, but they're healing."

Her heart pounded like a hammer against molten iron, trying to wield her. But she refused to be reshaped. Furiously, she wiped at her stinging eyes.

The baby was fine. Everyone was alive. That was better than she'd thought. They were healing and Peri was adjusting.

Still, she couldn't let herself feel relief.

"I'm going upstairs." Natalia scurried away, leaving no room for her father to argue.

On the way past, she stole the half empty wine bottle and drank without care, stumbling into her room, more from the mess than intoxication.

Paint splotches dotted her wall - she had been planning to redecorate but hadn't found the motivation to even pick colours, let alone pick up a brush. Her bed was rumpled, at least ten more pillows than necessary scattered over it. Her carpet was plucked in one corner but it was hidden beneath dirty laundry. Even her wardrobe doors were splayed open, clothes slung haphazardly inside.

Natalia slumped onto her bed, spilling drops of wine along the sheet's edges. She dug her phone out of her back pocket. At least ten messages and missed calls lit the screen. She ignored them all, deleting them without reading.

What she did look at was two pictures in her phone's album. The first was of her and Peri descending the stairs in Atlantis together, dressed up for the Flower Parade. She sniffed and flipped to the next, taken later that same evening. She and Jasper were dancing. Their bodies were tight yet they smiled, though the expressions weren't as bright as Natalia knew they could both be. Their photo had been taken *after* their awkward little encounter by someone they hadn't seen.

They're ok.

Fresh tears burned once more, Natalia swigged the last of the wine and dumped the bottle on the floor. She heard it fall but didn't care to pick it up. Rolling over, she dialled a number.

Ten minutes later, Noah arrived, standing in her bedroom doorway like he didn't quite know what to do with himself. He had a little patchy beard and moustache growing. The braces were gone, and now so was the retainer. He wore a yellow and white checked shirt that slung off one shoulder and his loose jeans were rolled up at the ankles.

Natalia knew how she looked in comparison. Ratty and unkempt hair, circles under her red eyes, a slightly hollowed face and body, and a "throw it on" outfit. Bronze sheens and lights didn't touch her much – she was paler than before too.

She wondered if Noah felt like he was staring at a Monster.

She dreaded what he had to say. So when he opened his mouth, she hung onto her breath for the attack. There wasn't one. All he said was, "You rang, Princess?"

They set up a film and scrambled into her bed together – really, Noah did most of the work. The set-up was the same as it had been for all of their friendship; movie, popcorn, and blankets. The only difference was the bottle of wine Natalia had found while making the popcorn.

"You're going to be incredibly drunk," Noah told her.

"I won't," she promised.

He watched her chug a third of the bottle. "I want to disagree."

"This is my second bottle and I feel fine," she said honestly. There was no light-headedness or blurry vision. It had been that way her whole life when alcohol had been involved and that should've been her first clue that she wasn't really Human, that she was different.

Noah took the bottle and drank. He pushed the bottle away, coughing. "How can you drink that stuff?"

Natalia shrugged again. "I like it."

"Remind me to bring something better to drink next time."

Next time. Natalia liked the sound of that.

With nothing else to say, they turned to the movie.

The further the film went, the more Natalia fell into Noah's side. It was a moment of weakness, a moment of conceding, when she sank completely so her head rested in his lap. As he began to stroke her hair, a single tear dropped from her eye. This time, she refused to wipe it away.

He didn't ask anything. Not why his messages went unanswered or why she'd wanted to suddenly see him today. And she knew he never would. He accepted her as she was, he always had. But would he accept her if she revealed herself as the Monster she thought herself to be? She didn't want to hold that answer, so knew she could never divulge her glass heart's truths.

But while she still had one friend, she clung to it. Even if she wouldn't admit needing and wanting him.

Eventually, the movie ended. Neither of the friends moved. At first, Natalia wondered if Noah had fallen asleep. Then she realised he was tangling his fingers in her hair still.

"Next time," he said quietly, "we should get take-away."

Next time, there were those words again.

"I think I could manage that," she agreed.

Noah's hands paused. "There'll be a next time?"

Natalia sat up and forced herself to look at him. She could see his apprehension but she could see his hopefulness too. For that alone, she said, "Yes."

"Good to hear, Princess. I'll try and fit you into my diary. I'm a busy man, you know? Between work and work, and not much else." He laughed, genuinely amused by himself.

Natalia swallowed the lump in her throat. "Work's going well?"

"It's fine. A little busy since you're not there." He glanced at the blank TV as if he'd said something wrong and needed to disguise it.

"What?"

"It's fine."

"Noah? What is it?"

There was a wince on his lips. "Alex picked up some of your shifts."

Natalia blanched. "Alex?"

"She came in the other week, saying she'd pick up your shifts if Katherine would let her," he explained slowly. "I don't know why."

"Katherine agreed?"

He nodded. "She's been working ever since."

Katherine hadn't mentioned that earlier, but why would she? She wasn't part of the "team". It did make Natalia wonder what Alex was doing. Did she need money? Alex had never had the clearest intentions, and this was just another blur to her overall picture. Natalia had been worried about Noah and Katherine struggling with the workload, but at least she knew they had help from someone trustworthy.

Noah shuffled to the edge of the bed. "I better get going," he said, and stood. "Early shift tomorrow."

She didn't follow but, when he reached the door, called, "Noah?" He turned back wordlessly. *Tell Alex I said hi.* "Thank you," she said instead.

He rubbed his chin. "What for?"

"For being my friend." Natalia touched her starry earrings, feeling a little awkward and embarrassed.

Noah's expression softened. "It's not a choice I can opt in and out of. Whenever shit happens, we stick together. I've always needed you more than you've needed me, so this is a little weird." He stuck out his tongue when she threw a pillow at him. "But I could get used to being needed."

Her heart weakened further. "I *always* need you, Noah."

"And I'm always here." He walked back over and kissed the top of her head. "For you to need me is special *and* troubling. Whatever you're going through, I'm here for you."

You wouldn't be if you know what I've done, what I caused. She saw Shadows, bodies, blood.

"Noah—"

"Princess," he cut in. "I'm on your side. You just have to call and I'll be here. For whatever you need. Whether it's a distraction, to figure this out, or for nothing but to waste a few hours."

He kissed her head again and checked her face over once more, and left. The door downstairs slammed behind him before Natalia could even formulate a reply to make him stay.

Natalia sat alone, her bed growing colder. He *had* been a good distraction. A few hours' worth of mindful peace - peace where no ghosts had come to haunt her. But those hours ended. She would always end up here.

She knew what Noah had been trying to say, she could read between the lines. But would she *ever* be ready? From what she'd heard, everyone was doing fine. *Better* even, without her there. All she had done was cause chaos.

Away from them, she could face what was coming without hurting those she loved more. She might be alone, but that was safer, especially for the Darby's. Because someone *was* after her, even if they hadn't come recently. At least now they couldn't use those she cared about against her.

Natalia hugged a pillow to her chest. As clear as it was that someone wanted her, she still didn't understand why and what for.

What makes me special? What could I be any good for?

For all she'd done, she was hardly any different from the Monsters she'd sworn to protect the world from. So what could anyone want from her? What would draw their attention to her?

As long as I stay away...

But spending time with Noah made her yearn for the others. The company of her friend had healed the smallest part of her, but it wasn't enough to heal the wounds cut into her heart and soul. Still, she would take those pieces to her grave if it meant protecting them all.

She touched the wine bottle to her lips and willed herself to get drunk as she drained it. She didn't. Just another curse, another thing taken from her. *Lemonspark*, the word whispered through her mind, followed by the memory attached to it.

Jasper.

The urge to scream clawed up her throat. She suppressed the need but did throw the wine bottle. It smacked against the floor and the entire bottom broke off, glittering in the fading light that seeped through her curtains.

She slid off the bed, curling her knees up. Pain raced along her joints and organs. It wasn't physical pain, but it felt like she was being held hostage underwater. The shaky breaths did nothing substantial to fill her lungs.

Through tired eyes, she could see bronze dust rise from her skin. Zoning back in as it drew her attention, she stuttered a gasp and scrambled to her feet.

The Heaven's had landed in her room through her dust. Her bronze had created several constellations; no space was untouched by her unbridled power. The dust floated in bronze waves, shining and dancing and controlling until it was all she could see. Her bedroom was gone, vanished, leaving her in darkness with only the stars as companions.

And then it changed.

Through the dusted stars, an image appeared. A bronze woman. Dust-made flowers were woven through her long hair. She smiled and drew closer. The woman's hand reached out and her knuckles grazed Natalia's cheeks.

She disintegrated on impact.

The dust settled into nearby constellations again, with Natalia at the centre of the universe she had summoned. Who had that woman been? Why was Natalia's heart pounding like never before? She touched her face and found her cheeks wet.

Once again, the dust began to shift. A man came forward next, and Natalia knew who the dust had drawn instantly. The wavy hair said it all. The smirk was extra. Natalia didn't need the dust to shift and change colour to see green eyes or freckles, her mind did that for her. Her lips twitched at the corners; she always *had* compared his freckles to constellations.

She grabbed her blade from its hidden place and sliced through the image. And Jasper was gone.

However, instead of giving up, the dust persisted cruelly. Next came a Calefaction; it didn't roar or stomp, only watched with glowing eyes. Natalia's body refused to turn from it, but she did step back. And she did try searching for a way out, holding onto her blade with all her remaining resolve.

How were her powers doing this? Was her dust supposed to create space-scapes and then mould visions? Was this even her doing or was something else controlling the dust? Was that possible?

The beast melted.

Her tiny stars stopped shifting and pulled her back to their centre. Out of the blackest edges, a Shadow crawled out. It weaved through the dust like it meant nothing.

It had red eyes.

Nothing else had a colour other than bronze, but those red eyes burned, and Natalia's eyes widened at the sight. This Shadow was *real*.

Natalia whirled around and lunged for where she thought her window might be. The Shadow had other ideas, ensnaring her ankle in its hand as she attempted to escape. She was slammed into the ground and her dust came raining down around her.

As she reappeared in her room, the Shadow didn't leave. She was lying in a puddle of bronze, a Monster hunching over her.

"Your dust allowed me here," the Shadow said. It used a voice Natalia had heard elsewhere, and she somehow knew that it didn't belong to this Monster – it was too alive.

"I didn't allow you here," Natalia managed to say as she struggled.

The Shadow's grip tightened. "There is magic here and not just your dust," it claimed, head turning away from her.

Natalia kicked but it was useless. "There is *no* magic!"

The Shadow ignored her. "It is protecting you. I could only come because you created a literal space that anything magical could walk through. That's what your dust did." It turned back to her, eyes glowing. "You're powerful, more than you even know."

Nothing's protecting me, except me!

She wanted to scream the words. There were no guards, no swords, no friends, and certainly no magical protection. *If* there was magic, surely she would've noticed some, and she hadn't. She grabbed at her blade, which had conveniently fallen beside her.

"You may be beyond my reach, and my Shadow *will* die—"

Natalia stabbed towards the Shadow and it was a direct hit. It tumbled into a pile of black ash with a single lilac petal falling on top.

She scurried away, hiding beneath the window where no one could see if they peered in from the balcony. She summoned her blade and held it out as she hugged herself.

She sobbed silently.

There was her proof that someone was still searching for her. It had been in her *room*. The very space over the last month that had become sacred because it had been the only place left untainted by bad moments so heavy they soaked into the walls.

As willing as she thought she was to accept that someone wanted her, clearly her head had thought one thing and her heart felt another.

If she had the will, she would've called the Darby's there and then, begging for their forgiveness, pleading with them to put a barrier around her house, not for her but for her father.

Yet she didn't. She didn't deserve their kindness or help, so she remained on the floor in a huddled mess. She refused to move in case something returned. She didn't call for her father, hoping he was blissfully unaware of what had just happened.

She cried, clinging to her blade like it was the only lifeline she had.

Wounds of a Thousand Hearts

Zoe came inside and chucked her skates down, and shushed them when they made noise like it hadn't been her fault they'd clattered against the floor and wall.

She cursed when the stair light turned on.

"Zo?" Her mother's sweet voice called.

"Right here," Zoe answered. There was no point hiding.

"It's one in the morning! Get to bed!"

Zoe ran up the stairs two at a time and zipped past her mother, shutting her bedroom door as quick as she could. Her mother sighed on the other side. The hallway light turned off, the glow vanishing from the crack at the bottom of the door, and footsteps padded away.

"Zo-zo."

Zoe slammed the light on, nearly shouting before she remembered the time. She showed her brother who lay sprawled across her bed her middle fingers. Noah laughed quietly.

She walked to him and slapped his shoulder. "I could've had a 'eart attack."

"Heart," he corrected, like always.

"What are you *doing* in here?" The bed squeaked as she joined him on it.

"Camping out."

"Hiding from mum?" she challenged.

Noah sat up. "While you were out..." He trailed off. "How did that go?"

"How did going out go?"

"That's what I asked."

Noah folded his arms and Zoe groaned, seeing how unrelenting he was. He wouldn't be the first to answer anything. "She was fine," Zoe said. "But it's not going to work out."

He studied her. "So you went skating, with your friends?"

"After the date was over." She slumped back, taking the spot he'd been in, and draped her head over the edge of the bed. "Now tell me what you were goin' to say."

"Going."

"Whatever," she dismissed easily.

"I saw Natalia."

Zoe bolted upright again. She looked into the eyes that were mirrors of her own. They were as much alike as they weren't. His hair was neatly kept and hers was fluffy, slung in a single braid. Her skin was as black as his, though she wore gold shimmers on her high-cheekbones to accentuate it. She had a piercing, a small silver hoop, in the top section of her ear.

Noah seemed to want to say more but looked conflicted.

For months, since his secret trip to wherever-land, it was like he'd had something to hide. He'd never said where he'd gone or why he'd neglected to tell their parents, and he'd definitely not said why he'd gone. Zoe might've been sixteen – seventeen on the twenty-second of June – but she was sure she'd understand whatever was going on. If only Noah would tell her.

"She's not doing so great," Noah continued.

"How *not great* are we talking?"

"Before today, I hadn't seen her for over a month."

Zoe grimaced. "Has she told you what's going on?"

He shook his head firmly. "No."

Sounds familiar. And Zoe was Hell bent on finding out *what* was happening. She just had to be careful. She wasn't above following Noah; she'd already crept behind him in the shadows to several places but there'd been nothing.

One day he'd slip up and she'd be there, ready.

Zoe flicked her braid over her shoulder. "Just be 'er friend and she'll come when she's ready."

"*Her* friend," he corrected.

Noah got off the bed and left, vanishing without a word. She had nothing to say to him to make him stop. The door closed behind him gently.

Evangeline nestled into her favourite reading chair with her back to the window, the sun beaming in behind her, and cracked open a poetry book titled *A Kingdom of Queens*.

Reading had always been her most precious down-time activity. Reading poetry was the sweetest. The best kind had been what her husband used to create. He'd found recognition because of it, especially back in Atlantis.

His ashes rested there now, his own lines etched into one of the memorial walls below his name – "*The body may leave, but our heart and soul linger in others, and so we never die*". To anyone else, it sounded morbid. But Evangeline saw the beauty. It meant that as long as someone out there remembered a person, love kept them alive. The words served as a reminder that love was precious, no matter the length of time together or apart. And though he was gone, he was still with her.

As were their children.

She closed the book and glanced at the mantle, at the few brown, black, and white framed photographs. One held all five members of the family together – Evangeline had been forty then, as had her husband. Their youngest, the twins, Damien and Maddison, were barely older than toddlers. Patrick, the eldest – he was five years older than his siblings – had already started to want to wear his father's top hat everywhere.

With every passing dawn Evangeline missed them. They were never far from her mind. Or heart. While the pain remained – for true pain over missing loved ones never vanished, either – her love for them kept her going.

A long time ago she'd faced the facts. She'd been some type of Creature first – it was still uncertain *what* exactly – and had then been bitten and turned into a Vampire. That Creature type alone lived longer than most if uninjured or unkilled. Now she was paying that price. And then tenfold for the anomaly she'd become.

Anger no longer raged inside at the thought. She'd been incredibly lucky to have a family in the first place. Never had she imagined she'd be able to have one, not after everything, not even with Witch intervention. And yet, she'd been blessed by the Seven Gods with three wonderful, *beautiful* children.

One day, she knew she'd be with them again. Reunited where all Creature spirits are said to connect at the gates of Heaven upon death. But until she could go, she lived on, gathering stories she would eventually share.

Someone knocked at her door.

Not many people knew where she lived these days. Only the Council, Gold, and now Sarah and James Darby. They still had no idea who *exactly* she was, but they were in charge of a Fairy who wasn't quite a Fairy it seemed, so she'd given them her residency in case they needed to contact her. After all, she knew about difficult cases.

She went to the door, book still in hand, and called, "Hello?"

"Message, Madam," claimed a voice outside.

She wanted to laugh. No one called her "madam" anymore. "From whom?"

"Gold, madam."

Evangeline opened the door to a pasty male, no older than twenty. He stretched out his hands to prove he carried a yellow envelope. The boy raced off the second she took it. Shaking her head, she closed the door again.

What's Gold sending me now?

She put her book onto the shoe-rack, tore open the envelope, and read:

My dearest Eva,

I do hope this finds you, if not, I will drain the life out of my messenger boy. I would've sent this via the clouds, but I have both run out of your magic – which I must ask you for a little more of to have in reserve – and no longer trust in who watches the skies these days.

Evangeline knew what Gold spoke of.

The incident with Natalia. The poor girl had been stolen and trapped, and was said to be wanted. After all Evangeline had experienced, she could believe in why Gold didn't trust in certain things these days. If Natalia was being hunted, then who knew the extent of what they'd do to get their hands on her.

Instead of pondering all her questions about the situation, she read on.

I feel our new friend with wings needs guidance – I do not know what with, why, or how I know, only that I do and feel so strongly that we should offer ourselves anyway.

I also sense a storm on the horizon and it is not to be a pretty one. If what we've already seen and heard of is the smallest measure of what's coming, I suspect our friends will need our hands and hearts.

I hope this receives you well.

Always,
Your golden friend.

P.S. I implore you to eat or burn this once done.

The last time Evangeline had been around the girl, she'd been performing a pregnancy test on her friend, the mermaid, Peri. Even then there'd been something almost *charged* about her. Even with Evangeline's back to her, she'd felt it.

A storm indeed.

Gold knew what it meant to ask Evangeline to join him. But she knew he wouldn't ask unless he saw no other way. She'd left the world of actively fighting many years ago, she still remembered the steps. Accepting this would throw her back into the thick of it all for the first time in about one hundred years.

She sighed heavily, the weight of her decision already forming above her.

Bending, she lit the fireplace with a snap of her fingers and threw the note into the roaring red and orange flames. As the paper crackled, the untouched, silently picture watched her from the mantle.

The vibrant colours would've been comforting had they not been covering patches of rust.

Somehow, Natalia knew she was dreaming. She didn't appear like a ghost, more like a fully-formed girl walking her memories while unconscious. But that didn't alleviate the pain or settle her stomach.

She'd been here in real-life once since the incident at the yard, just yesterday – a month and a half had passed since the actual incident and returning to it. Yet this place was imprinted on her mind enough that she saw it even when asleep.

Towers had been made of the shipping containers that imported and exported goods from Venderly. A crane that lifted them to and from the ships sat dead, the claw swinging as it being blown. Gentle, lapping water trickled nearby.

BANG!

Natalia's head whipped around, her hair crashing around her shoulders. Something had hit a metal shipping container. What one? What was here with her?

The sound of footsteps overpowered her senses, capturing her. She tiptoed after them, using what little grace and elegance left in her body to her advantage.

She crept through the man-made maze of metal. Her hands swept over one container, touching the rough patches. When she realised what she was doing, she yanked back – she didn't need another cut, even in a dream, even if it wasn't real here.

The area ahead was open, spanning wide like the world was showing itself off. A familiar girl stood in the centre.

The girl was her.

Natalia stared at herself; the long hair, shabby clothes, and the built over a few months fighting figure.

But that past version of herself wasn't alone.

Kei – she was a Geminis, a Monster meant to be friends and on the Creature's side but really a traitor – was at past Natalia's side. Natalia wanted to shout. To yell at the Monster dragging her further away from her friends and family and closer to the docks. To shout in the hope that this would all stop and she would wake up.

The noise lodged in the throat, as if the universe was telling her how little control she had here. Whether it was because this incident had already happened, a mere memory, or that she literally had no power anywhere, or something else entirely, she didn't know.

Those ahead began to walk faster. Natalia's body shuddered watching them, remembering how tight Kei's grasp had been. It hadn't been the power of a threat that'd kept her walking. It had been fear. Fear and confusion. Two very powerful things.

Now Natalia knew what waited at the end of the march, the incident that had quite possibly incited something infinitely more dangerous.

She reached for her blade and found nothing. As a last-ditch attempt, she threw herself in front of past her and Kei.

Nothing happened.

Natalia read the quiet terror and betrayal on her own face, and the steely determination on Kei's. They never saw her, a ghost inside her very own memory.

She remembered now knowing what to feel or why this was happening to her. Her questions had gone unanswered.

Those three questions rattled around inside Natalia's brain, causing her to shiver every time her mind brought them up.

Helplessly, she watched her figure, along with Kei's, disappear towards a fate she was still only starting to unravel.

In anger, frustration, and pain, she screamed.

Peri stuck Archie's hand to her bare stomach. Tiny kicks rippled against his palm, and stopped nearly as soon as they'd started. It didn't matter. He couldn't stop smiling. Their little fish was growing and Archie was becoming more excited with each passing minute.

They'd had their six month scan a few days ago in Atlantis. It was a skill only mastered by a Vampire with a Crystal, but Witches needed to aid in capturing the baby on film. A woman named Evangeline had been the one to do it at a local centre - she'd been the one to confirm Peri's pregnancy in the first place - though she made it clear it wasn't something she did often.

The second they'd come home, Peri had framed the black and white scan, hanging it on the bedroom wall.

Peri flipped down her sleeping t-shirt. "What do you think?"

Archie cupped her face. "That you're doing a wonderful job." He kissed her swiftly but didn't pull too far back.

She laughed against his lips. "No," she argued. "What do you think we're *having?*"

Gender reveals, they'd learnt, with Creature babies were harder to do than with Humans. Just like with the pregnancy tests, gender reveals required a Vampire. Peri and Archie had decided to leave it a secret, though sometimes he wished he knew, so he could begin spoiling them - a purchase of rabbit covered socks *had* been made already.

"I don't know," he answered. He'd thought long and hard about it, but it didn't matter in the end. As long as they were healthy and happy.

"Neither do I." She brushed her growing bump. "But I'm hoping for a little girl."

"A mini you?"

Peri grinned like a shark swimming up behind a trapped seal. "My plan of having an army is beginning!"

Archie choked on a laugh. "If even just this one is like you, they'll be a handful." She swatted for him and he jumped away just in time. "You want a whole army of tiny menaces?"

"Well, maybe one or two more."

The look on her face was a nervous, almost embarrassed, one.

They hadn't discussed exactly having *one* child - they'd not been careful though, having not used any form of contraception - let alone expressing their wishes for the future. They might've been young, but most Creatures had families young, and Archie was ready. He was ready because Peri was ready. But if Peri wanted an army, or just a couple of terrors, he wanted it all too. As long as it was with her. *Always* her.

He extended a hand and she graciously accepted it, allowing herself to be pulled close, but not quite as close as they used to be able to get. She wiggled her stomach against his as she laughed. He wanted to kiss those lips that allowed her joy to be expressed, wanted to always hear her make those noises. He kissed the top of top of her head, then her temples, and settled then for holding her hand as she smiled up at him through her lashes.

At most, three months was all they had left like this. The baby's due date was September sixth. Creatures, more often than not, were born early. There were *very* rare occasions when that wasn't the case, usually because of problems, so Archie wondered if they'd make it to that expected date.

They moved through the house, carefully taking the stairs down to the kitchen. Archie helped ease Peri onto a barstool. She sighed as she sat. He went round the counter and slid some bread under the grill – Peri's preferred toast-making way. He grabbed the thick peanut butter for her and some sweet jam for himself.

After a minute, Archie flipped the toast and shoved it back under. "Have you thought about names?" He turned to Peri, finding her snacking on some grapes.

"I have," she admitted. "But none of them *feel* right. I wanted, if it was a boy, to name it after my grandfather, Mattias. He'd cared for me most out of my family, and I know he'd be honoured, but..."

"It doesn't feel like enough."

Archie had heard the stories of Peri's grandfather Mattias. He'd cared for her when she was sick. He'd thrown her in the sea and taught her how to change between feet and fin. He'd read to her on stormy nights. He'd bought her a scooter she used to ride up and down the roads and curves of Atlantis. He was all about family. He'd loved her when no one else had. Peri had said that her grandfather would want the love and care he bestowed upon others to be passed along, and leave his name as his – a partially prideful man, wanting to be known for who he was and what he did but not completely shared.

"He'd *sempre* said about using strong names, that they were important." She shoved in another grape as wetness brewed in her eyes. "Have you come up with anything?"

Archie shook his head. "Nothing."

"We'll figure something out."

"Maybe we should get some of those baby books people go on about?"

"What? So we can name the baby Rubella or Glorious or something?"

"They both sound like diseases."

"If you hate them, what about Cherry-Blue or Sixx?"

Archie laughed as Peri shoved in the final grape, grinning.

The smell of toast rose and reminded him where they were. He rescued the slices and gave Peri hers, a thick layer of peanut butter slathered on top. Despite her snacking, she munched through three slices – nicking one of Archie's.

The letter box rattled. Archie left Peri with his leftover crusts – he still wouldn't eat them, even at this age – and went to see what post there was.

Lying on the floor was a yellow envelope. He opened it.

My dear boy, Archie.

I do hope this finds you, if not, I will drain the life out of my messenger boy.

*I had specific instructions for this to be delivered to you out of the family –
you are the most reliable. Though, if this is Peri, hello my dear girl. I do miss
your blue smile.*

*Though this may appear odd, please do have your family around you in an
hour or so from when you read.*

*Always,
Your golden friend.*

P.S. I implore you to eat or burn this once done.

"Peri?" Archie called through.

"Sì?" She mumbled back, her mouth clearly full.

"Where's your phone?"

"My what?"

"Your phone!"

"Why?"

"And you might want to get dressed." He knew she wouldn't see this as him telling her what to do. If he ever said anything, it was an advisory, something she could take or leave as she wanted.

Archie heard a chair scuff and then Peri appeared in the doorway. "Why? What's going on?"

Waving the letter and preparing to set it alight with the green sparks under his fingers, he answered her.

Jasper watched his mother manipulate the Monster, folding it like a piece of paper. The Wiska's six legs contorted until they were all bent at nearly ninety degrees. It shrieked and cried in response.

Jasper, while he'd read about Wiskas, had never seen one. They were supposed to have magnetic-looking purple bodies and move like giant bugs – the same way a Scorpio did. Through his reading, he also knew they never travelled in groups of more than three at a time and lived in sandy, desert areas so they could burrow. Why, then, was this one here?

His mother waved her arms, making them cross at the elbows, and finished the move. The Monster's back popped. It fell apart, limbs turning to purple ash, the same magnetic purple as its body had been.

This had been an interesting shopping trip.

"Well," his mother said, brushing her hands together. She lifted the shopping bags again, though this time with some obvious discomfort in her left shoulder – she'd been caught there by a Wiska when it'd first attacked. "Let's get home."

"We need to move faster," Jasper told her, already walking on again.

She kept up. "Why?"

"Archie texted me."

"What did he say?"

"That we need to have a little family get-together."

Her eyes slid to him in accusation. "This better not be one of your party ideas."

Jasper smirked. "I don't have party ideas! And if I did, why would I tell you *before* it started?"

She averted her gaze, shaking her head. "Good point."

They turned down Opal Street and their house came into view. His mother sped up even more. Jasper let her go on ahead. He'd hoped for one *day* where the outside world wouldn't descend to some level of stupidity.

It seemed that wasn't going to be today.

Natalia swore to herself that if the person on the other side of the door knocked one more time, she'd smack them with that morning's Island newspaper.

As she swung the door in, the thought vanished.

Of all the people she'd been expecting, Gold hadn't been it.

His rich blond hair was slicked back, showing off a new cut just above his left eyebrow. The obnoxious monocle he wore religiously still sat on his face, enhancing his golden eye. His suit was black velvet today. Natalia grimaced, wanting to pull back at the sight of his fangs. The only reason she didn't was because he was sucking at a metal straw jammed into a juice box, looking slightly ridiculous.

"Why are you here?" Natalia asked bluntly, considering shutting the door.

"Good morning to you too, my dear," Gold replied. He removed the straw from his teeth, revealing a trail of red on his lips and tongue – had *blood* been in that box? She shivered. "I might say you look dreadful, just to even out the compliments, or lack thereof."

Natalia sighed. She hadn't meant to be so awful, she was just tired. "Sorry."

Gold bowed his head. "As am I. Though, may I make a suggestion?" She knew he would anyway, so nodded. "You might want to consider leaving the house. Maybe get some sun to touch you? It is summer, after all, and you look a little pale."

Natalia groaned. She knew how pale she looked. She moved out of the way of the door. "Want to come in?"

Gold stepped inside and wiped his shoes. He paced towards the stairs but stopped before climbing, sitting on them instead.

Closing the door, she turned to him. "Have I done something wrong?"

"No, my dear."

"I haven't seen you in—"

"A month or so, I think it is now." He pulled out his eccentric pocket-watch, observed something, and stuffed it back.

Natalia huffed. "Why are you here?"

Gold put his straw into his breast pocket and threw the box into the hallway bin as he stood, smoothing out his suit. "You seem to have gone missing from the world."

Natalia knew that. She'd been the one to remove herself from it. The glint in Gold's blue eye said that'd he'd suspected as much but could now read it across her face.

She shut her face down, keeping it as blank as she could.

"I'm here for you," he continued.

"To collect me?" she said, remembering the last time she'd said those words. From the smile on Gold's lips, he was remembering too. But that was a different situation, a different time.

"No, my dear. I'm here to take you to your Council review."

Natalia stared. The review had been pushed back more than once, though she knew it had to come around eventually. It was to check on the training progress, which there was none. She'd hoped to have more weeks of reprieve, more weeks to prepare for the truth to come out. Her heart hammered, and she touched her earrings, hoping to subdue the itch in her back by distracting her mind.

Gold stalked towards her. Natalia knew what would come next. They were going to magically jump to their next location - portals were only needed to access areas within the same plane of existence that didn't connect directly to Earth, like Atlantis.

She wondered, not for the first time, how Gold had magic to use.

Without warning, Gold stole her hand and they disappeared into nothing.

Natalia's stomach flipped. Not because her emotions still rested too close to the surface. Not because of the travel. Rather, because of *where* they'd travelled to.

The sofa was in the same place, though the cushions were now teal and ruffled. A lamp stood in the corner, switched on. Natalia looked at the floor and could envision the track lines her own feet had made the last time she was here.

It was exactly as she remembered. But there must've been a mistake.

She spun toward Gold, desperation driving her. She didn't shout but her anger was at the forefront in her whispered accusation. "Why are you doing this?" she asked. "How *could you?* There never was a Council meeting, was there? You..."

Tricked me.

She wanted to call it betrayal. But could it really be called that? She was in no immediate harm, though that could quickly change. Like the flip of a coin now held her fate, and it was still up in the air.

"There will be a Council meeting," Gold said, straightening his jacket.

"What is *this?*" Natalia wanted to yell, to scream, but couldn't risk being discovered. "*Take me home!*" Her voice dripped with hurt.

Gold shook his head once. "I will not."

Natalia searched for an escape. She could feel Gold's eyes watching her as if he saw something she couldn't. She felt a familiar prickle at the edges of her eyes. To stop it, she fixed her gaze on Gold again, this time coldly.

"Why?" She had thought him a friend, now she wasn't sure. "Why are you doing this?"

Gold's smile wasn't sad or condescending, or even pitying, it just *was.* "Because it's what you need."

In a blink, he'd thrown open the door and was gone. Natalia could do nothing except stare after him, longing to be anywhere else, wishing she wasn't here, in a place she'd tried so hard to forget.

"Hello?"

That one voice froze Natalia more than any others could have.

It was high-pitched and feminine.

Peri's.

Though her brain was conflicted, her heart wasn't. Natalia's feet moved until she was in the hallway. Her heart was all she focused on.

On the wooden staircase, stuck to the last step, looking like she'd seen a ghost, was Peri.

"Peri," Natalia whispered.

At the same time, Peri whispered, "Natalia."

The girl wore a long dress, a bump protruding from her stomach. Her black hair was cropped just below her ears, evenly cut all the way round and clips parted it from falling into her face. Her brown eyes were wide and unblinking.

The injury remained. Peri's entire right arm was *gone.*

A tiny stump suggested where the arm had been, ending just after her shoulder, enough left to hold up her dress. Stiches had sewn the wound together. Bruises still circled the area. Otherwise, it looked healthy. As healthy as a wound like that could be, a wound sustained by a Monster clamping onto an arm and tearing it off whole.

Natalia swallowed the rising acid. But it was Peri who spoke again. "Are you real?"

An unseen force behind them both unstuck their feet, shoving them together until they collapsed in a heap on their knees. Peri immediately started crying and Natalia's own eyes welled. They clung to each other as if they were each other's air.

"Natalia?"

Peri removed herself and before Natalia could say anything, she was captured in a thick pair of arms. They pressed into her, squeezing her tightly, her chest and spine cracking from the force. She heard them sniff and when the arms pulled away, she stared into watery green eyes.

"So *you* were who Gold was talking about," Archie commented. He brought her in for another hug.

Natalia hugged him back. "You knew I was coming?"

"Gold said someone was."

He let go and helped ease Peri up from the floor. Together, they looked older somehow. More mature. However, Archie didn't look too different from the last time Natalia had seen him, not like Peri did. He still had his lighter brown hair and hidden freckles - his muscles seemingly *had* grown though.

"I didn't even know I—"

She was cut off by the door opening behind her. Somehow she knew who was there. Her breaths drew short and unsteady. Her fingers grazed along the forever scar on her arm, tracing the shape tentatively.

Natalia turned slowly. If she thought Peri had looked like she'd seen a ghost, Jasper looked like he'd seen the dead come back to life.

Jasper gulped visibly. His eyes dragged over Natalia and, surprisingly, she didn't shy away. It seemed he needed to see her as much as she needed to see him. His hair was curly and slightly longer, a few strands tickling his lashes. More freckles than ever were sprayed across his face. His white t-shirt was definitely strained on his arms and chest, and not because of the bags he carried.

Like a gun being shot, both of them flinched.

He threw his bags aside and barrelled for Natalia. She squeaked as he effortlessly scooped her up, swinging her around the hallway. His arms were wrapped around her thighs and she had to put her hands to his shoulders to steady herself.

Jasper smirked, a sight that before now, Natalia never would've considered a comforting thing. Yet she was elated, lighter in her body after seeing it.

Natalia moved one of her hands to his face, holding him in return, and he leaned into the touch.

Her fingers glided along his skin. She traced them along his face until her thumb rested a breath away from his bottom lip. She stared at the pinkness of his lips, wondering if she dared touch them with her own. Instead, she looked up at his eyes.

His on eyes roamed in wander over all of her as if trying to establish whether she was real. Eventually, he stopped searching, staring right at her lips.

He leaned towards her and she met him. With fire and need, they kissed.

When they pulled back, everything seemed brighter. It was as if Natalia could see again, felt her heart slowly set free from the prison she'd locked it away in. Part of her still suffered from a hollowness; there was no denying the time and peace that had been lost and would never be recovered. But part of her, the part that now was feeling whole again, breathed.

"Welcome back, Fairy," he grinned.

She kissed his forehead, mostly his hair. "Witch."

He lowered her, his breath caressing her ear as he whispered, "I've missed you."

She shivered at the truth she could sense.

After all her fears about coming back to them, he truly had missed her.

Natalia turned to the others She cracked a smile and her cheeks ached because of it, heating too. Peri winked as Archie whistled.

Natalia's smile faltered.

After *everything* she'd done to this family, after everything she'd wrecked and ruined, they'd welcomed her back with open arms. No one had tried to harm her or send her away as she'd expected. There were no threats or moments waiting for an everlasting end. They'd given her the complete opposite, the opposite of what she felt like she deserved.

"How about we get a take-away?" Sarah suggested, closing the front door at last. Natalia hadn't noticed her come in, but there she was, blonde, suited, and smiling.

"Pizza," Peri groaned, practically drooling.

Sarah stared at Natalia directly, leaving her no room to escape from the weight of it. "Natalia?"

She could only nod, which was enough for the others. They passed her on their way to the kitchen. Archie gave her shoulder a reassuring squeeze as he passed. Jasper slipped by after kissing her temple, leaving Natalia to contemplate in silence.

Was this wrong? She'd been so openly accepted. It *felt* wrong.

I harmed them. I should be burnt alive, cast aside, buried under rocks for what I did.

But she also couldn't deny how good it felt being back, how warm her body had become. Yet she feared this was some play, that the torment and truth of what she deserved was yet to come and the Darby's were biding their time to get there. They wanted her to get comfortable in a falsity before they struck. Reel her in to let her go.

Even as the thought crossed her mind, she argued with herself. The Darby's weren't the type to play games with others. If they didn't want her here, she wouldn't have been allowed in.

If *they* were so open to having her back, why couldn't she accept herself in return? Why was there a constant buzzing in her brain? Everything bad was her fault, wasn't it? How could they not see it too?

"You coming, or are you going to stand there like a bloody lemon?"

Natalia glanced up the stairs. Alex hobbled down, her right wrist tied into an orange cast. Because she wore a grey sports bra, the strapping around her ribs also visible.

"Pretty bad, huh?" Alex continued, noting Natalia's lingering stares. "I have that unexpected dive to thank."

"I'm—"

"I suggest you *don't* apologise," Alex cut in. "Nothing worse than an apology where it's not wanted or needed."

"But—"

"No! Anyway, *that* injury to the wrist healed. I re-broke it in training. Apparently it wasn't as settled as I had expected." Alex bowed her head. "Glad you're back now though, Nat. Life's been boring without you." She winked before walking off.

Natalia didn't know what to say so said nothing, following Alex in silence.

The whole kitchen was already alive when Natalia steeping inside. Sarah was swinging her hips and twirled with Archie. They danced to music from the radio and the incessant banging of pots Jasper provided. Peri sat at the bar, laughing, waving her arm in the air.

Natalia watched them, silently observing but never interfering, on the edge enough to be seen but not enough to break in.

When the musical interlude was done, Sarah's smile focused on Natalia. "What about your family?" she asked. She must've seen the confusion on Natalia's face because she elaborated. "Would your dad and his..."

"Girlfriend," Natalia provided. In the last month, *finally* Katherine and her dad had made things official; he'd told her right away.

"Katherine," Sarah said, "And your friend, Noah? Would they like to come for pizza?"

Three phone calls and twenty minutes later, Noah blundered through the doors like he'd been coming here every day and his entrance was normal. Katherine and Natalia's dad walked in together, Katherine bringing something chocolate and orangey.

For hours, they talked and laughed and ate, catching up on the last month or so. In the strangest way it was as if no time had passed at all. As if nothing had gone wrong.

James was currently in Atlantis, apparently helping someone deal with their finances, but he'd be back in a day or two. Sarah was taking up very few clients to represent at the minute, wanting more time with her family. Peri and Archie were so close to welcoming the baby, with about three months to go at most. They were meant to be house-hunting, but Archie had caught the flu a few weeks back, pausing that search. Alex had been running along the beach more, cooling in the waters after. Jasper had kept up with training, mostly alongside Alex. She joked that he couldn't keep up, even after he'd cast a spell of speed on himself, to which Jasper said he'd only done it once and never would again since it scrambled his insides.

Natalia could almost forget what loomed above her.

Almost.

"Your review has been pushed back again," Sarah announced once the table was clear and they were all huddled by the new fire-pit outside. "By a couple of weeks, I think."

The fire crackled. "What're a couple more weeks?" Noah asked.

Natalia caught Sarah scowling, but it vanished as soon as it'd come. "It means the Council is busy with something else," she murmured, though everyone heard. Natalia didn't like the implications of those words. Swiftly, Sarah turned to Natalia, offering her a marshmallow to roast. "Some *good* news though," she said. "I've heard from Kiva."

Natalia's heart twisted. "Oh?"

"Her parents were burnt in Atlantis and their ashes were scattered into the waters. If they were Creatures, their names would've been etched into the large marble memorial walls we have on the outskirts of the city with their dates and sometimes a saying." Sarah looked saddened that Kiva's family hadn't had that option.

Natalia lost interest in the marshmallow, so left it to burn over the flames. "Oh."

"But Kiva's doing fine. She's been enrolled at the school in Atlantis and is living with her uncle and cousin whenever she's back on Earth. She said she misses you." Sarah's smile was kind, secure; it promised that things would be ok.

"Everyone needs to stop moping," Peri told them. "If you don't, I will push this baby out here and now just to fight you all until you stop pouting."

"You will *not!*" Archie's voice squeaked.

Peri laughed but did give Natalia a pointed look.

Natalia held her hands up. "I haven't fought since..." She didn't need to finish, though she was slightly wrong. She *had* taken out that baby Scorpio but that was hardly a fight.

Alex plopped her crispy marshmallow into her mouth. "You need to start again," she said. "Fighting, I mean. Get back into it, get better. Get *prepared.*"

More than anyone else, Alex had been there, in the thick of the last major confrontation at the docks. She'd taken more of the hooded figure's power and punishment than anyone else.

Natalia knew that figure wasn't gone. They would come again. And when they did, Natalia would *have* to be ready. She couldn't let what happened last time repeat itself.

To do that, she needed to be away from the Darby's. Her dad too. She needed to do this alone, to take the fight away from them to preserve those she loved. And their returned love only drove home the point more.

She snuck a glance at her father over the fire. He watched her. If she didn't know he was Human, she would've been convinced he was a Creature that could read her mind.

"Natalia." Her attention shifted back to Sarah. "There's something I wanted to ask." Her gaze swept upwards, the fire light shimmering in her stare. Natalia's blood ran cold. "I've heard, little things, about your wings."

Natalia froze. The stick and cremated marshmallow fell from her hand. She sat still as a statue, aware of the others around her. Her friends had been there when her wings had revealed themselves for the first time. A sweat broke out along her skin and she shivered. No matter what any of them said, or done by any of them, this was the moment Natalia had been dreading the most.

Revealing her wings felt like revealing a piece of her soul. And when the reveal had come, it hadn't exactly gone well... So what did that say about her soul?

"Have you used them?" Sarah asked delicately.

"No." Natalia's voice shook.

"So, you haven't tried to fly?"

"Correct, I haven't."

"How do they look?"

She shook her head. "I don't know." Her stomach twisted. It was a half-truth since she hadn't seen them entirely, but she knew the general basics.

"Do you remember what wings are supposed to look like?"

"They're supposed to be cut into four sections, each nearly completely full with the same colour as our Fairy dust, though there may be a few clear spots."

"Are yours like that?"

"No."

For a moment, Natalia thought she had spoken. But when she looked up, Jasper gave her a small smile. *He* had answered.

"Natalia?" There was a pause before Sarah continued. "Can we see them?"

Natalia stared at the fire, willing it towards her and hoping it would consume her. But the flames refused to lick her skin or even flush smoke her way.

Despite her entire body tilting on a new axis, she took several breaths and then stood. She counted her breaths and turned away, not wanting to see anyone's horrified expressions. There were no holes or slits in her t-shirt, and she wondered how this would work *if* her wings appeared.

She rolled her shoulders and felt a tearing sensation spread through her back. She bit her lip to keep from screaming. Suddenly, a *pop* released all the building pressure.

She didn't turn. The reflection in the doors ahead showed the proof of what had happened.

They glistened. Two halves, four sections, all clear with a few tiny specks of bronze.

Her glass wings.

3

Glass Parts

$\mathcal{H}$OW ARE THEY REAL?

Noah has seen his best friend, his sister-in-arms-through-life, in many forms before. The shy and quiet school girl. The girl determined to ride a bike despite crashing many times. The girl who claimed she'd take on anyone who bullied him. The girl who aced her classes and exams. The girl who only drank wine at Christmas.

This was just another version of Natalia.

Still, he stared.

With the fire-light casting an ominous glow, her wings came alive. Noah thought of dragonfly wings – four sections, the top halves being smaller compared to the bottom two halves. Squinting at them, he searched for the hint of bronze that should've coated their expanse, observing mere sprinkles of it in thin dashes.

When Natalia turned back to them, tears streaked her face, and her expression flickered with pain as if shed expected this reaction but it still hurt nonetheless.

Noah threw himself from his chair. He ran forward, swaddling her in his arms. She whimpered and hugged him back weakly.

"You're ok," he whispered gently. He wondered who wouldn't be hurt at having to reveal themselves, to prove themselves to be different from what was expected. "I've got you. I've always got you."

Shuffling behind them caused Noah to pull back from the embrace, though he still kept her in his arms. Natalia nodded, saying that it was ok, but he took her hand anyway. They moved together.

Jasper was on his feet, eyes transfixed on Natalia – his expression wasn't anything nasty, just simple curiosity, and something else Noah couldn't place. He walked towards them, unspeaking.

Noah peered round Jasper briefly to steal a glance at everyone else. It seemed that no matter how long someone had been in this life there were still things that could shock them. Noah could see it, the hints of intense surprise shining through.

Jasper reached them, and Noah took his cue to step aside. Jasper ran his hand along a wing-blade and Natalia shivered. Noah grimaced at the intimacy.

"Are they heavy?" Jasper asked.

"I don't think so," she responded, her voice low but steady. "I don't have much to compare it too."

Jasper ran his hand over the other side's peak. "What do they feel like?"

"Light." Natalia looked to Noah and he offered what he hoped was an encouraging smile.

Noah knew from what he'd been learning – Peri, Alex, and Sarah had been giving him not very secret lessons – that Fairy wings weren't meant to appear like this. They were supposed to be luscious and airy, perfect for nimble flying. Natalia might've said hers felt light, but they appeared cumbersome and heavy, almost solid. The bronze dust inside appeared minimal and fair while the rest of the sections seemed see-through and glass-like.

Without meaning to search him out, Noah's eyes landed on Tony. His hands were in his lap, fingers tanged with Katherine's.

This couldn't be easy for him either. Natalia was Noah's best friend, but Tony was her *father*. From the way his eyebrows were creased and the corners of his mouth were turned down, it clearly pained him to see Natalia struggle. He'd known she was a Fairy, his wife had been one, but no one could've predicted the wings' appearance.

Noah hadn't been at the docks on the day of the kidnap and fight. Peri had relayed the details afterwards of how a hooded figure had come for Natalia. But that couldn't have just been about Natalia's wings, could it?

Natalia wiggled her shoulders as if to rid herself of the wings but they remained, stubbornly glinting. "I can't hide them," she admitted. She bounced on the spot, clearly agitated. "They never wanted to come out before and now the fucking things want to be out all the time."

Alex winced as she sat up straighter, her unbound arm curling protectively around her middle. "It's like the wolf shift."

"Something tells me she's not a wolf," Jasper mused.

Alex stuck her middle finger up and kept it aimed at him as she spoke. "After you're bitten, you want to change all the time. But it gets easier to control with time and practise."

"We'll help," Peri offered.

Natalia forced a smile. "In your state?"

Peri made a startled noise. "State? *State?*"

"Condition?" Natalia tried.

Jasper made a digging motion. "You're going down further here."

Natalia's face pinched like she'd eaten something sour.

"*Stato? Incredibile!*" Peri gave her a cutting glare before folding her arm over her baby-bump, relaxing back into Archie; he wound his arms over her shoulder and kissed her temple. "Besides," she grinned now, "I didn't offer myself specifically. I only offered the promise of help from the collective."

"Take the help." It was the first time Tony had spoken and he sounded strangled. "Do what you must to help yourself," he added. "Do what you have to do to *protect* yourself."

Noah could hear the words left unspoken. *Do what you have to do to protect yourself because I cannot lose you, too.*

She nodded firmly. "I will." She looked at Jasper sincerely. "Will you help me?"

"We all will," Peri cut in. "Now," she snatched up the bag of marshmallows, stuffed two in her mouth, and then proceeded to talk, "can we get back to eating?"

Alex winced audibly as she stood. "I'll help you now," she said, stalking over to Natalia as everyone else returned to the fire. Even Jasper moved away to give them space, though looked over his shoulder every so often. Noah kept doing the same too.

Natalia caught him once and Noah flinched, mouthing "just checking". Alex noticed as well and moved them toward the shadows of the house.

Whatever Alex did, it worked; as she and Natalia came back to the fire, her wings were gone. There was a small smile on Alex's face but not Natalia's, Noah realised.

She'll be ok, Noah told himself. *She has us. She has* them.

Natalia sat herself between her dad and Archie, who was wrestling his girlfriend for the bag of marshmallows so he could pass them around. Peri stole one last handful and put half in her mouth at once, fighting to stick her tongue out as she did, and Natalia let out a shallow laugh.

Without the brilliantly shocking glass at her back, Natalia seemed more like herself, more like the version Noah knew. But he knew the *real* Natalia included those wings, doomed or not. And doomed seemed right with all that was coming because of them, and because of her. But what was it? Why was it coming?

Noah stared into the fire, watching the tendrils dance and wishing he could be more help in finding the answers to fight back.

"Can't you sing for us?" Jasper pressed for the fourth time.

Peri wished she had her trident to hand. "No."

"Can't? Or won't?"

She sneered. "Both."

Peri possessed a beautiful singing voice and wasn't afraid to use it, or say so. However, since becoming pregnant, it hadn't sounded nice at all. She'd tried once in the shower and it'd sounded like she was gargling water.

In the Human world, Mermaids or Mermen were often confused for sirens, and they didn't exist – they were made-up by sailors of the past. Merfolk voices could manipulate emotions, but only a rare handful of them owned the power. They couldn't lure people to their deaths, only enhance an idea that was already present. So while the basic idea of sirens was correct, the "Creature" behind it differed slightly.

"Spoil sport," Jasper said, pouting.

"If you want to hear someone sing," Peri shifted positions, "*you* do it."

"I wouldn't want to upset you by being better."

"Please." She shifted again. "Be my guest. I have no concerns about being upstaged."

Jasper laughed and sat back. Archie chuckled at Peri's side; he knew too well, as Peri did, that Jasper couldn't sing a single note.

Everyone went back to warming their hands. Despite the earlier summer heat, the evening had chilled considerably. As Peri moved her feet closer to the fire-pit, her mind couldn't help but find words and a tune now that the idea had been planted.

From the deepest seas, to the highest hill,
We watch over lands of all.
The hearts of Creatures are set free,
Upon the even fall.
They will go on to rise and rise,
Above our clouds as doves,
Above Earthly ties, and forever becoming loves.
To keep their precious life flowing,
And to move them on the path,
Through dust and voice we sing we must.
Forever in peace we wish them off,
As their light here fades.
And for them we must keep fighting on.
Within night's deepest shades.
And so their song is sung.

Her grandfather had been the person to teach her her first ever song. It was called the *Song of Creatures* and meant to be sung at funerals by a choir.

Anxiously, Peri looked around at the relaxed faces and slumped bodies. What had made her think of that song now? No one was in dire circumstances. Sure, Alex was busted up and Peri's baby due date was looming, but there was no immediate danger or death to require a funeral song.

Peri refused to admit she was scared of her approaching date. However, she *could* admit that the sight of Natalia's wings had rattled something inside her. Something a little dark and unsure. She'd known, like the others, Natalia was different, and glass wings were certainly that. But they left behind more questions.

Without a doubt Peri could say trouble was bound to show up soon. It wasn't Natalia's fault, far from it, but it would be stupid to think she wasn't attached to it somehow.

Archie draped his arm over her and she tucked into him. Across the fire, through the flickers of flames, Peri watched Natalia sit uncomfortably. Red and blue strings surrounded the Fairy, strings Peri, and no one else present, could read.

Deep sea blue meant confusion; she was probably confused over what she was doing here and whether it was a good idea, and what everything in general meant. The blush red was blame, or guilt. Peri scrunched up her face. What did Natalia feel she had to be guilty over? What had happened or changed that made her feel that way?

She never got to question it further as a bell rang out from inside the house.

Using Archie as a stabiliser, Peri clambered to her feet. He rose to his own feet afterwards, pressing a kiss to the top of her head once up, and she smiled at him.

The ringing grew more intense and everyone stopped.

"Monsters!" Sarah called out.

"Oh bloody *great*," Alex huffed with a growl.

A whisper in the air told Peri to look at Natalia. The girl's face was whiter than ever, even against the colours of the night. Her eyes were cast down, hands visibly shaking.

Peri wanted to slap herself for not understanding the problem. Natalia had changed because her situation had changed. She'd gone from being the Human to the Fairy. She'd suffered the Council's scrutiny only to find out they weren't the worst things out there. The random Monster attacks had also turned out to be not so random, rather designed to trap her instead.

Natalia stood to leave and that was when Peri spotted the thick obsidian line.

Fear.

Natalia didn't want to hear the word no, to be told to stay out of this fight. If these Monsters were here for her, then she would go to them. This was *hers*.

She felt for the blade she constantly had strapped on her person, today by her hip. A safety crutch. The handle was familiar to the touch, the gemstones smooth and rough in her palm. Her dust could only do so much and she couldn't even stand the sight of her wings – not that she could use them – so the Creature blade was her only weapon.

Jasper had gifted her the blade. Every time she stared at the bronze gems, she was reminded of him and the memory attached to it; the one involving candles and his lips on hers. They'd shared a moment since, in this house, mere hours ago, but that just hadn't been the same. She still held him at arm's length. She *had* too.

She refused to allow the hooded figure to use anyone she loved against her, even if it hurt her so desperately to stay away.

Natalia gave every single person a stern look, inaudibly telling them she would be joining this fight. No one moved to stop her. Alex shifted as if the look forced her to – her bones cracked like surface ice on a lake. Natalia couldn't meet Jasper's eyes so instead looked at Archie, who nodded once. Her dad offered a sad smile.

Without so much as a whisper, they left, leaving those who couldn't fight behind.

Because of tight pathways and road works, they occasionally had to squeeze together in pairs or single-file. At one point, when she was beside him, Natalia dared to steal a glance at Jasper. He wasn't looking, a lazy smile on his lips. Her heart hitched. She wished that smile was directed at her but it wasn't, it was for the thrill of the fight.

She tore her stare away.

Back in the garden, Natalia had felt Peri's eyes on her. Had her friend seen her fear and regret, her *pain*? Keeping everyone safe meant hurting them by pushing them away. If that made her a Monster, then good. She'd happily play the Monster if it meant her friends lived.

But was this attack even about her, or just a generic bombardment?

They flashed by the local primary school and Natalia caught a swift glimpse of the sea beyond it.

Being in the school district, where Natalia and Noah had first met, forced her to look around. With a muttered curse, she realised he was there among them. He must've slipped in silently. She wanted Archie to jump him back to the house. Who had let him steal his way into the group? He was *Human*, and with next to no training.

"Fuck," she hissed to herself, her grip on her blade tightening. Now she had one more thing, one more *person*, to worry over. She only wanted to ensure everyone's safety. Why did they have to make it so difficult?

She went to shout at Archie when the smell of wet dog slammed up her nose. She blanched and seconds later so did the others. "Noah?" she yelled. He stopped and turned, thick eyebrows raised. "Stay behind me."

He pinched his nose as he walked to her, breathing rapidly. "What *is* that?"

Natalia drew her weapon. "Something you don't want to get hit by."

"What?"

"Just don't touch the slime."

"Slime?"

As soon as he'd said that, a Siltapolia appeared from behind a lamppost.

Then another.

And another.

In seconds they were staring down at least twenty of the same Monster type.

Archie moved forwards first. He huffed as if already done with the situation, crackled his knuckles, and then spread his hands.

Green light exploded from him like a tidal wave and it rampaged forwards at his control. Several Monsters turned to ash on impact.

Alex dove throughout the group of Monsters next, yapping and snipping. Natalia wondered if biting the Monsters burned her. She didn't seem to react as if it did but Alex wouldn't likely admit otherwise.

Suddenly, Noah gripped onto Natalia's shoulders. A Siltapolia had come up in front of them while she'd been watching the others. It tilted its head as if questioning her. Natalia didn't care to be scrutinised though. So she slashed out and the Monster folded into ash, no goo involved.

She spun round to face Noah, relieved to find him unharmed. He spoke first. "I want to fight like that!"

She blinked at him. "What are you even doing here?"

His eyes darted from left to right like he was searching for backup. "I wanted to help?"

"And how do you expect to do that?"

Noah's face lit up and he rummaged in his trouser pocket, drawing out a thin silver bullet. Natalia gave him an unimpressed look. But when Noah clicked the top of the bullet, it transformed into a metre long pole, tipped with a clear spike.

"A *spear?*" she shrieked. "Where on this Island did you find that?"

"Peri gave it to me a week ago. I carry it with me all the time now. She said it was a generic weapon and it might not work against all Monsters, but it's a start." He shrugged, drawing the weapon into both hands. "Alex said she'd teach me how to use it, but even then I don't know how good I'll be. You know me, princess. I'm not much of a fighter."

Natalia's lips formed a thin line. "Seems like I need to have a word with the girls in this family."

"They're only—"

Natalia didn't let him finish. She grabbed his sleeve and swung him away from her.

The approaching Monster, however, wasn't a Siltapolia. Glowing red eyes drifted down the street.

A Shadow.

Natalia froze, her body chilling all over. A Shadow showing up now proved this attack wasn't random.

"Out here," the Shadow croaked, "you have no barrier around you."

Natalia took a step back, stepping on Noah's foot. He didn't yelp or even whisper, just held onto her shoulder and inched back. "I don't know what you mean," she managed to say. Cold sweat ran down her back.

"You do."

There's magic here... It's protecting you.

That's what the last Shadow she'd encountered had said; the one that'd come into her house, claiming her dust had allowed it there. Natalia wasn't convinced, and none of the Darby's had said anything on the matter. But *was* there magic around her house that protected her and those inside? Was someone hiding that or was the Shadow lying? They weren't exactly the best things to trust.

The Shadow crept forwards; its soundless movements ghostly. Natalia raised her blade higher, holding out her other hand too in a 'stop right there' kind of way, but even she could see it shake slightly.

Natalia gritted her teeth. Magic or not, she wasn't in her house now. There was no barrier or protection here, for anyone. That included the Shadow. And it seemed to realise that, eyeing her blade more seriously.

The fight echoed behind her, and she could sense Noah so well she could feel him shaking. She tuned it out. "What do you want?"

The Shadow's red glare raked over her. "You are healing."

"I was never injured."

It looked as though the Shadow attempted to smile but quickly abandoned the idea. "Some injuries aren't always worn on the surface. But you did have some physical injuries too, didn't you?"

She resisted the urge to touch her T-shaped scar. "All this time and you still speak through someone else, through *Shadows*."

Natalia cut through the base of the Shadow's head, and it disappeared.

She wiped her blade against the thigh. She was done being the puppet and captive of someone she couldn't see. As much as she wanted the fight focused on her, there was no chance she was about to just hand herself or whatever it was *they* wanted over. Not when *they* wouldn't even show or identify themselves properly.

If *they* wanted Natalia, they would have to come for her themselves.

Natalia turned back around, and choked.

Three Shadows surrounded Noah. He must've pulled away enough for them to circle him. She felt stupid for not noticing.

The Monster's eyes flickered to her, their brightness burning. Natalia stepped forwards, a warning, yet they didn't back away. Thankfully, that meant they didn't move closer to Noah either.

"I am far away," said the Shadow on the left. Its voice was hollow, empty, but Natalia knew it was the same voice that was speaking as the last. "I'm tending to other business, but there are those here for you Prince—"

Natalia lashed out again. As she went for the third, she saw Noah coated in black ash, his spear fully extended in open air. He gave her a weak smile but a question hung in his eyes – what was going on?

Natalia looked away, unable to conjure an answer. "Nice stabbing."

Noah laughed. "I'm not sure if that's inspiring or worrying."

She wanted to joke back but the words tasted stale. Noah shouldn't have to be defending himself. She surveyed the rest of the carnage along the road so she didn't have to force a reply.

The Darby's continued to fight the remaining Monsters; only a few Siltapolias remained now the Shadows were gone. Thankfully none of them appeared injured and the surrounding area seemed undamaged. Natalia felt herself breathe a heavy sigh.

Noah touched her shoulder, and she turned to face him. "Princess—"

"Don't," she cut in. The word stung from how it's meaning, its *value*, had been twisted and tainted. "*Please* stay here. If something comes for you, you stab and yell and stab and yell."

"Stab and yell," he nodded, gripping his spear tightly.

"Otherwise, hide." She sighed. "You shouldn't be here, and I shouldn't be telling you that." She sighed again and stood up taller, pressing a kiss to his cheek. "Love you, Noah."

He nodded. "Love you too, Princess."

This time, the word didn't sound so cruel.

With one last smile at Noah, she ran from him and straight towards the brown wolf. Alex struggled with four Siltapolias at once. She kept snapping her jaw and growling, but it did little to deter the Monsters. She swiped her paw and caught one. The Monster hissed and lunged, right into Natalia's blade.

The manoeuvre earned a satisfied nod from Alex. Together, they then finished off the other three. Alex ran off immediately afterwards.

Natalia followed her rapid movements to Sarah who appeared to be fighting the air. Natalia squinted for a better look, and barely noticed *something* as thin and light as smoke.

Crack!

Natalia touched her cheek, the skin stinging. The impact had come out of nowhere. As she drew her hand away, the next attack came and sent her flying into the air.

She screamed, wanting her wings to free themselves, just this once. But they didn't.

She fell and crashed into something that groaned. Rolling off, she turned to see Archie sprawled out flat on his stomach. His body had broken her fall.

Brushing herself off, she stood and reached down for Archie. He accepted her hand though nearly pulled her back down in the process. Once up, he looked her over.

"You ok?" he asked.

Nodding, she looked across the road. "I got hit but I didn't see the Monster. I think it's the same thing your mum's fighting."

Archie looked over to Sarah, squinted, and grimaced. "They're called Maddners. They can form and change between states of existence." He brushed the dust from the road off his clothes. "One minute they're solid, the next—"

"Smoke."

He nodded. "Weapons don't usually work because they don't physically form long enough."

"Only long enough to smack us across the road. Fucking brilliant." She touched her still stinging face. Then her fingers slipped to her earrings. "What do we do?"

He looked down at her from the corner of his eye. "Fairy dust traps them in a single, *solid* state. *Then* weapons can be used."

"What about magic?"

"Only dust and weapons."

Natalia called her blade to her - she'd dropped it somewhere between flying and falling - and it returned to her palm gently, oddly cold against her skin. "So I need to trap it."

"They're incredibly fast."

"And impossible to see." She didn't like the odds.

Archie nodded and she sighed. Why were the Monsters getting harder to beat? Couldn't they be something easy for once? Like a mini mushroom with legs, maybe?

"A mini mushroom sounds fun," Archie teased.

Natalia blinked up at him. "What?"

"You said it out loud." She groaned as he chuckled. "That's *far* from the craziest thing I've ever heard. I live with Jasper, remember? I'm used to the weird and ridiculous."

Nodding, she looked back to the fight. *I guess the Monsters are getting harder to stop because they want me more each time I get away.* She shuddered at the thought.

Knowing Archie followed, Natalia raced back to where Sarah was still swatting the air. Diving in was a mistake as Natalia was immediately thrown to the floor. She peered up and her eyes *truly* opened to see what was there.

A Monster that resembled the stories and folklore of abominable snowmen stared between Natalia, Archie, and Sarah. The fur wasn't quite white but silver. Two spiralling horns protruded from either side of its head, the needle-sharp looking tips pointed towards the sky. Oversized hands, easily three feet in diameter, were swung wide. But the rest of the Monster was small, which would've made it easy for the Monster to change between states of being.

The Monster zeroed in on Archie and Sarah who still remained on their feet, fighting. Alex darted in from the side but was swatted into a nearby garden before she could even growl.

Natalia drew a handful of bronze, shining dust in her palm. In the past month, she'd realised she could create it not just on her face, but in her hands too. She crept forwards, hoping neither Sarah nor Archie would draw attention to her.

Once she inched as close as she dared, Natalia threw the dust.

Though she could already see the Monster it began to appear more *real*. Long tusks grew out of its mouth upwards to its nose and its fur shimmered.

The Monster's eyes locked with Natalia's and she gasped. They were piercing blue.

She didn't see who killed the Monster but she watched it waft away in the breeze.

Natalia's heart-rate spiked as she glanced around the street. *Another* failed attempt to kidnap her had just played out – she was convinced that was what it had been. It only solidified her hunch that there would be more later on. One that would lead to more desperation, more danger.

She had to get away.

With everyone distracted searching the area for other Monsters, Natalia ran to Noah, grabbed him by the arm, and dragged them both into the night's peace.

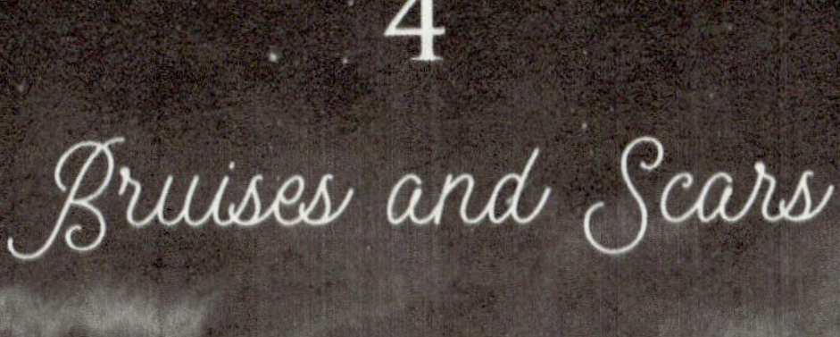

4

Bruises and Scars

ALEX'S RIBS HAD NEVER ACHED SO BADLY. Worse yet, as Peri started unwinding the bandages Alex felt were holding her together, the stabbing pain that restricted her breathing grew more intense. She eyed her reflection in the hallway mirror, her gaze settling on the black and purple bruising that'd spread down most of her right side.

Peri's fingers barely touched the skin and Alex yelped. "Shit!" Peri drew away quickly and Alex glared at her. "Do you have to?"

Peri stared back, her expression equally as stubborn. "Do you want me to see if you've broken any *more* ribs, or not?"

Alex grimaced. "Just... be careful."

"Really? There go my plans of pressing you with a silver butter knife next."

"See what happens if you do that."

"I'm being as careful as I can."

"I know," Alex sighed, relenting. She knew Peri really wasn't out to hurt her on purpose.

Peri shook her head and went about carefully touching the skin, feeling for any damage. Needle pricks of pain exploded along her flesh at every touch.

Alex didn't breathe too deeply again until Peri wound fresh, thick bandage around her middle. Once tied, Alex grimaced and lowered her baggy white t-shirt.

"Thanks," she muttered.

Peri tucked her hair behind her ears but it fell back round her face almost instantly. "I *hate* being left out of these fights," she replied sourly.

"Thank the Gods you weren't there!"

"Was it *really* that bad?"

"More Siltapolia than I've seen in one place before. It was a swamp-fest of tar and wet-dog smell, and that's *me* complaining." Alex nodded at Peri's stomach. "But you were left out, as you put it, for good reason."

"*Si.*" Peri sighed and rubbed her stomach. "You're right. And it's just for a few more months. But that doesn't mean I can't miss it."

For once Alex would like to sit out. As much as she enjoyed the fight, she wanted a moment to heal in peace. Just once, then she'd hop right back in.

Peri however had a little bit of a different situation. Creature pregnancies, Alex had learned, were more delicate than a Human's. Peri had benched herself to make sure all would be well with the baby.

Peri slumped down on the hallway bench beside Alex. "I don't miss the Monsters," she admitted. "I know I'll have to go back to it, there's no doubt about that. Those sons of bitches need to be sent back to the Hell they crawled from and I want to be a part of nailing their coffin lids down. I just miss being a part of something, being helpful."

Alex knew that feeling. It had always felt like she'd been born to fight and at least now she was putting that anger and desire to good use.

"But, right now, I would *kill* for a peanut butter sandwich."

Alex grunted as she stood. "Well, we better get you that sandwich before you collapse."

They stumbled together into the kitchen, no clear idea on who was leading or who was supporting as they both relied on each other. It was almost hilarious. At first, the girls hadn't gotten along. Alex hadn't wanted to see her brother's heart get broken – there were stories about the De Costanzi family's ruthlessness. It turned out that listening to rumours only gave half of a story. Peri *was* ruthless, but not with her heart or Archie's.

The girls murdered several sandwiches each. As they fell back in their seats, full and content, they relaxed.

"Know what you're having yet?" Alex asked a minute later.

Peri smiled and looked down at herself. "Not yet."

"Any ideas?"

"Any healthy baby will be perfect."

The way Peri looked or rubbed her stomach was so simple yet protective. Alex couldn't help but wonder if her birth mother had ever been like that. She doubted it since she'd been tossed aside at the first chance for a drink. And no one else had cared since, not until Sarah.

"But," Peri continued, "as for what Creature? I have an inkling it'll be Merfolk."

Alex pictured Peri's dark grey fin and scales but in miniature. "You do?"

"There's just *something*."

"Have you thought about how..." Alex made a motion with her hands, creating a visual tunnel with them in between her legs.

"How the baby's going to come out?" Peri laughed. "Probably painfully. Most Human births are, and Sarah's already told me a Creature birth is no different in *that* way. Though a water birth should make it a little less painful. Something about my body relaxing like it's at home. Archie's terrified. I'm not sure why or what of, whether it's because of the pain he knows I'll face or the goop and blood."

Appearing out of nowhere, Noah came swanning into the

kitchen, grinning. "That'll be your sex life ruined, then. It'll put him, and maybe you, right off. Welcome to the grossed out by sex team." He laughed and Peri joined in.

Alex, however, cringed. "Let's *not* talk about that. Archie's my *brother*," she said, making a gagging noise to support her point. "Anyway," she cut her stare back to Noah, "what are you doing here? Haven't you got your own home to go to?"

Noah folded his arms. "I was attacked tonight too."

"Did you use the spear?" Peri asked. Noah nodded.

"How many kills?" Alex challenged.

"One," Noah answered a little shyly.

Peri smiled. "Not bad for someone who hasn't been taught any physical fighting styles yet."

"Nat dragged you off before we could say bye to either of you," Alex said. "We didn't even notice you were gone until you'd literally *vanished*."

Noah moved to stand opposite the girls. "Your mother rang me, wanting to check for injuries. I was at home when she did and left right away. Princess doesn't know I'm here."

"Princess," Alex snorted.

"Why *did* she drag you off?" Peri asked, ignoring Alex.

He shrugged. "But I'm all clear, if you care."

Alex held up her hands. "I didn't ask."

"Terrible. Maybe you should?"

Alex began to smile. Her first interaction with Noah had been after he'd run head first through a portal to Atlantis. Either he was brave or incredibly stupid. The jury was still out on which. But since then, he'd stuck around.

Ever since the dock fight, Noah had been actively coming to the house to learn more about Creatures and Monsters. Usually, Peri taught him. Recently, however, he'd asked about learning to fight. Peri had given him a generic weapon, but that was as far as it'd gone.

Though Alex *had* promised to teach him how to use it.

Alex drowned out the conversation as it went on some tangent. Instead, she listened to the heartbeats upstairs. The slow and gentle beat belonged to her mother, and the unsteady and twitching one belonged to her brother.

Jasper had come home void of expression on his face. Which meant one thing. He was feeling too much. Whenever his emotions got the better of him, Jasper would hide, hoping to create a mask so thick no one could see through the cracks. But Alex knew what to look for.

Some of those cracks had begun to heal when Natalia had come back into their lives, a whole month after becoming absent. Yet Alex could still sense that she was holding something close to her chest, as if she had many cracks of her own and was trying to keep them in place.

The weight of her wings was extraordinary.

The others gathered around her, like spectators at a zoo. Dread sank into Natalia's stomach.

"They're..." Alex started but couldn't finish.

Jasper's hand reached out and fell through the air just before her. "Glass."

Natalia choked on her sobs; no one paid attention to her cries. The smell of smoke surrounded her until her brain could only see the colour grey. The weight at her back was nothing compared to that in her heart and soul.

"How is this possible?" Archie asked the others.

"It can't be," Alex replied.

"But isn't it there?" Jasper said to them both. "It wears the wings as if proud of them."

"I wouldn't be," Alex laughed unkindly.

"I'd burn them off," Jasper agreed.

"But how did it make them like that?" Archie pressed.

"It doesn't seem clever enough to do that on its own," Alex said. "And they may be hideous, but they're still too good for it."

Natalia folded her hands into fists to stop them from shaking as those around her argued.

This wasn't how her wings were supposed to be. They were meant to be bronze and shining. Not glass with little specs of bronze trapped inside. After all the waiting, they'd come out mutilated. What had happened?

Why am I different?

Natalia twisted away from her spectators and bent over the edge of where she stood. A river beneath her and in it she caught her reflection. Only her wings were different; they were charcoal black and burning.

Natalia threw up into the bin. She'd tried and failed to make it to the bathroom. Thankfully, her bedroom had been equipped.

Once done, she wiped her mouth on a clean towel – that, too, at her bedside for exactly this reason. Reaching for the nearby cup of water, she sipped, the acidic taste diluting with every swig.

This wasn't the first time she'd been sick after a dream. In fact, it'd become a regular occurrence. She wanted to stop, she did, but how could she sleep without dreaming?

Gradually, the queasiness subsided and she was able to pull herself, and the bin, into the bathroom. She cleaned up and finished the rest of her water.

Creeping downstairs for a refill, she heard no snoring and sighed. Her dad had gone to work already.

She turned on the kitchen light, finding the room a mess. Dirty plates and a tomato laced saucepan sat beside mugs and glasses. Splatters of sauce coated the tiles above the oven. A few cupboards were open. Water spots had dried on the window, and a dead bug had crusted on the windowsill. Natalia let herself smile. They were her reminders that life was real and it would continue on, a bleeding part that had seeped from one version to the next. But she could never *quite* return to the false Human life she'd had.

A gentle weight then pulled her a step back, and Natalia knew instantly what had happened. She didn't need to look into the window's reflection to see what had happened, but she did anyway.

There swayed her wings, not fully bronze and light as they should be, but rather empty and stoic.

Natalia swung round and threw her glass with a yell. It shattered against the wall.

She didn't stop until at least several plates and more glasses had been thrown. Desperation led to a chair being tossed, but it bounced off with no damage done. The hammering in her heart never stopped.

Despite it being well into the night, and despite the possible dangers that could be lurking, Natalia threw open the back door and ran. She hoped, for one single second, that there really was a protective spell around her house.

She threw herself into the furthest corner of the garden, the bushes swallowing her.

No longer able to contain the sobs, she let them out, but all was dry. It was like her body could no longer give what she wanted it to, could no longer offer the release she needed to grieve what had been and what was to come. The fight earlier had been a reminder that things were coming and they wouldn't stop, not without her.

Natalia's wings were glass, there was no question in that now. But her heart was too, and it was nearly broken.

Creeping around the house was easier when the world slept.

Noah barley made it across the landing before Zoe slipped out of her bedroom behind him. She folded her arms. Noah pulled a face, trying and failing to hide the pile of books he carried.

"What you got there?" Zoe nodded at his overflowing arms.

"Some stories," Noah answered. He flashed the spines.

They were indeed stories, ones from their childhoods. Noah was doing his own research. He knew now what parts of these books were correct and false. Armed with knowledge, he was collating all the information from both sides, of Creatures and Monsters.

He'd enjoyed the last few months of lessons with Peri were fun, but there was a lot to remember and a lot to discard, and Noah wanted to get it right. This wasn't to impress anyone. It was to make sure his life stayed *his*.

Zoe looked unimpressed but undeterred. "What are you doin'?"

"Doing," he corrected. "A research project."

"You're not in school anymore. You don't *have* research projects."

Shit. "I'm doing it for myself."

"Why? What for?"

"Someone's nosey this evening." It was a lame distraction and Noah cringed.

"It's quarter to two in the damn morning," Zoe told him. "You're sneakin' around like a burglar and when I question you 'bout it, you get sketchier."

"Helping the library with a kid project," was all Noah managed as a lie before he scurried away, face hotter than ever.

He barged into his room and shut the door behind him to keep his sister out.

He'd known Zoe was suspicious about him; Hell, he'd be suspicious too. He'd tried avoiding her and thought he'd been doing well. Until tonight.

Very few Humans knew of Creatures and Monsters; that had been lesson number one. Noah was one of the few privileged to know, and as much as he wanted Zoe in, she couldn't be. Not unless she was brought in another way. And after the stuff he'd seen, after the way he'd fallen into all this, he didn't want her here.

Archie groaned as Peri rubbed the cloth over his sore back. He arched when she did it again, wanting to get away from her forceful approach, but that didn't stop her. Part of him was glad, in the morning he'd definitely appreciate it, but right now his skin was raw and his muscles were screaming.

"I can wash myself," he said, turning round in the shower, squeezing his shoulders up and arms in to make sure he made it round.

The bathroom was a normal size family one, the shower inside a bath they had to climb in to, but there was more than enough room. Being bigger than others though, Archie had to be careful how he moved so he didn't knock the shower-screen or send the bottles on the bath's rim overboard.

Peri raised an eyebrow. "I know you can. But have you considered that I want to do this?"

He pulled her into him. "I have."

"And you're constantly looking after me right now," she argued. She kissed his chest and then looked up at him. "Let me do this for you."

"I like looking after you."

"Archie!"

Groaning, he gave in and did as Peri instructed. From turning back round so she could continue to rub into his wide shoulders and back, and then having him face her so she could rub his arms and chest with a lavender scrub.

The fight hadn't been too bad. There'd been a more concentrated load of Monsters than Archie had seen before, but nothing terribly overwhelming. Natalia's dust had been a help in defeating the Maddner and having his mother there too, working her magic, had given them an extra edge.

But Archie had still come away with aches and pains. The Siltapolia hadn't burned him with their goop, and most of his injuries were a result of the Maddner they'd unexpectedly encountered. His mother had said he'd broken a finger, which was now strapped up – the water was slowly peeling the tape away and it would need replacing – and he'd been hit several times in the upper half of his body. He was just grateful no one had hit him *lower*. One had tried, but Alex had gotten to it before the hit could land.

Peri peeled away from him to put the cloth on the edge of the bath. Archie moved to her and noticed how much steam was in the bathroom even with the fan on. They'd probably been in there twenty minutes, the water on half-power so it wouldn't go cold as quickly, though clearly they'd built up enough heat.

No matter what she did, Peri was beautiful. Archie had never thought any differently. From the first time he'd seen her in school right up to now. It had been a normal crush kind of way of thinking back then. Now, she had a true beauty to her that was like a drug to his system and he could never get enough of it.

Carefully, he touched Peri's bump. She immediately looked up at him, one eyebrow raised and a smile on her lips. He caressed the skin, staring right into her dark eyes.

"Is there something I can help you with?" she asked.

"I don't tell you enough how beautiful you are," he whispered, leaning closer.

She laughed and it sounded beautiful. "You tell me nearly every day."

"Nearly every day isn't good enough."

"For me, it's more than enough, *amore*."

"*Ti amo*," he whispered against her lips. "More than you know,

I love you."

Peri pressed herself closer. "I know very well how much you love me, because it's exactly how much I love you." Just from watching and hearing Peri, Archie could very well believe sirens were real. She'd ensnared him after all. "Is this you saying you're done with the shower?" she asked.

He kissed her, and her arm snaked around his neck. He groaned at both the weight of her on where he hurt and because of her in general.

Pressing their temples together, he murmured, "Let's get out of this water before it or you gets cold."

They slipped out, turning off the water as they went. Archie wrapped Peri in a soft towel immediately. She giggled as he wrapped his arms around her from behind. He kissed her cheek, leaving his lips there for a few moments longer than necessary. She reached up and touched the side of his face. He turned into her touch, kissing her palm, and then kissed her cheek again.

Archie wasn't done, however. Because he still held onto the sides of the towel, he let his grip go slightly. It began to fall away. It moved just enough that Archie could see the top of Peri's breasts. He bent and kissed the side of her neck, trailing lowered to her shoulder, moving slower with each peck.

Peri could heal any and all of his wounds any day.

"I don't think I'm going to feel the cold now," she whispered.

In one movement, Archie lifted Peri in his arms, ignoring his body's protests. Listening first, when he heard no one nearby, he charged out of the bathroom to make it into the bedroom in six quick steps. He swiftly kicked the door shut behind him.

Jasper had found the book of spells on his parent's bookshelves. Magic didn't require active spells that much anymore. Most Witches had better control to not need help. It was odd to find books like this one outside of libraries or schools, or even Atlantis. But he knew he came from a long line of Witches, and this book was probably a kind of heirloom which was why it was with his family still.

He flicked through the pages carefully. The edges of each page were yellow, while the inside paper was stark white, a complete contrast of where light had seen and where it hadn't. He noticed that the further he turned, the harder the pages were as if they hadn't been used as much before.

There was nothing he was looking for in particular. It was just an outlet for his anger and frustration. He often turned to his magic when he was at a lost for what else to do. He was always searching for a way to progress it because he didn't believe he'd reached his limit yet, and what better time to start than when he was annoyed at something else and wanted a distraction?

Jasper stopped on a page randomly and read the thinly written words. It didn't explain much other than the spell's purpose.

Clapping his hands together, he climbed to his feet, standing with his legs shoulder-width apart. The magic in him drew close to the surface until he saw his fingertips glow pink. He looked over the spell once more. He wouldn't pretend to know what he was doing, especially when it came to casting because he had never really done it before, but part of him was excited to try.

Under his breath, he muttered, "*Take the real, twist the feel. Take the small, grow it tall. Take the seat, give it feet. Take this chair and place a mare.*"

And then he released his power.

One of the training room chairs immediately began to change. It shifted this way and that, looking like it was melting, until it disappeared into the cloud of pink Jasper had made. There came a stuttering noise and then some scrapes.

Jasper pulled back and the smoke cleared, revealing a pink horse.

The horse swayed its head this way and that as if to show off the pink shine to its hair. Even though it stood far away, Jasper could appreciate both the beauty and raw power in the animal. Muscles grinded as it lifted a foot and scuffed it against the floor several times.

He wanted to whoop and leap with joy, but was conscious that it was late in the night. He wasn't sure exactly what hour the clocks were saying it was, but he knew that people in the house wouldn't appreciate his celebrations right now.

"Calm down, Fairy godmother."

Jasper whirled round. Alex was sat on the bottom step and amusement lit her face. She was strapped up from nearly head to toe with bandages. There even seemed to be a new plaster under her chin.

The horse trotted to Jasper's side, poking its nose into his shoulder. He reached up to stroke it. "Alex," he greeted. "Where's everyone else?"

"Busy with something else or in bed," she dismissed quickly with a wave. "What are you changing next? Maybe a pumpkin into a carriage? Mice into men? What about a house into gingerbread? Throw things in reverse for a laugh."

"I was just testing out a spell."

He looked up at his creation and smiled, but it faltered. There was always a pay-off for magic and tiredness had creeped into his bones. It was a heavier sense than what he was used to. Maybe older magic, because it was more direct and specific, not just thoughts and feelings and motions wrapped into one. A heavier exchange.

"Why?" Alex questioned. "You don't need spells."

The horse nipped his skin and he yelped. The horse chuffed, and he sighed, turning back to his sister. "I wanted to see if they could still be done."

She rose up from the steps with a loud, long groan. "I would have assumed they could be," she said. "Magic's moved on, but it hasn't changed *that* much that something wouldn't just stop working altogether."

"You don't know. There could be a spell to summon a dragon and that might not work anymore."

"That spell wouldn't work because dragons aren't real."

"What if there's one to make it real?"

"Do it then," she challenged. "Bring a dragon to life."

"I can't do it right now!"

Her eyebrow rose. "Why not?"

"I'm out of practise."

"If you're out of practise, I'm out of shape. And I'm in the best shape."

It was Jasper's turn to raise an eyebrow. "You look it," he said, indicating to her many current injuries.

Alex sighed. "Fine. I'll let you win that one."

"You'll *let me* win?" He laughed once. "I don't think so." The horse pulled back from his touch to nudge his back, managing to push him a step closer to Alex. "Will you stop that?" he muttered to the horse, before reaching up to stroke it again.

Alex nodded at the animal. "How long does your little spell say that thing will last?"

Jasper peered down at the book and then back up. "It doesn't."

"Are you serious? We could be stuck with a horse, forever?"

"Don't you want a pony?" he teased. "All little girls do."

Alex's glare could've melted metal. "Say that again, I fucking dare you." Jasper didn't dare, choosing to remain silent instead. "What were you really doing? And I don't believe your bullshit for one minute about wanting to try an old spell."

"You should believe it," he said.

"And yet I don't."

Jasper folded his arms across his chest. He hadn't expected someone to come down to the training room this late at night and discover him. He wasn't *lying* to Alex; he really had wanted to try out more magic, to feel more power. But he hadn't told her the whole truth either.

The horse sniffed in Alex's direction and then reared back. "I don't think she likes you," Jasper commented. He touched his palm to his creation and the animal calmed slightly.

"Well, she can join the list," Alex said. "Anyway, why would anyone write and need a spell to change a chair into a horse? Doesn't seem like the most advanced magic you'd want to remember."

"Movability?" Jasper answered, though wasn't sure of his own words. "The book didn't say how old each spell was. Maybe horse upkeep when the spell was written was expense and they couldn't afford one permanently. Or to use in a quick getaway? Make the immovable move."

"Are you going to try and ride it?"

"Do I look stupid?" Jasper sighed. "Actually, don't answer that. I don't need you to."

"Did *you* want a pretty pony and wished really, *really* hard?" Alex teased, her mouth twisting up at the edges. "Is that why you picked that spell?"

"I flipped to a random page. And there are worse things to have."

"Is that why you're down here? To avoid the worse things you have?"

Jasper fixed her with a stare, but once against didn't answer. His heart thudded loudly in his chest. How close Alex was to the truth was worrying.

"Alright then." Alex prowled closer. "If you won't tell me why you're really here..."

Alex gave him exactly one second to figure out what she was about to do before she did it, and he was still too slow.

Her back arched and a growl tore from her throat. The snapping of her bones echoed. Brown fur grew over every inch of visible skin and claws replaced fingernails.

Jasper stared at Alex's wolf form, and then backed up.

She launched at him the second he moved.

Her right foot tipped him backwards, the claws grazing his skin, but somehow the horse he'd made nudged him mostly out of harm's way. He looked at it, curious. Alex didn't do anything to the horse and nor did the animal retaliate, but it had definitely moved him aside enough to avoid being hurt worse than a few tiny scratches.

Jasper had chosen the wrong moment to think about it. When he looked back at Alex, she was already running for him again.

Stretching his hands out, he dug for his magic. It bounced around until he let it free. Ropes fell from the ceiling and chains rose from the ground. Alex snarled and dodged in a zigzag motion around them. Jasper grunted, forcing more and more to form, ignoring how the tiredness he felt seemed to overtake the energy he had.

Leaping over the last few obstacles that sprung up too slowly, Alex caught Jasper and they tumbled to the ground. He groaned as he sat up again. But Alex beat him back down, a paw to his chest.

Alex nearly always seemed to know what Jasper needed. He was wound inside too tightly, too much like a coiled spring over what had happened at the last Monster fight, at how Natalia had just run away before it had even ended. He knew he wouldn't be getting answers as to why any time soon. And so, right now, he needed a distraction. Magic was just one avenue. Fighting was another.

The horse trotted into view and Jasper sighed heavily. Alex snapped her jaws and snorted quick breaths out of her nose.

Flattening his palms to the ground, Jasper felt for the pipes beneath the house. His magic seeped out in search of them. When it locked on, he smiled. Then he closed his palms.

Explosions thundered. Alex jumped off him immediately,

and he scrambled to his feet, readying his stance again. All he'd down was sent his magic out to knock against all the houses' pipes simultaneously. There would be no damage, just noise and shock.

And Alex realised that a second later.

She snarled and barrelled forwards. Jasper swung round the horse, using it as a momentary barrier. But it didn't work. Alex skidded beneath it, right at his ankles. He yelped as her sharp canines caught a piece of his ankle. He darted away and looked down, and saw blood rising out of one short gash.

"I hope you're sorry!" he half-yelled.

Both Alex and the horse chuffed in shared amusement.

With his heart pumping hard, Jasper slipped around the room as Alex chased. He knew she could've easily caught him, she was much faster than he was, but she allowed him to stay one step ahead.

As he closed in on the steps, he barrelled up two and then jumped back. He barely missed landing on Alex's tail by an inch. Grimacing, he dived for the spell book he'd used, scooped it up, and flipped to a new page.

Only fire Nymphs were supposed to be able to control fire to its greatest capacity. Yet Jasper landed on a page indicating to a Witches spell to create small balls of the fire. He had to be fast. Alex was already coming for him again.

"*For all that's water, don't make it rain. For all that's dire, serve me small fire.*"

In the palm of his hand, a pink flame burned to life. It hissed and spat, and Jasper gawked.

Alex skidded to a halt, then backed up a step. Jasper laughed and waved the fireball towards her. She shook her furry head.

The horse whined, pointing its nose at the fireball. Jasper raised an eyebrow, but the horse persisted, up until the point it stopped. In one breath, it keeled over sideways and in a puff of smoke was transformed back into a chair again.

Jasper looked back at his hand and saw what the horse had been indicating too. The fire was now no longer pink, but red and burning. And then he felt the scorch of it.

"*Fuck!*" he hissed as he let go of his hold.

The magic and flame died at once. But it had already burned.

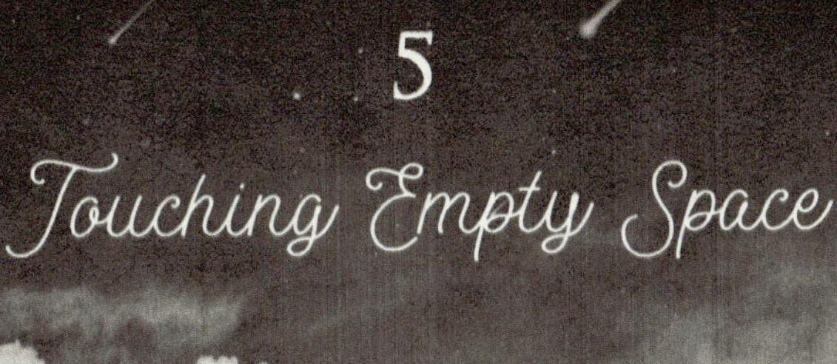

5

Touching Empty Space

GOLD WAITED PATIENTLY, one leg crossed over the other, while Evangeline disposed of the Snask.

Her blade arched neatly and cut the neck.

Huffing, she shuffled to the Snask's side and grabbed under its grotesque scales, tearing the head from the body. But she didn't hold onto it in triumph. She was still the same woman, still the girl who hated to hurt anyone and any *thing*. Even Monsters. Though she knew now that they needed to be disposed of.

Throwing the head to the leafy grass beside the lake, she sat beside Gold. He reached into his jacket pocket and drew out a handkerchief, passing it without even looking. Green slime coated the upper part to her purple dress and Gold didn't want to see the piece ruined. Evangeline seemed to notice at the same time and took the offering.

"You can hardly tell that you've been away from the field for one hundred years," he commented.

"I may only teach," she said, still cleaning, "but I am hardly away from it all as you claim."

Gold's smile was gentle. "You are not as involved as you once were."

Evangeline tried to hand back the messed cloth and Gold shook his head. She set it on fire.

After the girl had retreated in on herself, she'd barely re-emerged over the years. It was a shame. Gold thought Evangeline was a rather good fighter, one this world needed, but she had never been for this world. Strange circumstances had brought her into it. And while she did refuse to leave it completely, teaching those in Atlantis in classrooms and through books, she didn't venture out into the bigger Monster fights like she once had.

Gold surveyed the stagnant water before them. "This park is beautiful. I can see why you chose it."

Evangeline stiffened. "We've been here before."

He glanced at her for a moment before facing the lake once more. Then he saw it. The little boathouse across the water, with its twisted columns on either side of the red door.

They'd met for the first time here, in London. Evangeline had been mostly unconscious and hadn't known who had helped, until she'd laid eyes on him again. Gold saved her life that day; a young girl who'd come along for a stroll with the wrong person. Gold had taken her to be healed after the incident and then had sent her away, to the best place he'd known, to keep her safe. For what she found there, it hadn't been a complete loss.

"Do you remember it?" Gold asked, less delicately than he would've liked.

Eva's fingers traced the two permanent dots on her neck. "Sometimes, but never much."

He took her hand firmly. "And look at you now, my dear. Look at the life you've had since."

She turned to study his face. The same Evangeline who always evaluated.

Today, her wavy hair was tied atop her head, yet a single curl hung down the side of her face. The blue of her eyes matched the sky. Like this, it was hard to see her for her true age. She was timeless.

She dropped her gaze to their hands. "I know your note the

other day meant more than you taking some of my magic," she said. It was Gold's turn to stiffen. "And I know this meeting isn't just so you can remind me of old times."

"I don't quite see what you mean, my dear."

"You wanted the walk. You sent the note."

"You magicked us both here," he countered. Gold stroked the back of her hand with his thumb. "Why *did* you choose this place?"

Eva shrugged at that. "I lived most of my life indoors, in *that* house, and later Atlantis. This park is one of the few places around here I remember." She looked across the lake. "This is *your* plan. The location doesn't matter. If you have something to ask, *ask.*"

This was no longer the girl who was born in the countryside and lived a sheltered life. No longer did she hide or stumble over words. She'd always been strong; it had just taken a few magical moments to bring it out.

Gold ran his tongue over his fangs. "My dear," he said calmly. "These people are going to need a lot of help, a lot more *hands on* help."

He watched her gulp. "What are you saying, Gold?"

"You cannot deny how deftly you disposed of that Snask, as if it were no more than a nuisance. There is much you have to offer, much more than I."

Despite not needing to, Eva took a steady breath. It was times like this when Gold wished he could see into minds, read thoughts and glimpse the words etched behind eyelids. These two had been tied together for over one hundred years. Yet Gold still could not predict what Evangeline would say or do. It was a quality he'd always enjoyed from the outside, but up close, it made him uneasy.

"You want me to get involved?" she asked, still not meeting his eyes.

"Haven't you already been?" he countered.

"By your hand, not mine. This is quite a lot you're asking of me."

"If I thought it untrue or unnecessary, I wouldn't ask." He offered her a smile though she did not look. "There is something *big* going on, something ungodly."

"Who are you to speak about Gods or the ungodly?"

"The Seven are still believed, even if not by me."

Gold have never believed any of the tales about the Seven Gods. Never once had he been given reason too. He'd been alive longer than most and had never heard so much as a faint whisper from them.

"I can feel it in the air," he continued, undeterred. "I think you can, too."

"Can you know that?"

"I cannot know if you feel what I do. But I swear to you that there is something, and when it comes, they will need help from both of us."

Eva shuffled in her seat and drew her single curl back behind her ears. "I will give it thought."

She stood and disappeared in a cloud of grey, not once looking back.

Gold took off his monocle to clean it on his shirt. He'd thought this place was beautiful moments ago, and still did, but something about the world itself felt *dimmer*.

He sincerely hoped Eva would give his proposition some thought, because he feared it might not only be Natalia and the Darby's that required assistance. Just maybe, the whole world did.

Tony was convinced something was following him.

It wasn't until he reached the café and stared into the reflection that his thoughts were confirmed correct. He turned and drew the small, plain blade the Darby's had gifted to him. The Monster sank closer and Tony spotted the glowing red eyes. But as the Monster looked at him, it stopped. Its eyes narrowed like it was squinting, trying to understand who he was. Tony shivered.

Nothing happened and the Monster left.

Tony considered chasing it, but decided against it for two reasons. He had no combat training, besides the bare minimum from *years* ago, and this Monster could've been trying to lead him into a trap.

He tucked the blade away slowly, heart pounding in his throat in anger.

The bell on the café tinged as he pushed it open. Passing by a busy Noah, Tony stormed out to the back. He paused by the windowsill, eyeing the fresh cookies cooling there.

The uniced side of a knife came down on his hand before he could steal one. Katherine laughed. With her distracted, he stole a sweet treat, tasting the raspberry tang on his tongue.

Katherine stopped laughing but couldn't quite manage to keep up the scowl on her face as he ate. "What good thing did I do to earn this visit?"

He pecked her pink-painted lips. "Nothing."

Suddenly, her hand suddenly shot out and grabbed the handle of the blade he hadn't quite hidden well enough. "What happened?"

Tony glanced out towards the store-front. "There was a Shadow," he whispered.

"A Shadow?" Her voice trembled.

"Right by the door. It followed me. I don't know how long for."

Katherine's eyes widened with alarm. "Did you deal with it?"

"It looked right at me, yet wanted nothing to do with me. I didn't *have* to deal with it." He touched her hand and took back his blade, tucking it away properly. "It went away on its own."

"As easy as that?"

He nodded. "It saw me and just left."

Katherine gulped visibly. "That's not normal."

"I'm aware of that."

After all, the Shadows had been the ones to haunt Natalia, a Monster hoard turned collection crew, controlled by something else.

Had this Shadow been stalking him as a way to get to her? If so, why did it just float off when it saw Tony instead of attacking? Whoever was pulling the strings, they were willing to try and snatch a young woman right in front of everyone, and kill without remorse, so they'd hardly leave a father if it meant reaching their goal.

The Shadow was gone for now. Tony was sure it would return, or something else would, but mulling over why any Monster was present wouldn't get him anywhere. He'd take the small, momentary blessing while it was offered.

He pointed to the white box on the counter. "Someone's birthday?"

Katherine sighed, knowing he was distracting her, but went along nonetheless. "Yeah. A customer put in a special request. A sunflower designed vanilla cream cake."

"That sounds delicious."

"I'll make you one for your next birthday."

He smiled. "Will you?"

Katherine put down her decorating knife and touched his hands. He responded by drawing her closer. They'd been dancing around each other for years, so to have her this close, still seemed so unreal at times. He wondered if one day someone would pinch him and it'd all disappear. Their lips touched and as soon as they did, Tony heard a cough. He smiled against Katherine but they pulled back. Noah stood awkwardly in the doorway, shuffling on his feet.

"When you're *quite* finished," said Noah, doing his best to not look.

Tony snorted. Sometimes Noah sounded and acted so much like Natalia it was hard to tell where one started and the other ended. He supposed that's what happened when two people shared lives for so long.

"Are we ruining your day?" Katherine threw back happily enough.

"I should tell you to get a room."

Katherine shook her head and peered at the clock. "On a break?"

"Yes." He hesitated.

"But?"

Noah moved aside. Tony gasped.

Tucked into the shadows of the bright café, was his daughter.

Since going to the Darby's almost two weeks ago, Natalia had locked herself back in the house. Something had spooked her back into hiding. He'd tried talking to her about just doing something, but her old ways of one walk a day had settled in again.

Tony's first thought was that something was wrong. Remembering the Shadow, he let go of Katherine and scanned Natalia for any signs of attack.

Nothing, he thought. There wasn't even a faint scratch on her skin.

"Natalia," Katherine greeted calmly.

Natalia stepped further into the kitchen. Though her wings weren't present, Tony could almost envision them; the was bronze encased in glass.

"Katherine," Natalia responded. She looked at him briefly, a ghost of a smile tugging the corner of her mouth.

"Grab an apron," Katherine commanded gently.

Natalia did as instructed and Tony let out a sharp breath. *This could be the turning point.*

His mind flickered to the Shadow again, and he turned away from his daughter, a single tear welling in one eye.

What is normality now?

No one mentioned Natalia's absence as she worked, but she knew they'd all been thinking about it.

Several times, Katherine looked like she might throw her arms around Natalia but halted at the last minute. If she *had* hugged her, it would've been acknowledging that something was wrong. While there *was* something wrong, gravely and detrimentally so, Natalia's visits to the Darby's weeks prior had proved to the still-doubtful part of her that she wasn't entirely alone.

She could work and have friends, but deep down knew that there might come a time when she would have to leave them behind again to keep them safe.

The tram-ride home was steady, lazy. Other passengers clearly hoped for a breeze in the blistering summer heat's dead, humid air. Those walking along the paths sweated visibly and bugs could be heard buzzing around the dying grass and drooping flowerbeds. Windows of passing houses were thrown wide open.

Today had been a record high for a Venderly summer and the café kitchen had been stifling. Weirdly, Natalia had barely felt any of it.

She rang the little bell beside her and jumped off the back of the tram when it stopped. She crossed the road and waved at the driver to let them know she was out of the way. The driver pulled the bell and set the tram off again. She rarely used the tram, but today she'd decided to spare her legs the ache.

Unlocking her door, a smell assaulted her senses. She sniffed the air, peering around cautiously. When she looked down, she noticed a sunflower trapped under her foot. She picked it up. A few petals fell off, yellow and bright.

Did someone squeeze it through the letterbox?

As she moved inside and closed the door behind her, she realised there was another sunflower further down the hall.

"Hello?" Natalia called wearily.

She always cursed at people in horror films for calling out, like would the attacker really respond? But now she understood. It was so *they* could warn the attacker that they knew they were there.

Before Natalia could count, she had collected a handful of flowers. Finding herself in the kitchen, she put them in the sink.

Something shuffled behind her.

Without blinking she brandished her blade in one hand, whirled around, grabbed and forced the attacker against the wall with her free hand. Only, once she had blinked, she realised it wasn't an attacker.

"This is becoming a bit of a *thing*," Jasper joked. He peered down at the blade. "At least it's an upgrade from a spoon."

Natalia retreated, putting her blade down on the table. "You scared me to death!"

He pinched her shoulder, making her yelp. "Clearly you're alive."

"I could've cut you!"

"You would be responsible for the healing afterwards, it's fine."

"It isn't fine!"

"How about next time, to make it fair, I'll push you against the wall with an axe?"

"I thought you were an attacker."

"Do those kinds of people often leave a trail of flowers to follow? Something I find rather sweet and romantic? If I do say so myself."

Natalia sighed and he laughed, the noise filling the small space. Jasper lowered himself into a chair. His hair hung lower on his face than usual. His green eyes lacked some of their usual spark, and his freckles appeared less vibrant. Natalia's eyes travelled lower, and she caught a glimpse of white peeking out from beneath the collar of his t-shirt.

"You're hurt," she realised.

"I'm fine," he dismissed.

She slid into the chair beside him and took his hand. He stared at their entwining fingers as if he couldn't believe it. Her face heated.

They'd kissed plenty of times yet this moment felt more intimate.

She stroked circles on top of his hand. "What happened?"

"That last fight." He pulled his hand away. Natalia shrunk back but quickly straightened as he pulled his t-shirt off. Four bandage patches covered him from the base of his neck to torso. There was also a burn to his palm, she noticed, as he flung his clothing aside. "I got burnt. I did my healing thing with the candles in the training room. Clearly it wasn't enough."

That fight happened two weeks ago. Two weeks he must've been suffering. "Why didn't you come to me?" she challenged.

He blinked, obviously confused. "What?"

"I've never tried..."

Natalia reached out, touched the highest patch, and peeled it away. Jasper didn't try and stop her.

A vicious, red welt branded his pale white skin.

Drawing dust took effort but she made the bronze come forth. Jasper's eyes widened and his hands began to come up defensively. She moved to fast though, sticking her palm directly over the mark.

Jasper's hand encased her wrist as he pulled air in through his teeth. Natalia hated the idea of him being in pain, and it made her heart ache to think she was possibly making it worse. But as Jasper's noises faded, she realised his grip had loosened too. Taking a deep breath, she removed her touch.

All her medicinal training, all her schooling to become a nurse, couldn't have prepared her for this. This *magic*. The welt faded to something no more than a white spot.

Natalia looked up at his face. He studied the burn. "Will you let me do the others?"

He glanced up, his eyes reflecting his trust in her as he nodded.

Natalia's dust worked. The two week old wounds shrivelled to pinhead sized dots; thought they didn't completely disappear, small dots were better than melting scars. Jasper remained silent as her hands spanned over his palm - the wound there seemed fresher- and upper-body. Eventually, her fingers touched the fist-sized scar. *That* made him react. He winced, but didn't try removing her hands again. She knew she couldn't help this mark; it was too scarred, too solid, and too old. So she moved along, winding her fingers along his skin, round his neck, until they were tangled in his already messy hair.

Jasper's hands snaked around her waist, pulling her close. Against her mouth, he whispered, "Not bad for someone who's never done that before."

She watched his lips. "You bought me flowers. Did you know they meant joy?"

"I hoped the flowers might give you some."

"You didn't have to."

He kissed her cheek an inch from the corner of her mouth. "I know."

"But, you did."

"But, I did." He brushed his lips over hers, a ghost of an action, enough to drive Natalia mad. "Anything for you."

Wholly and completely, she kissed him.

Fire burned along her arms and back, the itch of her wings threatening to explode spreading. But she ignored it. If they were to break, then so be it. They would break together.

They didn't pay much attention to their surroundings, until they ended up on the floor. Natalia didn't feel her back hit the ground, nor the weight of Jasper as he followed on top. He laughed and moved an arm out from underneath her to hold her side tenderly. Her fingertips focused on his new scars, gently touching them; they weren't ugly or pretty, but a memory and reminder of who and *what* he was.

"This is interesting," he grinned. "We've never been here before."

"Here?" she asked. "I've been in my kitchen before, I'm sure."

"Did you know your eyes sparkle?" he announced suddenly.

Natalia froze, fearing that if she moved the moment would end. He smiled like he didn't feel her tension. "There's a bronze twinkle to them. It outlines the brown."

Natalia cupped his face and brought him down to her. Closer and closer he lowered until they met again. One of his hands twisted into strands of her hair that splayed across the floor. The other hand went lower. Because it'd been hot, she'd worn shorts, and now his deft fingers traced up her thigh, stopping at the edge of the material.

This wasn't about them being delicate, nor was it about them breaking the other. This was them summoning each other's songs until they weaved together as a duet.

She wrapped her legs around Jasper's waist and found the strength to roll them over. He kissed the underside of her jaw, making her shiver as she put her hands on either side of his head.

Delicately, Jasper tucked her hair over her shoulder. "So, you liked the flowers?"

She kissed the tip of his nose. "Whatever gave you that idea?"

"Maybe next time you can get *me* some flowers?"

His hands touched her wrists and ran up her arms. She gasped when he pressed against her brutal mutilation, the T-shape scar burning as if it's just been freshly cut into her flesh.

Immediately, the moment disappeared and she yanked her arms from him. She clambered back, pressing into the cabinets and folding inwards.

"Natalia," he said, sitting up. "I'm sorry! I didn't mean to hurt you, please know that. "

"I do," she gulped. "I do know that."

"*Did* I hurt you?" he asked.

She shook her head. "No."

He scooted closer. "I'm so sorry."

"You didn't do anything but touch me. The memory sprang forwards on its own. That wasn't your fault either." She willed herself not to cry. "Does it get easier?"

"The less you think of them, the more they fade. They become blurry. I don't know if they'll ever go, but it'll be easier to see them." He pointed to the dots and the fist-sized scar at his throat. "I should know. I have lots of scars and lots of memories."

Natalia's eyes welled until her sight grew fuzzy. "You got yours in battle, not because you were a designed target of an attack." Jasper was quiet and calm, open to hearing whatever she had to say. She took a deep breath. "I'm different. Not just from you, but from fairies in general. From *all* Creatures."

No matter how far she thought she'd come, life still made sure she took ten steps back whenever there was a glimmer of hope.

Her scar reminded her she was special, that she was wanted, and that she had no answers. It told her that there might be a thing like fate and it worked against her. It served as a reminder of all the people she'd hurt and how much further she might still have to fall.

How could people believe being special was good? Natalia had only known it to be a tragedy. She didn't know who wanted her, why, or what for. What did the difference in her wings mean? What really was she?

Jasper reached across the space dividing them. Natalia let him drag her to his chest, tucking her there. He spoke softly. "You *are* different but you're still you. Still the girl that took on the Council with swear-words and anger. Still the girl who faced a Calefaction in an unknown City. Still the girl who danced in a kitchen on an injured leg. The girl that rescued another from a collapsing jail. The girl that fought *for* a Monster after they'd been torn apart by one. The girl that tried to fight the figure that wanted them."

She shivered against him. She'd forgotten none of those memories but now Jasper had spoken them, she could almost see them the way he did – with a shiny, *brave* edge. He pulled back to search her face.

"You're still the girl who danced with me," he continued, his comforting smirk returning. "So what if you're different from anyone else? Whatever's coming, we can work it out and face it together." He kissed her forehead with such sincerity and kindness it made her ache. "And, anyway, I like different. I like *you*."

Natalia kissed him and tasted the salt of her own tears. Without opening her eyes, she whispered one word, "Stay."

Jasper made a choking sound of surprise. "Excuse me?"

"Stay the night. Here."

"Oh, I don't know. Let me call my mum first."

For what seemed to be the first time in a long while, Natalia truly laughed.

Though she wanted to push Jasper away, to argue that this was her fight alone, Natalia knew he wouldn't be moved. Whatever she wanted, Jasper would stay by her side regardless. As would they others, she knew. She couldn't keep denying her own wants either. *But* she would protect them at any cost.

Natalia yawned and Jasper helped her to her feet. "That's the healing kicking in," he said.

"I'm pretty sure *I* healed *you*." She yawned again.

He led her through the house. "Healing uses a transfer of energy. Your energy passed into me to increase my natural healing rate."

"So you get better and I get tired?" They climbed the stairs.

"Mostly. A nap to a long sleep should replenish you enough. Just promise me you won't ever try and heal too much. I don't think anyone will have told you this but healing comes with a greater price than almost any other type of magic."

"What?"

Jasper stopped and captured her face in his hands. "If you try to heal any wound that's too deep or too *much*, you could exhaust yourself. You might keel over and never get up again. It's happened. Promise me you won't ever go that far. Promise me you'd only ever heal until you felt uncomfortable at worst."

Natalia's stomach pinched. "I won't, promise."

Even as the words tumbled out she knew she couldn't hold herself to them. How could she? She would do anything for those she cared about, even at the expense of herself.

Jasper, however, seemed to accept it. He opened the door to her room and led on. She watched him as a memory surfaced, making her cheeks flush. A memory of him walking into her room wearing nothing, his peachy arse perfectly on display.

"You should come over tomorrow," Jasper suggested. "Peri's been itching to have a movie night with you apparently."

"Oh?" Natalia tried to hide her grimace. Peri was the biggest reminder of what Natalia being different meant and what could happen because of it.

He smiled. "I think it'd be fun. A girlie night."

"I don't think you'll be invited." She managed to crack a smile.

"Shame. I think I'd giggle perfectly."

"Do you think movie nights are filled with talking about gossip and giggling?" Jasper raised his eyebrows, making her scoff. "Oh no. It's more like blood sacrifices and stuff. But I can't tell. It's for those invited to know and everyone else to never figure out."

"Maybe we can all have dinner together afterwards though?"

She rose on her tip-toes and kissed his jaw. "Sounds lovely."

Jasper turned around and halted. Natalia became overwhelmed and suddenly worried she'd over-stepped some line. Had she asked Jasper to stay too soon? But when she looked up at him, his eyes weren't on her, but on a burgundy dress that hung on the door of her wardrobe.

Natalia dashed to it and shoved it inside carelessly.

"It's a dress," he commented, though he could no longer see it.

"Well observed."

"One for any particular reason?"

"Peri and Alex made me buy it a few months back." And she had never put it away. Every time she looked at it, it felt like a promise she intended to keep somehow, if only to herself. She dropped her gaze. "I was going to ask you on a date. I had no plans but—"

Jasper crossed to her in a single step and cut her off with a kiss. "When things are settled, when we're all on a good footing again, *especially* you," he gave her no room to argue with a menacing stare, "then you'll get to wear the dress. I'll design the date. *I'll* take *you* out."

"Is that a threat?"

"Depends. Did you enjoy it?"

She laughed and kissed him solidly, but didn't deny it.

Letting go, she ran to the bathroom to change and emerged in grey shorts and blue sleep-top. Jasper was already tucked in her bed, half under the thin duvet, t-shirt still absent. One arm was under a pillow while his other patted the empty space beside him. Natalia suppressed the urge to run and jump into the space, moving gently instead. He wrapped his arm over her casually once she was settled beside him, ignoring the lingering heat of the day just to hold her.

Natalia switched the light off and the room drifted into mild darkness. The fan above them whirled noisily.

Jasper's lips pressed to her temple. "Get some rest."

Natalia didn't respond. He could probably sense the exhaustion already wracking her body, even before the healing.

He kissed her head again and she didn't need to be told a third time.

Her eyes grew heavier and though she worried about being so close to Jasper, as if her words and actions were possible poison, he had promised to be with her through this. She would do whatever it took to protect him. She cared for him *deeply*, but tonight she was glad he was here.

Her chest rose and fell at an increasingly steady rate. She breathed in the smell of rain. Moving one last time, she shuffled to press her back into his chest, and finally felt comfortable enough to swim down into the realm of dreams.

Excruciating pain cracked across her body. Yet the glass kept being pushed into her arm. Blood continued to seep from the purposefully made wound, tugging at her consciousness.

Natalia watching herself, aching to wake the girl who was so close to drowning. But she could only stare like a ghost.

Natalia traced the healed lines of the scar on her arm. She often followed the path of ruined skin with her fingers, though she didn't know whether she was drawing strength or bringing pain from the past in doing so.

As she looked up, she saw something.

The darkest Shadow she'd ever seen hovered above the waves. Its eyes watched the two bodies on the sand. Natalia realised with a start that it wasn't just watching but spying. They'd acted like foot soldiers before. But how often had they stood by and just watched?

Natalia had seen the hooded figure command them. Is that why they watched? Could the figure see through the Shadows? The figure had even appeared to speak through the Monsters, so why wouldn't they be able to do more?

But how?

In the time it took for Natalia to blink, the Shadow above the waves vanished. She searched for it but couldn't see it anywhere. She moved her attention back to herself as she heard a rich growl.

Alex's wolf had finally appeared and was now fighting the Monster that had just moments ago trapped past Natalia's body with its own. That left past Natalia time to stagger to her feet. She took several shaky breaths before charging into the fight again.

Natalia caught the other version of herself flexing her fingers as she ran by.

The glass that had been inserted inside her arm fell to the sand with a soft thump.

Jasper lay awake. Not because he couldn't sleep, but rather because he didn't want to. A beautiful Fairy rested beside him, tucked against him, and *she'd* been the one to ask. He wanted to take her in as much as possible.

He'd been in a situation like this before with another girl, but those feelings then had been nothing like these. Then had been nothing but a wavering spark. But this felt as if a whole firework display was constantly exploding around him.

He knew what people said about him, that he jumped into bed with anyone. That was far from the truth. He had to have feelings for the other person first, *strong* feelings. Because of that, he'd only been here once before, and that hadn't lasted long. He'd been the one to end it after a few months. They'd been young, smaller in themselves, discovering who they were and what they wanted – it hadn't been each other.

This, with Natalia, felt *right*.

He'd heard his brother and Peri talk about the idea of soul mates plenty of times but he'd never believed them. Now he might admit that he was starting to believe.

Suddenly, Natalia started panting and her dust flew around the room like the beginnings of a bronze sand-storm.

Jasper rose out of bed and tried shaking her awake – he'd heard that shaking people in nightmares was a bad idea, but he'd rather keep his head attached than she lose hers inside a never-ending darkness.

Her eyes burst open and her dust rained around them, falling like glitter. "What's happening?"

"You were freaking out," he told her. "Are you alright?"

He could faintly see her touch the scar on her arm. "I was dreaming," she whispered. "I dreamt about when I got this." He got the feeling she was omitting something. "Otherwise, I feel fine."

"Maybe you need to come round earlier in the day tomorrow?"

She shuffled to sit up. "What for?"

"Just to make sure nothing sinister is still stuck in your arm," he answered, half-lying.

Of course, there *could* be something residual in her arm that had caused her terror and reaction. He'd heard of it happening before. But Jasper felt in his gut that this wasn't that. Her unconscious mind had reacted to something. He wanted all aspects checked- the physical *and* mental *and* emotional.

For now, he let it slide. She really did need sleep. She needed to heal as much as him.

He kissed her temple and pulled her back down, flinging his arm over her like a protective barrier.

"Don't leave," she muttered.

He held her tighter. "I won't."

Jasper knew exactly when she fell asleep again. Like he wanted to convince himself this was real, that he really was with her, he whispered, "I'm here," over and over until he, too, finally slipped under.

6

Hell is Easier

ZOE SIGHED AND ROSE FROM THE BED, her pleasant dreams already slipping from her mind. She flung her knotted braid over her shoulder and stumbled into the bathroom, almost falling under the warm steam of the shower.

Dawn hadn't yet risen; Zoe almost always woke before it, and wouldn't try to fight it. She'd start the day earlier, often with a walk. It was a way for her to clear her head, to brush off the night's cobwebs. Dressing in simple shorts and vest, she towel dried and re-plaited her hair, then headed out.

The warm air clung to her, but Zoe took it in her stride. She didn't need to be at work before midday, so she had plenty of time to take things slow. The nearby stretch of beach came into view. The patch of sand was small, but she slipped off her shoes and padded to the water's edge anyway. The soothing coolness touched her toes and she sighed. She revelled in it gleefully before walking on.

Further along, Zoe noticed something lying by the water. As she moved closer, she could see it was a person. But it didn't look right. Zoe squinted and then gasped. The person's head was *in* the sea, their face barely visible, and their body on top of the sand.

Zoe dropped her shoes and ran. She grabbed the person's shoulders and hauled them sideways by the top of their t shirt. When they were clear of the water, she sank at their side. Visually, she couldn't see anything hurt or broken.

Brown eyes burst open, the body springing up. Zoe flinched. The girl blinked as if they'd sensed it. She had light brown eyes that matched her bronze skin – which had spots of bruising – and her hair dragged against her shoulders. Her lips, Zoe noticed, were reddish. She forced her gaze up to the nose and then eyebrow stud.

"Can I help you?" The girl blurted.

"'Scuse me?" Zoe asked, dumbfounded.

"Can. I. Help. You?" she repeated, taking slow pauses between words.

"*You* were lying in the sea. *You* looked like you were drowning!"

The girl ran her eyes over Zoe's face, making her own soften. She could've been sixteen or twenty-five; she had that sort of fresh look to her features. "I was cooling off," she simply explained. Her accent was definitely American, though Zoe couldn't place where. "I been for an early morning run and decided to rest before running home."

"You 'ung upside-down in the ocean to cool off?"

The girl let out a throaty laugh. "Let's just say, sometimes it's the only way."

Zoe didn't know what that meant.

Suddenly, the girl sprung up. Zoe clambered after her. With dawn finally breaking over the horizon in pinks, Zoe realised the girl was someone Noah had been hanging around with.

Noah hadn't spent much time divulging where he'd been swanning off to after work, only that Opal House and its occupants were involved. The recently new residents to Venderly Island were his friends.

The girl was Alex Darby.

"You're a Darby," Zoe spluttered. She grimaced at the awkward response.

Thankfully, Alex took it well. "A Darby indeed," she agreed.

"You know my brother."

As if that piqued her interested, Alex ran her eyes over Zoe's entire body. "Noah?"

"I'm Zoe." Alex's mouth quirked and Zoe tried to stay focused. "He told me about you."

Alex scraped her fingers through her sodden hair. "He told us about you."

"He did?"

"He wasn't wrong when he'd said you two would pass as twins. You're just shorter."

Zoe smiled. Her and Noah were inches apart – him at five ten, her at five six. It had always been a game about who would grow taller. Plenty of marks in the kitchen doorway had called it a close race right up until a few years ago when Noah had finally grown, and stayed, taller.

"What do you do when you hang out together?" Zoe asked, blurting something for the second time that morning. "He never tells me, just comes home and squirrels away with books. He says it's for a kid's library display?"

Alex gazed across the scarlet sea. "I don't hang out with him that much," she said. Her body swung back around, her face closed off. "And even if I did, it's not up to me to tell someone's baby sister what they get up to."

"*Baby sister?*" Zoe half shrieked.

"Maybe ask him what he does?" Alex asked.

Zoe composed herself despite the heat still stinging her face. "I *have* asked him."

Alex shrugged. "I don't know then." She walked off, but ten paces away turned back. "Don't forget your shoes," she called, continuing on as if they'd never spoken.

Zoe snatched up her shoes, fighting down the urge to chuck them in Alex's direction. Just thinking that made her realise how like child she'd acted. She groaned. Alex maybe had a point with her "baby sister" comment.

But she didn't entirely trust Alex either. How could a person barely "hang out" with someone who came over to their house as often as Noah did? She had to have more interaction. Unless she buried herself in her room and never came out, which *was* possible, but doing that every time?

The sand flicked into the air as she kicked it.

I'm going to find out what everyone's hiding.

Natalia stood in front of a door she'd passed through many times before. Yet her mind twisted it until it resembled a swirling portal to somewhere dangerous.

Jasper rapped his knuckles against the wood and then unlocked the door. It swung open, revealing Archie; his expression gave away nothing.

"You stayed out," Archie commented. His gaze darted to Natalia, so quickly she almost missed it. "*All* night."

"I did." Jasper pushed past his brother, took off his shoes, and leant up on the wall casually. "Next you'll be asking what I got up to. Would you like all the juicy details?"

Archie snorted and turned to Natalia. "Morning, Nat," he said, his voice smoother. "I hope your evening wasn't *too* disappointing."

Natalia laughed, the sound bubbling up from her chest. Her night hadn't been disappointing in the slightest. It was one of the best nights she'd had in a while. Someone had stayed at her side, someone who knew the darkness and had helped her chase it away.

A hand clamped down on her arm and her laughter fizzled. Natalia blinked, looking up to Peri's blue painted grin.

Natalia looked at Jasper and he offered her a quirked smile.

She wondered if he knew about her fears and how last night he'd beaten them back. Could he sense that ever since she'd discovered her wings and how *wrong* they were, sleep had eluded her or it'd been torturous? Not to mention the shadows she saw in every corner when she was awake. Did he know what he had done and continued to do for her, even if he wasn't aware he was doing it?

Peri let go of Natalia's arm, only to slide her hand down and link her fingers with Natalia's. "Can we get this meeting over with?" she asked. "I want to steal this girl!"

Natalia's heart thudded in her ears. "Meeting?"

"My dearest Fairy!"

In the living room doorway, with fangs fully extended, Gold stood proudly. As usual, he wore a demure cobalt blue suit, darker blue shirt beneath, and the monocle around his golden eye.

Natalia's gaze shifted to a blond boy imitating a statue at Gold's side.

Her eyes lingered on the boy, but when he didn't move, she turned to Gold. "I should've known," she said. He grinned. Seeing his fangs, she realised, no longer frightened her. After all, she'd seen much worse now. "I should infect your eyes with dust for what you did to me the other day."

In a single breath, the tip of a long sword pressed into the base of her neck. The statue boy stared at her from the other end. "You will not speak such things to our crowned Vampire Prince," he hissed, his voice gravelly as if he rarely spoke.

"Whoa!" Peri came to Natalia's side and pressed her hand to the blade, forcing it up and away. "If anyone's getting out a sword here, it's me. I haven't fought anyone in a long time but I'm still capable."

The boy blinked. "In your state?"

Peri's eyes flashed with anger. "*More so* in my *state*."

He blinked again before fully removing his blade, tucking it behind his back. Peri looked like a ball of fire. Archie approached her, and her temper simmered after a few whispered words, the tension seeping from her shoulders.

Peri knew her skills and power, and it was to the seven Hells for those who tried to stop her from protecting the ones she loved. Though she wasn't training now, she wasn't useless. She had years of experience to fall back on, and the second her baby arrived, she'd be swinging around her trident again. She believed in her Purpose and wanted to make the world safer.

"Dears?" Gold called to them, clearly amused.

"Crowned Prince of Vampires?" Jasper said back, equally amused. "A little pretentious, don't you think?"

The boy beside Gold twisted. "More impudence." Natalia caught a flash of brown-gold flecks in his eyes as they turned from her towards Gold himself. They appeared to communicate silently.

Gold shook his head firmly. "They are my friends," he said, rather dramatically so. "You are not to hurt them. They don't need *lessons*. And I'm not the Prince of Vampires. Just a very old one who sometimes takes others under his wing." The boy looked dismayed but said nothing. Gold faced the rest of them again, smiling. "This is Aero," he introduced, swinging an arm widely so his palm lay flat under the boy's jaw. "He's another Vampire. We both work for the Council."

"You're being punished by them."

It took a minute for Natalia to register that Archie had spoken. Kind and sweet Archie who rarely called anyone out on anything, good or bad.

Gold nodded so slowly she almost missed it. "That is how anyone comes to work for the Council, unless you're one of the Seven. It does depend on the crime," Aero stiffened as Gold continued, "and the punishments vary, as do the time scales on the debt that must be paid. But sometimes working for those who convicted you is better than the offered alternative."

No one deserved to be forced into service for the Council, crime or not. Natalia's heart went out to Gold *and* Aero - sword incident aside. She remembered the Council all too well; how cold they were and how the faceless were also heartless. Natalia couldn't imagine giving herself over to the Council, so what desperate decision had these two made?

Alex wandered into the room then, looking like she'd taken a shower. She sniffed around Aero cautiously and backed up again, grimacing. Natalia wanted to ask what was wrong but Gold switched gears in conversation.

"The Council sent us personally—"

"When don't they?" Natalia said before she could stop the words. Her eyes flew wide, though she could glimpse Jasper's hardly restrained smirk.

The Vampire was undeterred. "They sent us personally to find out the explicit details on what happened the last time a Monster struck these shores." Suddenly, the room dripped with coldness despite the summer heat. "Plus, I had my own inkling that I needed to come."

All the breath Natalia had left escaped her when Gold's eyes latched onto hers.

She ran with ice and blood, with fire and dust, with good and bad. Gold had obviously seen something that brought him here and would have, Council approved or not. Natalia was that reason, that *something*.

The worst part was that he wasn't wrong. She'd been hiding, cowering from herself *and* the truth.

I burn.

A chorus of gasps erupted.

Horror set in as Natalia realised she'd spoken aloud. Swallowing her fear, she spoke; it was too late to hide the past anyway.

"On the beach, when I was dragged away," she touched the

permanent scar on her arm, "when I got this?" She showed the T-shaped lines on her skin. "I never told you properly what happened. Alex rescued me—"

"Damn right I did," Alex interjected.

Natalia tried smiling but it hurt. "You did. But how much did you see? How much did you *hear* before?"

Alex shook her head, her curls flapping. "Nothing."

"The Monster talked to me."

"The Geminis?" Archie's gravelly voice questioned.

"Yes," she responded slowly.

"What did it say?" Jasper asked.

Natalia reached for Jasper's hand and he gave it. "She told me I wasn't wanted by her, but by someone else."

"We know that," Peri said, not unkindly, but to remind her they'd all seen it.

"But what I didn't tell you is that she partly told me *why*."

Silence consumed the air.

Jasper broke first. She wasn't sure what he intended to do, push her outside and slam the door in her face? She couldn't have been more wrong. He folded her into him, like *she* was *his* lifeline, kissed her head, and then let her rest at his side with his hand still tucked into her.

Peri matched his movements seconds later, securing Natalia's other free hand in hers. She wanted to walk away but they kept her grounded and breathing. Her palms were sweating in theirs, but they didn't seem to care. Even Archie shuffled closer.

With the softest, most motherly voice Natalia had ever heard, Peri asked, "What did the Monster say?"

Natalia gulped. "That I burn the brightest," she breathed. The memory jumped to the forefront of her mind and she winced, pulling free from Jasper to grab her own arm. The scar seared and her eyes welled with fresh tears. "She said I burn brighter than my sisters and brothers. She'd said that no one wants me because *I* burn, but because I *can* burn. I don't know what that means."

She felt a flutter in her back and, before she could stop it her, wings burst free. Jasper and Peri managed to duck before their heads were smacked off their shoulders; Archie stepped in to help Peri up from her half-wobbled dodge.

Natalia staggered back, the room shrinking further as the walls closed in. "There's more," she forced out.

"Dear," Gold said, shaking his head.

She stopped him with a hand. Her entire soul quaked. "The figure at the docks. The hooded one? I think *they* are the one that actually wants me," she continued. "They said that they were coming for me, that I was important not just to them but to the worlds."

Gold moved with incredible speed to take her outstretched hand. He kissed it softly, almost protectively. Natalia shuddered as she watched his blue and gold eyes, and her wings receded. He smiled and moved aside.

She expected to see haunted expressions, but those around her smiled. Now they knew everything and they were *smiling*. If she had put money on a reaction, it wouldn't have been this, not in out of one million options.

"I will not tell the Council of this," Gold promised. His eyes turned firmly to Aero. "Nor will you."

Aero nodded. "I will not." He'd been so quiet, so still, up to this point, Natalia had forgotten he was there.

"Why are you so willing to help?" Natalia questioned, hands still shaking. "Earlier you wanted to teach me some sort of lesson and now you want to hide my secrets?"

Aero remained still as he spoke. "Because the Council have hurt enough of us for a lot less, and you are, as of now, innocent and undeserving of their fury."

Natalia wanted to have the world swallow her whole and never spit her out. How could someone call her and her friends impudent yet decide in the next breath she was innocent without any proof, only words? She'd never thought of herself as innocent, but had she really done anything *bad*? She'd cause her friends and family pain, but she also fought against Monsters and the wrongs in life.

When it came down to her, it didn't appear like there was a right answer.

And it made her think. What had the Council done to Aero? What had they done to Gold? What had the Council considered "bad" in relation to them? Would they see Natalia as "bad"?

She knew the answer instantly, and her back twinged.

"While we will not tell the Council of your wings," Gold said, pulling her from her mind. Natalia winced. "Or of everything that transpired at the shipping dock and yard, we *will* plant seeds. We will tell them that someone might be out there, after you, for who you are. A princess, a grand-daughter to the Fairy Queen. If we twist the truth, they may believe it enough to see what they want to see from it, and hopefully will come to see what *we* need them too in time. They then may arise to the occasion if something happens." His monocle shifted on his face as he tilted his head lower. "My dear? How have you been remembering those moments? You mayhaps would not have confessed unless urged."

"My dreams," Natalia confessed.

"You were prompted by your dreams to reveal yourself today?"

"I've been having nightmares."

"Nightmares." He sighed like it was a pleasant thought. Natalia shivered. "For how long?"

"Weeks." Several gasps sounded from the others.

Gold's fangs began to show. "Dreams have a way of trying to show us what we seek," he said, glaring past Natalia's head. "They show us truths we block. You are searching for answers on your very self, no? What you are? What is running amok around you? The only way for you to find your answers is to search your mind when there is no barrier blocking it."

"And how is she to do that?" Peri asked first.

"It's a process. I know of someone who will help," Gold replied.

"Sounds suspicious to me," Alex commented.

"Ominous indeed," Jasper agreed.

"Positively untrustable," Archie added.

Jasper snorted. "Untrustable?"

Archie shrugged as Peri giggled quietly. "It's good enough."

"It's pathetic," Alex told him.

"Yeah," Jasper said. "You could've said dubious."

"Iffy?"

Jasper pointed at their sister. "Even bloody *iffy* sounds better than untrustable."

"Could've said sceptical," Peri noted aloud.

"Sceptical!" Jasper and Alex chimed together.

Archie rolled his eyes directly at Peri. "You're not helping."

Peri struggled to reach up but managed to kiss his cheek, grinning. "I'm not here to help," she announced.

Gold ignored them all. "I will set things up."

Natalia barely nodded. "Ok," she breathed out.

If Gold was right, if her dreams harboured truths her conscious mind hid and locked away, what was there to show? How did they work, how could she unlock them? What did she already know that she wasn't *seeing*?

The Vampire continued. "Aero will remain in the area." Everyone stared at the boy, each with varying degrees of wariness. "He's under fewer constraints than I, and therefore may be of more use close by." Gold gave them all a curt nod. "Try to keep out of the Council's radar. The second they get wind of more Monsters turning up here, they will come. I will try and do what I can to keep them off your back for as long as I can and will try to find what they or anyone else knows. I will also try and set you up with my contact. But you must do what you can and more."

Unfortunately, Natalia knew Gold was right. He could only do so much.

Silently, Gold left. Aero gave a sneer before following. Alex reacted first, slamming the door behind them.

"Film?" Peri asked, already gripping Natalia's wrist.

Natalia had no reply. How could she sit still and watch a film at a time like this?

As she was dragged away, she grimaced. Not at Peri, but at the very idea of having to actively swim through her nightmares. Hell might be easier to transverse, with all its potential layers, than what her mind could conjure.

Peri sat on the floor, her back against the sofa, legs out, as film watching became house hunting. The rest of the family were down at the beach – Noah had turned up at some point and was with them. Peri had stayed behind and made Natalia too. Newspapers and a laptop were thrown open on the floor. The girls even had their phones out, scrolling through various sites. But Peri's discomfort increased.

Her growing belly was becoming a problem, even if she could now happily stack a plate of biscuits on top. She felt guilty for even thinking it, but the sooner there was no bump, the better. She was done being pregnant. She wanted her baby in her arms, and she wanted to be able to sit and sleep normally again.

"What about this?" Natalia pushed a page over. "It's down Ashturn Close."

Ashturn Close was on the Eastern edge of Venderly, in the same way Opal House was the top corner on the North-East side.

Peri examined the house. It looked decent; four bedrooms, two stories, a basement set up as a laundry room, and there was even a designated play-room on the ground floor. Peri adored the fact that it sat close to the sea, and the baby kicked as if they, too, appreciated the idea. There were quite a few rooms that could do with an update - the kitchen being one - hence the lower price. Archie had said he wouldn't mind a project. Not that they had time right now.

Only around two months remained of Peri's pregnancy. That was if the timings were right and no problems arose.

Peri's heart clenched. She didn't want to think about issues or her baby hurting in any way in She reached for her trident for comfort.

Did all mothers, Creature or Human, feel this way? Did they worry over every little possible thing that might not even happen? Peri only wanted her baby to be healthy and loved and full of joy.

"It's cute," she mused aloud, looking again.

"Or this?" Natalia handed over another paper. This showed a four bedroom down Olta Street.

Peri immediately shook her head. "We can't afford that."

They'd only just really started talking about moving out of Opal House. While she and Archie had enough funds between them for somewhere cosy, they couldn't afford anything extreme. Peri wouldn't have her parents to pass on her inheritance early, like they'd always said they would, because they didn't like Archie. To be fair, her parents still didn't even know she was expecting, though she doubted that would inspire them.

She tapped on the Ashturn house paperwork again. "I like this one, more than any of the others."

Natalia raised an eyebrow. "But the work..."

Peri knew in the end they'd spend more on the house, but they didn't have to do everything at once. "We could make it *ours*," she said. "We'll focus on what we need to start with, but we could really make it a home."

As she put a hand to her stomach, Peri caught Natalia's eyes follow until they landed on the space where her other arm used to be.

The pain, Peri had gotten over. She'd lost her hand once, not that she remembered it, so she kind of felt like losing that same arm to a Monster wasn't a big deal. It was simply part of the course of this life. Gold and Evangeline had done what they could but some injuries were permanent. She'd adjusted, as she always did, and Archie was never far from her side if she called.

"What?" Peri asked rather bluntly, rubbing her stomach as the baby kicked.

"What?" Natalia said back, eyes tearing upwards. A bronze sheen coated her cheekbones and the light that poured in the window illuminated them until it sparkled and shone around her.

"You keep staring at me. Mostly when you think I can't see you."

"I'm not—"

"Did I ever tell you how I lost my hand in the first place?" Peri asked, changing the direction of the conversation. Natalia shook her head in answer. "I mean, technically, it's not lost. I know where it is. Anyway, Mermaids grow scales over their legs when they fuse, and then over their chests. There is a rare condition that can make scales grow elsewhere unprompted, usually only in one other place, but it can spread across the body and become deathly. Unfortunately for me, one day I woke up and had a few scales growing across the back of my hand. Within days, dark silver covered the entire hand. My parents took me to the doctors in Atlantis where they diagnosed me with the condition, and decided the only way to stop the possible spread was to amputate." Peri shrugged at Natalia's worrying look. "I don't remember it. I don't remember even having a hand. I was barely a year old when it happened."

Natalia ducked her head and lifted it a moment later, eyes vaguely watery. Clearly something else was still going on, still eating away at the young Fairy.

Peri reached out and touched Natalia's hand. "*Amore*, what's troubling you?"

"It's not..." She trailed off.

"Then, what? Let me help you. You don't have to keep secrets."

Peri wondered if Jasper could see how Natalia was, how she still kept things close. He probably did. He saw more than most, not that he'd ever say. Those closest to him, he knew the best, and Natalia was growing to become the closest of all.

Peri could see it in the ways they looked at each other, how Jasper reacted when Natalia entered a room, how they talked as if everyone else had disappeared. He might not even know he did it. But Peri wasn't blind.

All talk of houses was forgotten when tears spilled over the edges of Natalia's eyes.

Peri had seen Natalia in so many forms before - angry, sad, fierce, happy, blissful, hurt - but never broken.

Natalia's voice cracked when she spoke. "I could've ended two innocent lives."

Every word Peri could have said died on her tongue. She reached out with her hand and heart, wanting to say so much. That Natalia did no such thing, that she wasn't capable, that nothing had been her fault and never would've been.

Shattering glass broke the silence.

The girls stopped, eyes hot on each other, as the noise repeated. Natalia sprang up and rushed off, leaving Peri on the floor like a helpless beetle.

She knew it was wrong to leave Peri stuck on the ground, but Natalia didn't feel bad. She was safer there, away from whatever was happening. The sound of something breaking meant someone or some *thing* had broken in.

Natalia stopped a few steps into the kitchen. The doors to the garden were only frames in the wall. Glass lay strewn across the kitchen floor, smashed into crystal teardrops.

A Monster, one she'd never seen before, slithered up to the threshold. It had the black, scaly body of a snake and the upper body and arms of a lion. The Monster reminded her of a Chimera, only a more twisted version.

She drew her blade and threw it.

The blade bounced off the Monster's body and clattered to the floor like it was nothing more than a twig. Hastily, she called it back and threw again, and again it ricocheted away.

A sniff behind her made Natalia whip round. Peri stood there, shaking her head. Her trident was nowhere in sight. It was then Natalia realised what Peri wasn't saying - weapons would do nothing.

The Monster slinked closer, a forked tongue flicking from its scaled mouth. Natalia shivered once before her body took control.

She paced forwards. Feet skidded behind her, and she glanced back at Peri. Archie stood before her, his body a wall she would hopefully be safe behind. She didn't want to ask how he'd gotten here so fast, or how he knew to come at all.

Natalia turned back to the Monster as the broken glass began to rise from the ground around them.

The first piece threw itself and cut through the tiniest gap in the Monster's scales. Another piece was flung, cutting another gash. The Monster cast out its tongue to hiss and the third piece sliced it clean off.

The Monster flopped, falling chin first to the ground. It shrunk to the size of a normal snake, the black scales muting to grey as its skin withered and wrinkled. Then, it crumbled to a neat pile of ash.

Natalia sucked in a breath when she heard her name. Fear

pricked the edges of her mind. But she faced Archie and Peri anyway. The pair shared a look, and then shared it with her. It wasn't until she noticed a piece of glass hovering beside her ear that she understood what the look meant.

She snatched the glass from the air, closing her fingers around it tightly. It bit into her skin but she didn't stop. She'd thought Archie had manipulated glass with his magic. When she glanced up at him, it was like she'd said her thoughts, because he shook his head. So, if not him...

Me.

The world tipped. She let go of glass fragment. It tumbled to the ground with several drops of ruby blood. The air grew thick and sticky.

Natalia stumbled back, crushing more glass beneath her feet. She kneeled down, gasping, choking on nothing.

"You can't." She slammed her fist into the floor, fighting the urge to scream at the pain. Her back seized as she fought the oncoming onslaught of her wings, sending shockwaves along her spine. "Please," she begged, voice scratching. "You can't tell anyone about this! I don't know what's happening."

Peri sidestepped Archie. "*Amore—*"

"If Gold thinks seeing my dreams will help figure this out, then they will. They have too." She had to believe in that. She had to believe there were answers. "My dust might've just controlled..." She swallowed and staggered to her feet, feeling about as confident as her wobbly knees. "I'm going to find out what's happening. But, please, you *can't* tell *anyone.*"

"Nat?" Zoe, Noah's younger sister, ducked under Archie's arm before he could stop her. She looked between Natalia, the ash, and the broken windows. "What was that thing?"

Zoe gaped as she took it all in. Natalia staggered to her feet. Where had Zoe come from? How much had she seen? Noah had promised Zoe knew nothing of this life, so how had she gotten in? Natalia's shoulder blades pinched again.

Peri shot Natalia a sympathetic look. "She's seen now," she said, rather gently. "I'll handle it." She strode out, dragging Zoe behind her by the wrist.

Archie walked to Natalia and flattened her to his chest without hesitation. He smelt of sea water and apples, nothing like his brother. Natalia fit awkwardly against him but clung onto him anyway. He stroked the back of her head, never stopping as she continued to cry.

"We promise," he whispered after moments of silence. "I can fix the window with my magic and send the ash away. We won't tell anyone what happened." He pulled back, just enough so she could look at him. The faintest of freckles were stretched across his face, not like stars, but like delicate decoration. "We'll keep this a secret. But you won't be able to forever."

Fate and the world weren't just playing tricks on Natalia anymore. They were trying to make her bleed from the inside.

A sleek tunnel of darkness formed ahead of her, one that showed no light at the end. She now had another secret to keep, the biggest one ever. A secret that threatened *everything*. And while Archie was right, that she wouldn't be able to keep this forever, for now, she needed to keep it locked. This was her fight. These were her questions and her answers to find.

She sank her weeping face into the centre of Archie's chest and he wrapped his arms around her again. It was all the comfort she could afford to have.

7

Apart at the Seams

"YOU LOOK LIKE YOU'VE SEEN SOME THINGS."

Alex sat beside the Zoe, the girl she'd unexpectedly met at the beach the day before, watching her curiously. The girl didn't move or turn her head. She sat in silence, picking at the edges of her nails.

Rain had come last night, but the day was already warm and humid again. It was barely past dawn, the low light taking the shadows with it, yet the heat had already begun to climb.

Alex hadn't questioned why Noah's sister had been in her house when she'd chased Archie back after sensing heightened distress, but Peri had explained it anyway. Apparently, Zoe had been spying on her brother to see what he was up to. Instead, she'd accidentally walked in on Peri and Natalia testing their power limits against each other. Archie had sensed Peri's distress through some weird relationship mind-link they suffered from after years of making googly eyes at each other and had gone home to check.

Or so the story went. Alex didn't fully believe it, but she also didn't want to call her family liars.

"What are you?" the girl asked, looking out at the waves.

Alex spread her hands into the sand, feeling the warm grains beneath her fingers. "How likely are you to scream?"

Zoe's head whipped up and her glare cut magnificently. "What are you going to do? You're not going to crush my body and grind my bones into bread, are you?"

"I'm not a shitty giant from a kid's story."

Zoe shivered. "Sorry."

"Do I even look *remotely* like one? I'm not short but I'm hardly twenty feet tall either." Alex rolled her eyes. "You know, if you're frightened of something that isn't real, it might be best if I *don't* tell you what I am, or what any of us are."

"I'm fine," Zoe insisted.

Alex wasn't convinced but went on slowly. "We're called Creatures. You've probably heard them be called the supernatural?"

"*Supernatural?*" Zoe cried. Thankfully no one was around to hear.

"Yes," Alex confirmed. Long ago, she'd thought that lying about who she was to the outside world would be easy. It wasn't. It was tiring. She had to constantly hide what she was to anyone who wasn't part of this world, and even then she had to be cautious. Her past often got spoken about back in Atlantis for what she'd done and how she'd become it. "For me, the term is Werewolf."

"A Werewolf?"

Alex rolled her eyes again. "Are you going to keep repeating everything I say?"

"Sorry." Zoe shook her head as if to clear it. "Noah knows what you are?"

"He does."

"How did he find out? What happened to him?"

Alex snorted. "He fell through a portal."

"A *portal?*"

"Again with the repeating?"

Zoe grimaced. "Sorry."

Pulling her hands from the sand, Alex brushed them against her legs and sat upright. "I guess you really must be siblings, since you both have a bad habit of walking into things to do with us."

"What happened?" Zoe pressed.

"It's a long story. You should ask him about it."

Before Zoe could say anything else, a long shadow fell over them. Zoe flinched and looked up, as did Alex. Alex groaned. The Vampire that Gold had brought along with him like a pet, the one named Aero, strolled up to them.

"My ladies," he said once he reached them. "Sorry for the intrusion."

"Are you?" Alex asked.

The corners of Aero's mouth turned down. "I come with news." He gave Zoe an unsubtle look of suspicion.

Alex pointed at Zoe with a nod. "She knows about us."

Aero looked between them. "And do we trust her?"

"'xcuse me?" Zoe stood and pushed a finger into the surface of Aero's chest. "Don't start talking about me as if I'm not 'ere."

Alex waited to see if Aero would draw his sword, but he didn't. He simply tilted his head. Alex raised her eyebrow from her position on the ground, mildly impressed.

"I apologise," Aero said a moment later. Zoe sat back down on the sand beside Alex, scooting closer to her than before. "I came to ask about recent Monster activity."

"Recent?" Alex's eyebrow raise turned mocking. "How recent are we talking about?"

"When Gold and I arrived back yesterday at his apartment, his Time Crystal glowed. It was one of a pair and the second had been left at the Darby's because of Natalia. It'd been triggered. I raced over this morning to ask if there was any disturbance."

Out the corner of her eye, Alex caught Zoe shuffling and a pink glean spread over her cheeks. "I was with Peri and Natalia," Zoe insisted. "Archie and the rest came after I was caught being where I shouldn't, but I didn't notice anything before that."

Aero faced Alex. "My lady?"

"Quit it with the *my lady* bullshit," Alex whined, glaring right back at him. "What time period did you drop out of? Seven Hells. You dress modern enough," she indicated to his boots, white t-shirt, and blue jeans, "but speak as if you belong in a time of kings and queens. I'm *not* a lady. I identify as female, as a she-wolf. Refer to me as *that*."

Alex watched Zoe's gaze pass over them both with unquenched curiosity. Her dark eyes flitted between the two and Alex's blood grew hotter when Zoe's gaze ran up and down Aero before resting on his face, but she couldn't tell why.

She pushed the weird feelings down, blaming the old blood feud between Vampires and Werewolves. There were plenty of historical problems between the two Creature types that always seemed to flare up in some way.

Aero clearly noticed nothing. "I was bitten and rose again in the twenties, if you must know," he said. "Not *quite* the time of kings and queens, and manners cost nothing, but similar enough. Gold took me under his wing after—" He stopped abruptly and Alex wondered how close he was to revealing how he'd ended up becoming the Council's busy-body.

"What else aren't you saying? With your original comment about Crystals, I mean." Zoe narrowed her eyes at Aero.

The Vampire pursed his lips. "You have an astute mind."

Zoe beamed. "I've been called many things, and astute has *never* been one of them."

Aero was silent for a few moments before he continued on. "The Crystal flashed something else, like a warning that it would be triggered again."

"When?" Alex asked, springing to her feet.

"Later."

"When later? Ten minutes? Ten hours? Ten years?"

"You should know how Time Crystals, or *any* Crystals, work," he said carefully. "They rarely give specifics. Time Crystal pairs can only be used three times. Once as a trigger that something's happened, the second for a warning that the last moment is approaching, and the last time itself? Minutes after the next time it triggers, the Crystal will burn itself out. That's why Gold sent me back."

"So he's watching the Crystal and can relay the message to you?"

"Either him or Evangeline, yes."

"Evangeline?" Zoe questioned, turning to Alex. She shrugged too.

"A friend of Gold's, one with far more skills."

"But why didn't you stay to watch it?"

"If I had stayed, there would possibly be no time to travel and be ready between the trigger and the attack. Records show that usually it happens within quick succession."

Alex heard what had also been left unsaid. Monster attacks happened all the time, but they were mostly random and unplanned. To alert a Time Crystal, something had to have been set in stone, a moment locked in time. *Someone* had to have set something.

How much time do we have?

"I have to go." Alex turned to the wide-eyed Zoe. "I'm sorry you found out about us so fast. Our house is always open to you, just as it is for your brother."

With that, Alex cracked and shifted, sprinting away. Not once did she look back.

Tony rolled onto his side and smiled at Katherine, who slept peacefully on the bed beside him. He reached out and tucked away a piece of hair that had fallen across her features. He knew she worried about Natalia as much as he did, she'd said as much, but things were starting to feel slightly more normal again – however momentary that would be, he would seize it.

Katherine stirred and Tony's hand stilled. She grasped his hand and pulled it towards her, kissing the palm. She faced him, putting her arm down and placing her hand on her exposed hip. "Good morning," she said, drearily.

Tony laid his head back on the pillow, smiling. "Morning. How did you sleep?"

"How did *you* sleep?" she asked back.

Tony raked his fingers along her side. "A little better," he admitted. "I still had the dream though."

"About Natalia's wings?"

Ever since the incident on the beach, Tony had been having a dream about Natalia's wings despite not having seen them until they'd all been together in the Darby's garden. When he'd first told Katherine, she'd said that dreams sometimes had a way of showing something to the person dreaming. But Tony didn't know what he was looking at.

Katherine touched his face. "Was it bad?"

"No," he answered. "You were there this time."

"What was I doing?"

"Controlling the waves. Natalia was hopping over them and using her wings to gain just enough extra height to fly." He couldn't remember whether Natalia was only trying to fly or if she was trying to fly *from* something.

"That doesn't sound bad."

"I don't think she knows how to fly." He'd barely seen her wings, let alone seen her use them.

"I'm sure she'll learn," Katherine told him. "We can teach her, somehow. Find a guidebook for dummies on how to use wings for beginners."

His hand stopped at her ribcage, right below her breast. "I wonder sometimes what it would've been like if you had come into our lives earlier. I know we're neighbours and friends, and we've always known each other, but *this*," he moved his hand an inch higher, feeling the goosebumps he created, "is slightly different."

"The Gods' have a plan for us and I believe now was the right time for us."

"You really believe in the Gods?"

"I do."

"Do you think they have a plan for Natalia?"

Katherine's smile turned sad. "I believe someone does."

Tony didn't believe in any sort of God, and seeing what they'd possibly put his daughter through made him even less interested in them. What sort of being would want a young woman to suffer? What did that say about the Gods – if they were real – that they allowed something like this to happen.

Folding back the covers, he leant over to kiss the top of Katherine's head. She caught the side of his face, bringing it to hers.

With a soft smile, she pulled back from the kiss and sank back into the pillows. Shaking his head, Tony went to shower. He let the water steam before stepping under it.

Maybe Tony didn't believe in Gods, but he believed in Katherine. He believed in himself. He believed in Natalia. Maybe that was enough. Maybe together, they *would* figure out what was happening to Natalia. Gods or no Gods, what did it really matter? They had something real to trust in.

Maybe, he thought.

His heart stuttered, as if he wasn't sure if he believed his own words.

Gold's door was brown. Of all the colours, Jasper hadn't been expecting brown. Though, he wasn't quite sure what he *had* been expecting. He knocked anyway.

It opened immediately, revealing Gold, who adjusted his monocle. He wore a lavish aquamarine silk dressing gown with white fluffy slippers on his feet. The corners of his mouth were tinted red and his fangs hung past his bottom lip.

"Am I interrupting?" Jasper asked, trying to peer round Gold.

"If I told you that you were?" Gold returned, raising an eyebrow.

"I would hope you would at least invite me in to wait in the parlour until you're finished rather than leave me outside."

Gold laughed. "I haven't owned a proper parlour in years. Not since my English Mansion."

"I can wait in the hallway? Maybe with a cream cake?"

Gold sighed and moved aside. "No cream cake here," he said. "And I just finished with my last task."

Jasper stepped inside and was met with stark white and black furnishings. The entire space was open-plan and modern. Again, Jasper didn't know what he'd been expecting from the Vampire, but this didn't quite fit his thoughts and preconceptions.

He walked further into the room, immensely aware of the grey-looking body lying face down in the corner of the room. Blood leaked from two spots around his neck, pooling under his chin on the otherwise clean floor. Jasper said nothing about it. He'd invited himself in, after all. Pointing out a dead body would probably get him kicked out. He just hoped Gold was well fed.

"Drink?" Gold offered as he moved to the bar across the room.

Jasper didn't look at the body, but the image lingered in his mind. "No, thanks."

Gold shrugged and made himself one, appearing on the sofa opposite Jasper a moment later. He swirled his drink with a finger. "Take a seat," he said, sipping. Jasper perched on the arm of the second sofa. "It's barely after dawn. I haven't even dressed yet."

Jasper kept his eyes focused on the Vampire. "You look fine to me."

"Flattery will get you everywhere, my dear boy." Gold smirked over his glass. "But I know you didn't come here to shower me with compliments. What did you come for? And why alone?"

Jasper sat upright. "I want to know what's wrong with Natalia."

Gold's face twisted with amusement. "How those who love, love so hard. It's our fate as Creatures, isn't it? To find love, sometimes young, and have it stick with us until we are so full we might burst."

Jasper blinked. "I didn't say anything about love."

And he hadn't, at least not out loud.

Since the night he'd stayed at Natalia's, Jasper had hardly thought of anything else. The way her hair sloped back from her shoulders. How her mouth remained slightly parted as she slept. The feel of her lips pressed against his. Her grip on him, like she'd break or fall apart if she let go.

There was desire, he knew it, and his heart wanted to be with hers, their whole beings entwined. He didn't know if she felt exactly the same, but he was sure of himself and of what his heart was beating for.

Was it love? That seemed such a childish, trivial name. Everything felt intense, like Heaven had come to Earth to bow before him. It was nothing like what Peri had explained, but how could anything so ethereal be so easily explained?

"I can see it on your face," Gold's voice broke Jasper's thoughts apart. "There's a shine to those who are in love. I loved like that once." A thunderous scowl laced his features. "It did not end well." As quick as it'd come, the expression vanished. "Back to Natalia."

Jasper coughed, hoping it gave him a moment to calm the flames heating his cheeks. "There's something going on."

"Is that so?" Gold downed the rest of his drink.

"After she explained everything to us the other day—"

"About her wings and the mad-one chasing her?"

"Yes," Jasper nodded grimly. "I still feel like there's more."

"It's as if she's split in two, torn by something I cannot see. And I agree there must be more, I sense it, but I cannot say what."

"You can't?"

"I'm good, but I am sadly not *that* good." He adjusted his monocle. "Like I said, seeing into her dreams will help her. They should hopefully provide insight and clarity to what's happening. Though, I am surprised to hear that she hasn't been influenced much by Mo."

Jasper raised an eyebrow curiously. "Mo?"

"The Monster that will help Natalia navigate her dreams, and those of others, is called Mo."

"Will Mo help? Will this plan work? Will she find her answers?"

"She should," Gold said, though his tone didn't sound as confident as normal. "Then we shall all know what we are really up against."

As Gold stood, Jasper stared. *What we're really up against.* Those words made it sound like there was a war brewing. Something *was* coming, and it had already torn so much apart in the relentless hunt for Natalia. Could there be a war? Jasper's stomach sank and his heart staggered out of rhythm for a few beats.

Gold reached his home-bar and turned to face Jasper, grinning. "Are you sure you wouldn't like a drink?"

"*Noah?*"

Noah stopped running and glanced around wildly at the sound of his name. The only people out were himself and Natalia, and she was at least fifteen paces up the road. Her voice would've been a distant yell at best, not a close whisper.

I'm just dehydrated.

Running laps was hard. Running laps in a small neighbourhood wasn't enjoyable. Running laps in the blistering height of summer, even earlier in the day, was just asking for the worst to happen.

He picked up his water-bottle from where he'd stashed it in the shade of a bush in his front garden and drank heavily, careful to sip and not to over-do it. The water wasn't cool, but gratefully wasn't completely boiling either. He even splashed a little over his face.

Why did I agree to this? he thought to himself. *Why couldn't I have started exercising in winter? Or just not bothered?*

He knew why, because Alex had advised him to start as early as possible. The sooner he got more athletic, the sooner he could begin to learn how other things. Not that the ultimate goal was to fight Monsters alongside the Creatures – that was too dangerous for a Human, which Noah agreed wholeheartedly with. The goal was to be able to run away fast and smart enough that he couldn't be caught.

He flopped down onto the curb, peeling his shorts from his legs and rolling his socks down. Sticking sweat drenched his body. At least Natalia didn't look much better off. Even though she was far away, beginning their next rotation, he could see how badly her t-shirt clung to her and how her speed had started to drop off.

"Noah?"

He twisted his head, searching again for who'd spoken. The air was too stagnant to have whistled to him.

"Noah?"

"What?" he barked. Then he realised Natalia was in front of him, bent-over and red-faced. "Sorry."

She half-fell onto the curb beside him, grabbing and drinking her water. "Are you alright?" she asked after consuming several mouthfuls. She pulled her green headphones from around her neck and dumped them, with her phone, beside her.

"I'm fine," he said dismissively.

"You've done well today. Six laps for your first go is great!"

"Still not sure it's worth giving up all that pizza for though."

Natalia snorted. "You don't have to give it up completely, you know."

"I'm hoping we can grab some slices later?" His stomach groaned. "Or now?"

"Now," Natalia climbed to her feet, "we need to shower and get moving."

Noah whined. "We do? Why? Does that mean no pizza?"

"We're meeting Peri, remember? For the house viewing."

"I'm pretty sure *you* are meeting Peri for the house viewing. *I* am going over to the house to listen to Sarah talk about Creature and Monster types."

"Sarah's a good teacher," Natalia defended.

"I'm not saying she isn't!"

"Come on." Natalia swatted at Noah's leg with her bottle. "And pick my headphones up for me? I'm too tired to bend over."

Noah laughed and grabbed the headphones, holding them out dramatically once he was on his burning feet again. Natalia shook her head and took her possessions as they began to talk back to Natalia's house.

Halfway there, she said something about racing him and took off. Noah was only half listening. He turned one last time, but could find not find the owner of the voice that he'd heard. It left him convinced that he had just been dehydrated and the voice had been a mirage in sound form, nothing more.

We seek beauty in the air,
We seek beauty of spelled fair.
Our hearts beat as once,
And in each other we come undone.
I do love my love,
Who swim in the skies a fair dove.
For our hearts are forever fond,
Of those we love; Family, our bond.

Evangeline repeated the poem over and over and over in her mind, her husband's words never losing the power to soothe her. It would've been better if he could be there with her. But he wasn't, and could never be.

The edge of her skirt rippled as either the ward-magic or the warm breeze made it. She knocked on the door, the hairs on her arms standing to attention. There was no immediate answer and she worried she'd have to knock again. Thankfully, she didn't have to.

She blinked in surprise. Of course it wasn't *him*, but the boy in front of her held a similar likeness. Even though she'd seen him before, those looks had been in brief passing, but now she could clearly see. He had the same lazy smile, the same charm in the one raised eyebrow, the same intrigued glint in the eye, though the colour was different –green, not brown as they had once been.

"Hello," the boy said. Despite the slightly different inflection to his tone, and the notably less English accent, even the voice was similar in depth and pitch.

Evangeline straightened her back. "I was asked by Gold to come by," she explained, blinking quickly a few more times. "My name's Evangeline."

"Evangeline?" The boy's green eyes swam.

She nodded firmly. "Evangeline Morgan."

With the door left open, the boy dashed off.

Evangeline stepped inside in the absence – no Vampire needed to be invited in any more than anyone else. The light in the hallway was low for such a sunny day and the dark wood absorbed most of the light, keeping its tone low.

As quick as he'd gone, the boy raced back into the room. Evangeline hadn't realised before how tall he was, or how he appeared sharp around the edges like a needle made Human. He was *so* familiar. Yet, the freckles on his face were something else; they were something closer to *her*.

The boy slammed a yellowing scroll down onto a nearby cabinet. Evangeline knew the parchment but hadn't seen it in years. Her hand reached out to touch the perfectly cut edges. She knew the scroll could only extend at the will of magic; it would never tire or wear. Any ink spills would disappear, and the writing had to be done with a proper quill. It was only yellowing because it would've been kept in the dark over the years, not proudly basking in sunlight like it was meant to be.

Evangeline knew all that because the scroll had been hers.

"Evangeline Morgan," the boy muttered, unfolding the paper with a wave of his hand. He traced his finger along it, guiding up and stopping at the near top. "I *knew* it sounded familiar." He looked up at her. "You're Evangeline *Darby*."

All at once, the past collided with the present.

Though she didn't need to breathe anymore, Evangeline still choked on the air she took in by habit. The boy looked oddly pleased with himself.

"You're one of us," he said. "Aren't you?"

Evangeline managed a nod. "I was, a long time ago."

The boy pulled up the parchment and let it curl in his hands. "I found this the other day when I was forced to clean and open the last of the moving boxes in the loft." He rolled his eyes dramatically.

"It's the family tree. The one I made."

"*You* made it?" The boy gaped at her. "You're the woman that's been helping Peri and you never said?"

"Years ago, I started documenting. I kept it up for the longest time. Once I finally passed it along, I made sure the family would always be recorded."

"But why did you stay away?" the boy asked. There was no indication of hurt in his voice, no betrayal, just a level of wishing to understand. "You've helped us before now. But why haven't you come to us properly?"

Her throat grew tighter. "I kept losing people. Some by old age, some by Monsters. When my grandchildren passed, I separated from the family entirely. My heart couldn't bear it."

The boy cast his eyes down. "I'm sorry. No one should lose anyone."

"I even changed my name back to the one I was born with, the one I had before marrying." She gave him a small smile. "As time went on, the happier I became again. But I also became numb, too. Gold was the one to teach me that life carried on. It may not be the life I was once used to, but it had its way of persevering. But that's our entire Purpose, isn't it? To make sure love and life continue on. I found that, over time, though I might lose people, I could gain them as well. So I came back into the world. Slowly, by teaching in Atlantis at first."

"And now here."

"And now here," she repeated, nodding.

"I know it must hurt," he said. "Losing people, I mean. But Gold's right. You might lose them, but you'd still have their children, and theirs. You'd still have your family."

"*For our hearts are forever fond, Of those we love; Family, our bond,*" Evangeline recited aloud. The boy raised his eyebrows. "It's true. I hadn't seen that before. I'd been too hurt and ruined. Now I see differently. Immortality is both a curse and a gift. But I leaned that while some things may hurt in the end, they're worth the joy at the time. Love is worth it *all*."

"Well, I'm sure if you stuck around, you'd meet the rest of the family. *Your* family." He grinned. "The Darby's persevered."

"It seems they did indeed." Evangeline let the bubble of laughter free. "But I don't know if you're still my family, or if I'm yours."

"We share blood and we once shared a name. That counts for something."

How could this boy, who surely hadn't long ago entered adulthood, be so wise? It really was like looking into the past.

"I'm Jasper." He stuck out his hand. "The prettiest part of this lineage."

Evangeline took his hand, shook it, and let go. "I must admit, I was a little startled when I first saw you. You look so much like my husband. Except for those eyes and those freckles. *We* share those."

Jasper laughed. "Not that family reunions aren't fun, and you're like my great-great-great grandmother—"

"I think you're missing a few greats."

"But you said you were here to help?"

Evangeline eyed him steadily. His gaze focused on her, something in his voice drawing her in. It wasn't desperation or urgency. It sounded like *hope*.

She didn't know how well Jasper and Natalia were tied, but it was evident he cared, and quite a bit. And now Evangeline was here, promising to help the best she could, with all she had to offer – which was quite a lot, thanks to her not being just *one* Creature. She'd brought the hope right to his doorstep. She prayed that she could indeed prove to someone else that the world wasn't always so dark, that there *was* hope.

Jasper led her to the living room, and she knelt in the centre. Carefully, she withdrew her Crystals from her bag. As she arranged them in a circle, one caught her attention.

"Is that supposed to be flashing?" Jasper asked, pointing to the larger, red Crystal.

"No," Evangeline answered, reaching towards the smooth, pulsing stone. "It's not."

"What is it? What's it doing?"

Evangeline prodded the Time Crystal. Gold had given it to her, saying it needed to be watched, before he'd sent her here.

The door swung in before she could reply. A girl with manic hair and two facial piercings panted in the doorway. She zeroed in on Jasper. "I've been looking for you all morning!" she cried. "Where have you been?"

Jasper raised an eyebrow. "Here and there."

The girl bared her teeth. "I don't care to ask about where that is. I have something to tell you." Opening her mouth to speak, her eyes shifted to Evangeline before settling on the pulsing Crystal. "Is that what I think it is?"

"A Time Crystal," Evangeline confirmed.

"Is *anyone* going to tell me why this Crystal is pulsing and why we're panicking?" Jasper asked.

"Time Crystals are always in pairs," Evangeline explained. "They show what was and what will be. They're rare, however, and must only be used if deemed necessary because of extreme cases."

"And it's flashing because..."

"It's showing Natalia, right?" the girl questioned. "She's in trouble, isn't she?"

Evangeline reached towards the Crystal, and it melted into nothing under her fingers.

"*This* is the house!" Peri squealed.

Natalia, Peri, Archie and Noah – whose training with Sarah had been delayed – stared up at the white, five-bedroom house before them.

A garden path led up to the sunflower yellow door, and rose bushes grew beneath the front windows. A bird feeder sat on the front lawn along with a tiny, empty pond barely bigger than a puddle. The mailbox had colourful sunflowers painted on it, though they needed redoing, just like the outside of the house did. It loomed as high as the other houses nearby but stood completely separate too, and the noise of the nearby waves crashed against the shore.

"This is it?" Archie asked, unblinking. He looked slightly overwhelmed.

"It's beautiful," Noah said, equally awestruck.

Tears threatened to spill from Peri's eyes, and Natalia passed her a tissue before they could fall. Peri sniffed, nodding in thanks.

"It's like all my dreams are coming true," Peri mumbled behind her hands. Archie pulled her against him. "It might be a little run-down, but it's *everything*." She glanced up at Archie. "You could mow the lawn and I could have early morning swims. Our little fish could sit on the grass and play with toys and balls."

Natalia pointed at the pond. "You might want to leave that empty for a while, then."

"Unless they really are a little fish?" Archie suggested. "Then it's a perfect little holder, like a bucket."

Peri pushed away from Archie. "We are *not* putting our baby in a bucket!"

Archie laughed. "At least we'd know where they were." They all laughed at that.

Peri turned to Natalia then. "Thank you," she said.

"Why?" Natalia questioned. "What for?"

"For finding this place. I might not have ever considered it if you hadn't pointed it out."

Natalia could lie and say that it had been a bit of a gamble.

While five bedrooms sounded nice, and the price was good, those two things came with the fact that the house was completely stripped bare inside. That and how it sat on the East side of Venderly, a side that wasn't entirely well managed or developed yet compared to the West or North parts like where Opal House sat.

Natalia smiled. "Can I give myself a pat on the back?"

Archie kissed the top of Peri's head and looked over at Natalia. "You know, getting you to come see the house with us was just an excuse."

Natalia blanched. "What?"

"Both of us?" Noah asked, looking himself up and down.

"Yes," Peri laughed.

"We were hoping to get you both *and* Jasper together to tell you, but he wanted to stay behind. He said a walk didn't agree with him today." Archie rolled his eyes, the action so dramatic it was easy to see how the two boys were related. "But we have news."

Impatiently, Natalia asked again, "What?"

Peri reached up and adjusted her hair, revealing the electric blue hidden beneath the black. "We're having a boy!" she cried.

It took a second for the news to sink in. When it did, Natalia screeched and launched herself at Peri. The girls hugged and twirled together until Peri grabbed Archie and Natalia grabbed Noah, forcing them to join. The four of them squealed until Peri split apart, clutching her stomach, saying she felt queasy.

"I thought you didn't want to know?" Natalia questioned when the world stopped spinning.

"We had an appointment weeks ago," Peri said. "Before everything happened."

A sick feeling rose in Natalia's stomach. She knew Peri meant before she'd lost her arm, before chaos had erupted and carved a permanent mark against all their names believed in fate - before Peri and Archie's the near-death.

Natalia's back twinged and she touched her star-earrings to sooth herself. She needed to remember that people *had* died that day. But, guiltily, those deaths didn't hurt as much to think about the possible casualties that could've been Peri and her baby.

Archie and Peri went off to make plans for the house and Noah kept running his fingers over the sunflower mailbox. Natalia remained blank. She tried to force a smile every time one of them looked at her. Her face ached from the falsity of it.

Despite what she was dealing with right now, she was *trying* to be good and happy.

Noah bumped his shoulder against Natalia's, waking her from her sad stupor. "Can you believe Zoe knows about all this now?" he whispered, indicating to Archie's green magic as he swirled some rose petals around Peri.

Before their morning run, Noah had mentioned that Zoe had gone to him last night, full of nervous energy, to say that she knew his secret. When he hadn't been able to deny anything, she'd literally exclaimed "*eureka!*" at him.

Noah sighed. "I'm just glad I don't have to keep lying to her," he said. "Do you know how horrible it was to hide all this?"

Natalia nodded, knowing full-well how it felt. She was still hiding things. The moment Zoe found out replayed in her mind like a looped piece of film: the window shattering, the Monster coming forth, Peri cowering, and the glass raising and slicing the Monster. At the time, Natalia had thought Archie had done the fighting. He hadn't. *She* had. And she'd made them all promise to stay silent, even Zoe; just while Natalia figured out what was going on. But the more she tried to understand, the more this rabbit hole never seemed to end. The dream-seeking idea was probably her last hope.

She opened her mouth to speak as the ground beneath quaked. Instinctively, Natalia pulled Noah behind her. Peri and Archie raced toward them.

Near the middle of the road, a long crack formed. With another rumble, a whole chunk fell and disappeared somewhere below.

"A sink-hole?" Noah asked innocently.

"That would be nice," Archie commented sourly.

Clawed paws appeared from the hole, and they hauled up the black and scaly body.

Natalia's heart pounded and her mouth ran dry. She'd never been fearful of much, besides spiders, but these Monsters were beginning to test those limits.

"Monster," Noah pointed out unhelpfully. "What is it?"

The Monster slithered forwards, moving away for three smaller ones to climb out of the pit. Natalia's palms became clammy. "I don't know," she mumbled. "They remind me of Chimeras."

"You're not far off," Archie said. "That ancient name comes from this Monster, we think."

"Not the time for a History lesson, *amore*," Peri said.

Noah touched a hand to Natalia's shoulder. "Have you seen them before?"

Instantly, she remembered the last Chimera and the piece of glass she'd somehow commanded to slide between its scales and rupture its flesh beneath.

Natalia drew out her blade. The weapon was weightless in her hand and it throbbed like a piece of her heart rested inside. She secured her grip on the handle.

The second biggest Chimera pounced first.

Archie met it evenly, his green magic warping around the Monster. The magic restricted the thrashing movements the Monster tried to make, so much so it partially attacked itself.

Seeing Archie' magic as an open attack, the other two smaller Monsters charged after him. Natalia could hear Peri shouting violent encouragements in the background, and she fought to maintain a straight face.

The biggest one began to drag its claws into the ground, pulling for Natalia's attention. Her grip tightened on her blade further.

Taking a steady breath, Natalia propelled herself forward.

Her blade collided directly with the Monster's scales, setting off a vibration that jolted her arm. The Monster didn't care. Its paw cut through the air, snagging her already permanently damaged left arm. She yelped and jumped back, but not before the forked tongue of the hybrid Monster whipped against her neck. Stinging burst around the area immediately.

Flinching, she bent away, clutching at the affected area. "Fuck. Shit. *Ow!*"

The Monster went to attack with its tongue again. She lowered her hand and attempted to stand straight, but her legs wobbled in protest.

Once the Monster was in reach, she raised her blade and managed to slice the tongue clean out of its mouth. The Monster hissed and slithered back, toppling into the very hole it'd clawed out of.

She turned to Peri, trident raised, wildly stabbing the air before her to hold back a Chimera; though the Monster didn't seem to be advancing. Noah was at her back, his spear raised. Archie only had one Chimera left, shrouded in a cloud of his green magic; meowing drifted from it like an oversized house cat had been stuffed inside.

For a moment, Natalia wondered if they might actually win.

It was her mistake for thinking so.

The darkness encircled them without warning.

Natalia's bones turned hollow and her skin chilled, hairs standing on end. She peered back towards the hole and dread wormed its way into her chest. Shadows emerged from the hole, swarming like locusts.

"Noah?" Natalia called.

"Princess?" he half-shouted back.

She didn't scream or even look in his direction. "Run."

Feet slapped the ground in response, and Natalia sighed with relief. If nothing else, Noah would be safe.

Natalia heard a second pair of feet and whirled round. Peri waddled severely a few paces behind Noah. Why Peri had decided to leave too, Natalia didn't know, but was glad. The darkness wouldn't take either of them today.

"You must know, you cannot win this."

Natalia turned, finding herself face to face with one of the Shadows "I like my odds," she snapped back, aware of the throbbing at her neck.

The Shadow managed a ghostly laugh. "Do you?"

Archie slayed his Monster and stalked towards Natalia. Like it was nothing, he dragged the Shadow apart. The ash disappeared in a puff of green smoke.

Another Shadow stepped up to where the last had hovered. "I have the answers you seek, you know." Natalia glared at the Shadow, hoping it came across as a threat and not curiosity. The Shadow held out a hand. "You need only follow."

"Why does it sound like some old Fairy tale you're told to stay away from as a kid?" Natalia asked Archie jokingly. The corner of his mouth quirked into a smile but otherwise he remained focused and simmering with magic.

The Shadow continued, "You cannot win. But you *can* survive."

"She'll survive *and* she'll win," Archie promised the Shadow. Natalia's heart thumped hard at hearing his comment; he believed his words and she felt it.

"So sure, Witch-knight?" the Shadow teased.

"Witch-knight?" Archie commented back.

I can win, Natalia thought. She *would* find out what was wrong. She *would* find out why she was different. She *would* discover who wanted her, why they did, and what for. And she *would* stop it all.

She would prove this *thing* wrong.

Evil might have a moment, but good would come to last.

Natalia threw her arm out, blade first, and collapsed.

Hands grabbed at her body, raising and twisting her until she faced the sky. She searched for *what* had caught her. A Chimeras face bent over her. There was a strange look in its solid black eyes, something she couldn't quite place. Was it sympathy or a wish for death? She guessed it was the second thing, but the way this Monster held itself, gaze steady, somehow said it was sorry for what it was doing. Natalia didn't understand it.

The Chimera moved away, its face being replaced with the haunted black and red of many Shadows. They had done something to her body; it was as if she'd been turned to stone. All her limbs were heavy and stiff, immovable. What had they done? *How* had they done it?

She took shaky breaths and heard a loud thump. For some reason, the Chimera drew near again and gently aided her in moving her head to see. Her gaze found Archie face-down on his new front lawn.

"I told you." Natalia's head was released, and it fell back. A Shadow peered down, smiling. "You cannot win."

Natalia slurred her stream of curses.

"I would rather have you willing, but since you refuse to come on your own, I *will* take you."

Its hand rose and plunged into her chest. Fingers wrapped around one of her most precious organs. She gasped like she'd been thrown under the surface of an icy lake, choking as the fingers around her heart squeezed more ever-so-slightly. The pain in her neck dulled in comparison.

"You are a beauty," the Shadow mused, its smile casual as if they'd been friends once. "Your blood is special, and so are you."

Natalia heard the faint sound of feet followed by a clang, like metal on metal, but it was too late. The hand inside of her squeezed and the tender organ surrendered. The darkness she hated surrounded her until she was swallowed by it completely.

8

Morpheus

ARKNESS. BLOOD. SURRENDER.

Natalia screamed and thrashed, legs kicking, arms flailing, lungs burning.

Something cold slapped against her forehead, and hands pushed her shoulders down. Panic forced her eyes open. Wildly, she looked around and immediately stopped fighting. Freckles designed into the pattern of stars became all she could see.

"Morning." Jasper's smile was kind, soft. He removed his hands, his eyebrows pulling into the centre of his forehead.

Natalia's eyes flurried around the room nervously, searching for the Shadows.

"There's nothing here," he promised, drawing back her attention. "We got to you. You're *safe*."

She looked at herself. Though the bed and clothes weren't hers, she was certainly somewhere safe. A chair sat off to the side, a blanket half strewn over it. Natalia peered up at Jasper. Had he been the one using the chair as a bed? Had he been keeping her company even when she didn't know he was? Her cheeks flamed at the thought.

"How's Archie?" she managed.

Jasper carefully repositioned the wet cloth on her forehead, moving it lower to cover her eyebrows. "He's ok. A few bumps and bruises, but he'll be fine."

"How did you—" Her voice cracked, and she stopped.

"We stopped them," he stated. "We found you, thanks to Evangeline. Well, we found Peri and Noah first. *Then* we found you." He touched her cheek. "Those Monsters are gone. They won't be hurting you anymore."

Natalia shifted uncomfortably, swallowing the thick lump in her throat. Jasper made it his mission to help her sit, then handed her a glass once she was upright.

"How did you stop them?" she whispered.

"Do you really want to know?" he asked, and she nodded. "You're one of the bravest people I know."

She stared at him. "I'm not brave."

"I happen to think you are." He reached out, smiling, and rested his hand on top of hers. "They'd stolen some magic, we think. It had paralysed you completely. Me and Archie had to tear those Shadows from you together. We each had to grab a half of one and pull at it. The one that had grabbed your heart to make sure you stayed still and under their control easier, we had to be even more precise with. But we got them. I swear to you, Natalia. They're gone. And there's no Shadow poison inside of you either. Mum took care to make sure there wasn't."

Natalia didn't know what to say. Her cheeks, her *body*, had never felt hotter. She raised her drink to her lips, living for the coolness if brought her.

Jasper let go of her and walked to the door as she sipped, yanking it open. "Alex?" he called. "She's awake!" Natalia winced at the loudness. Jasper grimaced at her. "I'm sorry."

She touched her temples. "I didn't know I had a headache until now."

"I should have assumed you would have one." He returned to Natalia's side, sitting on the edge bed. "Alex said she'd help you shower and dress. That is, if you want that?"

That sounded familiar, only last time it had been Peri who'd helped. Natalia inspected the room. A memory surfaced when her gaze landed on the desk and mirror. Like an old film, it showed her two girls at the desk, one brushing the other's hair, and a boy coming in to complain that his room had been taken from underneath him.

"This is your room." It wasn't a question.

"The chair's Archie's," Jasper commented, nodding to it. "I don't think he's noticed it's gone yet. He can't be mad at me though. I needed it. I had a patient to oversee."

"I'm not a patient," she argued.

"You're in bed, with a glass of water and a cloth on your head, looking like you might throw up. I'd call that a patient."

Natalia gave up. Her stomach was roiling and a dizziness was rising to accompany the headache. "Are you willingly going to give the chair back?"

Jasper grinned. "I'll at least consider it somewhere down the line."

"How is it that I keep ending up in your room?"

His eyebrows rose. "Would you rather be somewhere else?"

She laughed and winced as the pain in her skull thudded. "I like it here."

"Maybe you'll choose to stay in it on your own terms next time?"

Natalia liked the idea of that, remembering how it felt to be pressed against him and held all night, waking with him at her side. "Just as you chose to stay at mine?"

"You gave me an offer I couldn't refuse."

"Then maybe you should pass me one *I* can't refuse?" She took a final sip to hide her smile as Jasper's smirk lit his face. "And, anyway, out of the two of us, aren't I the better nurse? I mean, I *am* studying—"

She hadn't studied for weeks. When her last test results had come in, she'd barely looked at them. There were practicals she needed to do still, but hadn't yet scheduled them. Most of her class attendance had been online. Her teachers had been more than happy to help and oblige. But because everything had been pushed back multiple times at this point, it was becoming more of a slog to continue. So instead of trying, she'd just stopped, ignoring all the emails and notes her teachers sent.

"In our world," Jasper took her hand and stroked the back with his thumb, "we need healers as much as the Human world. You could get your Human qualifications and transfer them to Creature related ones?"

"I can do that?" She'd never considered it before.

"We get injured, *a lot*. Occupational hazard of the job. But we do sometimes suffer from the same diseases as Humans, and from ones they don't have, too."

Could that be my future? she wondered.

If she passed her courses, could she really transfer over the skills? Would she *want* too? She'd always wanted to be a nurse, and knowing she was also a Fairy with dust that could sometimes heal, it seemed like she was fated to become one. But what were the logistics? Creatures had mostly Human type anatomy, from what she knew. Would healing them be similar, or at least easy enough to learn? What about the Monster related injuries she'd have to deal with, how many of those would she need to know the signs and symptoms and treatments for?

What would my dad say? What about Katherine? Noah

She stole a glance at the boy sitting on the bed; his eyes were downcast, focused on her hands.

Where would I be based? Atlantis? Mentally, she snorted. *The Council would probably stand in my way. I have to give them reason not to.*

"I'll consider it," she said genuinely. "There are a few, *tiny* other things I need to worry about first." She already had so much to handle that thinking about a career wasn't possible. Maybe one day, but she had to get through whatever was happening around her first.

Jasper smiled. "I know, and I'll be with you. Now and after."

Alex blundered through the door before Natalia could reply, grinning like a wolf, almost tripping over her own feet despite her usual sturdiness. Jasper tossed his sister a suspicious look before planting a surprise kiss on Natalia's cheek. Smirking, he strode towards the door and shut it behind him.

Natalia wondered how much Alex had heard as the girl helped her out of bed and guided her to the bathroom. Once Natalia was in the water, Alex declared she'd be outside and Natalia would have to call her when she was done.

With a sigh, Natalia sank lower, wishing she was in the sea so the salt could cleanse her skin and the endless waters could wash her away.

Twelve cloudy white Crystals were spread six inches apart and formed a half-circle.

Since the kitchen in Opal House was the biggest open space inside – the basement practise room was too enclosed for what they were about to do – Archie had helped prepare it to be the optimum space, as had Jasper. While Archie wasn't as well practised with his magic as his brother, he could do a variety of simple and semi-difficult things decently enough. Furniture movement fell into that category.

Archie's magic pressed the table flat to the wall with the chairs stacked on top. The island counter moved to touching the cabinets, blocking them off. And the lights ascended into the ceiling in case they needed height.

Once the work was done, Jasper strolled in from the garden, brushed his clothes, and sat himself down as if he'd been in the room all along. Archie rolled his eyes at his brother, but he didn't see.

Tiredness crept in and along Archie's limbs. He sighed. It was nothing a good few minutes rest couldn't fix. The magic he'd used hadn't been extensive, not like a fight where he'd sometimes need a long nap to recover, but it was still enough to unsettle his heart and wind him slightly. While he caught his breath, he watched.

Evangeline lit the three blood red candles at the north point of the circle with a match. Archie stared, confused. He'd seen her ignite her fingers before. Why was she using matches to light the candles instead of her magic?

Archie didn't voice the question, and instead looked to Noah who sat beside Evangeline. He seemed eager to help, but he was still Human, and though he'd been learning all he could, there were still things he couldn't aid in and never would be able to.

Both Noah and Evangeline had stayed the night, both unwilling to return to their houses after the incident. This morning, the second they'd gotten news Natalia had woken, Archie had called Tony - he'd stayed at his house because, while he had the best intentions, and his heart was in the right place, his help and interference might've caused more distress and problems. They'd had no idea what they'd been dealing with, not until the moment Natalia had woken, so hadn't wanted to take any unnecessary risks. The call had ended with Tony promising to come over as soon as possible.

"They'll be down in the moment," Peri said, stumbling into the room.

Archie went over to her immediately. "I've got you a chair."

"I'm fine," she protested.

He wrapped an arm around her shoulders anyway and guided her to the remaining seat. Peri's stomach grew by the day, and though she wouldn't admit it, she was starting to struggle. Her feet were swollen constantly, she had heartburn throughout the day, and this morning she'd complained about being constipated. Archie made sure she wore slippers without socks, despite it being summer, and gave her the medicine she required for the other things.

Peri sat slowly with his help. "*Ti amo*," she whispered.

"I know, and I love you too," he said. He pressed a kiss to the top of her head and ran a hand through her silky hair. Peri peered up at him, smiling. "*Come va?*"

Her grin widened. "It needs work, but you're definitely getting better."

Out of the few things they had finally settled on, having their little fish learn English *and* Italian was one of them.

Though Peri hadn't lived in Italy, in the town of Manarola, since she was three, she'd still been brought up with her family's language. That very same family who *still* didn't know she was pregnant. It was another of Peri's choices – she'd asked Archie if he thought what she was doing was right, and he'd agreed.

"*Sto bene, grazie,*" she assured him.

He kissed her gently. "As long as you're sure."

"I am," she nodded. "But I'm worried about Natalia."

As if hearing her name had drawn her in, Natalia walked into the room, Alex close behind her. A chill settled into the atmosphere of the room. Archie couldn't stop himself from staring, and apparently neither could anyone else. Except Evangeline, who pulled Natalia from Alex. If Archie didn't already know Natalia was a Fairy, he would've discovered it by looking at her in that moment.

Natalia's long hair was piled on top of her head, a black headband keeping stragglers out of her face. Bronze coated her cheeks, the dust twinkling under the lights. She wore an old dress - white with red poppies at the bottom - that'd been Peri's, but unlike the clothes she'd borrowed last time, this dress fit better. Archie narrowed his eyes. The dress fit almost *too* well. Natalia had lost weight from her shoulders and her face, making her appear even smaller, and that *wasn't* a good thing.

Archie's attention shifted to the Fairy blade at Natalia's waist as her hand hovered over it. She moved gracefully with Evangeline as a guide, like she was dancing rather than walking.

Jasper neared Natalia. "Fairy?"

"Witch?" she called back.

Jasper frowned. "What happened to your arms?"

Natalia swung round, allowing Archie to glimpse the red lines dented into her skin. She touched the scar on her arm briefly before touching the new, smaller scratches. "Oh," she *sounded* surprised. "I must've gotten them when that Shadow attacked."

Noah got up and walked to her, touching her hands. "It *did* look like the Shadow grabbed you."

"I've never seen them scratch before," Archie said.

"Neither have I," Jasper admitted. "But it's possible."

"For how evil those bastards are, I would say it's *more* than possible," Alex added.

Archie glanced down at Peri, whispering, "*Sono loro...*"

"*Si,*" she whispered back.

So they're not marks of a Shadow, Archie thought, eyeing Natalia again.

The attack before last, the one in this house... They had seen the fallen glass. They were the *only* ones – Peri, Archie, and Zoe – who'd seen it here. And, though they'd not been aware at the time, it was clear that Natalia had been cut by it.

Archie studied Natalia. Maybe a few cuts *were* the work of a Shadow, but they blended with those from the glass. But she'd lied seamlessly. Most Fairies had a tell, a way of showing the world they were lying. Natalia expressed none from what Archie could see. Her cheeks hadn't even blazed more.

Honestly, he was starting to believe she really *was* different.

Evangeline cut past Noah and Jasper, looping her arms around Natalia. "Shall we begin?" she asked forwardly, but not unkindly.

"My dad?" Natalia asked, looking around.

"He's coming," Archie told her. "I rang him and he said he'd be right over."

"He'll be here before the spell is over," Evangeline comforted mystically.

"You'll be fine," Alex grinned. "You're not *that* helpless. Even if you think of yourself as a little duck, we're the wolves on your side."

Noah scowled at Alex. "Nothing's going to go wrong," he said.

Natalia nodded to Evangeline, and Archie could see the hopeful glimmer in her expression. "What do I need to do?"

Evangeline ignored the question, staring straight at Noah. "I know you are her friend, but you cannot be here."

"Why?" Noah asked. "Is this another one of those stupid anti-Human rules?"

"Those rules aren't stupid, *amore*," Peri said softly. "Those rules are there to keep you safe."

Alex opened her mouth but Noah cut her off with a stiff finger. "Don't you dare call me a little duck too," he warned as his lips twitched at the edges. Alex laughed but stayed quiet.

"The type of magic I am about to perform must not be observed by a Human," Evangeline said. Her face changed; kindness fading to sadness and regret. "It may damage you, change your very *being*. The same as Monster's damage cuts people differently, even between Creature species, some magic works differently around mortal hearts."

Noah grimaced. "I *would* like to keep my mortal heart."

Natalia opened her mouth. "Noah—"

"You'll call me," he cut in. "You'll call me when you're done. Just," he kissed her cheek, "sleep well."

Noah walked away, stopping to touch Evangeline's shoulder - it was an appreciative touch, a thanks for putting him first even if it upset him. The door clicked behind him.

Evangeline waited a moment before guiding Natalia towards the Crystals. She made her lie down, her head within the semi-circle, her arms out, palms up. She then sprinkled something over the top of each Crystal; Archie was reminded of sand, but with a golden shine.

The lights in the room shuttered out, basking them all in a hollow glow of candlelight. Archie reached for Peri, finding the hand she'd put up for him. They clasped each other tightly.

"Close your eyes, child of the stars," Evangeline whispered. "It will aid your journey."

Archie squinted to see Natalia close her eyes but knew the second her head tipped back that her spirit was gone.

Red.

It burned the sky and covered the sands. Even the light was crimson, casting everything under its spell.

Natalia turned this way and that. The last thing she remembered was saying goodbye to Noah and lying down. She didn't remember drifting off into sleep, though she was sure she had. No place on Earth could hold so much red, so where else could she be but in a dream?

There was no caress of a breeze here. Natalia realised then that there were also no smells or sounds. She searched for the call of a bird or the scent of a flower, but there was nothing. She lifted her hair and it fell right back to where she'd picked it from. Everything rested, sitting like it'd been stopped in time but had been stripped back to its basics.

As she twirled again, a vision of white caught her attention. She stopped and stared. Just ahead, a white bed with white drapes swaying in their own wind sat in the endless and dry ruby sea. She headed towards it.

Reaching out and touching the netting, the drapes slipped through her fingers. She bent to feel the white sheets next, and discovered them to be rich silk. Her hand sank into the soft mattress as she pressed into it.

What was this bed doing out here? Where had the bed come from? Natalia had seen nothing before and she was sure she'd looked in this direction first, not that she could tell what direction it was exactly. It was like it had materialised out of nowhere.

"Magnificent, isn't it?"

Natalia yanked her hand away and spun round. Drawing her blade, she held it out ahead of her in warning. She hadn't even realised her blade had travelled here with her.

A figure appeared on the horizon. Natalia kept her stance as they approached, confident in her ability to fight back if need be.

The newcomer spread their arms and spoke with a voice that carried across the rest of the distance. "Do I not please you as I am?"

As the figure drew closer, they shifted. In a cloud of white smoke, a female appeared. Curves ran along the length of their body. They were completely naked, blonde hair waving in the same wind that affected the bedding but nothing else. Natalia blinked in surprise.

The woman pursed her lips. "Still no?"

Clicking her fingers, more white smoke appeared. This time what emerged caused Natalia's heart to fire up.

Jasper.

He was as she'd seen him before; wrapped in a towel that hung at his hips, his bare chest and stomach on display. The scar below his neck shone with a viciousness not even the background scenery could replicate. His hair wafted in the breeze and his green eyes were fixed on her, life pulsing behind them. Even his freckles danced.

Jasper reached for her and she let him. His hands felt familiar to her hips when he put them there. Slowly, he lowered his face and their lips touched. Natalia gasped against him.

She broke away and slapped him, hard.

White smoke puffed in front of her, clearly to reveal a new face and body. This one was entirely unfamiliar and yet Natalia saw it as the truth. Whoever or whatever this was, this was their real face.

Hair the colour of chalk touched their shoulders. Legs were tucked into white flowy trousers while the torso was beneath a buttoned shirt. Strangely, *their skin was almost iridescent, as were their eyes. Though it was unusual, it seemed to fit somehow. They didn't shimmer, just existed.*

Natalia held her blade up again, stepping back to put some distance between them. "Who are you?"

"Is that how you speak to those you kiss?" they asked.

"I don't just go around kissing everyone I meet!"

"No." The person looked Natalia up and down slowly. "I'm impressed. Even with that kiss you felt something was off. Not many can break through my illusions. So I suppose the slap was warranted, and what a slap it was!" They sounded almost gleeful.

"It didn't feel right, and yes, you did deserve the slap!"

The figure's smile burst with brightness. "That's what signing your heart over will do."

Natalia blanched. "What?"

"Giving your heart to another ties you to them. No one but you can break that bond, and so anyone else and everything else is wrong. Your heart works out that the illusion – the person – isn't the real thing. The figure moved, pushing their chest up to the tip of Natalia's blade, grinning like this was the most fun they'd had in a while. "You slapped me because your heart told you I wasn't the real person."

Natalia didn't know what to say to that, so instead asked, "Who are you?"

"I suppose proper introductions are in order." They moved off the point of the blade and spun in place twice, as if to give Natalia the opportunity to fully look them over. "Gold asked for my assistance. I am here to seek out what you need from your dreams." They bowed. "I am Morpheus. But you may call me Mo."

Natalia stared openly. Did the myth of the Greek God come from this person, or did this person get their name from the myth? This being certainly acted the part, from what Natalia could remember of the stories she'd learnt at school years ago.

"This is my original form," Morpheus continued. "I can shift between

anything you want or anything you need. For that, I hope you will refer to me in neutral terms of they or them as my body shifts as well as my state of mind and heart." They wiggled their neat eyebrows. *"I am of Morph-kind. Yes, that is what we're called. I was the first and I am now the last. Not because my brothers and sisters and children were reckless, but because we were hunted."*

Natalia lowered her blade slightly. "So, you're a Monster?"

Morpheus spread their arms wide. "Indeed I am, and I'm not ashamed of that."

"You're here to help me?"

"The best I can, yes."

"And you know Gold?"

They smiled; something flashed in their eyes but it was gone before Natalia could identify it. "I do."

"Then," she tucked her blade away at her waist, though didn't move her hand too far away, "I'm Natalia."

Morpheus' smile relaxed at the edges. "I know, young one. Gold told me. He relayed what to expect of you and what to help you with. He said you were a vision, but he'd never mentioned how much of one you truly are. Maybe one day, I'll become you."

Natalia shivered at the echo of words she'd heard before.

I want to be inside your skin. I want to walk within your body. I want your gifts and your powers and the way you make yourself look like the night's sky.

Those words had burned themselves into her mind, forever carved in a sea of their own blood. She touched the scar on her arm, tracing the fracturing lines with her fingers.

"I mean no harm." Morpheus held their hands up in surrender, in apology. They must've seen something in her face, Natalia realised. "I may be a Monster but I am not monstrous. Gold and I only wish to help. I'm the only one that can help. At least with this part of your story, child of the stars."

Natalia took a deep, calming breath. "What do we do?"

"First, I need to go over a couple of rules."

Morpheus went past her to the bed and lifted an over-sized, brown leather book. It floated in front of them as they flicked through the pages. Before Natalia could catch a glimpse of anything, the book snapped shut and disappeared in a puff of white smoke.

"I can help you through your dreams and memories," Morpheus said, their tone more serious than moments ago. "Yours and those of others, past and present, but I cannot influence what you see. You must find what you need on your own. I cannot control the dreams that appear. Only you can. I can guide you on the path once you've chosen it, lead you through to it, but you have to desire to find it first. Whatever you're looking for," they stared at her then, a glint in their iridescent eyes, "it is here. But you must go to it. I will not take you."

Natalia nodded, trying to filter the onslaught of information in her brain.

Morpheus could show her what she asked for, but she had to ask first. She needed a goal and Morpheus would walk beside her as they went. She had to make choices, accept responsibility, and Morpheus would help see it through.

Morpheus was her companion, not her leader. They were her helper, her guide, not her controller. They were in this together, not as two separate people.

Who am I? she thought. How did I become like this?

How was she supposed to find the answers? They were complicated questions. But she had to think of a way.

"Now, wake up, young one." Morpheus had moved and cupped her cheek, holding it as if they held a glass of fine wine. "You may return in your dreams to me now. It will take you no effort at all."

"How?" she asked.

"Just think of me and I will come and meet you." Morpheus let their hand drop. "I will see you soon, child of the stars."

Natalia felt her body fall backwards despite the fact that she wasn't falling at all.

9

Divided Down

NATALIA'S EYES FLEW OPEN AND SHE GASPED. Her head smacked against the floor in her panic and she winced. She had to wait until the ceiling stopped spinning before sitting up.

The room around her was bright and full of colour, and somewhere completely different to where she'd been moments ago. She searched for familiar faces and found only Alex, Peri, and Evangeline who continued to pack her things into her bag as if nothing had occurred.

Natalia swallowed, her throat dry. "Where is everyone?"

"The boys?" Peri asked. When Natalia nodded, Peri's eyes cut to Evangeline briefly before returning to her. "They had to leave the room, *amore*."

"What happened?"

"Or, rather, *Jasper* had to leave."

Natalia scowled. "Why?"

"Nat," Peri called in warning.

Alex grinned as she answered. "You tried to slap him."

"*What?*" Natalia shrieked.

"You tried slapping him and when you couldn't, you screamed until he left. It was quite entertaining. Shame I couldn't film it."

"Your generation's responses to things are unbelievable,"

Evangeline muttered.

"Morpheus," Natalia spat. "He tried tricking me. He tried to pretend he was Jasper."

"And it came through." Evangeline's voice had an unmistakable edge. She zipped her bag and waved her wrist, making it disappear. "You need to be careful when you go down to see Morpheus. Though they are a Monster, and no doubt a trickster, they are kind. But despite that, their powers can reach into this world. Little trickles can come through. They won't always and won't ever be anything major, and you won't need to tie yourself down every time you plan on seeing them, but just be careful of what you or they do." She rose and traipsed past them to the door.

"Wait!" Natalia clambered to her feet. Evangeline stopped. "You tell me that *after* you send me to them, and just leave?"

The woman didn't turn but did answer. "I was only explaining the possibilities to you because it had already happened. They won't happen often."

"Shouldn't you have warned me about *all* things *before*, like some terms and conditions bullshit stuff?"

"Perhaps," Evangeline agreed.

"*Ma non l'hai fatto,*" Peri said in a sing-song voice. Natalia wouldn't begin to pretend she knew what Peri had said.

"But yes, I am leaving," Evangeline continued. "Not forever. You will see me again."

The room had been scrubbed of any evidence that a spell had taken place. Evangeline must've packed away the Crystals or they'd fizzled out and died on their own - Natalia knew there were limits on most of them for how often they could be used. The tiniest red dot had dripped to the floor, the only remnants remaining from the blood red candles that had been burning. Natalia could just about see it, but she had to strain her eyes. Even the smoke from those candles had wafted away, leaving the air fresh once more.

"Morpheus said that I only need to fall asleep to see him again, is that right?" Natalia asked.

"Yes. Now that you've made a connection, you simply need to fall asleep and you'll find one another when you need to."

Evangeline practically threw herself out of the door. Natalia watched the empty space she'd occupied in bafflement. How could she be so blasé? She could see how Evangeline and Gold were friends.

Dizziness overpowered Natalia's mind. She went to sit, but she missed, landing in a heap on the floor. The room didn't move but she certainly did. It was like her bones were vibrating independently to the rest of her. Raising her hand, she saw that it didn't physically shake, but everything rattled below the skin's surface. It was invisible to everyone but her.

All the past moments where things had just been dumped onto her – from being told she was a Fairy, to maybe not being one after all, to learning that someone with power was hunting her – came rushing back into her mind. This was just one more thing to add to the pile, but now the pile was tumbling in on itself.

Natalia's breathing grew shallower. Her heart thumped inside her throat and thick bile rose to the back of her tongue, making it hard to swallow. Whistling overpowered her hearing. She could smell the candles that no longer burned. The ceiling morphed into crimson skies and she saw shadows twitch everywhere.

"How about something hot to drink?" Alex suggested, creeping closer.

"Actually, she looks like she needs a bucket," Peri commented. "What about a glass of water?"

"I can open a window?"

"I need air," Natalia agreed.

Arms enclose around her, pulling her body up, and a moment later the warm July air suctioned against her skin.

They lowered Natalia into a chair she'd never seen before. Alex knelt in front of her a breath later; the lines of her face were tucked into a scowl, giving her a more animalistic look.

Natalia remembered suddenly that Alex had worn Gladiolas flowers back at the Fairy Parade in Atlantis. The flower had reflected strength, and every person who went to Parade wore a flower that they knew would represent what they wanted from the coming year. Natalia had been confused before, but now she understood. Alex was already powerful outwardly. Natalia could see now that Alex had worn the flower to show that wanted inner strength.

She wanted that for herself now too.

Minutes passed by. Natalia listened as seagulls and car horns echoed in the near distance. She breathed steadily, relaxing her grip on seat's arms, and tapped her feet gently to her heart's rhythm until she was certain it was slowing.

Alex gave her space until her tapping stopped all-together. "Do you need anything?" she asked cautiously.

"No. I think I'm fine," Natalia gave the girl a small smile. "Thank you."

Alex waved her off. "Take your time. There's no point in rushing."

Natalia wanted to laugh. "Unfortunately, time doesn't seem to be something I have an abundance of."

"Maybe not, but you still have time to breathe and clear your head."

"What do you suggest?"

"You're the doctor, aren't you?" Alex's mouth quirked. "What would *you* suggest?"

Natalia sighed. "Time."

"So give yourself time. Take the rest of the night off from worrying. Go home, watch a movie. You'll never get anything done if you're angry or upset or confused all the time. Sometimes, the only way forwards is to stop and breathe. I know enough about that to share the advice."

Natalia grasped Alex's hand, finding it smoother than she'd expected. "Thank you, and I mean that."

"I know you do." Alex stood, pulling away and shaking her head so her hair flew free. She ran her hands through it to make it even wilder. "Is there anything you would like?"

"You don't suit being a butler," Natalia joked.

"Does that mean I can drop the act?" Alex snorted. "I don't want you to start thinking I'll look good with a bow-tie and will hand you drinks every time you snap your fingers."

Natalia laughed a little, too. "I would never think you'd just hand me a drink."

"Not unless I spit in it first," Alex winked, grinning.

"Remind me not to take *anything* you offer." Natalia shook her head, though her smile waned. "But I think you're right. I need to go home and rest."

Alex nodded again. "I'll get my brother to walk you. Will you be alright for ten minutes while I get him?"

"I'll be alright for ten minutes."

Natalia was both relieved and slightly disappointed when Alex left her in the summer heat. Peri stole the silence to come see her for a moment. They spoke briefly, Peri asking and making sure Natalia really was alright. But the pregnant girls' body suffered under the heat and sunlight. Natalia told her to go and cover herself, so Peri pressed a kiss to Natalia's cheeks and wobbled inside.

Jasper appeared in front of her minutes later, his shadow sending her into its shade. He held out his hand and Natalia took it, letting him pull her to her feet. She would've normally argued that she could make it home on her own, but she didn't want to walk alone this time.

"Shall we walk, madam?" Jasper bent his elbow for her.

"We shall," she said, accepting his arm.

Together, they left the house. Natalia grew more exhausted with each step. Her shoulders ached, her knees shook weakly, and her head grew heavy.

They made it home without incident. If there was ever a time to jump out on her, it would be now - she was almost too tired to fight - but nothing came. Relief flooded her. The front door of her house loomed ahead.

Jasper detached his arm but held onto her hand. "Go get some sleep." He bent down and kissed her forehead. He balanced her, a coldness in summer, a warmth in winter.

"I will," she assured. "I've just got to ring Noah first." She hadn't forgotten.

Jasper nodded and moved his eyes away, not looking at her. "I know it's unfair of me to ask, especially now, but what *is* happening? Someone had me thrown out of the room."

She grimaced. "I swear I didn't know I was going to try and slap you in real life."

"But you wanted to slap me in your dreams?"

"Morpheus pretended to be you."

Jasper smirked. "I would've slapped pretend me, too. There's nothing better or quite like the real thing."

Natalia sighed at the familiar, comforting smirk on his face. "Morpheus is the one who's going to see me through my dreams, and other peoples," she explained. "They can help me access the answers I need. They can't bring them to me, I have to decide what I want, but they know what I seek is there. But I think that means I also have to dive through some parts I don't necessarily want to see," she said, realising it as she spoke.

He closed the gap between them and pressed his forehead to hers. "If it makes you feel safer, anytime you want a sleep-over, I'll be sure to set you up in Alex's room." He laughed when Natalia lightly swatted at him. "Natalia, if you want us, want me, at any point ever, say something. I'll be there."

Selfishly, she wanted to ask him to stay now, but was that right? Was it unfair for her to want him? He didn't deserve to go through all this, and her heart ached to think about him suffering alongside her. She tried to think how she might feel if their roles were reversed and honestly couldn't decide.

"I will," she repeated.

"Good." He bent and kissed the corner of her mouth. "Go dive into that bed, talk shit with your best friend, and we'll see you tomorrow?"

She stood taller and kissed the underside of his chin. "Do you really think you can get rid of me that easily?"

He grinned. "I hope not."

Natalia walked to the door and looked back when she got there. Jasper was already trudging off. He waved behind him like he sensed her, then marched on. She smiled and went in, and shut the door behind her, pressing her forehead to it.

Noah kicked his feet up onto the desk, crossing his ankles. "Are you sure?"

Natalia sighed. "I'm fine," she replied, voice a little robotic through the phone. "You know I'd tell you if I wasn't feeling great. I just need some rest."

"Rest?" He raised an eyebrow even though she couldn't see. The sunset beyond his window illuminated the walls in gold. "It's barely seven. *And* you were asleep for part of the day already."

"My body and brain do not care that I had a semi-power nap."

Noah had answered the call on the second ring, and Natalia had immediately jumped to share with him all about that'd happened. She'd said she'd met this Monster - Morpheus - who Gold trusted.

Noah was dubious about trusting a Monster, especially after the last one had turned their faith back on them.

"Then go to sleep," he told her. "Are you waiting for my permission or something?"

He heard her snort. "Fucking hell no."

"Put that pretty princess head down to snooze."

"*Still* with the princess thing?"

"From now until forever." He grinned to himself.

"What are you going to do?" she asked instead of hanging up.

"Taking a shower is top of my list. I think Zoe's cooking tonight. Her famous pesto pasta is on the menu."

"Damn!"

"Maybe you'll get an invite to this exclusive club next time." He laughed, then stretched and pulled a face at his own stink. "But seriously, a shower is *needed*."

"How many laps did you bloody do?"

He shook his head. "It wasn't just laps."

Noah was slowly increasing his "workout routine" daily. He always started off by running laps by the road, but today he'd stretched the circuit to include the next road over to. Then he'd taken to doing some sit-ups and the minimal count of five squats before his legs felt like they were going to fall off.

The slow progression had been Alex's idea.

"You go get your shower," Natalia told him, yawning. "I'll go get my beauty rest."

"Make it a long one," Noah joked.

"What are you trying to say, huh?"

"Oh, nothing," he laughed.

Natalia snorted again. "I'll speak to you in the morning."

Noah could picture his best friend's smile. "You better!"

She was silent before adding, "Noah? Thank you."

He sat upright, pulling his legs off his desk. "What are you thanking me for? I haven't done anything besides give you a cool nickname, take the piss out of you because you're tired despite having done nothing, and then telling you to be careful around the Monster you just met..."

Feelings aside, meeting a Monster called *Morpheus* was about as bad and hilarious to him as knowing a Vampire called *Gold*. No one could've made that up.

"For being there for me," she answered. "For listening and being my best friend."

Noah sighed, smiling. "I'll *always* be your best friend, just as you'll always be mine. You know this. I know this. So now you can sleep easy."

"Night, Noah."

"Night, Princess."

The phone went dead and Noah threw it onto his bed, where it bounced but landed without harm.

A gaggle of laughter echoed in Noah's ear suddenly. He searched for the source, but his window was closed to keep the cool air of his half-working AC in. Even his door was mostly shut.

Noah?

He jumped off the bed, causing his phone to fall to the floor. He cursed and picked it up.

The best friend.

Noah's head shot round again. The mirror that was pressed against the wall at the end of his bed at an angle – he hadn't gotten round to putting it up yet, it was new – seemed darker, the reflective surface swallowing light instead of bouncing it.

Cautiously, he crept toward it.

Noah?

His door flung open and Noah yelped, jumping away from the mirror. Zoe stood in the doorway and raised her eyebrows at him. "You good?" she asked.

"Perfect," he answered. "What's the matter?"

"Dinner's almost ready. I've been yellin' at you. The parents will be 'ome—"

"Home," he corrected.

She waved a hand. "They'll be back in a bit so you might want to take that shower. You smell like a sewer, and that's being unfair to the sewers 'ere." She darted away before he could respond.

Noah huffed, peeling off his socks and his t-shirt, and walked into the bathroom. He let the water run for a few seconds before stripping completely and stepping in. The coldness felt good against his skin.

Clearly he'd heard his sister yell for him but the layers of their house had degraded the sound. That had to be it. That had to be why the voice calling his name had been weird. It *had* to be Zoe.

But when he climbed out of the shower and wrapped himself in the nearby yellow towel, he didn't look in the bathroom mirror's direction. There was a wound knot in his stomach.

Gold had lived in many places around the world, yet had never felt comfortable enough to stay anywhere longer than fifty years. He was old, way past the age most thought him to be. He'd seen world wars, civil wars, and watched many people die. He had been around when the Eiffel Tower had been built, had seen Julius Caesar be stabbed, and helped to rid Egypt of locusts more than once.

No one believed him about any of it, except the Eiffel Tower bit.

He sauntered through to his cosy living room carrying two mugs upon a silver tray. He had always loved this house, hence why he'd kept it, but had changed his name on the agreements every so many years to make it look like it was being passed down through the "family". Though he liked it, tucked into the outskirts of England, he could never stay. This was his escape house; a place to welcome him, not keep him forever.

Setting down the tray, he clicked his fingers. The girl he'd wished to see appeared in the room. Oddly, she was scantily dressed. She gasped like she'd run out of air and hastily attempted to cover herself. Gold averted his gaze and hastily took off his dressing-gown, slinging it at her.

When he stopped hearing fussing, he turned. "Come and sit, dear girl." He patted the royal red and gold chair beside him.

Natalia, now dressed in Gold's favourite blue dressing-gown, drawstring tied tightly, scurried to sit. She crossed her legs beneath her, and folded her arms over her chest. Besides her hands and feet, and maybe her ankles and neck to her face, the borrowed clothes she wore covered her completely.

Gold studied her. Darkness underlined her otherwise shiny eyes. Her skin had a peachy-pink flush to it, and an underlying gleam of bronze too, though that could've been a result of the unexpected travel here. The ends of her long hair were damp, all of it hanging just past her elbows now.

"I hope there's a good reason for this," she mumbled.

Gold walked over to the matching chair and sat. "Were you in the middle of something?"

Her cheeks flushed. "I had just gotten out of the bath!"

That explains the lack of clothing.

Gold didn't smile. It hadn't been his intention to take her while she'd been compromised. He grabbed the blanket he kept folded on the footstool before him and threw it to her. She caught it and tucked it over her body like an extra layer. While it was summer and nights were warm, shock could do interesting things. He could only imagine how quick her ruby blood was racing around her body as her heart willed it to.

"Gold," she sighed, "where am I?"

He perched on the edge of his chair to pass her a mug, then sat back with his own. "*This* is my adorable little farmhouse in the adorable English country-side."

Steam wafted around her face. "You own a farmhouse?"

"I have for years." He sipped his tea and sighed at the delightfully sweet taste. "Isn't it quaint?"

Natalia looked, for one moment, like she had a million things racing around in her head – Gold could see it in how she narrowed her glazed over eyes. "So, two things? Three things?"

He nodded. "Go on, dear girl."

"How did I get here?"

Gold wiggled the fingers on his free hand. "I still possess some residue magic, bottled and given to me a long time ago. I simply made you *jump* here. Remember, portals are for off-world travel. It allowed movement within the same Veil, the same plane of existence, to worlds that barely touch ours, like Atlantis. Jumping is travel within the same world but not long distance. Though, I suppose Venderly to England is quite a distance. Not the biggest jump ever made, but... Do you feel ill? Queasy?"

She shook her head. "Is Aero about? He's not going to jump out and see me like this next, is he?"

"My dear, Aero would have a wonderful breakdown seeing you dressed as you are. I don't think I'd recover from the hilarity of that. But no, he is not here. He is back in Atlantis. He'll return eventually. The Council will want another pair of eyes on you beside myself soon enough, I'm sure."

Natalia brought her mug to her lips. "Why am I here?"

"I wanted to ask if you'd been acquainted with Morpheus yet," he admitted. His undead heart didn't stir, but knew it probably would if it could. "I want to know how it went, how you are."

Lowering her mug, she looked around the room. Gold watched her in silence, he hadn't changed anything about it in years.

The old writers' desk was as cluttered as ever, and the old typewriter which had once belonged to Evangeline's husband still sat in the corner. A bookcase stood on the left of the desk and a table to the right. A fake potted plant rested behind the door, and the room itself was splashed with greens, reds, browns, and golds, as if it were some quaint thatched cottage and not a long farmhouse of brick.

"It went as well as expected," Natalia said after a moment.

"And how did you expect it to be?" Gold chased.

"Confusing."

Gold laughed, surprising himself at the notion. "Morpheus is notoriously confusing. I am assuming they shifted shapes before you?"

She nodded. "I apparently tried to hit Jasper in real life because of it."

"Brilliant!" Natalia shot him a sharp look and he quickly adjusted, "Not brilliant!"

Natalia sighed. "I just wonder, will it always be so confusing? Is this going to be a hopeless venture of getting lost in dreams and memories and spirals?" She played with the rope of the dressing-gown, then moved to play with her starry earrings that somehow cast large illuminations. "How can it be good to be how I am? Nothing good has happened around me yet and—"

"Nothing?" Gold cut in.

Huffing, she reconsidered. "A *few* things."

"Then don't say it's nothing. There are nothings in this world and your life has barely known them. You may have bad moments, bad days, weeks, but you haven't had an all-over bad life. The few sour and hard moments do not over-power the sweet and soft."

"I just mean that things keep going wrong around me and bad things *keep* happening, so whatever I'm seeking surely won't be any less. *Glass wings* are just the first indicator."

Gold stared at the girl. She reminded him of another; one equally as scared of the future because of who they were and what they could be given time. But they had choices. Fate couldn't take that from them, so they weren't hopeless. Natalia had choices too.

"Who says your wings are bad?" he challenged. "Who got to decide that?"

She looked up at him, her eyes wide and full of emotion. "I don't know—"

"Then don't try and let someone else decide."

"But—"

"Things may seem bad and complicated right now, but they won't always be. Fog always clears. So, while you may have bad moments and might have to see some bad things, they'll lead you to your answers. Those answers, dear one, will chase away the bad because you'll understand and accept and learn." Gold smiled and for once hoped his fangs stayed back. "You're a good person and a good Creature, and *so brave*, Natalia Whitebell, child of the stars."

"That's just it though. I don't know if I *am* a Creature."

"Maybe not," he agreed. "But being a Creature isn't always in one's blood or appearance. It's *what* you are, what you do. You'll always be a Creature and I know you'll always fight. You'll fight for your duty, but more importantly, I know you'll fight for your loved ones and yourself. That's what makes you a Creature. It's your heart. You just need to find your whole truth."

He watched her throat bob, her eyes swimming. "My truth."

Gold reached out towards her, tucking her hand into his. "And you *are* good, Natalia. I can promise you that and swear it upon my undead heart. You are *so good*."

10

Living Dreams

ERI'S ARM CAME FREE FROM HER BODY like it was made of no more than stuffing and cloth. The Monster threw her down, playing with the arm like a toy. Archie dove for her, surrounding Peri like a barricade with his body as she grew paler by the second.

Natalia walked through the scene with stunted steps.

She'd not been witness to these moments the first time around – no memory had scarred her brain – yet everything played as if she had. Guiltily, she was glad this wasn't her past.

"Is this what you wanted to see? I cannot imagine why."

Natalia turned towards the voice as the Calefaction flicked Peri's arm into the air and jumped to catch it. Morpheus came striding up to her, their form different yet again. They had blond hair in tight ringlets and a white toga accenting their waist with a golden belt. They looked even more out of place than Natalia.

"You don't have to watch this," Morpheus told her. "You can pull something else forward. Think of something else you wish to see, change the scene at your command. I can then walk you through to that new moment."

"What do I change it to though?"

Past Natalia burst onto the scene before Morpheus could respond. Natalia watched herself like a leaf in a storm. She could remember the moment clearly, the memory resurfacing as it played out in front of her.

Morpheus clutched their hands together. "Change it to what you want to see."

Natalia closed her eyes as Morpheus' hands closed over hers. When she opened them again, the scene had indeed changed. They stood on sand, waves gently pushing up the shore towards them. This stretch of beach appeared clear of other presences.

Or so it seemed until Natalia moved.

Another version of her was there again. They stood up off the sand, arm bleeding. Natalia touched her scar as she watched, the calloused skin rough beneath her fingertips. The Geminis Monster she'd been attacked by was already gone. Alex was too. Even their shapes and shadows had long disappeared.

Natalia watched her past self flex her left hand and wrist.

As if sensing a shift, past Natalia looked down and flexed once more. Natalia watched herself and gasped as the shard of glass that had been stabbed inside of her skin simply fell to the sand. Past Natalia looked away like it had never happened at all.

Natalia woke in a bundle of sheets, sweating and gasping for air. She kicked them away, intending only to roll onto her side, but went too far and tumbled to the floor. Her body ached as she pulled herself up again.

What had that dream meant? Morpheus' power worked on helping her find something she wanted to see. Intention and want could draw out the memories and dreams she searched for, allowing Morpheus to lead them through to it. But why had Natalia wanted to see *those* scenes? What intention had brought *either* of them forward?

The scar and area around it were numb. Touching the T-shape, Natalia wondered...

She'd always assumed the glass shard had wormed its way out

on its own; come loose from inside the skin somehow. But knowing what she did now it seemed unlikely, especially since there had been no other internal damage. A single thought lit like a torch in the night.

Could she somehow have cast the glass from her own arm?

The front doorbell rang, and she gasped in surprise. She gathered herself up off the floor and raced to it. She cracked the door open just a slither, willing her heart to slow back to normal.

"We come with gifts," Peri cooed, holding up a heavy-looking bag. If the smell was anything to go by, they'd been to the market and had picked up breakfast.

"And *great* humour," Alex added, grinning from behind Peri.

Natalia ushered them in, Noah popping his head around the corner as she did. Natalia engulfed him in a hug. Only when he wiggled to say he'd had enough did she let him go.

While the others set up the food, Natalia ran back upstairs to wash in the sink and change for the day. She brushed her hair into a ponytail and wrapped a golden ribbon around the band for a bonus. If she'd learnt anything from Gold, it was that Fairy's valued style and decoration, and it was time Natalia embraced that.

She glanced briefly in the mirror, grimacing.

For three weeks now, when she wasn't awake, Natalia had been in and out of her dream-states. Sleep hardly happened peacefully or without dreams that didn't include Morpheus. *That* meant she'd barely slept soundly, and when she did, only in brief spurts here and there.

Her reflection stared back, unaffected by the exhaustion firmly hooked into her being. She no longer looked hollow but the dark circles under her eyes hadn't vanished and neither had the new paleness.

Natalia sighed. Three weeks she'd been trying to discover a meaning behind them, but there had barely been anything useful.

Why can't I find anything? I didn't expect it to be easy but... I at least thought I'd be a little better off by now.

Turning away, she hopped downstairs, the sight of friends a welcome distraction.

Noah dished out the bundles of food until pancakes, waffles, syrupy bacon, fried potato slices, berries and oats, were splayed out across the counters. It smelt wonderful, like sugar and spice and all things good for the soul.

They all squished onto the tiny table, eating buffet style. Natalia picked at her food more than the others. The perfectly crisp bacon cracked in her mouth, and the pancakes were light and fluffy. But nothing tasted quite right, like something had dulled their flavour.

"Zoe knows everything I know now, I think," Noah announced. He moved from the table and stuck the kettle on for drinks. "She's been in and out of my bedroom for the past week trying to get me to explain it all in what she calls," he made air-quotations, "*Human terms.*"

Alex pointed her fork at him. "You better be telling her the *right* stuff."

"There's wrong stuff?" Noah scowled.

Alex shoved two rashers of bacon in her mouth at once. "The stereotypes," she shrugged.

Natalia pushed her plate away. "How's she taking it?"

"Well enough, I think." Noah opened the cupboards, pulling out four mugs. "She's never really asked *much*, only that she wants to know whatever she is allowed to know. She understands there are rules and Humans can't know everything." The kettle flicked off so he began to pour, and once done he handed them out.

Peri lifted her mug, the steam bringing colour to the end of her nose. "I don't see the problem," she said. "I don't know why the Council are shutting Humans out. Yes, it's not their Purpose to be in *this life*, but our war can affect them as much as it does us."

"You know the Council thinks lesser of what they don't understand or like," Alex said darkly. "They think lesser of what they cannot control."

"Maybe so, but Humans have *sempre* been involved. Monsters can still hurt Humans, or infect their lives."

Natalia held her mug between her hands. "My dad's Human," she reminded them.

Peri nodded. "*See.*"

"Oh," Alex sipped her drink, "my eyes are *wide* open. The Council are just awful bastards with small minds and small dicks on their heads."

Natalia scoffed, sipping cautiously. "How do they exist? How do you even become a Council member? There's one for each Creature, right? Who even helps them get those positions of power? And there can't just be them ruling, they have to have other Creatures help keep their screwed kind of order."

Peri's face twisted in confusion. "No one really knows how to become one."

"No one? So it just happens in the dark of night?"

Alex rolled her eyes. "Sums those bastards up. Hush-hush, up each other's arses, you know."

Peri shot Alex a scornful look and then sighed, lowering her mug. "As for the help, the Council have a force. They're kind of this world's police."

"Really?" Natalia asked.

"They're called The Society of Souls."

"Society of Souls?" Noah questioned. "S.O.S?"

"Should be S.Y.S for Save Your Souls," Alex mocked.

Peri looked at Natalia. "Back in Atlantis, after your trial, you were knocked out at carried away. The Council didn't touch you."

Natalia's eyebrows shot up. "*They're* the ones that stunned me and locked me up?"

"Save Your Fucking Souls," Alex repeated loudly into her cup as she drank.

"They are," Peri said, ignoring Alex. "They follow the Council's orders without question. Those that work in the Society are their own body. They have an Academy and everything."

"So the police had a baby with the army and it's called S.O.S?" Noah asked.

"Near enough. While other Creatures may take on jobs outside of their Purpose, like Katherine and her bakery, or James and his financial advisory, if you're in the Society, that is usually your top priority. If you take down Monsters, yay, great, but their main concern is upholding the rules and the Council's wishes. To them, Monsters are a secondary concern. They are the law's right hand."

"On that insightful note," Noah put his mug down, "and speaking of Katherine, I need to get to work."

He rose and kissed Natalia on the head, then did the same to Peri who laughed and Alex who huffed out of her nose. Natalia smiled. As much as he'd accepted her and this world, the people around her had accepted him back.

At the door, he added, "Have a lovely day, princesses." Then he was gone.

"Lovely day?" Natalia asked.

"Did he just call me a princess?" Peri questioned at the same time.

"I already *know* I am one." Alex sat back with a smug grin.

Peri placed her hand onto her ever-growing baby bump. "That aside, we *are* going to have a good day and I'm going to hear no arguments about it." Knowing her trident was probably close-by, no one argued.

Breakfast ended not long after. They stored the leftovers in the fridge and put their shoes on for the day out, which had been explained to Natalia in about two rapid sentences. They caught the tram into town, making the journey easier for Peri. Once down Main Street, the girls went into every shop possible. When they arrived at the salon, Alex snatched up Peri's bags, made an excuse about some training she needed to do, and left without a goodbye.

Natalia and Peri entered and were immediately treated like prestigious guests; they were given drinks and cake and cool packs for their foreheads and backs. When a beautician came over and asked how Natalia wanted her nails, she picked out a light grey that would be topped with silver flecks. Peri chose a thick blue to match her lipstick. As their nails were left to dry and their feet were soaking in petal-topped water, the girls were left alone. Natalia put her head to the back of the chair, sighing. She couldn't deny that this was the calmest she'd felt in *months*.

Natalia glanced over at Peri. She had her eyes closed, but cracked an eye open and peered over at Natalia, as if sensing her gaze. "Everything alright?"

"Fine," Natalia said, her stomach pinching slightly. "How are you?"

"Fed up with being pregnant." Peri laughed. "My feet constantly ache now and are nearly *sempre*," she clicked her fingers, "*always* swollen. I'm tired all the time. *Hungry* all the time. I need to pee every five minutes. Bras don't fit me properly anymore, and my clothes might *look* good, but what's underneath is a whole fucking mess."

"You've not got much longer now, right?"

Peri's blue-lipped smile was electric. "About a month. But is it bad that I want it to hurry up? I know you shouldn't wish days away, Seven Hells I know, but more than anything I just want to hold my little fish."

Natalia smiled back at her. "Have you thought of a name yet?"

"This little fishy is going to be a Darby."

"Not a—"

"De Costanzi?" She shook her head. "I don't want my parents

to have any claim on him. I'm still not even sure if they know I'm pregnant or not. *I* certainly haven't told them, but the Council might have. They know, at least. I had to tell them, for the upcoming maternity leave payments and to notify them of a new Creature. You know how they are about records."

Natalia knew that Peri's dislike of her parents came from more than their lack of love for Archie. She switched the conversation slightly. "What about the rest of his name?" she asked.

Peri's brightness returned. "We *think* we have a name."

"And?"

"I'm not telling you yet, *amore.*"

Natalia fake gasped. "Unbelievably unfair!"

Peri's joyous laugh reached her eyes. "Originally, we weren't going to find out what little fish was going to be, so *this* will be the secret we keep. You can find out his name the day he's born, just like everyone else."

If I'm still around then, Natalia thought.

Natalia diverted her gaze quickly, hoping Peri hadn't seen her thoughts in her eyes. She didn't know exactly where her last thought had come from, only that it had appeared with the strength of a scream.

With how weary and on edge she already felt, it could easily be the sleepless and dream-hopping nights that killed her before any Monster ever could. Or *maybe* the Monsters that hunted her, threatening her, *wanting* her, would get to her first after all.

It was a race, a deadly one, with an end in sight that Natalia couldn't quite reach.

Once their nails were dry, the beauticians returned. Not long after the girls were back out in the heat, but on their way home.

Natalia burst through her front door into the shade, Peri two steps behind her. Though it was only marginally cooler inside, she welcomed it.

Natalia kicked off her shoes. "How about a drink?"

Peri shook her head firmly. "How about you get yourself dressed instead?"

"Dressed? For what? I *am* dressed." She pointed to her shorts and vest.

"No." Peri's eyes roamed over her. "I am *not* letting you go out in that."

"Letting me go out? Where the Seven Hells am I going, Peri? What's going on?"

The Mermaid gave no answer, shooing her up the stairs in silence.

She pushed into her room and stopped. The usual mess she'd left this morning had vanished. Doors and draws were closed. The clothes on the floor were gone. Even the curtains were pulled back. Clearly, someone had been in here, and recently.

All that remained of the previous clutter was the familiar pillows, sheets, and a very notable dress spread on top of the bed.

Natalia whirled on Peri. "What have you schemed?"

"*Schemed?*" Peri held her hand up in surrender. "I've done nothing you hadn't already thought of, *amore*."

Natalia blinked, her gaze shifting between the dress and Peri. "A date? With Jasper? Is that what today was about?"

"What? I wouldn't dare get you out of the house under the pretences of a girl's day when I really had ulterior motives."

Natalia turned back to the dress, ignoring the blatant grin on Peri's face. A strange flurry of butterflies settled into her stomach. "I can't wear that," she whispered.

"Why not?"

"He's seen it before."

Peri huffed. "Jasper will still think you're beautiful."

"No." Natalia faced Peri again. "I wanted to wear it because it was different, something new and probably unexpected of me."

"Ah, *merda*." Peri pulled out her phone. "Just give me a minute, *amore*."

Peri was on the phone for minutes and then clicked it off. She promised Natalia there was a plan and before she could count to two hundred – she actually tried too – there was a knock downstairs. Peri went to answer it and came back with a bag in hand.

"It's a good thing we have a wolf on the inside," Peri laughed, revealing dress option B.

Natalia was pushed into the shower before she could comment on the dress and dragged out again. She walked back into her bedroom to have her hair made-up, and when it was, Peri began to root through her drawers.

"Oh!" Peri pulled out some white undergarments from one drawer. Natalia's face flushed furiously. "Although..." Peri turned to look at the new dress she'd thrown onto the bed. "You'll have to go braless."

Again, Natalia was subdued into silence with a single look as soon as she opened her mouth. Peri passed over the knickers and dress, swearing that it would fit. Natalia chose to trust her and went into the bathroom to change. Once ready, she stepped out to a one woman round of applause.

Natalia had seen her reflection. Her long hair had been pinned to on top of her head in a curled spiral with thick white clips, some strands pulled loose to frame her face. Simple mascara and peachy lipstick dawned on her face; bronze livened her cheeks. Her favourite star earrings – she never went without them – shone like actual stars in her ears, moving when she did.

Then there was the outfit itself.

The stark white dress hugged the middle of her thighs in two layers – an under-layer of some soft material, and an over-layer of fine material like silk. Split spaghetti straps held it up on her shoulders but the dress did show off some cleavage where it slithered down between her breasts. Matching white sandals adorned her feet.

Appearances made Natalia look like she'd pieced herself together carefully. She didn't *feel* that way, but at least she outwardly portrayed that sense of togetherness.

Peri slid up beside Natalia. "He's waiting for you," she whispered.

Natalia gulped, suddenly nervous and tired and full of energy all at once. "Where?"

"Take the little path behind your fence and down the narrow slope."

She turned to her friend. "What about you?"

Peri waved a hand. "Never mind me! Get that gorgeous arse *moving!*"

Natalia bolted. Though she was far from healed, she had enough of herself back to *want* again. And this was something she wanted, more than anything.

Just as Peri had said, Jasper stood at the bottom of the narrow slope behind her house.

A white shirt stuck to his upper body, showing off his slim yet tightly muscled shape. Sleeves were rolled up to the elbows and smart navy trousers were bunched up at the knees. His bare-feet had sunk into the sand beneath him.

When he spotted her, his distinct grin lit up his face. She took in the way his green eyes were faint in colour because of the bright sunlight beaming above them, but his freckles still stood out. Clearly he'd seen some sun recently because his hair was blonder than before, his skin more bronzed.

Slowly, Jasper's eyes raked over her. Natalia did the same back; he was tall and lean and a little bit sexy right now.

Natalia kicked off her sandals and closed the distance between them. She snaked her arms around Jasper's waist, watching his face the entire time. He stared down at her, carefully taking in her every move. She smiled and stood up on her tip-toes. They met in the middle, their lips the finish line they crossed together. He tasted like salt, as if he'd been swimming in the sea, and smelt of soap and sweet apples.

His thumbs crushed into her hips, his hands holding her against him. A rush ran through her body at the touch.

Jasper pulled back and pressed his forehead gently against hers. "You look stunning," he mused. He let his gaze drop, straight down the front of her dress. "*Stunning!*"

Natalia laughed. "You are *unreal.*"

"Unreally handsome."

"That's not a word." She looked him up and down, drawing out her study as slowly as he had. "You scrub up rather well too."

He ran his thumbs over her hips in little circles. "The hottest couple in town."

"On the entire Island, if you please."

Jasper let out an echoing "HA!" as he entwined their fingers and drew her further onto the beach.

Round the corner from the ramp was a nook. A blanket had been spread across the pale sand, rocks holding down the corners. The cutest picnic hamper sat to one side, a buried bottle of something beside it. Jasper sank to the blanket first, guiding Natalia down as she held down her dress, not that anyone unwanted was around to spectate if anything unfortunate happened; the beach here was deserted.

Jasper turned and opened the basket, pulling out two boring kitchen glasses which instantly became better as he produced the bottle of wine he'd stored in the sand. Natalia sipped and the tang bit her back, and she liked it.

"This is beautiful," she told him.

Somewhere beyond their line of sight, the sun began to dip low on the horizon. A golden-orange tint glimmered over the Earth, and the gentle breeze engulfed the air around them. The waves blue waves splashed along the beach in a peaceful lull.

Jasper touched Natalia's free hand, drawing her attention back. "I promised you a date, didn't I?"

"You did." She swallowed. "But I also promised you one. Secretly, anyway."

"I'll make you a deal. How about you plan the next date? You can surprise me."

"I think I can manage that."

"I don't need to mention that everything you do surprises me then?" He took the glasses, stuck them down a few inches into the sand, and pulled her close, rucking up the blanket beneath them. She tucked into his side, his lips brushing her ear. "Because you do surprise me, Natalia. Every day."

She let out a nervous laugh. "I hope that's a good thing."

"Oh, it's *definitely* a good thing."

Natalia tilted her head back and stared up at him. The world quieted around them, giving them the space within it to exist. "Tell me something," she whispered. "Tell me something about you that would surprise me."

For a moment, he thought. "I used to be scared of ladybirds," he blurted.

Natalia sat bolt upright and laughed. "Ladybirds? *Really?*"

He nodded, grinning. "One night, when we still lived in Atlantis, I found a whole load of them. They were flying around my room, crawling over my toys, probably mating on my window! It was horrible! Apparently, I tried screaming the house down."

"I'm more of a spider-hater kind of girl."

"At least they don't have wings." He fake shivered. "Tiny little buggers."

Natalia shivered at the thought of spiders with wings. To keep her mind at ease, she met his gaze again. "What else?"

"Are we playing twenty-one questions after all?"

She couldn't help but remember the first time she'd ever really spoken to Jasper. She'd been in his room after she'd been attacked by a Calefaction; her right leg twinged at the memory, though the scar itself was now gone.

Those versions of Jasper and Natalia were long gone.

Jasper's face came back into her field of vision, a smile in his emerald eyes. "What's your favourite colour?"

"A little basic," she mocked. She knew what he was doing, he was distracting her, and she appreciated it now as much as she ever had. "Purple, though I don't mind a soft peach. You?"

"Blue, but the scale also slides into green too. Favourite film?"

"When I was younger, there would've been no arguing that it was Barbie Swan Lake." Jasper snorted and she laughed, too. "Now? I'm not really sure. I've watched most of the current Marvel cinematic universe movies with Noah, since they're his favourites."

"I was *super* into Toy Story. I used to see if my toys would move at night. Mum even caught me once tying up my teddies so they couldn't escape."

She beamed. "That's *adorable!*"

He huffed a laugh. "Hardly. Potentially worrying, I'd say. Between that and the ladybugs, it's no wonder I had some sleepless nights as a kid."

"All the same, *I* find it adorable."

"Of course you would." His green eyes lit with amusement before shifting, flickering with mischief. "Let's get a little more interesting, shall we?"

She raised her eyebrows at him. "Where is this going?"

"You'll be fine," he said, smirking.

"At any point I can say no?"

"Of course. You can always say no and I will *always* obey and respect it."

"Or lean over, grab the wine bottle, and use it like a weapon."

His laugh bounced around them. "Sure, Fairy. If the idea makes you feel better, I'll let you keep it." He even reached behind him and plucked up the bottle, sticking it into her hands with a grin before leaning back on his arms casually. "Who was your first kiss?"

Natalia sighed. "Noah."

Jasper had the audacity to make a choking sound. "*Noah?*"

"We were about fifteen. Neither of us had kissed anyone before, so we decided to do it with each other. We were comfortable enough as friends to try and to get rid of the stigma and pressure that a first kiss had to be perfect." She rolled her eyes, though began to smile. "It was actually funny. I'm glad it was him. But we both agreed there and then that we weren't meant to be anything more than friends." She shrugged. "In fairness, Noah decided the whole idea of sexual intimacy wasn't for him at all. What about you?"

"Her name was Emma." Jasper shuddered. "I wasn't into the idea in the first place. Since then, I've worked out that I'm not into much with a person unless there's an emotional connection first. But, at the time, Emma kept sucking at my lips like some deranged octopus. I had to push her away to get her to stop. The worst bit is that we were about fifteen too, not five."

Natalia leant forwards and started making hideous kissy faces with slurping noises. Jasper swatted the air between them to deter her, but she wouldn't relent until he cupped her face in his hands.

His stare became magnetic. "What else is there to you?" he whispered delicately. The previous jovial mood fell away.

Natalia let go of the bottle and touched his wrists. "Are you asking me or yourself?"

"Both."

There was no room to respond as he pressed his lips to hers.

Natalia felt like a teenager again - technically she still was at eighteen - but one who was kissing their first crush. The butterflies in her stomach wouldn't cease - but they weren't rapid and anxious

- and nor would the intoxicating dizziness that washed over her whenever Jasper touched her.

But they weren't teens and this wasn't some silly crush.

This was far beyond that.

They'd risked their lives together, held their hearts in each other's hands. Natalia had heard people say "you know when you know" about another person, but she'd never personally thought about it. Until now. Now she felt it, that this was *big*, two souls connecting on some deeper and resounding level.

His hands dragged down her arms to her sides and then slowly rose higher to hold near where her wings would sprout from. She leant into him, shaking slightly, wrapping her hands around his neck to touch the bottom strands of hair, twiddling them in her fingers.

As Natalia dragged her hands down to Jasper's shirt, her fingers grazing the buttons, the ground beneath them shook. They burst apart, wildly searching around.

"If this is what I think it is..." Jasper trailed off as the ground rocked again before a Poena came trundling around the corner. The glob-like mass shuffled, wobbling the ground with each footless movement.

Natalia unveiled her blade, taking it out of the thigh strap. She stole a glance at Jasper and found him smirking, eyes darting from her exposed thigh to her face. Her cheeks heated. He looked like he was about to say something when two more globs appeared behind the first.

The three Poenas gained speed.

In panic, Natalia launched her blade. It managed to snag one of the Monsters, but because she'd not aimed, all she'd done was cut a chunk out of it; the slice that looked like a cube of jelly fell away and melted into ash on the sand.

The three Poenas stopped. Before, they hadn't appeared focused on Natalia and Jasper. Now they were zoned and locked in. Yet they stayed there, unmoving.

"I can't use magic," Jasper whispered, his green eyes watching the Monsters. "They'll just absorb it and maybe rebound it. I can't risk that. And I don't have a weapon. I didn't think our date would require one."

"Can you distract them somehow?"

"I might be able to use a little, harmless magic." She nodded in agreement, and pink light darted toward the Monster trio.

The Monsters scattered then regrouped, racing together towards the source of light. As one of the Poena touched the pink strobe, sucking it into its see-through body, it began to glow a deep pink.

Jasper threw more light at the Poena as Natalia threw her blade. She sliced off parts of them chunk by chunk, but it was slow going. Natalia knew she needed to take them head on but couldn't guarantee how safe it would be for either of them if she tried.

Her wrist tingled as her blade returned to her yet again and she glanced down at the scar. Suddenly, she remembered something and whirled on Jasper.

"Glass!" she hissed.

He threw a quick glance at her. "What?"

"*Glass*. It works against Poenas. Don't ask how I remember." She pointed to the wine bottle and glasses. "Can you break them and throw the fragments?"

Natalia turned from him, not waiting for his reply as *she* became the distraction instead. Watching her blade fly through two Poenas at once was somewhat satisfying. She almost smiled, but stopped herself as she saw something green shine at one of their feet.

Curious, she squinted at it, focused on it. It disappeared.

But as her blade returned to her palm, so did something else.

She gasped as her fingers closed around it, and he glanced out the corner of her eye to see if Jasper had heard her, but he was still focused on breaking the glass around him into little bullets.

Natalia opened her hand, spying the piece of glass that had come back with her blade. *Did I just call that to me?*

To test her theory, Natalia dropped the green glass in the sand and then called for it. She prayed it wouldn't come. But it did, floating right back into her palm.

How am I doing that? I can't do that! I can summon my blade because it's mine. I can bring my dust because it's mine. Glass isn't mine.

The memory of the Darby's kitchen window resurfaced like an all-consuming tsunami, her mind showing her how she'd handled that glass to ward off the Monster from herself and Peri. Her dream resurfaced too.

Natalia threw down the green glass and kicked sand over it furiously, burying it deep. This wasn't the first time she'd commanded glass. It wasn't even the second. *That* was what her dream had been showing her, she realised. The glass hadn't simply fallen from her arm. No, she'd *commanded* it out. Knowingly or not, she'd pulled the glass out of her arm on her own.

Despite not remembering first-hand, she'd seen her memory, and how could she dispute that or her experiences since?

"Ready!" Jasper called.

Natalia nodded without looking at him. Her blade went hurtling towards the Monsters again, lodging into one's side. An invisible string attached her to her blade, a connection through Fairy dust. She focused on it, pushing the dagger deeper.

The blade sank through the Monster, making a *pop* sound as it burst all the way through to the other side. The Monster wobbled and melted into a pile of jellied ash.

One of the other two Monsters left was plastered with coloured shards of glass. Natalia watched as it stupidly flicked a jagged piece with a see-through hand. It caught itself enough that the entire Monster caved inwards before spraying the sand with goop.

That left only the lit up pink one. Natalia saw that Jasper was running out of glass. She called her blade back, poised to move whenever he did.

In unison, they commanded their items. The glass and blade struck the Monster's centre simultaneously. The pink Poena grumbled, and looked vaguely in Natalia's direction. She quickly saw why.

The wine bottle had been brown and the glasses were clear. Natalia blade was silver and bronze. But there, stuck directly between where she assumed its eyes would've been, nestled a green shard of glass.

The Monster tipped forwards and gently folded into ash.

"No rest for the wicked around here," Jasper joked once it appeared they were safe. He wiped himself clean of as much goop as he could before striding up to Natalia. "Are you alright? You look like you've seen a ghost."

Did he not see? She looked right at him, and he stared back with careful consideration. "I wonder what got it in the end," she said, tearing away her gaze and calling back her blade.

Jasper scanned the now empty beach. "Well, there are only two options: your blade or my glass." He laughed and pulled her in to kiss her head despite the mess and grime covering them both. "Good job on thinking up the glass by the way!"

"I'm sure it was something Alex said," she replied, her stomach twisting.

Natalia reached up and kissed the underside of his jaw, and then stayed there, tucking her head into him to hide her face.

Since he hadn't said anything, she assumed Jasper really hadn't seen the green glass. She stuck her hand behind her body and willed the glass to come. She waited, but nothing touched her palm. She scowled in confusion and tried again but still as nothing came. She hoped that was because it had disappeared with the Poena.

How did I do it? How can I call glass?

Jasper kissed her head again, drawing her away from her mind. "Speaking of your blade, you kept that hidden." His tone was playful.

She tipped her head back to look up at him. "I always have it on me."

"As you should." His smirk widened. "But tucked against your thigh? In *that* dress? That's awfully dangerous."

She smiled back. "I rather like it though, don't you?"

"It's definitely not bad."

"Maybe one day I'll show you up close *exactly* how it attaches and detaches."

"One day?"

She stood on her tip-toes to whisper against his ear. "Who knows how close that day really is?" She pushed her body against his and felt him shiver against her. "Could be a lot sooner than you think."

Jasper whistled and teasingly kissed the corner of her mouth. Natalia dodged his next kiss, laughing, and tucked herself back into him, more comfortably this time. He grunted, and she smiled as she touched his chest, spreading her fingers across it to feel the muscle below. He held onto her back, his other hand covering hers on his chest, and she wondered if his heart thundered as loudly as hers did.

Staring out to sea, her eyes welled until a few tears broke loose.

As the two of them stood there, letting the world calm itself, Natalia couldn't shut off her mind. Her endless questions of who she was and what she could do overwhelmed her, as did the recently discovered proof showing what she was capable of. A knot formed at her throat, slipping around her neck.

But she *would* find answers.

She sniffed and wiped her eyes. She had to find them, now more than ever. If not for herself, then for everyone else.

11
A Taste of Life

THE RAIN WAS COOL AND REFRESHING AGAINST ZOE'S FACE. Every time a droplet landed, she'd let it stick, unwilling to wipe away the water after such a hot day. She only put her shirt on so she wouldn't have to carry it, but made sure to roll the sleeves up as high as they would go.

She tip-toed down the street barefoot until she found a bench. Sitting, she brushed her feet with her hand, then slipped on her socks and skates. Once they were laced up, she took off.

Not wanting the night to end early despite her shortened date, she took the long way home via the beach. It might've been raining but it wasn't storming; it was the perfect time to steal a moment of calm before returning home.

The noise of the waves rippled inside her ears, the sound running interrupted as the people had long gone home now that it was night-time.

Zoe shook out her hair, the strands matted and damp. She'd been toying with the idea of cutting it short. The idea was growing with each minute.

A growl cut through the serenity. Zoe strained her neck as she whipped it back and forth in search of the source of the noise.

She skated down the path to the colourful little beach-huts that lined the shore. As she turned towards the dead bushes, she spotted a shape. Her defences went up immediately and she backed up. But as the growl came again and the shape produced itself fully, she let out a heavy sigh. The shape morphed with cracks and groans until Alex Darby appeared from the mass of fur.

"You're hiding in a bush because..." Zoe trailed off.

Alex detached her leg from the mess of brambles and branches, shaking it out. Zoe averted her gaze promptly when she realised the other girl was naked. Zoe shrugged off her oversized shirt and handed it over. She felt Alex take it.

"I'm fine," Alex grumbled.

When Zoe turned back, Alex was covered, but not well. The shirt was done up by two buttons and the bottom ended right at the top of the girl's thighs. At least Alex's wild hair covered most of her exposed chest and neck.

"You're still looking," Alex told her.

Zoe coughed and forced herself to concentrate on Alex's shadowed face. "Just making sure you haven't got any injuries," she lied.

Alex tucked some hair behind her ears and raised her eyebrows, accenting her piercing. "Why would I have injuries?"

"Why were you in a bush?"

"I got stuck," Alex shrugged. "And even if I *did* have injuries, which I don't, they would heal pretty quickly."

"Righ', wolf abilities."

"Why did you give me your shirt? I don't feel the cold and its summer."

Zoe swallowed. "You were naked, on the beach."

Alex fixed her with a questioning look. "Wolves have no issue with being naked. We change so often it's inconsequential. Clothes also shorten our fur if we leave them on when we shift." As if something occurred to her, Alex strode forwards. Zoe backed up until her legs were pressed into the low wall that separated the path from the actual sand. "Now it's my turn to ask the questions. Why are *you* out so late?"

"I'm on my way home," Zoe said.

"It's past midnight."

"I'm seventeen," Zoe said, as if that explained everything.

"I'm twenty, what's your point?" Zoe didn't answer, because really she didn't have a point. Alex huffed and changed the course of the conversation. "Where have you been so late?"

Zoe pointed to her skates. "I was at the skating rink with some mates."

"And you're only now leaving?" Alex crossed her arms causing the shirt to lift up and wrinkle at her mid-section. Zoe didn't dare look lower. "I don't believe it."

"Is it any of your business?"

"No." Alex grinned wildly. "But it's fun to find out."

Zoe matched her stare. "Why are *you* out so late?"

"Patrolling. My brother and Natalia were caught by some Poenas earlier. I was seeing if there were more."

"Could you see much from the bush?"

Alex huffed. "I ran down part of the cliff and my foot got stuck at the bottom, ok?"

Zoe nodded and backed down, her shoulders deflating. "Were there any Monsters?"

"Not that I could see." She shook her head, her hair falling from behind her ear. "Want some company on your walk—" She stopped abruptly and smirked. "Your *skate* of shame home?"

The hairs on Zoe's body all stood to attention at once. "*Wha'*?"

"I can smell two perfumes on you and the lingering smell of sweat." Alex grinned but it wasn't wild or wolfish anymore. "Don't worry, I don't judge. Good for you, actually. Nothing to be ashamed of really."

It was Zoe's turn to snort. "He was ok but nothin' special."

"So you're not going to see him again?"

"Hell fucking no. Maybe I'll see his sister instead."

Alex raised a curious eyebrow in her direction but said nothing. She turned away and Zoe went to speak when the shirt came away. Alex's back was on full display, all tight muscles and small white scars, and...

Shit.

Zoe reached for the shirt but missed, and it fell to the ground. She snatched it up quickly, diverting her attention as she remembered that Alex had better senses than her, and the way Zoe had stared was bound to be detected.

"I wouldn't mind the company," Zoe answered Alex's earlier question. She didn't put her shirt back on, just slung it over her arm and clung to it like it might stabilise her somehow.

Alex nodded and bent over, her bones visibly shifting under skin. Zoe gritted her teeth at the change, her stomach squeezing. She wondered how Alex could do it so often without feeling nauseated or pained. When the shift stopped, Zoe stared down at the brown wolf from before.

Alex bared her teeth in some imitation of a grin. Zoe edged closer. Looking into the wolf's eyes, Zoe noted that the colour remained – the light honey-brown that was Alex in human form stayed while she was a wolf too.

Maybe being around Monsters won't be all bad because I have the Creatures?

She had been worried, *terrified*, after her last encounter with a Monster. But staring at Alex and seeing how her eyes never changed, how she still seemed to be *her*, smothered a layer of that worry. Creatures were harsh, but Zoe could see them still as Humans, unlike the Monsters.

Alex bounded off. Zoe looked to the sky and realised the rain had stopped. She hadn't even noticed.

Taking a second to breathe, Zoe followed, her skates clacking and gliding on the ground as she tried to catch up.

The double layer of peanut butter wasn't enough, so Peri added a third.

She bit into the toast as she worked on Archie's. She couldn't wait for him this morning. Her hunger was too immense. Soon, Little fish settled down with his kicks, clearly satisfied as well.

"Morning, Peri."

Peri shuffled to face the speaker, a piece of toast half hanging from her mouth. Noah waved as he walked into the room.

"You're early," she mumbled as she chewed.

"I didn't mean to be," he said. "Katherine didn't need me at the café today so thought I'd stop by for a lesson now instead of coming later." He looked unsure, nervous. "Is that ok?"

"That's more than fine, *amore*. I have been telling you for weeks that you can stop by whenever you like."

"Ok, good. I didn't want to intrude."

"You never would be." She smiled at him. "Would you like a drink?"

Noah walked to her side. "I'll make them."

"I was just going to get some orange juice," she said, relenting and awkwardly sitting on a barstool. She was grateful for each day that passed, bringing her closer to the end of this pregnancy and the return of her independence.

Noah fetched a glass of orange juice and water for Peri. She smiled when he placed them in front of her. Whether she asked for it or not, he would nearly always get her a drink when he was over, and she would always drink them.

"What would you like to start on today?" Peri asked as she sipped the cold juice.

Noah picked up his bag and took out a notebook, flipping through the pages quickly. At first, Peri had been agitated at him for taking notes, but who was she to deny him his best way of learning? He aced whatever she threw at him, so something was clearly working.

Finally Noah stopped on a semi-blank page and pulled out a pen. "Last time we left off on Crystals? About their uses and powers."

"Ah," Peri nodded. "I remember *saying* that, but really I don't know much about Crystals."

"They can only be used by Vampires, can't they?"

"Mostly. There are a rare few that can be used by others."

"And you said the practise was old?"

"Old-fashioned," she corrected.

Noah looked at her, innocent eyes gleaming. "But they're used to determine pregnancy, so how is that old-fashioned."

Peri took a sip of water. "*That* isn't considered old, but nearly every other use is. Same as verbal magic and potions for Witches. It's not used much now. General intention is the way forward. If we still used spells or potions, the magic cast would have to be so precise and careful to make sure there was no bounce-back."

"Right." Noah began to write. "Where do Crystals come from?"

"All over," she answered. "The ones we still use are from this world, this *plane* really."

He stopped writing and looked at her. "But you *can* get them from elsewhere?"

"I don't really know, but it's been recorded and we learnt at school that a few Crystals over time were accidently brought through Veils to this plane of existence by Monsters. Those Crystals tend to be the ones that burn up after one use and, for obvious reasons, are also *super* rare."

He nodded. "Obviously."

Peri opened her mouth but was cut off by her phone. She grimaced at the displayed name.

Madre.

Peri looked at the clock and wondered why her mother was phoning and wasn't out at sea. Her parents religiously went swimming this early each day, but never in the same space of water.

Noah peered over at the still ringing phone. "Are you going to answer it?"

Peri sighed and clicked "*answer*" on the screen, putting it on loudspeaker.

"*Madre,*" Peri acknowledged.

"*Figlia,*" her mother responded. "*Come te la passi?*"

"*Sto bene, grazie. Tu?*"

"*Così-così,*" her mother answered.

"My friend is here, *madre,*" Peri said, switching back to English for Noah's sake.

"And which friend would that be?" her mother questioned.

Peri ignored her question. "Why did you ring?"

"Is it illegal to want to speak to my own daughter?"

"No, but you never ring. You swore off speaking to me, remember?" Noah's eyes widened and Peri waved a hand at him.

"*Bugiarda!*"

Liar. Her own mother had called her a liar. She gritted her teeth and steadied her resolve. "Oh? I'm still with Archie." Immediately, the phone-line went dead and Peri sighed, locking her phone. "And my point is proven."

"I'm sorry, Peri," Noah said. He reached over and touched her hand.

"I don't even know why she rang."

"Maybe she just wanted to talk?"

Peri let out a sad laugh. "She's had plenty of chances for that. I ask her why she rings and she cuts me off when I bring up why she never speaks to me in the first place." She pushed her phone away. "She doesn't even know I'm pregnant."

"But you're about to pop!"

"I am, and I cannot wait. But my parents don't know because they don't spend long enough *trying* to know. This is the first time either of them have tried to speak to me since getting pregnant and she cut me off before I could say anything."

"Well, it's their loss. Who needs them anyway? You have a great support system around you here."

Peri leant to kiss Noah's cheek. She watched him beam as she pulled away, making her laugh. Noah was a kind soul; Peri could sense it radiating off him.

"Now, back to Crystals," she said.

"I'm guessing there isn't a Crystal to fix family relations?"

"Fixing relationships takes hard work and effort and time, not spells and potions and fins."

"That's me told." Noah picked up his pen but looked back at her. He already had a soft, open face, yet somehow, it morphed to become even gentler. "Seriously though, is there anything I can get you?"

Peri shook her head. "Let's just keep going with your lesson."

"You're the teacher."

She dug around and pulled out her trident, flicking it to its full size, leaving it on the counter. "This is a threat so you don't forget it."

Noah gulped and Peri genuinely couldn't tell if it was real or dramatic. "Yes, ma'am!"

Both of them laughed and then settled down to learn.

In those quiet moments where Noah read or scratched down more notes, Peri vowed to not become her parents. She refused to carry on the De Costanzi family tradition of being ruthless to everyone, including themselves. That was not what she wanted for her little fish. That vicious circle was being cut there. Her little fish would know happiness and she would do anything to give it to him. Whatever it took.

Workmen pushed through the house. The echoing noise of sawing, drilling, and scraping could be heard halfway down the street. Archie observed them. They'd made an offer on it immediately and, with no other interested parties, it'd been sold to them – something to do with the old owners wanting a quick closer. Updates and work had begun as soon as Peri and Archie had been handed the keys.

In all the madness the world had thrown his way recently, it *was* unnerving to try and settle down a little, but if they didn't try now, when? So while the going was good, Archie was seizing his chance.

However, it was odd that they had been given this long period of quiet to try and settle. The Monsters had been oddly absent recently. But this was a small Island, and they could appear anywhere at any time...

"They're finished for the day now, *amore*."

Archie turned to see Peri waddling through the mess. Once at his side, she kissed his cheek then wiped his skin with her thumb, probably to take away the blue marks she often left.

Peri had been at the family home for the morning and here at their soon-to-be family home this afternoon. Archie had errands to run throughout the day, but he'd come over to his new house to check the progress and meet up with Peri.

"We could stay here tonight?" she suggested. Their room was one of two fully completed, though there wasn't much furniture yet.

He smiled at her. "I like that plan."

Peri glanced around. "This place is going to look amazing when it's *all* done. Our own little sanctuary." She smiled, leaning into him.

"You know, I disliked the idea of coming to Venderly to begin with," he admitted, aware that Peri hadn't known his true feelings. She shuffled to stare up at him. "But I'm glad we did, and I'm glad you decided to come with me."

Peri's eyes welled. "I think I would've come after you no matter what."

"More than anything," he stole her hand and kissed the palm, "I'm glad we're *staying*." He kissed each finger in turn. "I thought that maybe you'd want to return to Atlantis eventually, to live there. That's where I always pictured us."

"Where you are is my home, *amore*."

"So you don't want to return to Atlantis?"

"Here is where I want to be. Look around us, *amore*. I have the sea and you have the land. There's this beautiful house and our family lives just down the road. We're surrounded by lovely things and lovely people, soon to be joined by one more. I want to be *here*."

He beamed. "Yeah?"

"Atlantis served its purpose, it helped me meet you and your family. But it was never really home for me." She sniffed, tears clouding her eyes. "My *nonno* was kind and caring. The rest of my family, not so much. I would've moved eventually. You simply stole me away and I let you."

"*Ti amerò sempre.*"

Her smile was every bit beautiful. "I will always love *you*." Without warning, Archie carefully wrapped his arms around her and lifted her bridal style. She laughed, throwing her arm behind his head. "Where are we going?"

He didn't answer. He moved them through the house and up the stairs, right into their bedroom. There, he sat her on the bed carefully.

Bending down, he lifted her feet and slid each shoe off gently. Once they were discarded, he gripped onto her legs. Archie smiled as Peri watched him with curious eyes.

He kissed the skin, his hands and mouth wandering higher with each touch. When his hands reached the band of her underwear, he grinned up at her flushed cheeks and closed eyes.

Archie stood and tipped Peri back. She gasped but he covered her eyes before she could open them and climbed over her. "Are you ok?" he whispered.

"I am," she said. "But you won't be if you stop."

He laughed. "I won't. Not unless you ask." He leant closer to her ear. "But I don't think you will."

Moving back down her body, he slipped his hands back under her dress. He stole more kisses, gently roaming his hands around her centre. He could feel the heat of her and he loved it.

Shuffling, he pressed his lips to her inner thigh. Peri gasped. He laughed, nipping the inner flesh. She whimpered in response, and her hand touched his head, holding him in place.

Archie slid his hand beneath her and pulled her underwear from her hips first, pushing her knees apart after. He dragged his mouth closer to her centre until she jolted in delight from his touch. The grip on his hair tightened as he continued. Each time she moaned, it was music to his ears.

She came apart beneath him.

Peri reached for him, grabbing the neck of his t-shirt and hauling him up to kiss her. He laughed against her mouth as she moved her hand down, fumbling with his belt. She bit his bottom lip and with a single look made him undo his own trousers.

"How do you want me, *amore?*" he whispered after removing them.

Peri climbed up the bed and rested her head on the pillows. "Right here," she said, pulling at the edges of her dress.

Archie moved up to meet her. Balancing his weight on one arm, he moved up behind her. Slowly, he kissed the side of her face, her neck, even her shoulders. Peri grasped him and made him hers.

They built up to the edge of the cliff together. Peri tipped first, dragging Archie with her through shattered breaths and stuttered heartbeats.

Cautiously, he pulled away and nestled beside her, wrapping her body with his protectively. She wiggled to get comfortable, laying her head back into his chest. Their breaths were the only sound Archie could hear.

Archie looked up at the ceiling. He hadn't lied when he'd said about imaging him and Peri back in Atlantis. But now it was clear they would stay here, on Venderly, and they would make this house their forever home. As he stared up, Archie imagined the Heavens beyond, and begged the Gods silently that forever actually meant a long time.

"What are we watching?" Tony looked at the flickering TV and scowled. "The *news?*"

Natalia shrugged. "I wanted to see what the weather was going to be like tomorrow."

"Hot, hot, and bloody hot?"

She accepted the cup of tea he handed over. "You're not wrong," she said. "We must be due a storm soon though. All this pressure has to be building up."

Tony nodded in agreement and sat beside her on the sofa, sipping his devilishly sweet tea.

They'd spent the afternoon together, just shopping around town for some new bits for the house – paints to update a few rooms, a new mirror for the bathroom, a plant for the hallway – and it had been nice, and spending the evening together too made it feel like old times. They didn't always get to relax and spent much time together now that they both had their own busy lives.

Tony put his cup down on the wonky coffee table and leant back, the news droning on in the background. "I never asked." Natalia looked across at him. "How did your date go?"

She considered her answer for a moment. "It was fine, *good*, you know."

"Am I not going to get any more out of you than that?"

"How did you even know I was going on a date?" she asked instead.

He scratched his greying, itchy beard. "Peri told me."

Natalia sighed. "Of course she did. What else did she say?"

"Just that you and Jasper were going down to the beach for a late day picnic. She asked if I could give her the house so she could help you get ready. Conveniently, I was already at work that day."

"It went well." Natalia didn't meet his eye but he caught her smiling into her cup. "Peri put me in this beautiful but *ridiculous* dress."

"Not the burgundy one I remember you buying?"

"No. Jasper had seen that one before." She shrugged.

"You wanted something a little more special, which Peri provided. I get it. I was young once."

Natalia's eyes, her *mother's* eyes, stared at him. "I suppose," she said, bending to put her own mug down. "Is this really something you want to hear about? I mean, it's something I'd tell friends but..."

Tony smiled. "It doesn't matter how old you get, I'm still your father. I want to know how your days have been, how your dates are, not details." He cringed at the thought. "But I do want to know if you're *happy*." He would give up his own joy if it meant she could take it for herself.

"Dad." Natalia gave him a wide-eyed smile like she used to when she was young. "I promise you, I *am*."

"Jasper's treating you right? He's not trying to do anything or force you into anything?"

She snorted. "He wouldn't stand a chance at trying anything like that. Not with me. I wouldn't let him. The threat of the other females in his life finding out if anything happened is also sure to stop him. They'd cut him into ribbons, no questions asked. But he wouldn't even think of anything like that. Jasper's a good guy."

"If you're happy, then I trust you and I trust you'll do right by yourself."

Natalia drew a cross over her heart. "I can certainly promise you that." She yawned.

Tony smiled at her. "Why don't you take your drink upstairs? Go run a bath and get to bed. You have work in the morning, right?"

She nodded. "I think I will."

"I'll give you a lift in since I'm working, too. Normal time, half seven?"

"Yeah." Natalia stood and picked her mug up.

On the way, Tony caught her wrist, pulled her down slightly, and kissed her cheek. "Love you, my little Natalia."

She laughed. "Love you too, dad. See you in the morning."

He watched her vanish upstairs. A minute later, the pipes began to rattle, telling him Natalia was running a bath as he'd suggested.

Tony settled into the sofa, stretching his legs, and flicked through the TV channels until he found one he could watch without fully focusing. Late night TV wasn't always the best, but he wasn't tired enough to attempt sleep yet.

He didn't know how long he sat there before a faint tapping echoed behind him.

Quietly, he peeled himself from the sofa and crept through to the kitchen. The dim light was still on, just as he'd left it, and nothing else was out of place. Even the tap was turned off. He frowned. He'd been convinced the noise had come from here. There was no sign that Natalia had gotten out of the bath either, though he grew increasingly unsure.

Until the knocking came again, at the backdoor.

Tony flinched, his heart racing. He grabbed the nearest thing he could – a small knife – and touched the door handle. Counting down from three, he wrenched it open.

Nothing was there. Not directly anyway. But his gaze caught on a shape further down the garden. His stomach twisted uncomfortably.

This is a trap. It has to be, he thought. *Why else would anything climb into his garden, knock on the back door, and then run to the centre of the grass? Why not just knock on the front door and be seen?*

Despite his better judgement, Tony stepped outside. The door shut behind him,

Tony traipsed across the garden that had only recently been restored. Out of the corner of his eye, he saw her bedroom light on and wonder if she would be able to hear him should be need to call for help.

Eventually, he stopped. His knife fell to the grass, lost to the ground for the night.

"*Azalea?*" he choked in surprise.

Tony had not seen Azalea Whitebell since his wedding to Lavender. The women were non-identical twins, born mere minutes apart, and had grown up inseparable. But when Lavender had dismissed her responsibilities as Heir to the Fairy throne and Kingdom, Azalea had been crowned. It had been a surprise that she'd shown up to the wedding at all. She hadn't been around at all after.

But here she was, in his garden after all these years, illuminated by a glow of her own making – her royal blue Fairy dust.

Azalea didn't look any different than she had that day, maybe just a hint more aged around her facial features, but not in a bad way. Her round face held deep-set blue eyes, extenuated by thick lashes. Blonde hair twisted about her thin neck and shoulders, a heavy-looking sapphire necklace at her throat. She wore a toga-like dress; white with a band of blue and gold at the middle.

"What are you doing here?" Tony asked. He looked about the garden anxiously. "Your mother isn't coming, is she?"

"She is not here," Azalea confirmed.

Tony nodded, relieved, fixing gaze on her once more. "Why are you here?"

"My mother may be travelling, but I do not have a lot of time. She will be back soon," Azalea said. She stepped forward, her movements appearing like she was floating without her wings present. "Did you know she forbid me from seeing you?"

Tony shook his head. "No, but it makes sense." They were both tense, he noticed. The years of no contact were like a wedge between them. He wanted to warm to her, to treat her like a sister-in-law, but this woman was unknown to him. She had just been a name and brief memory for so long. "Did she tell you she came to see us herself a little while ago?"

Azalea nodded. "She did, and it was unfair. How dare she tell me not to see my own twin's family yet see them herself?" She glanced down at her joined hands clasped hands briefly. "I apologise that it has taken me so long to come."

He narrowed his eyes in suspicion. "There's no hidden agenda behind this? Your mother isn't going to jump out of a bush and hit me over the head, is she?"

She stared coldly. "Certainly not!"

"Well..." He debated saying that her mother *certainly would* do something like that, but decided against it. "You know your sister had a daughter, that you have a niece?"

Azalea peered over his head. "I hadn't known until the other month," she admitted. "I apologise for that too, but you must understand. My world is closed off, my life even more so. My guards only speak of things happening on a grand scale, like Monster attacks or breaches to our land. My advisors talk only of duty to the land and to Fairies. The staff chatter but only about their lives. My own mother hardly ever even looks in my direction. So until my mother spoke of her visit, and of seeing you, I had been in the dark."

Lavender and Azalea had been close, Tony knew, so it must've hurt them both to one day have a sister and no one a dawn later. Queen Primrose wanted the future queen to grow without confliction and without restraint. She would've made the choice herself and closed Azalea out because Lavender had cut them off when she'd chosen a life for herself. The queen wanted to shut Lavender out more than she'd ever done to them. Choosing a life for oneself over what the queen had wanted would've been the ultimate betrayal to her, and so everyone was to be punished.

Azalea looked back at him. "What is my niece's name?"

"Natalia."

She smiled, and her dust glinted brighter. "Lavender always said that if she were to have a girl, she'd name her Natalia."

"She did. Natalia Primrose."

"She chose mother's name to be her second?" Azalea blinked in shock.

"After meeting her, I was just as shocked."

"I suppose you would be, yes. I also heard that you kept our last name."

"It kept me closer to Lavender and closer to my daughter."

Azalea's smile returned. "I came here to give you this." Tony hadn't noticed a little purse on her wrist until she pulled something from it. He took what she offered; a small cream coloured bottle. "It's perfume, for Natalia."

"Perfume?" Tony questioned.

"For a *very late* birthday present." Azalea sighed. "It's the same subtle vanilla and juniper one her mother used to wear. Junipers also mean luck and protection to us. I thought Natalia might like it, to know her mother better."

Tony took off the cap and sniffed, the memory of Lavender

instantly consuming him. He'd never known there was juniper inside, but having something floral made sense. His heart squeezed in his chest as he replaced the lid. "Thank you," he whispered. "I'm sure she'll love it."

"I hope so. I also hope one day I will get to meet her. I had thought that might be tonight, but I see tonight I am too late."

Tony turned and saw that Natalia's bedroom light was now out. "She's a good kid, I know she'll want to meet you," he said, turning back.

The Heir to the Fairy throne nodded once. "Let that day come."

"Just, knock on the front door next time."

"I only came out here to keep from being noticed. But next time, I will tell my mother of my plans and do as you ask."

"But—"

"She cannot banish me and leave the throne empty. I will always be her Heir while I live." Azalea wove her dust in the air before them. "I came to tell you something, too. You are aware that I was married a few Earth months ago, yes?"

Tony nodded. "You mother had mentioned it. She'd said that'd why she hadn't seen Natalia's trial in Atlantis."

"One more thing I regret." Azalea moved her hands to her stomach. "I wished to tell you that soon, Natalia will have a cousin."

"A cousin?"

"I am carrying a child."

"Congratulations to you and your husband."

"Thank you." Azalea moved her hands aside and looked at to the cloudy night sky. "Unfortunately, that means I must take my leave." She sighed heavily. "I had even shorter than I expected, but any time was better than nothing."

"Look after yourself, Azalea."

"I will, and I will try to come see both you and Natalia soon as well. Please, look after yourselves."

"We'll try."

A red portal opened behind Azalea – a Witch with red magic had to have opened it for her. She cast one last glance up at the house before disappearing into the light red swirls. The whole thing closed behind her.

Tony sighed heavily and turned back to the house. He stood at the sink, intending to get a drink. But couldn't move. In the end, he turned the tap off.

"Dad?"

Tony whirled around to find Natalia in the doorway. He hadn't heard her, but there she stood, hair dripping over her shoulders.

"Who were you talking to?" she asked.

He rested against the counter. "How much did you hear?"

"Nothing. I could just see you from my window."

For several counts of his heartbeat, he debated about telling her, or what to even say. In the end though, he decided that it would be all or nothing, and it had to be all. Natalia had had enough secrets in this life. No more.

Tony spent twenty minutes explaining. He even handed her the birthday present Azalea had asked him to; Natalia smelt it and smiled like she recognised it, though he knew it wasn't possible, not really. He even told her that she would soon have a cousin, a family she might be able to see, and she practically beamed. Her bronze dust rose on her cheeks like she'd dunked her face in a bucket of glitter.

She was happy, that was clear, and he was happy to see her that way.

12

Of Creatures and Monsters

HE NEXT MORNING, all sweet and floral smells were replaced with that of mint.

Katherine had asked Natalia to bake it into every muffin, even some of the cookies, with a mix of chocolate and sometimes raspberries. Both Natalia and Noah were hard at work, doing whatever they could to keep the morning rush pleased.

Gradually, as midday came, the customers dwindled. That meant they could finally take their break.

They sat outside the front doors on little chairs, propped under an umbrella that was far too big for the space. Natalia sighed in content. Her feet ached and she was clammy all over, but business was good. Busy enough that Katherine had called Alex in for a few hours that morning to help her run the counter so Natalia and Noah could do the baking.

Natalia caught a whiff of something vanilla and thought back to the night before, when her father had given her a gift from her Aunt. A bottle of vanilla and juniper perfume, just like her mother's. Even though she had no memory of her mother, she could imagine exactly how it would've been to have cuddled up to her and smell that powerful yet subtle concoction.

Noah groaned as he sat in the spare chair. "It's Hell," he whined.

"I'm in Hell." He kicked off his shoes and socks, letting his feet bathe in the sunlight unprotected.

"You haven't done the Christmas rush here yet," Natalia said. "*That* is Hell."

Noah whined. "I don't want to think about Christmas."

"It's cooler at that time of year."

He groaned again. "You're a cruel, cruel woman!"

"Nat?" Katherine's head popped out of the door, dangly earrings wobbling. "Have you got a minute?"

"No rest for the wicked," Noah joked.

Natalia smacked his shoulder on the way past. Katherine led them just inside to the main café floor, where all the windows had been thrown open at the beginning of the day. Not that it made much, if any, difference.

"What's up?" Natalia asked once Katherine stopped. Katherine pointed.

Archie stood by the kitchen door, rocking on his heels. When he spotted her, he grinned and waved. She waved back.

But her eyes were drawn to the people at his side.

A man, probably in his late twenties, and a younger girl stood side by side. The man held a clipboard and wore a long coat despite the weather. The girl had several pins stuck on her chest. Both of them stood to attention, their noses stuck in the air.

"Natalia Primrose Whitebell?" the man asked, referring to his clipboard for her name.

She folded her arms over her chest. "Who's asking?"

Somehow the girl stood even taller. "We're from the Society of Souls," she addressed formally. It was strange, she appeared to be maybe only a few years younger than Natalia, yet acted as if she was older. "My name is Crystal-Rose, this is my instructor," she pointed to the man, "Warren. We're here on Council business."

"And Archie?"

Archie grimaced. "They dragged me along."

"The Council wants your progress tested," Warren announced, louder than necessary.

"Now?" Natalia questioned.

It'd been at least a week or two since the mention of the delay. Natalia knew her testing would've come around eventually, but she hadn't thought about the Council finding a date so soon. She had *also* thought, mostly in hope, that maybe Gold or Aero would be the ones testing her, but maybe they'd been around her too much to remain impartial.

Warren lifted his chin. "Your review is long overdue."

"That's fine," she said. "But why is Archie here?"

"We need to test you alongside someone you've been training with. Archie Darby just happened to be the person we came across first."

Again, Archie gave her a grimace. She nodded at him, knowing it wasn't his fault. He was simply doing as he was told – no one defied the Council or their underlings – and she would have to do the same.

"We should say," Warren continued as Natalia went for the door, "this is the first phase of the review."

Natalia rounded on him and his little minion. "First phase?" she asked, voice squeaking in surprise.

Crystal-Rose nodded vigorously. "Oh, yes! There are two phases for review. If you pass this phase, you proceed to the next. Pass them both and you're fully cleared."

"And if I fail?"

"You won't," Archie declared rather loudly. Natalia shot him a grin.

"If you fail," Warren carried on like nothing had happened, "then you have to retake that part until you pass. If you progress and fail the second half, you only have to retake the second half. But you only get three retakes overall between the two parts, so I would suggest passing."

Natalia gulped, shoulder blades itching. She didn't like the idea of there only being three tries. She didn't doubt her abilities, not exactly, but everything depended on what was required of her.

I won't fail, she told herself. *I can't.*

Warren left the café, Crystal-Rose right behind him. Natalia half-turned to look at Katherine. The woman gave her a firm nod. At some point Noah had come along to stand beside their boss, and he nodded as well. Natalia smiled weakly.

Archie stepped up beside Natalia as they followed the S.O.S members. "I don't know what they're going to ask of us," he whispered as they walked. "We'll either have to work together or work against one another, but I'm assuming they won't get involved."

"I hope not," she whispered back. "Either way, I'm glad it's you that they chose for me to work with." She stole a glance at him.

Archie had always been kind and Natalia trusted him. He wouldn't go easy on her like Jasper might, but he also wouldn't top over the edge the other side like Alex possibly could. Archie would do what was required, no more and no less. Natalia knew he'd help her pass these tests – she wasn't saying the others wouldn't be capable – Archie simply knew a lot and so might just be her best hope in finding a way through whatever was about to be thrown at her.

Archie smiled fondly. "Me too."

"Don't go easy on me if we have to fight."

"I wouldn't dream of it, Fairy," he said, winking just like his brother would. Warmth spread through her, a comforting sense that things might just be ok.

"Why are they being so nice about all this? The Council, I mean."

"Technically they're the Council's workers, their little do-gooders," Archie corrected. "And you've heard the expression 'you catch more flies with honey than vinegar'?"

"They think I'll cooperate more if they're nice."

"You have to do these tests either way, but—"

Warren whirled round as if he'd heard, shutting them up instantly.

They walked onto the blistering beach. Once at the water's edge, Warren instructed them to discard their shoes. The S.O.S members had chosen a stretch of beach that was already closed off. Natalia assumed one of them had also hidden them from the public with some sort of spell.

"This will be a test of abilities," Warren announced, once again addressing his clipboard. The sun glared down hard, and Natalia had to shield her eyes with her hands to see him. "Previous to our meeting, I called upon a few Monsters. They are your targets for this phase. You must work together, but Natalia, our sole focus is you. We want to see what you can do, how you do it, and how you work as part of a team. Is that clear?"

Warren didn't wait. He clapped with his clipboard in hand, and the sand shifted at Natalia's feet. Archie displaced his weight, making himself lower. Natalia copied. The sand began to wiggle as something below the surface moved.

Suddenly, Archie threw a bolt of green to the ground. Natalia gasped as a slippery looking *thing* jumped out of the sand and landed on top of him.

Archie writhed, dodging every strike the Monster tried throwing. It snapped its weird flower-shaped head. The Monster was big, probably only a few feet smaller than a Calefaction. Natalia didn't know how to intervene or what to do. What didn't help was the fact that people were watching.

"Shit," Natalia mumbled, snatching up her dagger from under her t-shirt.

"No!" Archie cried.

It was too late.

Natalia's blade struck halfway up the Monster's green body. It twisted to her. From where she'd stabbed, a clear substance now ran down its side in a soft trickle. The head resembled a flower until it opened, revealing row upon row of yellow teeth. A giant lashing black tongue whipped for her. She dodged sideways.

Silently, the Monster shivered and then split in two.

Archie kicked his away as the Monster righted itself. He rushed to Natalia's side. "They're called Chiksaaz," he told her. "Blades do nothing to them."

Natalia called her blade back to her. "I'm pretty sure it made that one split!"

"Injuries make them split. The fluid they leak is like a poison to the outside of their bodies. It stuns them. The only way they can heal themselves is by pulling themselves apart, spreading the poison thin. The energy used in the split causes the wound to stop leaking and heal."

It was a lot to take in. Natalia shook her head. "If blades don't work, what *can* we do?"

"Honestly? I'm not sure."

"You're not sure?"

"I've only read—"

Archie was yanked sideways by one of the tongues. Natalia yelped, letting her blade go again in panic. She tried to call it back but it struck home first. The Chiksaaz shivered and divided again.

Shit! What do we do?

Natalia looked at her watchers and found them staring at the damned clipboard with their noses in the air. They would be absolutely *no help*.

She called her blade back and strapped it back to her side. *Right, no blades.* The problem was, she didn't know much about fighting with her fists. Alex had been training her, but she didn't feel like it would be enough. Despite that, she launched herself into the fight. In a perfect coincidence, one of the Monster's tongues looped towards her and she caught it, wrapping it into the crook of her elbow. It struggled, managing to partly wrap around her.

But her intention wasn't to kill it, only distract it.

Archie reached up and with a snap of his fingers, green light surrounded the tongue she had. He snapped his fingers again and the tongue went limp. Natalia fell to the sand.

"Magic works," Archie surveyed aloud.

Natalia brushed off the sand and got to her feet. "What did you do to it?"

"Snapped its tongue?" he said, not sounding very confident. "It felt like a limb, like how an arm would feel."

"Did you know magic would work?"

He shrugged. "I've never met them before."

Natalia opened her mouth as a new tongue wrapped around her middle. She slammed her fist onto it, but it wouldn't release. It yanked her backwards as if she weighed nothing, and her body hit the sand with a soft *thud.*

The grotesque flower-like Chiksaaz loomed over her. The thing even *smelt* like flowers; like freshly cut grass, like juniper. Natalia hated it even more.

The tongue lashed for her face. She turned away, only to feel her hair rising. She gasped, grabbing for it. The higher it was pulled the more her scalp began to sting. Natalia scrambled to her knees and then her feet.

"Don't fling them in the water!" yelled Archie. Out the corner of her eyes, Natalia could see him running away from four more Chiksaaz. Natalia stared back at her one.

"Can you let go of my hair?" she asked, unsure why she was trying to be polite.

Apparently, the Monster found her amusing, because it made a chortle noise. Natalia glared harder and sighed. Clearly this fight wasn't one of brawn or magic. Even the Monsters weren't really fighting, just lashing out and almost *guarding*. They only fought back, not instigate.

"Don't fight them!" Natalia yelled, hoping Archie heard.

Her Monster opened its mouth to make some sound. She tilted her head at it as much as she could, and it mimicked. She moved her head the other way and it followed again.

"Do you just follow?" she asked it. It made another noise. "Can you let go of my hair, please?"

Strangely, the Monster sucked in its tongue, dropping her hair.

"Thank you," she whispered, flatting her hair back down.

Crystal-Rose's voice suddenly screeched, "Did you *see* that?"

Natalia focused on the Monster before her rather than looking at her observers. It stuck its tongue out, but didn't throw it towards her.

If these Monsters only imitated their opponents, then they possibly weren't the threat.

Her cheeks heated, and she touched them, drawing off the bronze dust. Would that work? She stuck her hand onto the awaiting tongue that had come back out.

The Monster screeched. Natalia stole her chance and ran past it, and her body slammed into something hard. She pulled back, staring at Archie. Then she stared at the Monster she'd been trapped by.

Frozen. Unmoving. But not dividing.

"How did you do that?" Archie asked.

Natalia tried to keep track of the other Monsters racing towards them. "I stuck my dust to its tongue."

"We can work with that."

She peeled as much dust off her face as she could. Archie whirled his arms around his head. Sand and air flicked around them in a small storm, green lightning flashing in intervals inside.

On his mark, she threw her dust inside and he launched the mini tornado at the oncoming hoard. The storm washed over the

Monsters and they seized up.

"We've isolated the problem," she said. "Now what?"

Archie scowled. "The tongues seem to be the key."

"So we snap them off?"

He shrugged. "It's worth a shot, right?"

Natalia and Archie divided, heading to two different Chiksaarzs. There was no indication on how long the sleep would keep them trapped for. They could wake any moment, and she was getting in range of many rows of teeth.

Natalia hadn't paid attention before, but the inside of the Monster's mouths were green.

Like a plant. A plant that's alive.

It didn't have any obvious eyes, but it felt like the Chiksaaz was looking at her. She screwed up her face, and her heart thudded inside her chest. The juniper smell wafting from it was enchanting though subtle.

"I'm sorry," she whispered, unsure exactly why she was apologising. Maybe because it had never actually *done* anything wrong.

Releasing a breath, Natalia reached in, grabbed the black tongue, and pulled hard.

The Monster sort of gagged, which in turn made Natalia gag. The tongue came away with a thin coating of the Monster's poison at the base. Natalia yelped and threw it, but some of the poison flicked up. When nothing burnt or melted her flesh off, she sighed. It seemed the poison was only poisonous to the thing that created it.

She looked for the Monster and found herself oddly disappointed to find it already gone.

Warren approached her with his stupid clipboard, Crystal-Rose and her badges a step behind. They looked as much like pricks as they had before. Natalia would've preferred another Monster.

"Well done," Warren said, not sounding overly joyous. "I must say, that took more time than I expected. Any longer and it would've been a fail. But you passed, Miss Whitebell."

"Yay," Natalia said dryly.

"We will be with you in a few more months for your follow up task."

"I cannot wait."

Crystal-Rose raised an eyebrow but followed her leader, both of them leaving the beach in back-straight silence.

Weariness soaked Natalia's body, every bone and muscle crying. Her head throbbed. Her mouth was drier than the sand beneath her.

She sank to her knees.

Archie crouched down beside her. She wanted to tell him to not touch her but couldn't get the words out before his arms flung around her. He didn't immediately let go in disgust, so that was something.

"You did great!" he cheered.

"I mean, I passed," she said, breathing heavily to refill her lungs.

He pulled her closer. "No, you did *great*. Let yourself believe that."

"Ok, fine." She laughed into his shoulder. "You know what I also believe?"

He moved so he could look at her face. "What?"

"That I need a shower and a long ass nap."

Archie laughed. "I'm in agreement there."

"With what? That I need those things, or that you do?"

He scoffed. "I don't think you'd like my answer."

"What's that supposed to mean?"

"It means that you *definitely* need a shower."

She whacked his shoulder. "You're so rude!" she cried, laughing.

Archie laughed too and helped Natalia to her feet. Together, they hobble off the burning sand and struggled to slip on their shoes. Natalia was aware of the world around her as they began their trek home, but she was too depleted of energy to really feel it.

Two hours after midnight, the alarm rang out. It rang loud and clear; Monsters had arrived on the Island.

Jasper had been nicely tucked in bed, soft music playing in the background beforehand. With his parents away on business, he'd roused Alex from her deep slumber and had dialled Archie.

Archie had complained the whole time on the phone that he didn't want to disturb Peri – they were staying at their new house. Jasper had hung up almost immediately, needing every second to prepare, and Archie, thankfully, had appeared moments later, clearly sensing the urgency.

Wanting to rid his skin of the humidity, Jasper rubbed his palms together. It didn't help. If anything, the friction made him hotter than before. Summer on Venderly was uncomfortable at best, vastly different from Atlantis where the temperatures never boiled or froze.

The siblings stood under the starry sky, listening to the silent night. The crescent moon glowed a soft yellow illumination from its perch above.

"Where are we going?" Alex asked, eyeing her youngest brother.

Jasper stared back, wondering why it was his decision suddenly. "Towards the fight, obviously."

"*Obviously.*" She rolled her eyes. "But *where?*"

"You need to be more specific with your questions." He waggled a finger at her. "Especially when dealing with Fairies. They can manipulate your questions and words, you know that."

"Yes, yes," she dismissed. "I cannot give them room to speak freely. But, I'm not a Fairy and neither are you."

"I would make a very lavish Fairy."

Alex snored. "I strongly disagree with that."

"Seconded," Archie said.

Jasper huffed. "We haven't got time for this." He set off with a gentle run and the sound of slapping footsteps behind him said the others followed.

"Your girlfriend's a Fairy," Alex continued, catching up easily. "Has she used her charms on you yet? Avoided any questions by slithering out of them lately?"

Jasper smiled sweetly. "I honestly don't know if she knows *how*."

Guilt bubbled up inside him and he looked away. He had wondered about it. He'd considered all the ways Natalia was like a Fairy; her gracefulness, the natural dancing talent, the way she'd been drawn to nursing to help heal. And he'd thought about all the ways she wasn't one; how she wasn't charming, the way she didn't hold herself above others. Then there were her bronze wings...

"Speaking of your girlfriend," Alex fired up again, "where is she?"

"Yeah!" Archie pushed. "I thought this was an emergency."

Jasper looked over at them both. "Peri isn't the only one who needs sleep right now, so I thought it was best to let them rest."

They're exhausted, he thought. *Each for their own reasons.*

The siblings slowed to a stroll down Main Street. Halfway down the road, Alex's head jerked suddenly, her nose sniffing the air.

"What you got?" Jasper asked.

"Near the docks," Alex said, grimacing.

It was clear as they looked to one another that they were all remembering what happened last time they were at the shipping yard.

"The damage?" Archie asked.

"Six. A combination?" Alex screwed up her face. Her loose hair hung against her face thanks to the heat and it hollowed her out in the dark. "I can't tell what combination we're looking at, but I don't like what I feel."

Archie stepped in front her. "Which is what?"

"A hive of wasps swarming."

The siblings started into a run.

Mid-stride, Alex disappeared in one leap and her wolf appeared on landing. The brown fur was plastered to its scalp, ears flopping. Wolves could suffer from heat exhaustion as much as Humans, so Jasper made a conscious effort to watch Alex out of the corner of his eye.

The closer they drew to the docks, the more a buzzing zapped along Jasper's nerve endings. He rubbed his palms together again, allowing them to glow their pinkish colour as if to help chase away the unease. His heart pounded in his ears and his toes curled inside his shoes.

Alex had broken her wrist here. Kiva's parents – Humans, just protecting their changing daughter and wanting to help – had lost their lives here. Worst of all, this space had stolen part of Natalia. She'd been dragged here, sliced open, and had been told she was special to an awful someone for some reason.

Jasper ached and gasped with pain as if he'd been the one physically beaten and broken. Alex was his sister. Kiva was new to this world and Natalia's friend. Natalia herself... They hadn't exactly worked out the definition and dimensions, but he knew enough of what he felt for her. Her pain specifically more than the others poured into him.

Monsters came tearing around the containers stacked in the yard, shrieking and crying.

Archie climbed up the side of a container to gain the higher ground, and shot a bolt of green magic at one of the faster moving Scorpios. Alex immediately engaged two Kiffleggers – a blind, six-legged, floppy tailed, dumb Monster they'd not seen in these parts before. That left three other Monsters; one squishy Poena, one oddly small Scorpio, and one *very* angry looking Jij.

Jasper narrowed in on the Jij first.

He clicked his fingers twice, and then flicked his hand away from his body. He repeated the action, this time envisioning a cube.

As he flung his arms wide, the Jij became trapped inside a jelly-like pink cube. Its tiny arms clawed at the edges. When that didn't work, it started biting. Chunks tore away almost immediately. Jasper grimaced; he'd have maybe five minutes before it broke free.

"Jasper!" Archie shouted.

Turning at the sound of his brother's voice, he saw the small Scorpio had gone to join its bigger friend, flinging itself and sticking to the brown container Archie stood on.

Jasper flung his arms wide again and raised his palms to the sky. Pink light danced up his skin like winding vines. He waited one moment, two, until the Scorpio had nearly reached Archie's feet, and then dragged his arms down and away from his body.

Both mini and big Scorpios were torn apart and flung in four different directions.

Jasper gagged as the stench of compost rose up from the dead Monsters. He'd forgotten dismembered Scorpios smelt like that. Archie nodded appreciatively.

Jasper gave his brother a middle finger salute as he gagged again.

Archie rolled his eyes and then refocused on something Jasper couldn't see on the other side of the container. Jasper struggled to swallow and moved away.

Alex had already dealt with her two Kiffleggers, the dust floating along the ground, and was now growling at the Poena. Jasper let her. That would be the better Monster for her to fight anyway since she had no magic or gifts it could steal.

Instead, Jasper zeroed into his trapped Jij and summoned another box, this one bigger and thicker, plopping it around the one already there just as the Jij broke out. It looked between its new cage and Jasper as he bent down to face it at eye-level.

"Silly little things aren't you?" he asked, not expecting an answer. The Jij began to bite again. "But what's brought you here? You don't like the open."

It was true, Jijs tended to be found in areas that were highly populated and densely built. Some old Creatures said it was because they liked the taste furniture, liked biting and ripping it apart to chew as sustenance.

But they didn't seem to be trying to escape into town, where they could feed to their hearts' desire. Jasper could also assume that they weren't here for Natalia either, as none of them had even mentioned her or noted that she was missing. So then, why *were* they here? Normally, these Monsters didn't work together, yet here they were, fighting on the same side and acting like a dysfunctional though well-matched *team*.

Monsters, usually, weren't organised in any aspect *ever*. Had they suddenly grown a brain-cell to cooperate? Was their need to fulfil *their own* Purpose so great they'd activated some part of themselves they'd previous neglected that allowed this coordination?

Jasper glanced between his brother and sister, both competent and obviously winning. If this wasn't a ploy to get to Natalia...

He swallowed the growing lump in his throat. *Are they being controlled somehow?* He felt slimy all over. *Is this a test? Some sort of dry-run at getting them to move like separate but together parts?*

The Jij broke free of its prison. It raced for Jasper, and he tore it apart in one fluid hand movement.

If this *was* a test, he wanted it over with overwhelmingly conclusive results, ones that told whoever was conducting this they can't win. But what if this was just the first one? Would there be more? What would the variables look like next time? What was the point in all this? And if it was a test, they would have to end at some point for the real deal.

The pink light that surrounded Jasper died. *What would the finale look like?*

The scar breathed red. The Monster creating the permanent map upon the flesh was positively bursting with joy. Slowly, with each notch, the unconscious body beneath it was roused more.

Natalia watched herself, helpless to stop the attack. She tried yelling, screaming at the top of her lungs, just as she had done times before. But like every other time, it was no use.

Rapidly, the scene continued.

Past Natalia screamed and fought back, body writhing. The Monster reared back and, as it went to cut further, it was pulled off of her suddenly. The girl scrambled to her feet and looked at her arm, squeezed her fist, and the glass fell out of her flesh.

Everything shifted in a motion of wobbles and in sounds of static.

Natalia now sat at the Darby's kitchen table. Past her was there, talking with the others. The conversation hushed and the cupboards on the walls started to vibrate. But no one at the table noticed a thing, not one of them turning to it.

The scene switched again.

The Darby's kitchen reappeared, but something was different. Then Natalia felt it. A charge in the air, a heaviness in her movements. She gasped as she spotted the glass strewn across the floor.

On cue, the Chimera crawled up to the empty doors.

Past Natalia burst into the room just as the Chimera inched inside, a pregnant Peri at her heels moments later.

Peri's brown eyes were paler, as was her skin. She was usually so fearless, so ready to fight. Here, she seemed to have lost all of that. She held onto her stomach, splaying her hand out flat over the top like a barrier.

Natalia turned her gaze in time to watch her past self throwing her blade. Just like before, it didn't make a single dent. The Monster's forked tongue flicked out and Natalia shivered at the same time her past self did. However, it was like she shook off the fear. Her past self strode towards the Monster, only breaking eye-contact with it when Archie rushed into the room to shield Peri.

Glass shot through the air, leaving the Chimera hissing and twisting around on itself. Natalia watched her own face, saw how it didn't change. As the Monster opened its mouth, glass cut its tongue off. The Monster dropped, chin smashing against the ground.

"My, young one." Natalia turned in the direction of Morpheus. She flinched. Part of her had forgotten they were there, standing in the background, observing. "You are intimidating." They raised their eyebrows, a giant grin on their lips.

Natalia could hear her own voice begging in the background, pleading with her friends to not say anything about what happened. The pain, the horror, in her tone cut deep. It was so raw, so powerless.

Natalia squeezed her eyes shut like that would cut it all out.

"How about we change this scene?" Morpheus suggested gently.

"Not another memory," Natalia said, opening her eyes. "Please, not another one."

"No memory," they promised, holding out a hand. "Somewhere quiet and out of the way. Think of something good and I'll take you there."

Trusting them entirely, Natalia took their hand.

Underfoot, the red sand sifted as they landed. The sky overhead shone a slightly deeper crimson, but it was more relaxing to Natalia than anything else she'd just seen.

Morpheus led Natalia through the barren place, her hand in theirs, until they came to the draped white bed. Morpheus sat, swinging one leg over the other, before they spread backwards, bending one arm to prop their head up in their own palm.

"You may sit with me," Morpheus said, their grin growing a little wicked. "Or you could lay with me?"

Natalia stared. "Do you realise how that sounds?"

Morpheus tapped the covers with their free hand. "Beauty, I know exactly what I'm saying and I know exactly how it sounds. Take my words how you wish. Lie with me and gaze at the sky, or you may lie against me, skin to skin."

"*I'll just sit,*" *she insisted, perching on the edge of the mattress.*

Morpheus laughed, the sound comforting yet haunting in an otherwise empty place.

They sat like that, in silence, for as long as it took Natalia to calmly count to one hundred.

Morpheus, who had made a punnet of grapes materialise, tossed them into their mouth. They had changed their hair to a shoulder-length style of waves that was kept from falling in their face by a bushy wreath.

Natalia wished she could be as carefree. Watching Morpheus eat grapes, splayed out on a magically appearing bed, allowed her to see what life could be like. Only, it wasn't. And may never be. She had a Purpose. Even if there were calm moments between the bigger ones, there was always the inevitability of a storm rising. Not only that, but she had other worries too.

"Why haven't you hurt me?" The question ran from Natalia's lips before she could think to stop it.

Morpheus lowered the grapes and the dove vanished in a puff of feathers. The grin they wore was full of amusement, and somehow danger, like a lion that had cornered its next meal. "I was wondering how long it would take," he mused aloud. "I must admit, I had expected you to ask sooner. You keep surprising me, beauty."

"I didn't mean—"

"Of course you meant it." They sat up, tucking their legs beneath them. "You wouldn't have asked or said anything otherwise."

"I just meant..."

Morpheus stared, hard and cold. "You just meant what?"

Natalia edged away slightly. "I was told Monsters were bad. That Monsters want to kill and ruin." She sighed heavily, a memory surfacing. "Even the ones claiming to be on our side can't fully be trusted. I have proof of that theory."

Natalia watched Morpheus' eyes dip to her scar. She tucked her arm behind her body, and Morpheus' face softened.

"I understand," they said.

She blinked. "You do?"

"Creatures are told from the time they're tots that Monsters need to be cast from their world, sent back into the great beyond to never return. Yet here you are, conversing with one! How scandalous!"

"Think of the news headlines."

Their mouth quirked. "Oh, the horror."

Natalia smiled sadly. "It's just that I've had bad experiences."

"If I ever promise you anything, it is this: I will not harm you, Natalia Primrose Whitebell. You have my word and I lay my life on that oath."

Natalia's voice came out as no more than a whisper. "I believe you."

"Being a Fairy, I'm sure you can tell when I am speaking the truth. Some may be able to deceive your kind, but I will always talk honestly with you." They reached for Natalia's hand, stroking it with their thumb. "Trust me when I say that life isn't as black and white as the elders and those in power tell you it is. You can have both good and bad Humans, can you not? So you can also have good and bad Creatures, and Monsters. While, yes, the majority of Creatures serve the good of life and the majority of Monster-kind are mindless and thirsty for destruction, there are a few rogues that are devilishly wonderful and wish to do no harm." Morpheus winked. "We like the worlds how they are. We don't all wish to make those around us suffer, nor do we want to bring damnation and Hell across every plane. Some places deserve beauty."

"Is that why you're helping me? You don't wish to cause suffering and pain?"

"One reason, yes. I don't want to see Earth brought to its death by Monsters who have no right to do so."

Learning about Monsters from the Darby's was one thing. Actually talking to a real one was very different. Strikingly so. Natalia could see that Morpheus really was no different to her. They said "good" Monsters were rare, but Natalia would say Morpheus was one if anyone ever asked.

She shifted on the bed, scooting back and swinging her legs onto it. "Where do you come from?"

"Not this plane, though I have regrettably made it home."

"Regrettably?"

"Other Monsters killed this plane and created a path reaching here. I followed it." Natalia looked at them, and found grey eyes staring back. "But this plane can be linked to Earth, which is how and why you can reach me. There is a Veil, in real life, but enough magic can link us in dreams. That and it's part of my gift, to dream-walk or dream-seek, whatever you call it. It all allows me to aid your kind in secret, helping the fight alongside you without the snivelling Council getting their hands on me."

"So not all planes are this linked with Earth?"

"Oh no. Sometimes we must travel through hundreds of planes, shattering many Veils that separate them, just to steal a single glimpse at the Veil that leads to your world."

She scrunched up her face. "Hundreds?" she asked. "I think I'm lost."

Morpheus laughed. "Think of planes as Islands in an endless ocean, but with invisible walls concealing them. Earth, your home City, Atlantis, and the Fairy realm are all within one Veil. They are one Island." They roamed their eyes over her. "With me so far?"

Natalia nodded. "I think so."

"Now imagine loads of Atlantis' and Earths scattered about, all with Veils separating them from each other. Humans don't know of their existence and most Creatures don't know the vast expanse of what is there either. Slowly, however, these Veils are breaking. The few separate worlds are becoming one big one. Holes, large enough to crawl through, are cracking in the surfaces. No one knows if it's natural, Monster related, or a combination that's causing it."

"So where do Monsters actually come from?"

"Even I don't know that. The origins are from before even my time, and I am thousands of moons old. But the stories go that the first ones clawed their way out of Hell itself. However, most Monsters are actually born on different, ruined planes everywhere. They spend their lives crawling, trying to reach and unruined plane to harvest. Some make it far. Some don't."

"Are any of the Veils between those different planes still standing? Are there any others left besides ours?"

"Quite a few," they affirmed. "As I said, more than Creatures think, though not in a way they once were."

"Oh," Natalia whispered.

"Fragments of Veils are missing, or entire holes have been created. There is one Veil that barely has a side of it left." They patted her hand then, reminding her just how close they sat, and her cheeks lit up. "Don't worry about Earth. The Veil surrounding it is one of the strongest I've seen."

"But Monsters still get through!"

"Sometimes, yes. What you see are small numbers compared to what it could be."

Natalia didn't want to think about that. She thought she'd faced hoards, but if Morpheus was right, if the Veils kept breaking, things would only get worse.

"Creatures are working on a way to repair our Veil, right?" she asked.

"I've heard."

"Do you think they'll be able to?"

Morpheus took a moment and looked away. "Maybe," they said, facing Natalia again. "They might even be able to repair some Veils beyond their own if they tried. That would certainly halt the bastards in their tracks. It might even kill off whole types, or life to return to those other planes."

"What? There's other life?"

"Why are Humans and Creatures always so sure they are the only things around?" Morpheus shook their head. "Monsters exist, so might other life." Natalia didn't know what to say, so said nothing. "But I did not bring you here to speak of death," they continued. "Nor did I bring you here to speak on Creatures and Monsters. That was you."

"Then what—"

"I brought you here to speak of you."

Natalia couldn't fight the grimace she produced. "What about me?"

Morpheus brought Natalia's hand up to their lips and kissed it, before *returning it to her lap. "You have seen what you need to answer one of your questions now."*

She blinked. "What—"

"Don't play, beauty." They didn't sound frustrated or angry, only disappointed which was infinitely worse. "You cannot avoid this answer. You knew what you were doing when you asked for help. And I have helped. You knew the terms and asked for an answer. Now you have it."

"Morpheus—"

Their stare was once again cold, distant. "You know what you are."

Natalia rose from the bed, no longer wanting to be in Morpheus' company. She didn't know why she did it, but she started walking. The Red thrived around her. Morpheus didn't call out, but she felt their presence slip away.

Natalia bundled herself up and cried.

She remained like that until her legs cramped, her eyes ran dry, her throat was sore, her head ached, and her brain could think of no more reasons to let her continue on.

But she knew, in her heart, this wasn't the end.

Though she'd walked away from Morpheus, moved until she'd woken herself up, she'd only done it because they were right, and she didn't like it.

Now, she had one piece of herself. A clear-cut, *terrifying* sharp piece.

The need to lock it away was strong. She needed to keep it from the Darby's, from Jasper. She had to protect them in any way she could so it couldn't hurt them. They meant everything to her, so if that meant leaving and breaking them, then it was a price she would pay for the better ending.

It would cost *her* entire heart to do, but it wouldn't cost *them* their lives.

To test the picture of herself she had conjured in her own mind, she wiped her face and stood. She rolled her shoulders and her wings sprung forth. As always, they were weightless and barely noticeable, expect in her shadow that clung to the wall and the way bronze twinkled in the room.

Natalia snatched her glass cup from her nightstand. She threw it at her shadow and it shattered into tiny pieces.

Closing her eyes, she imagined the pieces floating upwards, in a sort of spiral, dancing in the light her dust gave off. She imagined them creating a soft vibration in the air, a crystal like dance.

Opening her eyes, she watched her thoughts become reality.

The shards rose off the ground and were sucked up by an invisible force, twirling them into a delicate whirlwind. A few bits knocked together, creating an almost wind-chime sound.

Natalia gasped and the pieces fell, breaking further.

She backed away until her back was pressed firmly into the wall, her wings aching at being trapped. But she couldn't slow her breathing or the way her heart pounded. All she could picture was Kei and the girl who'd stabbed glass into her arm. The two Monsters who smelt of vanilla and ice, wore faces like masks, and could control broken yet sharp things.

The room was suddenly too small, too close, too quiet, too still.

Indeed she had known what she was doing when she'd asked for Morpheus' help, but this had gone beyond anything she could've expected, beyond anything she could've *feared*.

This was her painful, *hideous* truth.

Tears wouldn't even come, banished in her horror. But her heart and soul fell from the precipice they hung over. They fell down and down until they broke.

Maybe some Creatures were bad and some Monsters were good. Maybe it was possible. But someone was already hunting Natalia and now she partly knew *why*. And none of it was good. Which, in turn, meant she could only be bad.

She'd seen the glass manipulation before. She'd seen the horrors and the destruction it caused. It was a trait. That too also explained that, while she had *some*, she hadn't acquired *all* that belonged to a Fairy.

Because she wasn't all Fairy.

She wasn't even a full Creature.

She was part Monster.

She was part *Geminis*.

13

Woven Truths

TONY STROLLED INTO THE GARDEN and encircled Katherine within his arms, kissing the tops of her pointed ears. Water sprayed from her fingertips, her abilities manipulating the droplets to land where they were needed.

Yesterday had been mostly spent moving her in. They talked about it for quite a while, and they'd finally decided it was the right time. So now box after box was stacked around the house. Old furniture had been sold off or given to charity. Last night had been spent unpacking the essentials and deciding which offer to take for Katherine's old house. There had been quite a few.

Tony had hoped Natalia would've had an input, not that any of it was her responsibility, he just wanted to include her in these things, but he'd barely seen her yesterday at all. He'd doubled checked before the move to make sure it was ok, and she had said she was fine with it, but he worried she wasn't.

He watched the water, part of him hoping he'd get splashed. The sun had barely risen, yet the heat of the day had already come in with aggression. Tony's top already stuck to him. He backed away from Katherine with one last kiss.

Katherine stopped sprinkling the water and whirled on him. "Where are you going?" she asked.

"To work," he said.

She wandered up to him, putting a hand on his cheek. "I suppose I can't keep you here all day," she joked. He touched her sides, slid his hands under her top slightly to feel her curves and grooves. "Do you think I could try though? Or would your bosses throw you out?"

He dipped his head closer. "Count yourself lucky that you're your own boss."

"Oh, I do." She rose and kissed the greying stubble along his jaw. "You better go get ready."

"Haven't you got work too?"

"Yes, but not until later."

Tony gave her a quick kiss and raced to shower and dress.

Once in uniform, he left his room and blinked. A very weary looking Natalia stood on the landing. He'd never seen her so scraggly before; her hair stuck out in every direction, eyes unseeing, and wore a smile that reached nowhere near them.

"Nat?" he called.

"Hey, dad," she said back.

"Are you alright?" He reached for her and she let him tuck her into his side so she was pressed flat to his chest. "You're not mad at me, are you?"

She shuffled and managed to peer up at him. "Why would I be mad at you?"

"About Katherine."

"Katherine?" Surprise travelled across her face.

"About her moving in."

"Dad?"

"I know it seems like it's happening fast and I only spoke to you about it a few times briefly... I want this. I want all of this, all of us together, but you're the most important thing to me. I want you to be comfortable with it all. If you're not—"

"Dad!" she cut in. "Katherine's been like a mum to me for bloody *years.* I'm happy for you both. I *want* you to be together and for you to be happy, for you to be happy together. That's every child's dream!"

"But yesterday..."

Natalia glanced down. "I know I should've come to help. I was busy with other stuff, mostly just catching up on all the sleep I've been missing."

Tony blinked, astonished. "You were asleep the whole day?"

"Not the *whole* day. Though, that *does* sound good." She managed a small laugh. "I'm sorry, dad. Katherine's good. You're both good. The whole thing is bloody good with me. Don't worry about being worried."

"It's my job as a dad to be constantly worried."

"Don't be. I'm ok with it, I promise."

"Then what—"

"Just training and work and stuff has been getting me tired. That bloody phase one test the other day didn't help either. Feels like I was hit by a train after that." The faintest smile crawled onto her face. "I just needed a day to myself."

Tony's heart felt lighter. He'd seen his daughter after plenty of solo training sessions. He could only imagine what group sessions or a Council assigned test would do to her. Training was taxing, mentally and physically. Let alone *actual* Purpose seeking...

"As long as you're ok," he said and kissed her forehead.

She nodded. "Love you, dad."

"Love you too, my Natalia."

She smiled and hopped sideways into the bathroom, gently closing the door behind her.

Tony trudged down the stairs and out to his run-down car. It spluttered to life after a few tries.

As he reached the end of the road, he realised something.

Natalia had said she was alright with him and Katherine. However, Natalia had never said if she was ok in *general.* Something was obviously bothering her. And it couldn't just be sleep deprivation.

In the rear-view mirror, he watched his house disappear. He turned to go back. But Natalia was a good kid and always had been. He was certain that she would come to him if it the problem was *big*.

Tony gripped the steering wheel and kept driving, his knuckles going white.

Nothing was better than the smell of fresh blueberry muffins in the morning. That's what Natalia thought anyway. Noah had always expressed that banana bread was better. This morning called for both, so they worked separately in the kitchen and took turns serving out front when needed.

When Noah next went out to the front of the store, Natalia sighed and stepped back from her bowl. She put her hands on the counter and slumped forwards. She took some deep breaths before righting herself, seconds before Katherine appeared in the doorway.

"Morning," Natalia said, hoping she sounded better than she felt.

"How are you?" Katherine dumped her bag, swapping it for an apron. Her beady eyes landed on Natalia. "Did you get much sleep last night?"

"Some," Natalia answered.

She'd slept for a few hours before meeting Morpheus, but after, she'd been too aware of her own shadow to move, let alone close her eyes again. The night had drifted on and she'd counted every second. There had been no peace last night, not after the horrors she'd learnt of.

"I think I'm just so overly tired at this point, my body isn't reacting anymore." Natalia winced.

Katherine smiled, sympathy written into her expression. "I

remember what that's like."

Natalia let out a tight sigh. "You do?"

"I once trained so hard I was in too much pain to sleep for nearly two full days," Katherine said. "It was fucking awful."

Natalia half-assed a laugh. "I can imagine."

"I must've looked like one of those cartoons you used to watch? Match-sticks in the eyes, tape holding them open, big bags underneath. Only mine were all invisible."

Natalia knew Katherine was only trying to be nice, so nodded. Her dad had assumed the same thing, that it was training beating her black and blue. But it wasn't. It wasn't completely *wrong*, just a little misdirect.

Mental battles were the *real* exhaustion makers.

Honestly and simply, she was tired of life.

"That was a rush," Noah announced as he returned. Using the back of his arm, he wiped the sweat from his forehead. "Easily a bus-load of pensioners and kids. When do they go back to school?"

"Two weeks," Katherine said as she passed.

"Who wants hot drinks on a boiling day anyway?"

"Apparently the very old or the naïve young," Natalia answered.

Noah scowled and flicked his teeth-retainer with his tongue so it popped off. He pushed it back into place with his thumb. "You know what I meant. Why couldn't they ask for a milkshake?"

"So you can stick your big head in the fridge for a minute?"

"Precisely, Princess!"

Natalia shuddered and turned from Noah, using the pouring of her mix into cases as an excuse to half hide from him. Joking had been nice, *normal*, until then.

If only he knew, she thought sourly. *If only he knew I wasn't a princess, but a Monster.*

While she might not want to wreak endless havoc, while nothing destructive was a conscious thought, it would happen to or around those near her, fulfilling the promise of what she was in front of them.

Suddenly she was reminded of the vow she'd been made to take months ago, the one the Council had expressed to her. A vow that had made her promise, in a way, to kill another Creature or Human if they ever became a Monster, whether in form or ideals. Her friends and family were also tied by those expectations. If they knew about her, what would they do? They were almost honour-bound to follow it. She shuddered. *Would* they follow it? Would they end her? Part of her was glad that it might be one of them, that someone she loved might stop her heart before things could get even worse.

Coughing to hide the lump in her throat, she turned into her elbow to wipe her eyes. Katherine rushed off to serve as more customers arrived. Noah rushed off too, saying he was getting them a drink. She took several deep breaths and went back to mixing her morning baking concoction. Noah returned minutes later and handed over a glass. She sipped at the cold water, eyes dry once more.

The rest of the shift drifted. Natalia focused on what she needed to do and avoided unnecessary conversation. No one seemed disgruntled by it. Noah and Katherine weren't too chatty themselves, sticking to their own tasks. They saw nothing and asked nothing more. She was fine because she said so. She was a Fairy and they couldn't lie.

Except, she wasn't one, not really.

Zoe let the girl kiss her cheek; she smelt of the cherry pie they'd shared for dessert. The girl waved and slipped into a car. Zoe waved but the second the car was gone, she sagged. It wasn't the *worst* date she'd been on, yet it was hardly top tier. Turned out her date's brother *was* the nicer one, better conversationalist too.

"Well, that was interesting," someone mocked.

Zoe whirled round to see Aero - the Vampire boy that the Vampire man Gold had introduced her to - perched on the nearby stone wall, legs swinging. "Are you seriously taking the piss?" Zoe asked. She didn't give him a chance to answer. "Are you spyin' on me right now?"

Aero adjusted the length of his sleeves nervously. "I wasn't spying on you," he muttered.

"It looks like you were." Zoe walked past him. He jumped off the wall and jogged to catch up. She sped up but he kept pace, so she sighed. "If you weren't spying, why are you here?"

"The Council let me leave Atlantis to come back and keep an eye on Natalia," he admitted. "The portal I was using opened up around the corner."

Suddenly, his head flicked in the other direction, his body freezing. He pointed, and it took a moment before Zoe saw what he was indicating at.

They'd walked along far enough that the beach was close. A *thing* rose up out of the sea, or was it the sand? Whatever it was, wherever it had come from, it had a purple-onyx body and landed with an almighty *thud*, and began to scuttle around with determination.

"What *is* that?" Zoe whispered.

"A Wiska," Aero answered calmly.

"Is it a Monster?"

Aero's eyes found hers. "You've never seen one before?"

Unprompted, Zoe's mind threw forth an image of the Monster she'd seen before, the one back in the Darby's house - it had gone to attack Natalia. But Zoe couldn't admit to seeing it. That would unravel someone else's problems, issues she'd agreed to keep quiet on.

But technically, she hadn't seen *this* Monster before, so saying that wouldn't be lying.

Zoe shook her head. "No."

Aero scowled. "Then you best stay out of the way."

"Oh, like *Hell!*"

He glared at her. "This is *dangerous!* It's not some game."

"I'm not trea'ing it like a game! I just don' like being told what to do by someone I don't know!"

Aero blinked wildly. "You have my apologies if you think I'm simply dismissing you."

"I don't think—"

"Creatures fight and Humans can, too," he cut in. "That is if they become trained, and are allowed to be. But I am aware that you are untrained, and I do not wish to see you hurt."

Zoe stared. Aero took her surprise as agreement and sprinted away. He ran so fast, Zoe had to blink several times just for her brain to cope with his movements. She watched as he approached the Monster, a blade he'd plucked from somewhere in hand. He seemed to dance around the danger.

What if there are more?

Cautiously, she looked around. Terror flowed through her body. While she didn't know the first thing about a Wiska, she *did* figure that the safest place had to be under the nearest piece of cover. Or maybe beside the person who had the gifts and weapons of defence.

That meant Aero was the safest option right now.

Zoe bolted across the sand, until she was flipping through the air. A moment later, the sand came up to meet her. It was surprisingly hard as she slammed into it, a sickening crunch echoing on impact, her bottom jaw slamming up in her mouth.

"Zoe!" the voice calling for her was shrill.

Rolling onto her back, Zoe felt a trickle of something slide down her neck. It slithered right into her ear. But she couldn't fixate on it because a Wiska was bearing down on her.

Powerful legs skittered about beside her head. Sand flicked

into Zoe's mouth; she let it dribble out in her saliva. Zoe knew that the Monster had somehow sprung up from nowhere at the perfect moment just to meet her.

At least now she had the answer to how she'd come fly.

Something incredibly fast dove into the Monsters' centre. It wobbled and teetered out of the way. When it stopped, Zoe caught a flash of a blade above her.

Aero's face appeared. He perched beside her, and opened his mouth just as the Monster came back. Right as it bent over them both, Aero sprung, shoving his sword upwards.

It gave Zoe enough time to scramble backwards. She watched as Aero left his sword vertically inside the Monster's jaws and then physically threw *himself*, clamping his mouth onto its purple neck.

Zoe's stomach turned as something squelched.

The Monster tumbled to the ground in a neat pile of purple-onyx ash. Aero wiped his mouth on his sleeve and turned to Zoe, appearing at her side a breath later.

Awe crept in as she roamed over him with her eyes. Sweat was notably absent from his body but he panted without moving his chest. His brows were heavy, scowling, as he looked back at her.

"Is it dead?" she asked nervously. His body blocked out the rest of the beach, not the she could focus on much else.

Aero nodded. "Weapons don't destroy Wiskas."

"You used your teeth."

"The fangs," he corrected. He changed the subject then. "Your chin. I heard it crack." Carefully, he leant forward and pressed a finger to the side of her face. She flinched, but not at the pressure of the touch. He was iced over. "It's split."

"Is it bad?" she asked. Her words came out with more dribble than she expected.

"I won't lie to you. It is."

Like all the adrenaline she'd be riding with had been zapped from her body, pain exploded along her jaw. Zoe's eyes watered heavily and she felt like a curtain was being drawn against her brain.

"I'll get you to the house," he continued, standing. "Blink once for yes, twice for no. Do you mind being carried?"

It took an egregious amount of effort to blink twice.

Aero bent and Zoe had to shuffle a little at his instruction so he could lift her - he managed like she weighed nothing. A few times he had to slightly adjust his grip, but she made no complaints. She couldn't. She could barely hold her hand under her chin as Aero told her to do so it would hurt less as they moved.

"I shouldn't have left you," he mumbled, walking on. He barely moved as he walked as if he was a living but walking statue. "If I hadn't left you, you might not have been hit."

"I... was... coming... for... you..." She forced out between winces, eyes welling until the tears fell ungracefully.

"*Why?*" He sounded pained. "You're *Human*. I shouldn't have engaged with you there, we should have just left."

"Your... Job... You..."

"Don't talk," he ordered. "Try not to do anything that'll agitate the wound."

They switched to firm ground and her teeth grinded together in her head. She cried out behind closed lips.

He looked down at her when he next spoke. "I apologise and I hope you can find it within yourself to forgive me for this. I just raced off, letting the action of my Purpose run me wild. Safety of others should've come first. *Your* safety should've come first." He averted his gaze to whatever was up ahead. "It is my fault and mine alone."

This had been no one's fault except hers. She'd been running towards him, stupidly thinking it would be the best place to be. If she'd listened to him, she wouldn't have been caught and injured by an emerging Monster.

She had to let him know that. He had to understand.

Zoe reached up, pressing her palm to his face. It forced him to look back down at her. Their eyes connected and Zoe felt her stomach shift with energy she didn't recognise. She couldn't tell him with words what she meant, but she no longer felt like she needed to.

Her arm slid from his face and rested back on her body as they went, Aero carrying Zoe towards help, and she swore his body temperature rose immediately after she shivered.

Evangeline had definitely been intrigued when Gold mentioned about having tea together. He hardly ever came around anymore, especially compared to the old days when he would turn up unannounced at any chance he got. But with the Council on his back, he was too tied up.

Over the years, Evangeline's abode had grown with her. A flat-screen TV was screwed to the wall. Electric lights came on at the flick of a switch, as did the gas heating. It was all a marvel, and she often wondered what her husband and children would've made of it.

At exactly at eight o'clock, the bell rang. Gold stepped inside when she opened the door. his monocle perched against his left eye – she'd hated that blasted thing for years. His suit tonight was black velvet with shoes to match.

"My dear!" Gold kissed Evangeline's cold cheeks. "It is lovely to see you as always."

Evangeline smiled. "You look well."

"I feel it!" he agreed. "And yourself?"

"Better with seeing you, as you would say."

"And what would you say?"

"That I am healthy, and it really *is* nice to see you."

Gold grinned, fangs elongating slightly. "You have never lost your sweetness."

Evangeline laughed, and turned away to make the tea.

When it was ready, Gold chose to sit at the glass dining table instead of going into the cosy living room. Evangeline didn't question it – she'd learnt not to over the last century – and just placed the teapot in the middle with two accompanying china mugs.

Gold waved his hand once Evangeline sat, making a third mug and a tray of biscuits float through.

She shot him a questioning look as the room shifted. Almost instantly the house fell away, leaving them in white emptiness. She closed her mouth with a sigh.

Completely unaffected by the change, Evangeline reached for the teapot and asked, "Whose magic did you use this time? Some of mine? You know I gave you that for emergency use only, not to summon biscuits and send us into the void."

The white void was a place secluded from everywhere, a pocket in space with breathable air. It wasn't quite another dimension or anything crazy, just an open doorway into another room – voids were never overly big – that only existed for the caster. Evangeline had always seen them as panic rooms for the magical. Any Witch with control and powerful enough magic could create one, and they could bring people and objects along with them.

Gold tapped the side of his nose. "A magician never reveals his secrets."

"*You* are *not* a magician."

"You always did keep me honest, dear Eva." He held his mug out so she could fill it, and then did her own. She replaced the pot and lifted her mug as Gold did, though he did not drink. "I will not reveal my secrets today on this. We are awaiting a guest." He nodded at the third cup.

As if called by Gold's words, a body materialised. The head grew long, brown hair that tied itself into a knot. The body grew more solid, clad in scant shorts and matching top, both silky-looking.

"Natalia, dear," Gold greeted as the girl fully formed. "Would you like some tea? It's an old flavour."

The girl shook her head. "It's too hot for tea."

"It's *never* too hot for tea," Evangeline argued, sipping and reaching for two sugar-cubes.

Gold poured Natalia a cup anyway.

Evangeline couldn't help but notice how smaller Natalia appeared compared to when she'd last seen her. Not in height or weight, but in the way she carried herself. There was a distinct lack of *her*.

"Is there a reason you asked me here?" Natalia asked Gold directly, her face flushing bronze. Evangeline looked at him too, wondering the same thing. "At least you gave me a few minutes of warning this time, though I'm still not dressed to meet people."

Gold waved a hand in rejection of her comment. "I wished to find how you were faring," he answered.

And you needed me for that? Evangeline thought. *Could you not have asked her somewhere else? Somewhere without me?*

Evangeline glanced sideways at Gold, finding him perched awkwardly so he couldn't look over at her. It was a block, him using his body like a shield. She frowned slightly. He only ever sat like that when he knew his eyes would reveal something.

Interesting. What do you want me for? She sipped again, narrowing her eyes further.

"I'm fine," Natalia responded.

Evangeline turned her attention back to Natalia. She didn't *look* like she was lying – there was no new flush to her face or any discomfort in her body-language – but Evangeline wasn't like any other Creature, so couldn't be fooled like them.

"Is that so?" she challenged. "How fine do you think you are? Are you eating? Sleeping?"

"Eating, yes," Natalia nodded. "Sleeping..."

Gold produced a pleasant smile. "Is Mo keeping you in your dreams too long?" Natalia nodded. "Well, you do need your beauty sleep, not that you are unpleasant to look upon as you are."

"You need *normal* sleep," Evangeline explained. "It will hurt you if you don't get some, exhaust you even if your body's technically resting. To actually sleep, you must banish Morpheus from your mind."

Natalia released her mug completely. "How?"

"Imagine building a wall between you and them, and sealing it so you're kept on separate sides. Your body and mind will then be allowed to sleep properly. However, I must warn you, that when you wake, the wall will reset. So try not to slip or you will exert more energy into building walls than resting to replenish."

"Mo will understand if you do not meet," Gold said, smiling with a gentleness that was usually reserved for Humans. "They will feel your wall and know you are taking some *you* time."

Bronze fluttered onto Natalia's cheeks again. "Thank you."

"Of course," Gold told her.

"What is it you wish to ask?" Evangeline said. Natalia's gaze whipped round like she'd been caught doing something she shouldn't have. "I was a mother once, so I know when there is more."

Natalia fidgeted. "Can I ask something?"

"I'm sure you're quite capable, dear," Gold said, cleaning his monocle on his jacket.

Evangeline glowered. "Go ahead, Natalia."

The girl nodded and took a deep breath, filling her lungs slowly in preparation. When she spoke, she did so quietly, as if worried someone might overhear. "How do I deal with something that can never get out or be known?"

Gold replaced his monocle, golden eye twinkling brighter than the blue one. He leant forwards, arms on the table, hands under his chin. "You have a secret?"

"Maybe," she said noncommittally.

"And you wish to keep this maybe-secret secret? From everyone?" Natalia didn't respond, only glared, and Gold sat back and drummed his fingers on the glass surface. "For that, you must create a lie so perfect with woven truths that your lie could be seen as nothing but the whole truth. The best lies are always made from sprinkles of truth. But you *must* be careful. Don't tangle yourself up in your own web and lose your way. Though, the saying 'the truth will out' was made for a reason."

I don't like this, Evangeline thought sourly.

She studied the young girl and watched as a brilliant bronze overpowered the brown of her hair and eyes entirely. Even her body began to glow with an ethereal shine. Evangeline suspected Natalia didn't know, but her and Gold certainly did – he was watching her too, one eyebrow quirking higher. They both knew Fairies could cast their dust but this seemed unnatural, otherworldly, *else*.

"The truth," Natalia seethed through her teeth, "will stay with me."

Gold snapped his fingers and the girl was gone. Evangeline's real room reappeared around her and Gold in the next breath.

While he set about cleaning up the uneaten biscuits and the empty cups, Evangeline sat staring at the now vacant chair. She couldn't help but wonder about how bad this truth was that it demanded to be so twisted and lied about.

Peri stared at the Darby family tree spread out over the table, pristine as if it had just been made.

There were so many Darby's written across the ever-extendable paper with enchanted ink. It only expressed when people were born and when they'd died, but still, it was incredible to see so much history. To see how the family had survived so long.

Peri touched her trident, flipping it over and over, as her stomach rolled from little fish kicking. Archie had added Peri's name to the tree a week ago. *Peri Sofia De Costanzi* was right there, in black ink, tied to his. And soon both their names would have a string from them.

The doorbell rang. Peri clambered for it, taking her trident with her just in case. She unlocked it and gaped. Her parents – the dishonourable yet honourable to only themselves – stood on the doorstep. As always, their noses were poised in the air and their eyes sneered down.

"Peri Sofia," her mother addressed. Her eyes moved from her daughter's face to her ever-growing stomach and her mouth hung open at the sight. "What *mess* have you gotten yourself into?"

Peri had decided days ago that she was too close to giving birth to even keep up with light throwing practise, let alone any other kind of training. But that didn't mean she wouldn't make an exception to prick her mother with a spike or two. Her blood boiled and her heart raced happily at the idea.

"I'm pregnant, *madre*," she stated boldly. "Hardly a *mess*." She placed her trident over her stomach protectively as if her mother might go to attack it.

"You will *not* speak to your mother with such a vicious tone!" her father croaked; his raspy voice scratched anyone's ears if they listened long enough to it.

"Or what?" she half-laughed. "You'll smack me? Send me to grandfather? Oh wait. You can't do those things anymore."

Her mother's eyes opened wider, hardly notable, but it was the first time in years such recognition had entered her demeanour. "Peri Sofia, *bambina*, *figlia*," she said, trying to call for her daughter with the softest tone she'd used in a *long* time. "You are *pregnant*. These are not games. There is a life inside you!"

Peri glared, all sense returning to her body. "I'm well aware of the life growing inside of me."

"I cannot listen!" her father yelled. He stormed away, hands covering his ears, never turning to look back.

Peri waved childishly at him. "Bye! Bye, *padre!*"

"You will be having *my* grandchild," her mother continued. Her skin was devoid of colour and Peri wondered if she was going to faint. "You are so *grande*. Were you ever going to tell me?"

"I tried to tell you on the phone the other day."

Like always, her mother mostly ignored her response. "What will my grandchild be?"

"A boy," Peri told her. She rubbed her belly and felt little fish kick back. "But I wouldn't start calling yourself a grandmother—"

"Oh *Seven Hells!* Not *grandmother*. Maybe *Nonna?* It's much more—"

"No."

Her mother stared. "What do you mean, no?"

"I mean, you can barely call yourself a *mother*, let alone anything else yet."

Her mother straightened. "There has been trouble reported on this Island recently," she said, her gentle tone slipping. "We came because we'd heard there was a string of Monster attacks."

"*Stai scherzando!* Nowhere on Earth is safe."

"But these attacks have been unusual. There is still time."

"Time for what?"

"To come to Atlantis with us. Protect yourself and," her gaze dipped to Peri's stomach, a flash of something crossing her face but it was gone a moment later, "your baby. It's safe there."

Peri scowled, tightening her hold on her trident. "If I remember right, Atlantis was attacked last time I was there."

Most Monster attacks were random; it was in their nature to be, as Monsters would break through Veils and appear wherever they could, and begin their tirade there. But for Peri's parents to have become aware of them, to know of something outside themselves... It unnerved her.

But what unsettled Peri more was that not a single attempt had been recently made to find and *take* Natalia. Something strange was in the air. It wasn't the amount of attacks. Rather, the lack of them suddenly. The world seemed to have been tipped upside-down, the dust settling too still.

"Protect—"

"Myself and the baby, you said," Peri cut in, her annoyance building. She pointed to the Darby's house behind her. "*Madre*, I've found and made myself a place here. I'm in the process of buying a permanent home for my family. The attacks might be unusual but they would be wherever I went."

"I can find you shelter, a new home. I could even find you a nice, young Merman. He would take care of you and—"

Peri laughed without humour. "I should've known," she hissed, finally letting her anger flow freely. "I should've *known* the *second* you saw me you'd try and drag me away. Whether you came here with honest intentions of protecting me from these attacks or not, you've ruined every chance now. I don't want some other man! I want Archie and my baby! We've gotten this far with it being just us. We can look out for ourselves and each other just fine. I'm staying." She moved back, ready to shut the door, but paused to add, "If I want you, *I'll* contact *you*. Otherwise? Stay away from me. Because it's clear you don't want me as I am."

She moved back and slammed the door with resounding finality.

Natalia's fingers traced across the smooth glass pattern. The sun and the moon designs on the front-doors had become so familiar that she hadn't thought about how distinguished they were in quite some time.

The door started to open and she yanked her hand back. Sarah, dressed in a lovely grey-check suit, greeted her with a motherly smile. The summer sun had also produced her freckles, just like her sons'.

"What a lovely surprise!" Sarah cheered, opening the door wider. "Come in, come in!"

Natalia stepped into the house. "Is Jasper around?"

Sarah's smile increased in size. "He's in his room." Natalia nodded and went to move, but Sarah quickly called, "Wait!" Natalia turned back. "It really is good to see you, Nat."

Natalia's stomach didn't twist as she said, "It's good to see you, too."

"I know these past months haven't been easy on you, but I can at least give you some good news."

"You can?"

"Besides the final phase in your testing, the Council doesn't need to see you in person anymore."

"Really? No more check-ups? Just one more test and that's it?"

"I spoke to them on your behalf, with a video of you training you let me record?" Natalia nodded – she could *just* about remember it being done, though most training sessions had become a blur after returning to them. Sarah continued. "They said you're improving enough that they're happy. They even said the final review won't be for another six months."

Natalia flew at Sarah and hugged her as tightly as she could. This woman was someone who'd come into her life and had worked some miracles. Sarah laughed into her.

Natalia would hate to let her go. She'd hate to let *any* of them go.

But for no she detached herself anyway and ran up the stairs, grinning. Right now, the Council were off her back. That was one less problem, but she had others. She *had* to play the part of a girl trying to be a Creature. She needed to be calm. She had to be quiet. She should be a Fairy. Everything depended on her wearing that mask and keeping her newfound secret, even if it tore her apart inside.

Courteously, Natalia knocked on Jasper's door before entering. Only, it seemed she'd walked in too soon because Jasper scrambled around his room, throwing an envelope onto his desk but not quite out of sight.

"Well hello beautiful lady," he said, throwing all his charm into his smirk.

"And what were you doing?" she asked.

"Nothing." He moved closer and kissed her cheek. "Well, nothing bad."

"If it's nothing bad, can you show me?"

Jasper wiggled his eyebrows. "Maybe it was something naughty."

"From an envelope? I didn't realise technology had gone backwards."

He laughed. "The beautiful lady is smart, too!"

"And persistent. What're you hiding?"

Grinning, he reached forwards and touched the stars that hung from her ears. "Have I told you how stunningly shiny these are today? Almost as precious as you."

Natalia couldn't help it. Her body warmed and she cracked a smile. "Jasper!"

"Natalia!" he cried back.

That was it. When he reached for her next, she sidestepped his attempt and dove for the envelope. Jasper made no attempt to stop her, keeping his green eyes focused, an award-winning grin on his lips. She took that to mean that she had permission to look inside.

In her hands were two tickets to see the famous *Don Quixote* ballet. *In Russia.*

The tickets fluttered from her fingers. Jasper came over, picked them up off the ground to put on his desk, and then surrounded her in his arms. Tears prickled her corners of her eyes.

"I wanted to surprise you," he whispered. "I *do* owe you a date since our last one was ruined."

"Jasper—"

"Say that again," he cut in, lightly touching his forehead to hers.

"What?" she asked.

He drew his face closer until their lips were barely an inch apart. "Say my name."

"Jasper."

He kissed her. With all the force and strength he could muster without being completely overpowering he kissed her.

And she closed her eyes and kissed him back with equal measure.

Natalia traced up his chest until her hands wound into strands of his hair. Without exactly meaning too, a finger got stuck so she had to tug slightly to free it. Jasper moaned against her mouth. She smiled into him and intentionally pulled a piece at the base of his neck, earning the exact same reaction.

However, apparently, Jasper wasn't going to be outdone.

He dragged one hand down her slide like he was tracing the whispers of a flame. The other hand pulled her to him until they fell back, landing on his bed. He manoeuvred them so he was above her, his body supported by his arms. She touched the strain and veins of his arms as his legs moved to open hers, the skirt of her dress fluttering open. He began to trace the inner parts of her bare thigh.

Breathing against her ear, he whispered, "Are you accepting my gift?"

Natalia pushed herself up the bed so she could rest herself against the pillows. Jasper followed her with his eyes.

"It's too much," she told him.

He crawled up the bed to her. "I'm going to have to disagree."

"A nice dinner would've done."

"It would not! That's boring and I *refuse* to be known as boring.

What if you went to Noah and told him I was a boring man? I would be shamed off of Venderly, forced to live out a solitary life on a farm somewhere cold."

Natalia laughed and put a hand to his chest. "Jasper, you are anything *but* boring."

"Well, that certainly *is* a relief." The freckles on his face were vivid, alive, and she touched them. He leaned into her touch and even shivered as she connected the dots. The emerald of his eyes didn't once leave her face. "I remembered how much you loved to dance, and even if you don't do it yourself anymore it doesn't mean you've lost all love for it." It was his turn to feel her face, cupping her cheek, and she surrendered to it. "And I'm not letting you back out. My parents are going to help us jump to Russia in October for the show, and then we're staying the night there. Plus, I *want* to do this for you." He bent lower, moving his hand to the side of her head. "I want to spoil you."

There were no words, so she didn't use them.

She grabbed his shirt, pulling him down onto her completely. She kissed him until they were both enraged with fire, and kept kissing him afterwards. She didn't feel like she deserved to be spoiled, to deserve Jasper, but as she dragged his shirt over his head, it must've been something right.

And while she knew it couldn't last, and *wouldn't*, she allowed herself these small moments as they kissed and laughed and as he dragged her from the bed to dance around the room in sickening circles.

14

Echoes Through Soundless Galaxies

"Come on! This is supposed to be a training exercise. Push harder!"

"I'm pushing as hard as I can!" Natalia yelled back. Her shoulders were pressed firmly against the immovable objects, legs crunching beneath her.

"The blocks aren't moving," Archie told her.

Natalia stepped away and folded her arms, sweat trickling down her forehead. "I'm well aware that they're not moving, Archie!"

"Alright." He raised his hands in surrender.

"No! You keep pressuring me to move them. I want to see *you* do it, if you think it can be done."

A challenging smile transformed Archie's face. He turned to the stack of five blocks – made of hard metal and wood and sponge outer-layer – and lowered his hands. Green smoke-like tendrils licked through the air. They swam to the blocks, snaking around them like translucent vines. Clawing and climbing, they grabbed hold and yanked. The top four blocks tumbled to the ground.

But Archie didn't stop there.

He raised his hands again. More green smoke, this time jade colour, punctured the centre of the blocks like arrows. The arrows were attached to Archie's palm by a thin, green string. He whipped them all at once and a thunderous *clap* echoed around the room. As he did it again, the ripples along the threads vibrated and the blocks flew across the room.

Archie turned to grin at Natalia. She rolled her eyes. "You're just like your brother," she grumbled.

"I hate to remind you that we *are* related," he said. "So we're bound to share some characteristics."

"But you came first! So whose characteristics are they really?"

He laughed. "Be thankful that it's not my brother teaching you today. I moved the blocks—"

"You *cheated*."

"I *only* moved the blocks," he said. "You know as well as I do that Jasper would've had them floating over your head, performing all sorts of tricks, before he crumbled them into piles of rubble that could not reform."

Natalia pouted. "You still cheated."

"I never said you *had to* use physical strength. You just assumed."

"You could've told me otherwise!"

"How would you ever learn if I led you through every step?"

She shook her head, hair falling free from its bun. "I thought you were the nice one."

"I am still the nice one."

"Conceited now though."

Archie laughed again, harder this time. "You know what I mean. I'm more patient than Alex and more focused than Jasper. For this kind of training, I'm your best option at actually getting any work done."

Natalia surrendered to that. "Fine, you win."

He nodded in appreciation. "Now, how about a break? You've been trying to push nearly one hundred kilos of solids for the past twenty minutes."

"Sounds good," she agreed, just as her stomach growled.

Archie raised an eyebrow. "Did you eat breakfast?"

"Small bites. I didn't want to be sick while training."

"A snack break it is."

Once in the kitchen, Natalia sat at the island. Archie grabbed things from cupboards and then picked the seat beside her.

"Oh!" Natalia cried. She snatched a bowl and a mini-box of cereal, and combined the two, eating them dry.

"Disgusting," Archie complained as she shoved in another spoonful. "Eating cereal raw. You are a criminal." He picked up the milk, poured it into a bowl, *and then* added some chocolate cereal.

Natalia grimaced. "And you just called me a criminal."

They ate in silence, munching through cereal, oranges, a whole punnet of grapes, and a small packet cheese that had apricot chunks. Natalia felt better afterwards; more awake, more energized. Not wanting to be sick that morning she'd only eaten a single round of toast. But now she didn't care and relished in feeling full.

Last night had been another bad one. Despite Gold and Evangeline's advice, Natalia hadn't managed to grow a wall inside her mind. Morpheus had awaited her on the white bed, splayed across it like some Ruler of an old world. While they never left that spot, no dream-searching, Natalia still woke with heavier exhaustion.

Archie began to tidy up. "How are you feeling?"

"Like I might explode," Natalia said, patting her stomach.

"Are you sure you've had enough?" He passed her the last red apple.

She rolled it back. "More than enough, thanks."

He shrugged and put the apple by the sink. "If you're sure." He leaned back against the counter. "Do you want to continue where we left off?"

"Which bit? The cheating at the exercise thing or the blocks can't be moved thing?"

"I didn't cheat," he reminded her, green eyes blazing like Jasper's did.

"Because I don't have magic, I declare you *did*."

"I declare that you're a sore loser!"

Archie sprinted off and Natalia nearly tore her trousers clambering after him. The smooth basement floor changed the second they stepped onto it, switching over to grass.

Natalia stopped. "What're you doing?"

"Making a few adjustments," Archie said, waving his hands.

Walls painted over grey. Grass grew taller. Cawing came from near the ceiling which now looked like a never-ending charcoal sky. Light drew back. Smells of brewing storms and forest dirt floated around. A metallic taste even entered the air.

"Physical strength is important," Archie declared as he walked back over to Natalia. "It's needed in a fight as much as magic or dust. Some Monsters can't be destroyed by anything but strength or being outsmarted."

"I don't think I'll be flipping a Calefaction onto its back beetle-style anytime soon."

"I'd be impressed if you did," he grinned. "But what I mean is, you can get far with basic attributes as much as gifts sometimes."

Natalia nodded. Sometimes there would be no fight because it was over before it began. If someone showed strength, fear would overpower the need to do anything but run. So if Natalia made herself look powerful and strong she might get away free. She had no idea *how* to do that, but Archie seemed to think she'd be capable of finding a way. He wouldn't have suggested this path of training if he didn't.

"Wait!" she cried. "You *did* cheat! You wanted to teach me to move those blocks on my own, under my own steam, yet you moved them with magic."

Archie laughed. "I concede!"

Natalia grinned. "I knew I was right."

"I was only trying to prove that they *could* be moved, that they weren't made of stone."

"If you're making a point, follow through with it next time. Use your own body if you're trying to get me to use mine."

Archie tipped his head. "Alright," he agreed. "Shall we try again?"

They began slowly this time; rolling small tires, straining against each other, even sitting and squatting against a wall. Once again sweat began to drop from Natalia's head and she let it.

Archie switched things up after an hour and asked her to begin pushing against his magic - a shield he made in front of his hands. Natalia did so, using her whole body in the attempt. She gained no ground, but lost none either.

As she took a step, her legs bent awkwardly and she immediately crumpled. The grass beneath her seemed to reach up to catch her, come to leech the last energy she had, because as soon as she touched the ground a wave of dizziness overcame her. Her hearing went fuzzy, her eyesight blurry, her tongue drier than if she'd eaten the sand off the nearby beaches.

Archie ran to her side. "Natalia? What happened? Are you ok?"

Natalia shook her head slowly. "I don't think so," she answered honestly.

"Tell me what's going on."

A ragged breath drew itself from her chest and fell from her lips in a wounded sigh.

The entire room around them dimmed to blackness. And out of it bloomed constellations.

Burning stars appeared and started to circle others. Other smaller stars danced in lights of purples and greens and pinks. The gaps in between were filled with shiny rocks; diamond, topaz, ruby, and sapphire. In tiny glimpses, stacked beyond everything else, were signs of copper and gold and silver.

The sight was enough to choke on.

Archie did. He coughed and gasped like he'd been flung into real space, and even clutched onto Natalia's shoulder to ground himself. She let him because she needed him equally as much.

"What is this place?" he whispered, reaching out to touch a tiny golden rock as it passed. It bounced off his finger but didn't seem to lose its course.

Natalia touched her starry earrings. "I don't know."

Archie pointed at another rock as it whizzed on, carefree. "Did you make it?"

"I don't know," she repeated.

"Natalia?" He looked at her then, consideration dancing across his face along with the light of the stars they were surrounded by – some had even begun to *circle* them. "Have you been here before?"

She nodded. "Yes. Once or twice. But I don't know how I get here or what..." She trailed off, unable to finish.

A tiny star of brilliant purple-onyx stopped before them. It zigzagged up to Archie, booped his nose, until it had had enough of him and flung itself into Natalia's awaiting hand. She absorbed its warmth, noting how this place responded to her. This place had never done anything to hurt her. In fact, it only ever seemed peaceful, almost kind like it knew her on some richer level.

"You have to admit," Archie leant over to peer at the star in her hand, "this place is *beautiful.*"

Natalia smiled and motioned for Archie to open his hand, before she realised the star. It went burrowed into his palm, accepting him as much as he was accepting this place.

"It has to be something to do with your power that brings you here, or creates this," he continued, his voice quieter. "Something to do with you, right?"

She looked at him, at his hand still on her shoulder like he'd fall if not tethered. "I thought you knew what Fairies were like."

"I thought so too, but you've proved to us that we don't."

"Right." She shivered inwardly and averted her gaze. "I don't know if I can get us back," she admitted, changing the subject.

"How did you do it before?"

Natalia grimaced. The last time, a Shadow had brought her out, saying she'd broken a barrier that had allowed it through. "I don't know," she lied, her stomach twisting viciously.

Archie opened his palm and gently threw the little star back into the sky. It hovered, just for a moment, before dashing off to join a cascade of the same coloured beings racing by in a whirring flurry.

Natalia wondered what Archie was doing when he lowered his hand close to her, but when his fingers pinched her arm and she yelped, the stars and beauty fell away. In a blink, they were back in the training room.

Natalia yanked her arm away, rubbing the sore skin. "Couldn't you have flicked my ear or something?" she questioned. "Pinching *hurts!*"

He pulled a face. "I didn't know how much pressure it would take. It's tied to you, after all, right? Sorry."

She sighed. "It's fine. It's not like I had a solution. It was a good guess."

"It was, and it worked! You better keep it in mind for next time."

Archie grinned and, just as if nothing had happened, they began their strength training once more. Natalia wasn't so cheerful though.

That expanse of space had come to her, pulled her in, and even though it was somehow gentle and kind to her, she didn't know what it meant. And she didn't know if it would stay that way 'next time' either.

Just when Tony thought the afternoon was going fine, the sky proved him wrong.

Hundreds of rain droplets poured from the dark clouds. The noise of them hitting the sea was wondrous, but the feeling of wet clothes sticking to skin dampened the enchantment.

Tony and Katherine dove for cover under a nearby veranda. It protruded a good few metres away from the life-guard hut it was attached to. Many other families along the beach were diving for cover at the same time.

"Looks like a storm," a man nearby said. He had his three kids with him, and they happily continued playing with the scraps of sand everyone had dragged along with their feet.

Tony glanced across the sea to where storm clouds were indeed blowing in. They were grey and thunderous. "We should probably get home before that comes in," he said to Katherine. "It looks like it might be a bad one."

Katherine nodded and they began their trudge back to the car. Their perfectly synced, supposed to be relaxing, day off together at the beach was done.

The engine splattered to life. They hit traffic at they drove, the car easing to a halt just as a text message came through. Katherine read it out and Tony moved to accommodate when the traffic began to move again.

Natalia's head peeped out of the Darby's hillside house before disappearing and reappearing again a moment later. She ran down the stone steps as best she could and slammed the car-door shut just as the rain picked up.

"Thanks for coming to get me," she said as they pulled away from the curb.

"I told you I'd pick you up anyway," Tony told his daughter.

He could see her smile in the rear-view mirror as she settled into the well-worn seats. There was healthy pinkness on her cheeks. The exhaustion around her eyes, however, was new. Someone outside might not have noticed, might have called it a blemish or a trick of the light, but Tony knew his daughter.

"Natalia—" he started.

"How was the beach?" she jumped in, catching his eye in the mirror and abruptly turning away from it. The darkness from outside covered her and the street-lights did little to penetrate through to uncover it all again. He sighed, focusing in on the road as the thick droplets splashed against the windscreen.

"I *was* building up the tan," Katherine said. "But clearly the Gods had other plans for me."

"The Gods made the weather?"

Katherine shook her head, laughing slightly. "No, but it's nice to blame something for ruining my day."

"Isn't that sacrilegious?" Tony asked. He was starting to have to squint at the road and slowed down as much as he could without actually stopping. "Can't the Gods hear you or something and strike you?"

Katherine snorted beside him. "For all the things I know Creatures have shouted at them and they've never listened too, I doubt I'll be struck by lightning for blaming them for the changing weather."

"Are they even there to listen?" Natalia questioned rather loudly.

"I've never seen a scrap of evidence to say they are."

"But people believe in them?"

"It's how our supposed story as Creatures began, so some still do. I think some people just like having something, *anything*, to believe in." Katherine sighed. "I know we came from somewhere and have a Purpose against all Monsters. *That* I feel in my bones. Everything else? I have no guts to believe in."

Tony finally careened down their road and pulled up outside the house. They waited a few moments in the hopes the rain would ease up momentarily to make a dry dash. It didn't. They had to cover their heads and bolt, piling in the house in one bundle. It took two of them to shut the front door against the howling wind.

Tony huffed as they entered the kitchen, shedding wet outer-layers as they went. "I think it really is going to be a bad one."

"I might have a shower now, while we still have power," Natalia told him. She left, the stairs creaking beneath her feet.

It wasn't unusual for power to cut off while a storm raged.

Lightning cracked outside and thunder roared two breaths later. Tony went to the window and peered out. He could barely see the bottom of the garden.

Katherine came and wrapped her arms around his middle. "I'm glad you're not at work," she whispered.

He twisted round and put his arms over her shoulders, touching his cheek to her head. "Me too," he said. "I think they'll be sending everyone home anyway."

Shops often closed during a heavy storm, sending workers home until they got the ok to come back. It became too much of a problem, too unsafe to continue if power was cut or doors blew in because of raging winds. The best thing to do was lock down. Tony remembered during *really* bad times when his supermarket had once closed for four days straight. Natalia had also been sent home from school and hadn't returned until a week later.

Most people who lived on Venderly were prepared for such cases. They had cupboards full of foods they could cook with hot water only, boiled by using a portable camping stove. Batteries were collected in full. Blankets and logs for fires – those who had them had the traditional sort here – were hoarded in the event it happened in winter.

Tony removed himself from Katherine and went to the freezer, pulling out four cheap pizzas – four cheese, pepperoni, BBQ chicken, and vegetarian. "Should I cook these?" he asked. "While still have power? If we don't eat them, cold pizza could hold up for tomorrow as well."

Katherine nodded. "I don't see why not. As you said, they'll keep if we don't finish."

They set about making food. The pizzas went in the oven and Katherine prepared some salad bits as a side.

Twenty minutes later, Natalia returned smelling like mangos, her hair stuck up in a twisted towel. Her starry earrings, ever in her ears, were back in now too, glinting even in the gloom. She smiled when she saw the food on the table and plopped herself down in her favourite seat.

"A lunchtime feast?" she asked, picking up a slice of pepperoni.

Katherine sat, as did Tony. They wasted no time in digging in. Once they'd finished, as they were about to clean the table, the lights turned off. Tony was convinced he heard Natalia gasp but when he looked at her, her face was neutral.

"At least it's not the middle of the night," he said. It was barely two in the afternoon and, while it was darker than normal, it was still light enough. Brighter yet when the lightning forked in the sky.

"I wonder how long it'll last," Natalia said. "I was hoping to see Noah tonight. We were supposed to be watching one of his films. One of the Thor's, I think?"

Tony cracked a smile. "God of Thunder?"

She laughed. "Sounds a *little* ridiculous right now, I know." The rain outside changed direction with the wind, lashing against the house. Natalia looked up at the ceiling.

"You've got a couple of hours before you were meant to go, right?" Katherine asked.

Natalia nodded. "A couple. I'll see how the storm holds, though I'm not holding out much hope."

For hours, they waited for the storm to end. But it just kept getting worse. At one point Tony was concerned that the house would flood as the garden out back and the road out front began to clog, the water unable to sink through the ground or drains. He had towels and buckets ready, and in intervals they kept checking for leaks.

Not a single drip fell from a ceiling or burst through any crack. Another cupboard door lost a handle and the small mirror in the bathroom came away from one of the hooks as an enormous rumble of thunder reverberated through the house, but nothing sinister happened.

To occupy themselves, they played games by candle-light. Card games, board games, silly games, music games, even brain games. Whatever they could play, they did. Until they became bored of that and ate some sandwiches to switch things up.

The night drew in slowly. Each moment it became more and more clear that the storm wasn't ending tonight.

Eventually Natalia went up to her room, claiming she was tired and wanted an early night. Tony couldn't blame her. She looked exhausted; she'd sat on the sofa with her eyes drooping every couple of seconds after the games had ended.

Tony and Katherine followed her up not much later. He laid down in bed, groaning as his head hit the pillow.

"Sounds like you've had a long day," Katherine giggled, lying beside him.

"Feels like it," he said.

He shuffled onto his side to see her, not that he could see much besides her faint outline. She was all curves and lines and grooves. He reached out, tracing the bare skin she'd left exposed. A breath of air passed her lips and it made him want to pull out the full sound.

"Go to sleep," Katherine whispered, tucking into him carefully.

Touching his lips to her head, he said, "Like I could with you this close."

She laughed into his chest but then pulled back. "But you need sleep. You've been wound so tightly since we got home."

It was his turn to sigh. "Did you see her today?"

"What, Natalia? Of course I saw her."

"Did you notice the way her eyes dropped closed for longer than usual or how there was a redness underneath them?"

A pause. "I didn't."

"I *did*," he said. "I've never seen her look so tired, not even when she was still dancing."

"Maybe it has." Katherine shifted again, this time putting a hand to his face and cupping his cheek. "She's been through a lot. She's *still* going through a lot! Between days spent training and nights finding out who she is, she's at the shop and still trying to prove she deserves this to the Council. I'll try and lessen her work-load if she won't slow herself down. Just so she has some time and peace to herself."

"Kath—"

"It's the least I can try and do. She's your daughter. But I care for her too, as if she was my own." Her lips touched his bearded cheek. "But you're not good to her if you're tired and worked up constantly. So, sleep."

Her words seemed to hold some kind of magic of their own, because Tony closed his eyes and felt his breathing slow, but never felt himself enter the dreamlands.

Tossing and turning, Zoe barely slept. The noise of the storm was one thing. The pain from the attack hadn't left yet, leaving her cursed.

Her whole body ached. Every limb felt detached and awkward. Her chest staggered with each breath, her ears ringing. Sharp pain lanced through her chin if she moved or used it too much.

The rumbling and crying of the sky made her finally think. The attack from the other day finally registered. She let herself realise it really had happened.

In the darkness, she clutched her chin. That was the sorest part of her body, where the pain was the sharpest. Nothing else compared.

Some invisible knife had been thrusted in, cutting through to the bone. Throbbing coursed up her jawline and around her mouth. There had been several moments of panic where she'd thought her teeth had fallen out, but after checking, she could see they were still firmly in her gums; there wasn't even a chip.

Her explanation for the injury had been a roller-skating mishap, which wasn't exactly uncommon. Noah knew the truth though. Despite what he'd kept from her, she couldn't do the same.

She rolled over, winced, and climbed out of bed. Her mouth was dry, so she went in search of water, snatching up her pink dressing-gown and putting it on as she went. She used her phone's flashlight to guide her since power had gone out a few hours ago.

The kitchen was still in chaos from dinner. She could see the outlines of pots, pans, and plates stacked on the counter-tops, waiting to be washed. Zoe rinsed out a glass before pouring herself a drink, letting the cold water slip down her throat.

A shape outside the window moved.

The glass slipped from between her fingers. She caught it before it hit the floor and placed it down on the counter, hands shaking.

Zoe backed away slowly. She turned her phone off, plunging her into darkness. She could hear her own breathing and it echoed around inside her mind.

The darkness outside shifted again.

This time, Zoe leant towards it. She knew it was a bad idea, knew that no one in a horror movie survived by *following* the bad, but she couldn't stop that single bead of curiosity from rolling.

Out of the night came the snout of a wolf as it pressed up against the back-door.

Zoe gasped, pain forgotten. She threw the door open and stumbled out into the ravaging storm.

"Alex?" She shouted against the wind and rain.

The wolf padded forwards, claws scratching the ground beneath.

It came close and pressed its snout to Zoe's outstretched hand. She ran her fingers through the fur and watched the wolf's eyes half roll back in its head.

When it shivered, it backed off and shifted.

Steam rose off Alex's bare shoulders. Zoe clambered out of her dressing-gown and approached Alex cautiously, laying the material over her exposed body. Alex smiled and put her arms through, wrapping the rest around her. But, just like last time, the item didn't fit, leaving most of Alex's legs exposed.

"Pink doesn't suit you," Zoe blurted. Shaking her head, she tried again. "Do you want to come inside?"

Alex looked over Zoe's shoulder. "I won't be here long."

Zoe folded her arms over her chest against the wind, hoping they provided enough of a barrier against the elements. "What did you come here for?"

"To see how your chin was."

Zoe blinked at her. It wasn't exactly surprising that Alex knew about it as it had been her mother that had patched Zoe up. But to have her come here, through a damned storm, just to check how she was doing *was* a little shocking.

"Sore," she answered. The wind whipped her hair into her face and it lashed against her injury. She grabbed for her hair, brought close to tears at how severe the stinging was, and continued to hold it out of the way.

Standing taller and rolling her shoulders, Alex stared down at Zoe with intensity. "What were you thinking, going near a Monster?"

For a second time, Zoe blanched. "Do you think I went after it on purpose?"

"You got injured by one," Alex shrugged.

"I didn't chase it!" The rain crashed around them harder, turning itself into a physical manifestation of the tension growing between them. "I happened to be in the area—"

"With the Vampire boy."

"Aero," she corrected. "Yes, with him."

"And you just *happened* to come across some Monsters?"

"He sensed them or somethin' and went after 'em. I stayed behind but started to panic, thinking they'd come for me. I moved towards him for protection."

Alex's eyes rolled. "Some protection."

"It wasn't his fault! The Monster just popped out of the ground and took me with it. I was flipped through the air and landed chin first. It was an *accident*."

Their eyes didn't unlock from each other; Zoe shivered as the rain chilled her skin and Alex watched her, eyebrow and its golden piercing rising.

"Well then," Alex said, clearly stumped.

"Yes, well," Zoe said, not knowing what else to say either. She coughed, clearing her throat. "Are you sure you don't want to come inside? I could get you a warm drink?"

"I'm not actually cold."

"Of course you're not."

Alex shook her head, ringlets of hair flying all over the place. "And I really meant it when I shouldn't stay. I don't know if you've noticed but there's a storm happening."

It whipped round them now, swirling and circling like it was trying to capture them. Zoe had to fight against the wind that wanted to shove her against the side of her house with invisible hands. She braced her legs shoulder-width apart and shielded her eyes with her free hand.

The edges of Zoe's mouth quirked. "So I've heard. Should you have come out in it?"

"I can't sit still for long." Alex's grin was fierce, but then it vanished. "I really did want to check up on you."

"And what's your assessment, doctor?"

"Doctor?" Alex snorted. "The only person close to that is Natalia."

"Natalia?"

"Fairies have a natural ability to heal," Alex explained casually.

She prowled forwards and Zoe's body went rigid as Alex stopped right before her, her hand twitching at her side, but it never moved. Her eyes roamed Zoe's face, unafraid, unashamed. In the dark, Alex's eyes were a heavy black, her face a rich golden brown.

"It seems to be healing well," Alex declared upon closely inspecting Zoe's chin. "Neat stitching. You'll barely have a scar."

"Your mother has steady hands."

"I know. She's put me back together more than once."

Alex's hair fell around her face like curtains and Zoe resisted the urge to push it back. Instead, she gripped onto her own hair tighter. The rain lightened suddenly around them, but they were soaked through already, not that either of them seemed to notice. The pressure in the air had built to such a crescendo it was threatening to rip them in two separate directions, and it was up to them to decide how bad the fallout would be.

"I should get going," Alex declared. She slipped the gifted dressing-gown off, standing proud and extremely naked. Zoe took the robe with a lump in her throat, careful to keep her eyes focused on Alex's face. "Try not to run into any more Monsters."

"I'm not planning on meeting one in an open field at dawn with pistols."

Alex's face shifted to something feral, wild, *free.* "I wouldn't *suggest* taking on a Monster, but if you wanted a few basic tips on how to survive an encounter in case one happens... Our house has its doors open."

"Like it does for Noah? You'd train me?"

Alex snorted. "Noah is more *mentally* acquiring the basics. We only gave him an extendable spear for fun and emergencies. It's not something he can hurt himself on. It's more of a blocking weapon anyway."

"But—"

"I'd teach you whatever you wanted to know."

"Whatever I wanted?"

"*Anything.*"

Zoe opened and closed her mouth several times, unable to properly respond. Her thoughts raced.

She had wanted to know what was going on with her brother, with Natalia. Now she had her answers. There wasn't meant to be an *after*. She'd never thought she'd get this far. After finding out, she'd been stuck in a weird limbo where she hadn't considered what else to do or what more there was for her to want.

"Humans aren't *strictly* aloud." Alex shrugged carelessly. "But I've never been one for rules."

Zoe felt the pressure of the air start to build inside her lungs. "Can I think on it?" she asked. Her voice sounded weak, even to her own ears.

Alex shrugged again. "You'll have to come over in the next few days." She nodded at Zoe's chin. "You can give me an answer then." She walked off.

"Would it just be you?" Zoe called out.

Alex stopped and turned. "I could teach you, or anyone else could," she called back. "Whatever you want."

Whatever you want.

Anything you want.

Zoe took in a sharp breath and blinked, and Alex had already disappeared. The rain fell in her absence, covering her tracks as if Alex had never been here, and the pressure finally released.

Noah tore off a chunk of banana bread and shoved it into his mouth. It tasted a little dry, but nothing a cup of sweet tea couldn't fix. Natalia sat opposite, picking her cherry muffin apart before eating. They sat cross legged on the floor in his room.

The night had been long. Noah could've sworn he'd heard every crash of thunder and every howling of the wind and rain. Light and power still hadn't returned now that it was morning. Technically, the storm was still happening outside. There was just a break in the worst of it right now.

Katherine had decided to keep the café closed for another day, saying there was no point opening only to be forced to close again when the storm returned to its max. She'd dropped off some day-old goods and Natalia before leaving. Natalia herself was only staying for an hour or so, just to see him, before she too would have to leave.

Light peeped through the window, tiny cracks of sunlight forcing their way through ashy clouds. The little rays caught the bronze on Natalia's cheeks and the ever-growing bronze in her changing brown eyes.

"These aren't half bad," Noah commented, taking a bite of a lemon muffin. "Could be better and not a day old."

Natalia smiled as she chewed. "I'll let you tell Katherine that."

"You can tell her. You *live* with her." Noah looked across at his friend. "How is that going by the way?"

She shrugged. "Katherine's always been in my life. The only difference now is that I see her in the mornings and without make-up on."

"I suppose it's nothing *really* new then."

Natalia shook her head. "How's the Zoe thing?"

He puffed out air through his nose. "It's nice that I don't have to hide it, but it still unsettles me that she's aware of all this, too. I found her reading my notes the other day."

"Is that such a bad thing? You know she wants to have whatever you do."

"But she also wants to be *involved* with everything. She's already been flipped by a damned Monster and slammed her chin enough that it needed stitches."

Natalia raised an eyebrow. "Do I need to remind you that you walked through a portal, *before* you knew anything?"

Noah chewed slowly, swallowed by silence. He chugged some water, swirling it through his mouth to clear his teeth, and then popped his teeth-retainer back in. "I worry about what she'll do," he whispered, suddenly conscious that Zoe might hear them through the walls.

"What are you worried she'll do?" Natalia asked, wiping her hands.

"Something stupid."

"Like?"

"Wanting to be trained, wanting a weapon maybe?"

"You wanted to train," she reminded him.

"Only to be physically fit enough to *run away*. I prefer the mental side of things more."

Natalia fixed him with a stare. "You've never thought about getting a weapon?"

"I have my staff, or spear thing." He indicated to the desk where the tiny weapon was resting, condensed to its pocket-size.

"But you don't want a bow and arrow? A sword?"

"I'm sure swords are great, and maybe I would want to swing one once, but I'm not cut out for fighting. I'll keep my metal, poking stick."

Once, back in high school, Noah had been close to getting into a fight. It had been a case of mistaken identity. Quickly the mistake had been realised and Noah had been left alone. That was as close to any action as he'd seen, besides recently.

Natalia twisted and when she turned back, her Fairy blade was in her hand. She held it out, sharp point down. Noah noticed how it glinted, the way there seemed to be magic *infused* inside. He could see one of the bronze stones on the handle; whatever was captured inside seemed to shift towards Natalia like it wanted to be closer.

"Take it," she offered.

Noah flinched back. "*What?*"

"It's my blade," she told him, though he already knew that.

"Where were you keeping that?"

"Today? My hip."

"And normally? Do you always walk around with that thing? What if you get stopped by the police? How are you going to explain a *knife?*"

She rolled her eyes, smiling a little. "It's a blade, not a knife. And I have never done anything wrong in my life to attract the police's attention."

"They might do a random check on you one day!"

"If that happens, I'll figure something out." She held the blade out further. When he wouldn't touch it, she dropped it onto the old sand coloured carpet by his legs. "Normally I keep it strapped to me somewhere. Depends on what I'm wearing."

Noah gulped, looking down at the blade. Tentatively, he reached out. He expected a vibration or a pulse from the magic inside, but there was nothing, no hint of magic at all. The bronze dust trapped inside the gems on the handle continued to swim towards Natalia despite his touch.

Suddenly, he remembered the bronze was *her* dust. The thought slammed inside his brain like a scream. His reaction was to throw the blade away. At the last second, his resolve returned and he didn't. Maybe someone could use the blade like a knife, but Natalia could control the blade completely without a touch.

Laughter filled his ears, a deep and hollow sound.

Noah glanced up. Natalia shook her head, her face scrunched

with humour.

"Something funny, Princess?" he asked.

She let out another soft laugh. "You're holding that thing like it'll eat you alive."

"I haven't had much experience with Creatures or their weapons, so..."

"How does it feel?"

Noah turned over the Fairy weapon, staring at it. It felt small in his palms, but tiny things couldn't be discounted. Fused with Natalia's dust for control, the weapon could be *deadly*. He wondered how many Monsters she'd sent back to Hell with it.

"Like I'm holding your blade," he said, voice wavering though he wasn't sure why. "Is it comfortable for you to hold?" The stones dug into his hand. He couldn't imagine getting a good grip on the handle.

Natalia raised her eyebrows. "It's fine for me."

"Because you're used to it or because it was made for you?"

"I wasn't there when it was made for it to be completely moulded around me."

"Maybe your little dust changes the blade to fit you?"

She tipped her head, still staring. "It's not the craziest thing it's ever done."

Noah went to ask what was when a loud crash of thunder rumbled overhead. He gasped and the blade slipped in his surprise. The very edge pricked the inside of his left index finger. He winced but it only stung as bad as a paper-cut.

"I guess that's the warning bell," Noah mumbled, closing his hand into a fist.

Natalia took her blade back and strapped it to her middle. "Do you want me to try and fix that?" She pointed at his hand.

"Have you healed anything before?"

"No, but Fairies are supposed to be good at it."

"You do have your medical training too."

"Yeah, I do." Her features slipped into a scowl. "I offered to heal one of Jasper's burns before. Apparently it was too far gone for me to help. But I healed his other, recent injuries."

"Jasper seems like the sort of person who enjoys having a scar or two for the story."

She laughed, loud and unexpectedly. "There was also that time with the candles..."

Noah remembered. Natalia had told him of the room of candles, of pink mist, of Jasper lying in the middle of it all with his magic. She'd brushed over the part where they'd *kissed* but Noah had caught on, forcing her to back-peddle. He'd laughed but also loved it for her. He was glad to see her so happy.

Opening and closing his hand, he said, "I'll be fine. It was only a tiny cut."

"If you're sure."

He nodded. "It's not that I doubt your nursing skills. I very much value them." She smiled and he smiled back. "I just don't think it's worth exuding all that energy on healing it when it'll be fine in less than a week. If I ever skin my knee or something, you'll be the first to know."

"How old are you? Five?"

"Older people can skin their knees!"

"If you say so..."

"Falling into roads *could* happen to anyone!"

"If you fall off a curb, I'm laughing, not fixing you."

"I would suggest going to Zoe to try and fix her chin but I don't want either of you to end up hurt."

Natalia nodded. "I should probably try on something small to make sure I can *actually* use the ability before I jump into anything else." The sky rumbled again, louder this time; the second warning. She climbed to her feet. "I should be going. Sounds like the storm's coming back."

"Don't fall off any curbs on your way back," he said, standing and folding her into a hug.

Natalia let herself out of the house just as the first sprinkles of rain came. Noah shut the door and returned to his room. Back in his safe space, he opened his hand, extending the fingers like petals of a blooming flower. A tiny line lay against his skin, the area around it agitated.

He sighed. "Of course the first thing I'd do with a real weapon would be to cut myself on it," he said aloud.

Within minutes, the storm came heavier than before and Noah flopped backwards onto his bed. He stared up at the ceiling, and his eyes followed the patterns his brain conjured in the textures.

Noah.

He sprang up. That voice was familiar but also not. He'd heard the gruffness, the *richness*, before. Why was he hearing it though? He was beginning to think that it wasn't just his mind playing tricks.

The cut, Noah heard.

Laughter, the same as before, came in as thick as thunder.

Noah peered down at his hand but couldn't see the cut in the growing darkness. Flexing his fingers, he still felt it.

As the rain and thunder and lightning returned with full power, he heard the voice again. It echoed, airier now, calling for him in a rhythmic chant.

Noah. Noah. Noah.

What was this voice? What did it mean? If it wasn't in his head, what could it be? Terror rose throughout him slowly, sending his heartbeat into an irregular pattern of thumps. He tried squeezing his eyes shut, tried to block it out, and even reached for his metal spear as if that could be all he needed.

Noah.

15

A Crack Across the Night

ALEX SIGHED. "AGAIN."

"I am trying, you know," Natalia retorted.

Alex scraped her hair back from her face with her long fingers, the strands tangled with sweat. "I know you are," she agreed. "But I'm telling you to try again."

Fuck, Natalia mentally cursed.

She flexed her arms and her bronze wings sprang free. The rush that came from extending them never fully settled.

Alex blinked several times. "I don't think I'll ever get over them."

Natalia laughed nervously. "Me neither."

Alex hadn't changed into her brown wolf yet, leaving Natalia curious as to why, but she figured Alex had her reasons.

One breath. Two. Three...

The girls threw themselves at each other.

The aim of the exercise was to get Natalia to fly. Nothing much had happened, but they were determined to keep trying until something did.

Normally, Alex wouldn't have been her first choice for a partner. She was abrupt and rash. But Natalia also knew that Alex would push her beyond what she thought her limits were, only stopping when there was actually no further to go. Everyone else would just worry

~ *278* ~

about her, about the circles under her eyes, about the exhaustion creeping around her body, about how she was one hit from crumbling in on herself.

It had been seeing Noah, and the urge to want to try and fix his little dagger-prick, that had driven her to ask for help. If she practised her powers, maybe she could heal wounds like a Fairy. Maybe she could fly too. She hadn't even tried in private, but she felt like she *should* be able too, that her wings had to be more than just decoration. And if she could master both...

The minute the storm passed and the power returned, Natalia had called Alex for help. Alex had instantly agreed. The arrangement had been set, and now here they were.

Their bodies smacked in mid-air. Only, something was different this time. Natalia's hand glided past Alex, her legs kicking like she was in water, and she seemed to climb *up* Alex.

Before she could take her next breath, she was looking at the world upside-down.

"Look at you, Fairy." Alex's face came into view; her ponytail was loose and her dodgy self-cut fringe – she was growing it out – had fallen out. "Don't let all the blood rush out of your head."

Natalia glared and hoped it looked fearsome. "I'm not hanging here on purpose!"

"Can you get down then?"

Natalia took in the world from this unusual vantage point. The most she'd done so far had been hover a few feet and glide through the air after being pushed from behind. This was nearly hanging from the ceiling like a bat, very unFairy-like. Her wings twitched in effort to keep her steadily there.

How did that work? How did it happen? she thought, trying to come up with a way to reverse it. *Why did it work now?*

She twisted from side to side and whatever trance-like state her body was in failed.

The safety-mats rushed up to meet her. She folded into a heap of limbs. Groaning, she flipped over, staring up at where she'd fallen from.

Alex reached down a hand and helped her back to her feet. "Not bad," she commented. "The landing looked rough."

Natalia rubbed her stomach, trying to ease the queasiness. "It was."

"It's the best I've seen you do so far."

"Really?" She wasn't convinced.

"Seriously. You managed to stay on the ceiling. I didn't have to push you up there. Next, we'll try *actually* flying." Alex snorted.

Natalia sighed. "Again?"

"Again."

Every time Natalia attempted a landing – if she even made if off the floor – her wings tucked themselves neatly away as if afraid they'd break. She set them loose again. They fluttered as she rolled her shoulders. Their weight no longer unbalanced her but they were still strange.

She was only beginning to accept that these wings were part of her, not separate entities. The colouring might've been unusual, but they were hers. She needed to treat them like an extra appendage, an elongation of *her*, not a thing to be commanded and bent to her will sometimes. They needed to be one together always.

Unsteadily, her feet began to rise from the ground. Alex backed up and pounced. This time, they didn't collide.

Natalia had mentally wished to dodge Alex's forthcoming attack. And she slipped right past Alex as easily as if she'd taken a step in the air, her wings beating at her back.

Alex gave no room as she dove again.

Natalia managed to side-step a second time. However, she went too fast and her wings tried to correct themselves mid-flight.

Instead, she slammed straight into something hard that made a winded *"oof"* sound.

Touching the ground and tucking her wings back, she looked up. Noah grinned at her, though the smile didn't quite reach his eyes.

"Thanks for catching me," she teased.

"Thanks for being *inches* away from the areas that would've *really* hurt," he said.

Natalia saw where his hands were cupped. "Oops?"

"Doesn't *quite* cover the near misfortune, Princess," he told her. "But, it's a start."

Alex wiped her forehead with the bottom of her t-shirt. "If you keep standing there, I'll give you something to be misfortunate about?" she offered.

Noah took a step back. "Maybe next time? I have a mental appointment with Peri first."

"Who is having great misfortune without me now?" Jasper's voice said at the same time. His body followed seconds later.

Natalia glanced up as he descended the last step. Jeans and a grey t-shirt covered him, and he was pulling a green hoodie on over-top. Natalia forced her gaze away when the jumper rucked up and showed off a piece of his mid-riff. Her cheeks flushed, and unfortunately she'd turned in the direction of Noah who raised his eyebrows with a smirk.

"Natalia almost hit Noah square in the balls," Alex explained bluntly to her brother.

Jasper winced. "That's not something you want to be trained in."

Natalia raised her eyebrow. "I didn't do it on purpose!"

"I've been hit once. Never again thank you."

Alex spun to Natalia, grinning wildly. "He said *thank you!* Did you hear that?"

"I did," Natalia said, pretending to note it on the back of her hand. "I'm writing down the date right now. Must be a first."

"Alright, alright!" Jasper held his hands up in surrender. "I said *thank you*. Let's move on before the world implodes when I next say please or..." He showed Alex both his middle fingers.

Natalia crept over to Noah. "You must *love* coming here sometimes."

He laughed quietly. "I've been to worse places."

"You have?"

"There's nowhere better than here." Jasper came over and looped an arm around Noah's shoulders. "Speaking of here, is the training done?"

Natalia ached from top to bottom. "I think so?" She glanced towards Alex.

Alex nodded once. "She's improving," she said, loud enough so everyone could hear. "We got her hanging from the ceiling."

Jasper's face lit with amusement. "The ceiling?"

"I say, if she keeps it up and we work on more balance and simple skills like take-off, then she'll have this flying thing aced in no time."

"Or she'll be a bat."

"Maybe another month of hard work?" Alex said, ignoring her brother.

Natalia gaped. "A *month?*"

"Few weeks?" Alex adjusted. "You forget. Most Fairies have this ability locked down by the time they're walking, if not before. You're learning as an adult. It's going to take time. It's not been natural for you for the past eighteen years. There's no shame here."

Natalia cast her eyes down. She had known flying would take time to master, just like any skill. So Alex was right. Learning as an adult meant retraining her brain as well as her body. But she *would* learn.

Dust was something she *could* use and had mostly mastered. Flying would give her an extra edge – though it wouldn't be unexpected to see a Fairy fly. And, though she hated to think about it, it would also allow her to fly away with attention, quickly leading the fight elsewhere in order to protect those she cared about.

"You picked up blade-throwing," Jasper reminded her. Natalia wanted to argue that she still wouldn't be able to hit a centre target without her blade to command, but settled for a scowl. "I'm sure flight will come quicker than you anticipate. You'll be a natural. When I'm right, I'll give you a race."

She raised an eyebrow. "How do you expect to race me?"

Jasper wiggled his fingers. "Magic."

"You're just going to grow some wings?"

"What kind do you think will suit me?" His mouth twisted into a smirk. "What kind do you want to see on me?"

She tried not to smile back but it was hard. "I'll win no matter what type you choose."

"Can we *not* flirt when there are other, innocent ears about?" Alex cut in.

Jasper moved his gaze to her. "I wouldn't call you innocent."

"Dickhead," Alex coughed into her hand.

"Asshole," he mimicked.

Noah stepped between them all. "If training's over, my sister's upstairs?"

Natalia wondered what kind of reaction she thought he wanted, and whatever it was, he clearly hadn't expected Alex to nod and walk upstairs without a single word.

Noah blinked. "I guess I better follow and hope they don't kill each other while I'm with Peri." He raced after Alex.

Jasper turned to Natalia. "Right then," he said, smile returning. "Time for you to try out one of your other skills." He held out his hand to her.

She clasped it and squeezed, letting him guide her towards whatever task awaited. She didn't know what she'd done to test two skills in one day, but she hoped the second would go better than the first.

Zoe huffed as Sarah inspected her jaw gently. "Is this going to take very long?"

Alex, who'd watched studiously from the doorway for a few seconds, laughed. "Are we keeping you from something? A hot date?"

"With some sexy pirates, yes," Zoe swallowed harshly.

Alex raised her studded eyebrow. "Are you into that?"

"I'm not going to tell you I'm not. Have you seen Pirates of the Caribbean?"

Sarah's fingers slipped away from Zoe's chin and she ordered her to lower it. Zoe's stomach recoiled at the sight of the discarded bandage; a thin line of old blood and the tiniest trail of yellow puss could be seen.

Sarah backed away with a kind smile, brushing past her daughter with a few whispered words before leaving. Noah appeared in her place followed by Natalia and Jasper. Zoe scowled; she didn't realise she'd become a spectacle.

Zoe watched Jasper touch Natalia's shoulder and whisper in her ear, then left. It only deepened Zoe's scowl. Was today the day of whispers and secrets? They were in a normal lounge, inside a normal house, not a soap opera set.

"Where'd he go?" Zoe asked.

"My brother?" Alex questioned. "He's going to meet the other brother. Archie. In the meantime, Natalia's going to heal your chin."

Natalia shifted uncomfortably. "I'm going to try." Her eyes met Zoe's across the room. "If you'll let me?"

Zoe wanted to touch her chin but resisted. "Have you tried before?"

"I'll leave you to it," Noah cut in, promptly leaving too. Part of Zoe was thankful; she didn't want an audience.

Alex shrugged. "I'll stay."

Zoe wasn't enthused at having an untrained person near her damaged chin, but she trusted Natalia not to do anything she knew she couldn't do. Plus, she was aware that Natalia had partly trained in nursing. Zoe nodded, accepting it.

Natalia approached carefully as if Zoe was some petrified animal. "I'll be honest with you," she said, crouching to inspect the injury. "I haven't done this before, to *any* extent, so I don't know if this will hurt or even work."

"Big boat-load of confidence you're supplying me there," Zoe teased, though her voice wobbled.

"Mum wouldn't have suggested Natalia should try if she didn't think she was capable," Alex chimed in.

Natalia whirled round from her spot on the floor. "*Sarah* suggested this?"

Alex shrugged, shifting her feet and trying to look disinterested.

"It's fine," Zoe said, her voice slightly stronger. "If her mum trusts you, then I do too. I also trust you'll stop if I ask or scream?"

Natalia nodded and reached out. Coldness immediately crawled spread along Zoe's chin. Tendrils snuck along the surface of the skin, gliding over the stitches.

Zoe hadn't seen her face in a mirror for a day or two now, but she'd been assured the closure of her chin had been done decently. She trusted Alex when she said that her mum was good at that kind of thing, but that didn't mean something undetected wasn't hidden beneath the surface. The thought made Zoe's heart pound.

The coldness turned to stillness. Zoe glanced at Natalia and swore she saw bronze glitter swim in her eyes but couldn't be certain.

"Know what I find interesting?" Alex spoke up again. Zoe's attention darted to her. Alex slinked further into the room, her dark eyes solely fixed on Zoe.

"What?" Natalia asked. Zoe had meant to ask but was rendered incapable.

Alex didn't redirect her gaze. "You handled that Monster so well," she commented. "When that Vampire boy brought you here, he'd said you'd been attacked by some, I think he said they were Wiskas, but you showed no fear. It was like you'd seen them before."

Zoe choked out a strangled laugh. "I can assure you, I'd never seen a Wiska before one flipped me like a fucking pancake."

Alex shrugged and sunk away again, and Zoe realised then that Natalia's hands had stopped moving. Zoe peered down and found Natalia already staring.

A silent conversation passed between them. Zoe's wording had been specific. She'd always been bad at lying, but technically she hadn't lied to Alex. Just because she hadn't seen a Wiska before didn't mean she hadn't seen a Monster. Because she *had*. One she'd promised to stay quiet about.

Zoe didn't know what Natalia was hiding specifically, especially around the people she supposedly trusted her life with. But bronze that was glinting in her eyes said there was something deeper.

Keeping her nod small, Zoe silently promised to keep what she'd seen secret. Natalia withdrew her hands and stood. "We're done," she announced, leaving without another word.

"She's not normally like that," Zoe explained to Alex, watching the door in her wake. "I've known her for years and I've never known her to just walk off without a goodbye."

"I think it's all the training," Alex said, her eyes on the doorway. "She's been pushing herself a lot recently." She huffed and looked back at Zoe. "I get the feeling that she's not the type to admit it, but I don't think things are going her way. I think she's being unnecessarily hard on herself for what she's not accomplished yet."

"You think she's being too hard on herself?"

"Months ago, she couldn't even release her wings. Now, she's trying to fly and is managing. She's *rapidly* improving. But I don't think it's matching up with her own goals and where she wants to be right now."

Zoe had known Natalia for as long as her brother had, and in all that time she'd never seen Natalia give up on something she'd wanted. Whether it was ballet, school tests, her nursing, *whatever*. Now this. However, the whole exhaustion thing was worrying. Even in the height of exams or dancing, Zoe had never seen Natalia to be so drained.

Zoe stood, but before she could go anywhere Alex trapped her, putting her legs on either side of Zoe's. She pressed a gentle finger beneath her chin, tilting her head up.

"Looks pretty good," Alex mused.

"Like new?" Zoe questioned, praying to whatever these Creatures believed in that Alex couldn't hear her heart race.

Alex ran her thumb over the skin. "You'll barely have a scar," she said, dropping her hand. Zoe didn't know if it was the stitches or Natalia that had fixed her – from Alex's gaze, she got the answer that it might be a little bit of both. "Next, we'll have you *killing* those bloody Monsters."

"Killing them? I don't think so! The only way in *Hell* you'll get me near them again on purpose is if you pay me."

"How much?"

"One million."

"Done."

Zoe blanked. "What?"

Alex cracked into maniacal laughter. "Do you *really* think I have that kind of fucking money?" She stood straighter and, before Zoe could reach out and touch the straggles of hair that were in her face, moved away. "It wouldn't hurt to train you though, like I suggested. In case you meet a Monster for a second time. Maybe for defence rather than attacking though?"

Zoe nodded, not trusting her voice not to correct her and say *third.*

Peri slumped at the kitchen island as Archie moved to the other side. They'd come over to the family house for dinner and Jasper had met them halfway down the road as he was coming back from town. Natalia and Alex were also in the house, just elsewhere, training.

Jasper smiled. "Natalia knows about the ballet," he disclosed casually.

Peri slapped the counter-top in surprise. "You *told* her? I thought you wanted it to be a secret!"

He stared at her. "I *didn't* tell her," he said. "She *happened* to come into my room at the exact wrong moment and saw the tickets."

"Do your reflexes need working on?"

"There's nothing wrong with my reflexes!"

"There bloody is if you can't hide some tickets with magic."

When Jasper had told Peri he planned to take Natalia to the ballet, she'd nearly cried – a combination of hormones and genuine joy. When she'd seen the tickets for herself, she'd been astounded and *had* cried. It did feel like a bit of the magic had slipped away now that Natalia knew of the surprise, but it wasn't all gone. And it would do them *both* good to have a night off to themselves. They were wound too tightly – rightly under the circumstances – but they needed time together, away from this swirling chaos.

Archie placed his hands on the counter, his arm muscles straining slightly; Peri only gawked. "At least there haven't been any attacks to stop you from setting up or executing the surprise so far."

Jasper shook his head at his brother. "Doesn't that seem odd though?"

Peri, regretfully, looked away from Archie. "It does," she agreed. "It's unusual to go this long without an attack, big *or* small."

Quiet periods were never taken lightly. Peri was grateful, especially with her due-date looming, but the absence of Monsters made her nerves prickle more than the threat of knowing they were just down the street.

"Odd isn't good in this instance," Jasper said.

Peri nodded, shaking her sharp-cut bobbed hair. "Though *madre* and *padre* had all the love in the world to visit and tell me that they'd heard of the attacks here." She glanced cautiously at Jasper and knew he understood the attacks she was referring to – the ones that involved Natalia.

"They better have brought a house-warming gift," Jasper said.

Peri snorted. "They came to tell me that I would be better in Atlantis, *safer* there."

"*Amore?*" Archie called to her.

Instinct made Peri touch her stomach, feeling for the little fight that was growing and worth more than any gem or Crystal. These days, Archie speaking in Italian – or trying to – meant he wished for her attention.

She'd told Archie of her parents' arrival, but hadn't brought it up since. His eyes bore into her now, searching her face. She shook her head. Her parents wouldn't be bothering any of them for a long while, nor had they brought a house-warming gift. And she certainly wasn't moving to Atlantis.

Peri went to lead the topic back to the lack of Monsters when a light floating string caught her attention.

Mild green thread led out into the hallway. Tension or apprehension.

Peri got up from her seat and followed the strand towards the front door.

The door opened as Peri approached. Sarah smiled at Peri as she stepped inside, then lifted her nose into the air. "I hope you boys aren't ruining another kitchen," she called, giving Peri a wink. The house *did* smell like something was currently burning.

"Once!" Jasper screeched from the kitchen. "I *nearly* set fire to one kitchen once!"

"One time too many!" Sarah raised an eyebrow and a hand, receiving the high-five from Peri. Sarah's face became solemn and she looked beyond Peri. Peri knew the boys had come in behind her. "I didn't come home early by choice," she told them. Recently she'd come and gone to Atlantis several times to try and do some lawyer stuff. "But neither did I come home alone."

The direction of the green thread became clear as Kiva stepped through the door.

Peri shuddered, not at the girl, but of the memory tied to their last meeting. It had to be one of the worst days in her entire life. The day Peri had lost her arm, and nearly hers and her baby's lives.

Her stomach clenched and she held onto it, swallowing back the rising bile. A phantom pain ran down her missing limb, making nerves that weren't there tingle and twitch.

But it wasn't just that. Natalia had spent that day being tricked by Monster after Monster. Kiva had lost both her Human parents because they'd been good people who had just wanted to help.

Standing in the doorway, Peri could understand Kiva's apprehension. But she *looked* good. Her shoulders were flat and her arms bore the start of building muscle. Her braids were gone, a tiny and course looking paintbrush ponytail now stuck away from the nape of her neck. Her skin was richer, the colour darker as if she spent all her time outside. The depths of her eyes were as beady as before.

With perfect timing, Natalia appeared in the hallway, Alex just behind her. She stopped like she'd seen a ghost. "Kiva?" A wave of hope entered her features. "Kiva? Is that really you?"

The girl nodded. "I didn't realise I'd changed so much that I wouldn't be recognised."

Natalia surged forwards, engulfing the girl in a crushing hug. When they pulled apart, Peri stole her chance to hug the young girl best she could with one arm and a giant bump. Only then did the others make their moves.

Peri shuffled to Archie's side and watched as Natalia went to Jasper's, looking like she would fall at any second if he wasn't near to hold her up. Alex left the room, her footsteps fading up the stairs.

Kiva laughed at Sarah's side. But the laughter stopped abruptly. "I wish I could say I've come to visit at a good time."

"Will you stay for dinner?" Archie offered.

"She might be staying for a bit longer than that," Sarah told him. Peri watched as Kiva's thread of apprehension grew. "I came back early because I couldn't actually get *in* to Atlantis. The borders are closed."

"Closed?" Archie questioned, eyebrows rising.

"I r-bounded off the walls. The portal wouldn't get me inside."

"Why?" Peri asked.

"There's no news as to why," Sarah said. "Nothing's coming in or out, no news and no people."

"They're pushing all the Humans out too," Kiva added.

"Pushing them out?" Jasper asked. "Why would they do that? I know there aren't many there, just helpers or whatever, and I know the Council are *knobs*–"

"Jasper!" Sarah scolded.

Kiva seemed unbothered by Jasper's words and shrugged. "I just know that I was there one day, ready to start the new calendar year at the school, and the next I was packing my bags."

Natalia, who had been quiet until then, said, "But you're not Human."

"True. But I wasn't about to stay when my uncle and cousin couldn't. When I found Sarah, they both told me to go with her. They wanted me to be safe and said that, whatever was happening, I needed to be with my own kind to face it. They moved to a village somewhere. I don't remember its name."

In that moment, Peri saw Kiva for the child she was. Puffy cheeks, round eyes, thin neck, short stature. Dried tracks ran down her face, obvious marks that she'd been crying. Mixed with the green lines tied around her chest, there was a cloud-grey - a sign of hurt - and why wouldn't that be there? She'd been moved from place to place and so had her family, all without explanation or help beside Sarah's intervention.

"You can still write to them, if you have their new address," Peri offered, hoping to ease the girl's worry. "And phone, since they're not in Atlantis anymore." Kiva nodded solemnly.

"I don't like this," Jasper muttered, but it was loud enough. Everyone held the same breath. "Why suddenly kick them out? Why close off the borders *now*? Some shits been shat and I don't like the smell."

"Jasper," Sarah sighed.

He shrugged. "What? I just don't like this."

Peri scowled. If the Council was kicking Humans out of Atlantis, there had to be a reason. But nothing sprang to mind. It was great to see Kiva, but the circumstances should've come with better terms.

"I don't like this or that I agree with you," Peri said to Jasper.

He beamed like he'd been given a new puppy. "You agree with me?"

"Makes three," Archie added.

Natalia's bronze shone throughout the hallway as she said, "Four."

The scorching weather had returned. Natalia's body sweated until the sun dropped beyond the horizon, and even afterwards it didn't cool much.

The Darby's cooked up a wonderful buffet barbeque for dinner.

Natalia barely ate her first plate however. Just a spoonful of potato salad, one spiced chicken leg, and some cucumber sticks.

It was decided over the course of the meal that Kiva would move into Peri and Archie's old bedroom – now that they had their own house – until whatever mess around Atlantis was over with and she could return to her family and her new home there. She told them that she'd been about to start school and had been doing some extra training to prepare, mostly weights and running.

When dinner was done and everything had been cleared, Natalia left. Jasper trotted alongside her, keeping her company on the walk home. Out the corner of her eyes, Natalia watched Jasper swing his arms dramatically. He was no different now to when they'd first met; she could just see below the layers now. It was her who had really changed.

"I appreciate when you stare," he blurted, turning round sharply to walk backwards so he could meet her gaze. His smirk brightened his whole face. "It makes me feel important."

She laughed. "To who? Is there someone around who thinks that so I can hand you over to them?"

"You little trickster." He tried to reach out and flick her nose, but she dodged under his arm, smiling. "If I didn't know any better, I would've said you wanted to be rid of me!"

Her smile widened. "Clearly you *don't* know better."

He fake gasped. "I shall leave then, if the lady demands it!"

Jasper turned back around to face the right way but left his hand out to her. Natalia stumbled up to his side but, instead of taking the hand, she high-fived it. His mouth opened and closed several times, clearly flabbergasted. She laughed and half jogged on. Jasper took a few seconds to catch up, and when he did, he tucked his arms around her waist and lifted her off the ground, spinning them both in a circle in the middle of the road.

He dropped her again, pulling her flush against him. His smirk melted as his eyes dipped all over her face, mostly to her lips, before returning to her eyes.

Natalia looked up at him confidently. "Well?"

"Well what?"

"Are you going to kiss me?"

"If the lady demands it?"

"Don't call me lady."

"Fairy?" he challenged, eyes alight with green fire.

"Witch."

He raised an eyebrow. "How about, since you have me here, *you* kiss *me*?"

Natalia wound her arms around the back of his neck and pulled her down to him. His eyes dipped to her lips again. When he looked back up, she smiled and moved closer, pressing her lips to his delicately.

His hands clutched her sides, capturing her in place. He deepened the kiss and her heart stirred as if it'd been asleep until now.

Jasper broke off and touched his forehead to hers, his breathing shallow.

Natalia wanted desperately to ask Jasper to stay tonight, a small voice in her brain telling her to keep him close. But he was already on baby furniture building duty with Archie and Peri this evening - he'd promised them over dinner - and she refused to take him away from family or deconstruct promises.

"Come over tomorrow," he asked suddenly.

She kissed the underside of his jaw. "What for?"

The tenderness in the next kiss was feather light. It was so delicate she wanted more. She grabbed his thin t-shirt so he wouldn't pull back before she let him. He smiled into her lips and just deepened the kiss.

It was intoxicating. From the way her heart fluttered, to the heat around them, to the way her body began to call out for his... She wanted the feeling seared it into her brain and written along her skin by his hand forever.

Jasper wound the loose strands of her hair around his fingers. "I was thinking about a beach day," he whispered, pulling back to talk against her mouth. He tilted his head and peppered kisses along her cheeks. The grip on her sides tightened, making her gasp. "I wouldn't mind seeing you in the sea. Water slicking back your hair. Sand on your skin."

"It would only be fair," she said, "since I have seen *you* naked."

Jasper let out a low laugh. "Whoa. I said nothing about being naked."

She smiled, gazing up through her eyelashes at him. "I suppose you didn't."

"But, if we *were* going there, maybe—"

Her impatience cut him off, the clash of the kiss nothing but force. She pulled herself against him at his stunned moan, moving her hands down his shoulders and towards his waist. He bit lightly at her bottom lip and she gasped.

Like a bucket of ice cold water had been dumped over her head, she remembered they were outside, in the open.

Slowly, she peeled away. Her cheeks heated as Jasper studied her carefully. Then he laughed, taking her hand again. He walked her the rest of the way in silence, then left with a kiss to her temple and a warm wave goodbye.

The whole way up to her room, her shoulder blades itched. It wasn't a reaction from her wings, she was sure of that. She fished out her blade and clutched it in her palm.

Looking out the window, nothing seemed amiss. So why did Natalia's stomach keep twisting, as if the world was lying about something?

"Nat?" She turned from the window as her dad appeared in her doorway, leaving a steamy bathroom with the door open. He was dressed but had a towel in hand. "You're home."

She couldn't help but smile. "Well observed, Dad."

"Cheeky!" He flicked her with the end of the towel. "How was your day?"

"Better than yours, I'd bet," she answered. He nodded in agreement since he'd been at work and there was no worse place to be when it was hot. Natalia took a deep, steadying breath. "Kiva's here."

"Kiva? The girl from Atlantis?"

"Uh-huh." Natalia explained the girl's situation briefly. Her dad listened without interrupting. "So now she's staying at the Darby's until the whole thing's fixed."

"The Council have made no effort to hide that they *dislike* Humans."

Natalia scowled. "What do you mean?"

"I mean, they've made it clear before that they don't like Humans present, but I wouldn't have thought they'd go as far as kicking those that help out of the City."

"Well, they have."

"So you say."

"The whole place is locked according to Sarah."

"Those on the Council may be arseholes, but I wouldn't have thought they'd just throw the Humans out to fend for themselves. Why not seal them inside too? The only known break-in happened months ago."

Her brain ached. "Okay?"

"Why close it now? Is something happening that we don't know about? For the level of secrecy, there has to have been something pretty major. As selfish as the Council are, they wouldn't shut out all Creatures and leave them to hang alone. Humans, maybe. But Creatures?"

"Are you talking about an attack?"

"I can't see another reason why they'd close the barriers without warning."

Natalia shivered. "Another attack on the most impenetrable place we know."

"Maybe sending the Humans away was to protect them somehow? Leave the Creatures inside, those best to defend, to do their Purpose when it was needed without the possible loss of other life." Suddenly her eyes began to water and her dad reached out, putting a hand to her shoulder. "Whatever's happening, Kiva's safe," he reminded her. "She's here, with the Darby's and you. They can help with her training and you can be the friend she needs."

"Her family *isn't* here though. They're who she really should have with her."

"Nat, do you really think Kiva and Sarah would've left her family without making absolutely certain they were well looked after and supported. Sarah probably set up a magical barrier around their new abode so that no Monster could cross it, keeping them safe inside."

"People have to leave their house at some point!"

"They do, but they are also aware of the stakes."

Natalia's shoulder blades itched and she wiped her eyes as something else occurred to her. "We assume it's an attack? One incoming or currently occurring, right?"

Her dad narrowed his eyes. "Probably."

"Do you think it could be a Creature *and* a Monster that's doing this?"

"Are we talking about them as if they're things working together, or things that come as one in the same body?" He studied her, face twisting into a scowl. "Because I don't know if that's possible."

The itch grew. "Which bit?"

"Any of it. Why do you ask? Why do you think that?"

"I just remembered that when I stood before the Council, they said Monsters could infect a Creature. They could change them until the Creature no longer resembled itself. I don't think that sort of person is after me." She swallowed thickly. "But my brain just made some sort of connection, I think? Like could it be possible for a Creature to remain as one *and* have Monster powers or something?"

"In theory, it's possible, but I don't see why it would cause so much trouble."

It's not the only thing causing trouble, she thought solemnly.

She was causing trouble. Her existence was a problem, and not to just her anymore.

"You must have Creature blood to get into Atlantis," he continued, clearly not visualising the same dark images as she was. "Plus, if it was a combination of a being housing two things, surely the Council would've found it by now."

"Hunted it," she murmured.

"Then there are the motivations. I can *almost* see why a Monster and Creature, working together in whatever way, would want to break into Atlantis. But what does it have to do with Humans? And what does it have to do with you? Why would some monstrosity come after you? I still can't figure that out."

"I never said anything about me."

"You didn't have to."

She looked up at him, at the defeat in his eyes, like he really had walked every possible avenue and had come back empty. She put on a smile. "I don't know either, dad."

He bent to kiss her head. "We'll figure it out," he promise. "But I don't think it's the same at all."

"You don't?"

"There is too much *why*."

She snorted. "The level of *why* has only grown for me over the last few months."

"We'll figure it out," he repeated. "No more worrying about it tonight though. I don't want to ruin your good day with theories and tinfoil hats. Change and we'll do something."

Natalia nodded and shut her door, putting her back to it. Only then did she drop her face to her hands and dry sobbed into them.

16
They Who Breathe Clouds

Natalia couldn't remember falling asleep, only waking. The sound of an explosion forced her out of her slumber.

She wasn't entirely sure it hadn't been inside her head until she walked to the window and climbed out to the little balcony.

In the distance, without question, were Monsters.

Her blade touched into her palm at her call. She let her wings free and, after taking a deep breath, stupidly threw herself from the balcony.

The ground rushed up, flashbacks to the last-time she'd slammed into the grass surfacing in her mind - her leg even twinged at the memory. But it was as she'd been told. If she thought of the wings as an extension of herself, she could make them work. She fell to the ground ungracefully but didn't slam face first into it.

When the world stopped spinning, she clambered up and moved on. Her legs pulsed as she ran. It didn't matter that the air was sticky or that it was well into the night. What mattered were the Monsters.

Eventually, she made it to the beach. Her feet sank into the sand and it forced her to slow as she looked around.

A small Calefaction stomped happily further down the beach. Its head lifted into the air and twisted in her direction. Twelve Shadows and an odd Monster tucked behind them all she'd never seen before did the same. They weren't fighting, not even amongst themselves.

There also weren't any Creatures. No Darby's anywhere.

Natalia halted. It honestly looked like she'd stumbled into some kind of Monster tea-party.

A Shadow slunk forwards, eyes glowing like lava. "There she is," it hissed. "Our little pride and joy. We chose this spot, hoping you'd see us and you'd come."

This is a trap. How could I have been so stupid?

She backed up, and all the Shadows did was tipped their head in one collective movement. Even the Calefaction simply watched.

Natalia's back hit something. Burying her surprise, she turned and her mouth broke open in a silent scream.

Eight spindly legs tracked up to a giant body of a spider. The top half, however, was that of a woman. Dark hairs grew from her neck and upon her two Human arms. Natalia gulped.

The woman glared, all eight eyes wide, its jaw clicking as it hissed.

From underneath her, to more versions of this *worst* kind of Monster sprang free. The younger spider girls grabbed Natalia's quaking arms and dragged her back a few paces.

Natalia kicked out, struggling, but the spiders were strong. To hinder her further, their "*mother*" sprayed something resembling webbing over Natalia's legs until they were tightly bound and uselessly limp, heels creating trenches in the sand.

Just when Natalia wondered what they were going to do with her, the spider-children dropped into the sand. She spluttered and hoisted herself up with great effort, focusing mostly on the spiders despite the other Monsters around her.

A Shadow swooped closer but Natalia was faster. Her blade tore free from her side at her silent command. The Shadow simmered into fine powder before disappearing into the sand.

"Is that any way to treat someone who wishes to talk?" the next Shadow said, stepping up to take the last one's place.

"I don't want to speak to you!" she called back, holding out her blade as a warning. The spider-girls scuttled back and forth.

"Ah." The Shadow created itself a hand, and waggled a finger. "And yet you were interested enough in what was happening here to *bravely* come. All alone."

"The others will know you're here."

"They will," it confirmed. "So I better speak fast."

Natalia didn't want to listen.

Unprompted her back itched and then her wings broke free. The spider-girls jumped back at the sight of them to hide under the bigger spider.

She tried to take off but the webbing around her legs still tethered her to the ground. She looked around, panic building in her chest. In a blur, she threw her blade and somehow managed to force it through three Shadows in one sail before calling it back.

She whirled on the spiders next. But then she paused.

In her hesitation, the mother spider shot out more webbing. Natalia cried out as her wings were forced together, stuck behind her back at an awkward angle – it felt like a twisted limb, one that was a fraction away from breaking.

"As I was *saying*," another Shadow seethed as it came forward. "We weren't planning on coming for you tonight."

Natalia tried to move but the pain shot through her like a spear. "Yet here you are!"

"And here *you* are, with us." The Shadow's smile was warped. "Our other plans didn't go right, so we came for you instead."

"You have something to do with Atlantis being in lockdown." The thought tumbled from her mouth uncontrollably. The Shadow's smile dropped, confirming her suspicions. "What did you do?"

"Nothing that we cannot try again, in time," the Shadow mused. "Your City might be locked for now but it won't always be. We can try and get what we need again." There was some sort of twisted satisfaction in the Shadow's fiery eyes. "It doesn't matter what order things get done in. In the end, we will need both."

So she'd been right about a Monster being behind the Atlantis lockdown and the attack being connected to her.

Fear coursed through her body as swiftly as her blood swam in her veins. She looked at the Shadow as it reached towards her. Its hands sought and clearly wanted to claim. But Natalia wasn't planning on being kidnapped anytime soon. Though her refusal would only end with pain, or at least harm, just as it had each time before.

She waited for it all: the wanting, the attempted claiming, the fighting, the *everything* in between.

Yet none of it came.

Natalia opened her eyes – she didn't remember closing them – and saw a brown wolf had replaced the Monster. *Alex* was panting exactly where the Shadow had been.

We will need both, her mind echoed. What was in Atlantis? Why was she needed? What connection tied them together?

Creatures scrambled out of the cover of darkness, wide-eyed and bright against the back-drop. The Monster's themselves exploded at the exact same moment as if they'd sensed it coming. Flashes of both sides came and went like fireworks, and somewhere in between it all Natalia thought she saw Jasper.

Her knife came as she desperately called it, carefully slicing through the webbing still holding her back. Once her legs were free, she moved to her wings. She barely breathed until the webbing fell away like layers of silk, her wings unharmed fluttered, and her blade rested in her palm.

Freed, she jumped to action.

Before she'd taken more than a few steps she sliced through two Shadows. The spray of their ash slapped her face; some went in her mouth, tasting of metal and dirt.

Suddenly, the ground rumbled beneath her and she fell to

its mercy, landing on her knees in the sand. Peering up, the three spider Monsters stared down with bulging eyes. Each set of eight legs scuttled as if restless.

One of the younger spiders leaned forwards and wrapped an arm around Natalia like a shield. The second one did the same on her other side. Together, they hauled Natalia to her feet but it didn't feel malicious or ill-intentioned.

The *mother* scuttled forwards, bending low. Natalia tried to not scream as the mother's furry hands tucked under her chin, forcing her eyes up.

The Monster's voice was calm, *soothing*. "We will not harm you, Princess. We never wanted too. We were only doing as we were told."

Natalia swallowed the rising bile. "Then why—"

"We were doing as we were told," the small spider to the right answered.

"We had to," said the left one. "There was no choice, *we* had no choice."

The mother spider let Natalia's chin go. "How?" Natalia whispered.

"Control," the mother answered vaguely. "We do not want what has been planned to come. Me and my daughters do not seek nor crave destruction. That is why we shall leave and I ask you to let us go."

"And you'll let me go?"

"Princess, we do not want to harm you. We never did." Natalia nodded and the mother spider offered a weak smile. "If we meet again, I hope it is for you to claim us on your side."

What does that mean?

As quickly as they'd appeared, they scuttled off towards the centre of town. Natalia couldn't watch them as they reached firm land. She shivered and averted her gaze, still fearful they'd change their minds, tie her up, and consume her as their next meal.

Noise drew her attention. Carnage had claimed the beach.

She went to take a step and stopped. A Shadow was floating in her direction. On reflex, Natalia let her weapon fly. What she hadn't noticed was the rock the Shadow had. The Monster threw the stone and it collided with the blade mid-air.

The blade shattered with an echoing *tink*.

"Fairy weapons," the Shadow tutted, "aren't invincible."

Natalia gaped at her now three-piece blade. "The rock—"

"Was enchanted with magic just to break your puny weapon. Now what do you have?"

In anger, Natalia threw herself. She casted out her glass wings when the broken pieces of rock and shards of her blade began to rise.

Natalia didn't know what she was doing – she knew her *type* could manipulate broken and sharp materials – but used the surprise to her advantage. She ploughed into the solid Monster a second before the shards did.

The Monster screamed.

Ash replaced the Monster, the only indicator it had existed, and the chipped bits of stone folded inside, all of it sinking into the beach. Her blade, however, dropped to the sand in more pieces than before but stayed on the surface.

Natalia bent over and heaved. Nothing came out but thick bile. Her stomach roiled and fought against itself. Tears burned at the edges of her eyes, a cold sweat replaced the overheating one.

When she was done, she wiped her mouth with the back of her hand. Heart hammering, she wondered how the Hell she'd just done what she had because it certainly hadn't felt like she'd been entirely in control. If she hadn't seen it for herself, she never would've known it had happened.

Something roared and Natalia braced herself. Through the chaos, there stood Jasper. His mouth was agape, his body completely still. Pink surrounded him like a barricade of purposeful magic. But it was easy to see that his eyes, his stare, was fixed firmly on *her*.

She did the only normal thing she had thought of since this had all started. She ran away.

What have I done?

Alex slammed Jasper into the minor cliffside wall, holding him there firmly. She'd never used her full strength against him, and this wasn't it either, but it definitely more forceful than before.

"Calm down," Alex snarled.

"Or what?" he bit back.

"I'll use *all* my force," she warned. There was a snapping of bones as her arms pressed him further into the wall, her shift close to the surface. "You know I'm an angry soul, but you *really* don't want to see it take over."

Jasper felt like his rage trumped hers. "Maybe I do!"

"You're a fucking idiot if you think that."

"How in the seven Hells can you know what I want?" His green gaze burned with emerald fire. He moved his sights to their brother "You *knew*," he spat. "You knew I wanted the truth and all along you had it! You kept it to yourself, knowing I wanted to help!"

He continued to struggle, to try and break free, but Alex slammed his back into the brick so several spots along his spine popped. The force she was using really was nothing he'd ever felt before. But it was *good*. He wanted that rage and that animalistic drive to pound him through the Earth's surface, all the way to the devils below, and he would fight them all the way down. Anger burned under his skin, igniting the ends of his veins and piercing his heart with both speed and accuracy.

All along his brother had known the truth. He could read it in Archie's expression, in his downcast eyes. Jasper had asked everyone for answers on what was going on, on how he could only help and support and hold a hand if nothing else, and yet there had been nothing.

"We didn't tell you because we were asked not to," Archie said after a painfully silent moment.

Jasper choked. "*We?*"

"Me." Peri stepped out from a behind a curve in the rocks. She must've sensed the non-Monster disturbance on the beach and had come. She stood there without a smile or even blue lipstick, looking pale and horrified. "Jasper?" He met her gaze. "You need to understand, *amore*. We didn't *ask*. We found out by accident."

Jasper stopped struggling all at once. Alex's grip loosened but she didn't completely let go. "How?" he asked. "How did you find out?"

"There was an attack, at the house."

"A Chimera crashed through the kitchen windows," Archie answered. "The glass went everywhere. It had *rained* glass all over the floor. And then it floating. Natalia didn't even know she was doing it until she realised *I* wasn't."

"You were attacked and it just happened?" Jasper questioned. His voice wobbled.

Peri looked away. "She had no idea."

Jasper let the sound of the nearby ocean wash over him.

"Nat begged us not to tell," Peri continued. "We had to respect that."

Jasper looked to his sister. "Did you know?"

Alex shook her head. "No, I didn't. But, now that you're starting to see sense, I can talk to you properly. You know Natalia must've had her reasons for keeping this secret. She must've been *terrified*." Her hands fell away but her body remained poised. "You saw what she did with that blade and the rock. You know what else has those powers."

All he'd wanted was to help. Natalia could've told him and

they could've worked through it, together. He could understand her reasons and he *certainly* could understand her fear. But that didn't stop Jasper's heart from swelling with hurt. Yet did he have any right to feel that way?

However, Peri wasn't done. "Who would want to admit to being even a small part of the evil we hunt every day?"

The evil we hunt, he mentally repeated. *I would* never *hunt Natalia.*

So Natalia could do some things a Monster could. That didn't make her one. She was far beyond what a Monster could ever hope to be. She was Natalia. *His* Natalia. The woman who had stolen his heart and continued to run with it.

He balled his hands into fists. There had to be some reason, some way she'd been able to do those things. Now they had part of the puzzle complete. But they were still no closer, none of them it seemed, to having all answers on what was going on and what it all meant.

Jasper broke free and stormed off. Tiny pink sparks erupted from his fingertips as he left, flickering to match his heavy footsteps.

The day's training with Sarah was finally done.

Noah slumped in a chair as everyone else stalked into the kitchen. He was tired but they looked exhausted, faces shallow and eyes half closed, mouths hanging open slightly and chests rising and falling rapidly.

Natalia was absent from the group.

"Where is she?" Noah searched the faces that were avoiding his gaze.

Alex stared above his head as she said, "She went home."

"Home? What happened?"

"We think the attack on the beach was a way to draw her

out," Peri answered. "Her blade was smashed to pieces but she still commanded it, as broken as it was."

Noah scowled. "Did the dust not fade?" He'd learnt about Natalia's Fairy blade from her. She'd said her dust allowed her to wield it. But how could she if the pieces weren't whole, if they couldn't all touch her dust, if they weren't all connected to *her*. "How did she use it?"

Peri reached out and clutched Noah's hand silently.

He glanced up at her. "What am I missing?"

With regret written in her eyes, Peri launched into an explanation of how Natalia had used her broken blade. The other two remained silent; Alex covered her face with her hands and Archie fussed with some candles that had a faint green flame.

Noah's heart strained in his chest and his body grew cold. "You're saying," he swallowed when Peri was done, "she's a Monster?"

"Not completely," Archie said calmly. His eyes met Noah's, sympathy dripping from him. "But she has, at least, Monster powers. We've seen it twice now."

"I refuse to believe she fucking knew!" Alex half-yelled.

"I think she would've told me if she had," Noah said, but the words sounded false in his own ears, he just didn't know why. "Whatever this is, she probably didn't know. She's been diving into her dreams to *understand*. It might not be like what we think it is. What she can do is one thing. How and why are two completely other questions."

Alex scoffed. "That's a lot more sensible than my brother."

Archie sighed heavily. "He was going to be upset."

"She didn't tell Jasper?" Noah gaped.

"You kept the secret from him," Alex accused at Archie. "You knew and you didn't fucking tell him."

"It wasn't for us to tell!" Archie cried. "We only held what we'd seen. We didn't know if that was the first time or the fifth time she'd managed it."

Peri removed her hand from Noah to stroke Archie's back. "What we need to do now is not argue and just be present," she decided, cutting through the fizzling tension. "We need to help Jasper and prove to him that we had no ill intentions, and we need to help Natalia understand and fight whatever is happening. We need to be there for them."

Noah opened and closed his mouth several times, trying to decide whether he was going to throw up or not. The urge bubbled inside of him violently.

"I'll take Jasper," Alex declared.

"No," Archie said. "*I* will take our brother. He might hurt you and I'd rather him tear at me for something I did than have him come for you for nothing."

"I'm a big fucking girl. I can fight."

Archie shook his head. "I'm well aware you can fight, but you shouldn't have to fight either brother because of one of our cock-ups."

She shrugged. "If you insist."

He nodded firmly. "I do." Alex shrugged again as Archie pointed to the candles. "I'm trying to find him now."

Noah moved his attention to what Archie had been doing. A Crystal swung between the green flames, and on its surface a blurry image formed. A picture was of a boy walking. *Jasper* beside some lavender bushes.

"He's at the hotel," Noah blurted.

Archie raised an eyebrow at him. "What? Where?"

"The rooftop bar, down Main Street. The new one on top of the hotel? It only opened a few months ago." Noah remembered being there, at Natalia's birthday, a moment that felt like another lifetime.

Archie blew out the flames, puffs of smoke wafting around his face. "I'll start there." He backed up and turned to Peri. "Do you need anything before I go?"

"I have Alex," she answered. "She can be the one to bow to my demands for a change."

Archie kissed the top of Peri's head. "*Ti amo, tesoro.*" He left through the back door without another word.

Peri waited a few moments before speaking. "It's all linked somehow," she said, scowling furiously. "Natalia being able to control a Monster power, her wings being like glass, the way she's being hunted."

Noah's brows creased and his stomach sank. How had this happened? How had Natalia become this and what *exactly* was this? But something gnawed at him, like an earworm but from a signal from the universe.

"I can feel her string now," Peri added. "It's growing stronger, even as she gets further away."

"What's it showing you?" Noah dared to ask.

"As of now? She's fearful and hateful of everything."

Noah's stomach hit rock bottom and his body shook. He ran for the bathroom, ignoring how his image in the mirror blurred for a second behind tearful eyes, and vomited in the sink.

"How was Bulgaria?"

Gold spun round at the sound of Evangeline's voice. It was airy, light, *troubled*.

They hadn't spoken for a few weeks, not since Gold had left for his little trip - there'd barely been time to tell her besides a small note. It had been a Council mission, though he was a tiny bit grateful for them sending him away. He couldn't lie to them or worry about his secrets being discovered if he wasn't around them. Not that he worried much, really. He'd had plenty of secrets over the years. And the only *key* secret that he'd had was long ago discovered, but only by sheer luck on the Council's end.

Though, his secrets these days were less selfish and more world-wrecking.

Evangeline was dressed in yellow and white, her hair tied in a knot, and a straw bag tucked under her arm.

"My dear," Gold addressed, moving aside to let her enter the house.

She entered and asked again, "How was Bulgaria?"

"Calm." Gold lead on to the living room. "I went to one of the markets just before I left."

"And the mission?"

"It turned out to be a Human messing with a Witch artefact. I got to them before the Society did."

The Society of Souls were the Council's police force. They were usually everywhere but had recently been pulled back because of closed borders into Atlantis, hence Gold being needed - not that there was room for him to disregard an order.

"Silly Humans," she muttered.

Gold's mouth quirked. "Silly indeed," he agreed, glancing at the woman who had been one. "This was silly too. Remember how Humans have always been famed for having magic, for sometimes pulling rabbits out of hats? This Human was pulling tortoises from a sock." He stopped at his home bar. "Drink?"

"No, thank you." She seated herself, delicately laying her hands in her lap. "I don't know if the Darby's have told you, but Sarah couldn't get in to Atlantis."

"No one has told me such things," he said, pouring himself a glass of fresh red.

"And when I tried, neither could I."

Gold whirled round so fast he nearly spilt his drink. "Tell me everything!"

Evangeline went on and Gold listened intently. She explained that it appeared the borders, the magical barrier, around Atlantis had been completely sealed and doubled in strength. Normally, portals allowed access, but there had been no points open, leading people to bounce right back.

"So, you tried after Sarah called?" Gold asked once Evangeline was done.

She nodded. "But she rang me *after* she'd found Kiva."

"How interesting. Why would they close it, I wonder?

"Your brain would probably be better at solving that mystery than mine."

"I've only ever seen it done a handful of times and none in the last century." He gave Evangeline a pointed look and watched as she grimaced. "There has to have been an incident."

"That's all I can come up with."

"What's also interesting is how you went to help."

Evangeline's glare could've melted glass. "Now is *not* the time for this argument!"

"Oh, it absolutely *is*, my dear. Sarah called you, and you went to see if you could make it through."

"I was already on my way to Atlantis."

"Your reluctance to make a decision on helping is wearing thin, don't you think?"

"I wouldn't say that. I would simply say that I am—"

"Eva—"

She held up a hand, stopping him. "That is not all I came to speak with you about," she said. "There is something else Sarah told me while I was in transit here."

"Two phone calls with your descendants in recent times? How wonderfully scandalous!" Gold grinned.

"It's something that's only just happened and Sarah thought that I might want to know or tell you about it."

"Don't make me wait all day for this news you bring to my door."

"It's about Natalia." Gold learned further in as Evangeline looked right at him. "She has a Monsters' power."

Gold choked on the air he didn't need to breathe. "*What?*"

Evangeline launched into another explanation.

At the most recent attack, Natalia had been discovered by Sarah's children to have been wielding rocks and shards of a blade – her own, which had apparently broken during the fighting. Those very sharp weapons had dismantled the Monsters successfully.

Gold fished for the right words but couldn't find any.

"The Council *cannot* find out," Evangeline whispered as if they might be overheard, even here.

"I'm certainly not planning on telling them!" This was one more thing he needed to keep locked inside. One more thing he *wanted* to keep.

"Sarah said that Natalia still has her wings and dust, so that at least makes her *part* Fairy."

Something inside Gold soured. "Part is not all."

Evangeline looked away. "How is this possible?"

"We know it's semi-possible to be *part* something. After all, you were made. *You* were possible," he said, giving Evangeline *the* look.

"But I'm only spliced together parts of Creatures." She smiled sadly. "Who would've gone further and done this to Natalia? Why would they have done it? It can't be for the same reasons as me."

"I don't know, and I don't like it."

"She needs to be protected."

"That she does."

Neither of them said any more. They didn't need to. Natalia hadn't even known she was a Fairy. To know she was part something else was entirely out of the question.

Gold stole his drink from the table and downed the contents in one, foul gulp.

Arms cuddled Natalia's body, cradling her in a warmth she hadn't known she'd missed.

Through blurry eyes, she looked at the swimming green above her. Freckles outlined them perfectly. A summer glow pinked the cheeks. Even the waves of hair had fallen aside.

"Jasper," she whispered.

But he didn't hear.

All of a sudden, her body fell through his arms and landed on the floor. There was no pain but an emotional weight settled over her as Natalia watched a past version of herself being carried onwards while the current her was no more than a stone in their already walked path.

Morpheus appeared at her side, offering a hand. Natalia climbed to her feet alone. She felt for her dagger, but it never showed up in her dreams. She'd never thought to question it before so didn't start now. But she knew she wouldn't see it again now, even in her waking moments. Her breathing hitched at the memory. Morpheus gave her a perplexed look but she couldn't be bothered to entertain it.

Natalia watched the past her and past Jasper weave through the streets of Atlantis. She could almost feel the pain she'd been in that night after the attack, and she could almost feel the stinging in her eyes that had come afterwards. Jasper had not once said a word.

She owed him several explanations.

"You ought to seek him out," Morpheus said, echoing her own thoughts.

But how could she even approach the situation? Saying "sorry" alone didn't carry the full apology she needed to give, yet neither did anything else. It was a place to start but not a place to end. She'd thought over countless suggestions from "I'm sorry I didn't tell you I was a Monster" to "I've been going through some stuff and wanted to figure out who I was before I let anyone else hate me too" but nothing sounded right.

She knew this was hurting them both – her not to trust him, him to not trust her, and her to not trust herself. A chasm had opened inside her heart, swallowing everything around it.

"I never lied," she said aloud. Morpheus turned towards her but stayed quiet. "I never once told him I was one thing when I wasn't. He was the one to call me a Fairy."

Morpheus' brows drew together. "But you never told the truth either. Even after you knew, which was, I think, before I said anything."

She sighed, the heaviness of the entire sky bearing down upon her. "I know."

"So, what are you going to do about it?"

"Do about it?" She peered up at Morpheus, at their grey eyes. "I don't think there's anything I can do."

They rolled their eyes. "I forget how young you are," they mused. "There is still so much you can do. Maybe outright apologising wouldn't seem sincere, but you could always try and explain why you acted the way you did, how you felt in those moments. You could try and tell him that you were trying to protect him, trying to set him free from the burden of having to choose."

Natalia's heart jumped.

Finding out she was somehow part Geminis had been the biggest blow to her life, tearing it apart, third to finding out she was a Fairy and second to losing her mother.

Creatures were meant to destroy Monsters, to cull and stop them before they could do harm to life and souls. She had wanted to distance herself from Jasper so he wouldn't be forced to choose between her and his Purpose – a Purpose that, by all rights, could see to the end of her. Would he even want her now? Maybe not. And while she hated the idea, permanent distance would make him safer.

Natalia turned from her past self, blinking back the growing sea of tears. She had the answer to what she was, but there was still a lot to figure out.

"I was in love once," Morpheus blurted.

Natalia sniffed and wiped under her eyes. "Who said anything about love?"

Morpheus snorted. "The actual curse you both suffer from which stops you admitting it to yourselves." Natalia had no idea what Morpheus was on about. Morpheus seemed to recognise that and explained. "Your boyfriend said the same thing once. Though, I cannot remember whether he said it to me or I heard it. But never mind. I was trying to comfort you by saying that I was in love once too and know how it feels."

Natalia hooked on to Morpheus' words. She knew how she felt about Jasper, she had for a quite a while. Some part of her body was holding on to life at the mere thought of Jasper, at the minor hope that things could be fixed between them, that this wasn't the end. But... Was that a fool's hope? It felt like it was.

"Oh," was all she said.

Morpheus' vision of themself shimmered. Grey eyes went black and the body crackled like TV static. Natalia tried to not shiver.

"Yes," they said. "But it wasn't all happy tidings. We were separated for what we are, for how different we were. We're kept apart in life and reality. The only place we may meet is here, in dreams, where we are neither whole nor incomplete."

"But you still meet? Despite being punished?"

"Of course we do. Love doesn't simply stop." Their shape shimmered again. "We were forced apart by the Council. This place became my personal Hell, which may sound odd for a Monster to say since most wish for nothing more than to have their own land. But Hell is bearable as long as you have someone by your side. I bear it for those brief moments I get."

"And where are they?"

"Up on your Earth. Our initials were engraved inside of a cell by my other soul who was kept there. Their crime was loving and being loved by a Monster. I know you have seen those letters."

M + G.

The thought sprang to Natalia's mind instantly and her mouth fell open. Morpheus' smile was kind. She could see the cell she had been in. Would she *be back in it one day, inscribing her initials?*

There was nothing "Monster" about wanting to love and live.

But here they were; the punished and the one about to be. Morpheus' punishment was solitary confinement. What would Natalia's be for being part Creature and part Monster? What would Jasper's punishment, or anyone else's, be for being near and aiding her for this long? What about her dad?

Morpheus' smile never failed. "I want to tell you to not be afraid of the Council," they said. "There is only so much unhappiness they can bestow upon you. What you do to yourself is far worse. Don't let that be so. Go and speak to your little Witch, Princess."

She shuddered at the nickname, but not in a way she had before. Somehow, to be called a princess by Morpheus, the last of his kind, felt like an honour of some sorts.

Natalia looked away, unable to stay at the shifting grey and black eyes that were so full of sadness and hope, and when she did, she spotted a red handprint floating in the sky. She'd seen it before.

Suddenly, pain lanced along her skin. Her body folded in on itself and she screamed.

Natalia was thrown from her bed and crashed down onto the floor. She gathered herself up and searched for any signs as to what had caused such a reaction here in the real world. There was nothing. That meant something had happened *inside* her head, inside her dreams.

The handprint.

Her father burst into the room and turned the lights on. The brightness burned and she looked away, but she felt the security of arms wrapping around her.

When she could look again, her father had pulled back slightly. Katherine stood just over his shoulder, a water-bubble in hand, ready.

"I'm ok," Natalia told them.

"You *screamed*," her father said. His hand touched her cheek, forcing her to look at him as he scoured her face. "You've not screamed in your sleep for years, not since you were little."

Natalia looked between the two of them carefully. "It was just a nightmare."

It took several more minutes of convincing before her dad was sent off to make hot chocolates and Katherine went to the bathroom. Natalia sat in silence, her light still so bright it touched every corner of her room.

Again she thought of the handprint and looked at the wall straight ahead of her, scowling.

Her visitation to her dream tonight had shown her travelling through Atlantis. She remembered Jasper carrying her, felt his arms around her. There had been tears, as she'd seen, but through them...

She sat bolt upright and went to snatch her blade, only to remember it was in pieces and no longer with her. But that wasn't important. She knew where she'd seen the handprint.

The handprint had been bloody and red and pressed into the barrier of Atlantis.

Aero slammed down the heavy-looking, leather-bound, tied up book. The spine was fractured and the pages appeared to have been stuffed inside.

Peri had seen this book before, once. It was lucky Aero could take it from the Library in Fairy. This *"Book of Monsters"* was one of a kind and kept guarded. It was *the* original. That was why it was protected in Fairy – anyone immoral looking for it would go to Atlantis, thinking something so important would be held there. Those in the know – Peri only knew because of her parents bragging they'd seen it once –

knew where to look. Hiring it required a Council approval. Aero had somehow managed to get the approval for a single day loan.

Peri knew each page must've had a copy, filed and hidden inside the Council building in Atlantis, just as a precaution, but she was curious as to why no one had tried putting this book back together with magic or something before.

"Can you open it?" Jasper asked as he leant over the table, staring intently at the book like it was his next meal.

The basement had been transformed into a useable room outside of training. Sand had been replaced by carpet, the area by a long wooden table, and candle-light lit the space in dark hues. The air smelt of salt and dust.

Aero glared at Jasper but did withdraw his blade. He waved the weapon over the buckles and straps on the book. Dried blood on the tip of the weapon transformed, coming alive in colour and sliding slowly down the silver. Aero dropped several spots onto the cover. An actual slurping sound resonated as the book turned red and the straps and bindings undid themselves.

"Now *that's* magic," Peri commented. Jasper fixed her with an affronted look and she shrugged. "You just wave your pretty hands around and pink comes out. *That* was special."

Jasper grinned. "You think my hands are pretty?"

Aero coughed. "It's not magic."

Peri put her hand to her stomach. "Then what is it?"

"I simply fed Monster blood to the book."

Zoe, who had been silent at the other end of the table, asked, "How does that work?"

Jasper peered over at her. "I don't think you want to know."

Her face hardened. "I think I do."

"Good girl," Peri muttered under her breath. Because she stood beside Jasper, she knew he'd heard but elected to ignore her.

"Don't say we didn't warn you when you throw up." Jasper

moved and placed a bin by Zoe. "Just in case. I'm not in the favourable mood to be looking after people. I make an excellent nurse but I make a better patient, and since he brought the Monster book, you'll be Aero's responsibility if something goes wrong."

Peri swatted at Jasper's arm. "*We* asked him to bring the book."

Aero bowed slightly near Zoe, and Peri raised her eyebrows curiously. His eyes scanned the book over her shoulder, his cheek close to hers. Peri caught Zoe following Aero with her eyes as he stood, cheeks slightly flushed. Peri's eyebrows rose a little further.

"When this book was created, it was to document all the Monsters that the world's Creatures had ever met," Aero explained. "Students of Atlantis, our Home City, were taught from this book. Knowledge of the various Monster types have been passed down thanks to these words, and still there are thousands we don't know about. Not even the eldest Creatures among us know of the true numbers and kinds in all the worlds. Some Monsters haven't been seen since their first appearance documented in this book. Some Monsters, we think, have yet to be witnessed even once, so we don't even know of them."

Zoe crept closer to the book and Aero. "What does that have to do with what you did?"

"The cover, bindings, and the glue holding the pages, is made from Monsters. Special magic helps to keep the "Monster" parts alive but no one knows what it actually is."

Jasper reached over and touched the edge of a page. "A spell conveniently lost."

"Quite," Aero agreed readily. "Blood of a Monster is required to open the book. It activates the magic on the book and also wakes the Monster so it can help us in return."

"Oh." Zoe looked a little pale. "I know Monsters are bad and everything, but it's still not nice for them to be used like this."

"Quite," Aero repeated.

Peri shuffled her feet and eventually had to sit in the seat Jasper whisked up. She felt queasy and uneasy, even though she knew the history.

Aero turned to Jasper who was practically climbing on the table for a better look. "What is it exactly that you're searching for?"

"Monster lore," Jasper answered, not looking up. "How Creature lore entwines with it. And Geminis'."

"Is this about Nat?" Zoe asked.

Out of the corner of her eye, Peri saw Jasper's head jolt as if the question had shocked him physically. She stayed quiet, shuffling her swollen feet inside her new slippers. Little fish kicked against her ribcage.

"And what am I going to do?" Zoe continued when she got no verbal answer.

"Didn't you come here to be checked on?" Peri offered.

Zoe touched her chin. "Partly. I also came to train but someone's turned the training room into a library!"

"I wouldn't be here if there was training happening," Peri told her.

Truthfully, she'd come to check on Jasper and have lunch here. She'd been roped into this madness when Aero had arrived at the same time as her.

"And what about Aero?" Zoe pointed at him.

Aero held his hands up in surrender. "Don't worry about me," he said. "I am only here to pass on the book. That was all that was required of me today."

Jasper flipped open the book and it sounded like it gurgled. He raised an eyebrow at it. "I suppose you could both help?"

"Will you take your bin back if I do?" Zoe questioned. Peri liked her indeed.

A smirk rose to Jasper's face. "You might want to hold onto it. You never know what you might read." He waved his hands and two more chairs appeared at the table in a puff of pink smoke. "Shall we?"

he said, handing out bundles of loose pages.

Zoe took a chair and sat. "What are we looking for? Specifically?"

"Anything," Jasper answered. "Just yell if you think you find anything relevant to Geminis' or mixed Monsters or something. As to narrowing *that* down, I'll let you know when we get there."

Everyone settled, fawning over their papers in utter silence. Peri had to bend awkwardly to sit and read, her belly getting in the way.

Apparently no one in the room was going to mention the fact that Jasper's left arm was in a sling, how bruised his knuckles were, and how mattered his hair on one side of his head was.

After the last fight, Archie had gone to find Jasper at the hotel rooftop. They'd fought verbally and then, according to Archie, Jasper had wielded magic he'd never seen before. He'd yelled about wanting to search for a Monster to fight, and then disappeared inside a cloud of pink. When Archie had found him again, Jasper's arm had been hanging at an awkward angle.

Blush red and obsidian strings – guilt and fear – were tied around his neck and chest so tightly it was painful to see.

Peri looked over at Zoe and then the bin. Maybe the Human wouldn't need it but with the way her own belly was beginning to roll, she was tempted to steal it for herself.

It'd been two days since the beach incident and Alex had had enough. She hadn't tried a stunt like this since Atlantis, but determination swirled through her as she crouched.

With a final breath, she raced forwards.

Her legs kicked off the ground and she bounded up the wall. Thanks to the wolf in her, she had an extra spring in her step, but that didn't mean she always made the jump. Her hands reached out for the platform above, but one slipped. Heart pounding like lead, she gripped on tight with the fingers that dug into the brick.

Kicking the empty air, Alex swung back and forth for momentum, and then finally securely latched on with her other hand. She hauled herself up the rest of the way. The wood creaked under her feet as she landed. Her body ached and her ribs screamed where she'd hurt them, but it felt *good*.

She wrapped her knuckles against the window. When it opened, Alex dodged the lamp that was thrown out at her.

"I surrender!" Alex cried out. "Don't hurt any more lamps!"

Natalia's head popped out of the window. Her eyes roamed over Alex as if checking to make sure she was really there. Alex waved enthusiastically.

Natalia's expression settled to neutral. "How did you get out here?"

"If you let me in, I'll explain it to you."

Natalia waved an arm and Alex followed her through the window.

She hadn't known what she'd been expecting of a Fairy's bedroom, or another girls bedroom that wasn't Peri's, but this didn't meet her expectations.

Bundles of clothes had fallen out of the wardrobe. The walls were void of much decoration. The bed was rumpled and unmade. Four empty glasses were dotted around the room. A mug sat by the windowsill, remnants of chocolate creating patches inside.

Alex turned to the equally dishevelled Natalia. Her long hair was wet and tangled at the ends. There was a spot on her left temple, small but still red. Her clothes hung on her awkwardly. Alex didn't know if they'd never fit or she'd just thrown something on.

At least she smelt of soap and... There was something else.

"What do you smell of?" Alex blurted. There was an undercurrent that cut through the clean smell, a sweet hint.

Natalia blinked, slightly taken aback. "I've just had a shower? So I probably smell of shampoo."

"No." Alex strode closer, sniffing. "It's sweet."

"Oh." Natalia moved to her wardrobe and drew out a bottle with a golden top. "It's a perfume. I sprayed it a minute ago to see how strong it was. It was a late birthday present from my aunt." Natalia put the bottle back. "She's mum's twin sister. I haven't actually met her. She came to see my dad and gave it to him for me."

Alex had been about to question the whole Auntie thing since all Natalia seemed to have around her was Tony and Katherine. Though, knowing who Natalia's grandmother was, it wasn't surprising to know that Natalia had never met her mum's family. They were Fairy *royals*. They had responsibilities back in their land and some people looked below those that didn't always stand at their shoulders.

"So, why are you here?" Natalia asked, not unkindly. She perched on the edge of her bed and patted a spot beside her. Alex accepted the seat. "And why are you climbing up the side of my house instead of coming through the front door?"

"Peri wanted to come," Alex said, ignoring the questions. "But she's too pregnant to travel far now. The trams are shut as well, some repair works or something, so she stayed home."

Natalia sighed. "Alex—"

"We're worried about you."

It came out, as simple as that.

Natalia blinked, the edges of her eyes watering. Alex sighed and leant towards the girl, wrapping an arm over her shoulders. The smell of soap and vanilla grew stronger, and Alex fought the urge to sneeze.

"It's true," Alex continued. She could hear and feel the thumping of Natalia's heart. "We *are* worried about you. All of us. We know what happened, and we know what you are." Natalia sucked in a breath. "But we don't *care*."

Natalia pulled free and stared, wide-eyed. "You should care, I'm a risk—"

"Bullshit," Alex scoffed. "That's an excuse. You're as much of a risk as I am." Alex cringed. "Ok, maybe I'm a bad example."

"Alex—"

"That doesn't take away from what you're going through, I know, but you have us on your side." She grabbed her own elbows, needing to do something with her hands. "Did you know Jasper went looking for Monsters to fight? And he's been trying forgotten *spell* magic?"

Natalia stiffened beside her. "No, I didn't."

"His arm's in a sling and his knuckles are pretty bad. He went to the rooftop bar and then to the beach for them. Archie had to go after him."

"Why would he do that?"

"Because he's angry." She paused. "He's angry, Nat, cause you didn't tell him when he thought you trusted each other and he's feeling guilty that he didn't work out what was happening to you so he could help you."

Natalia slumped. "He has nothing to feel guilty about. I didn't want his help, or anyone else's, because it puts you all in more danger. I thought I could handle this on my own. I thought..." She trailed off, hiccupping. Tear leaked from her eyes and she rubbed the backs of her hands against them. "It's not that I don't trust him, or any of you. I trust you all with my life. It's that I was trying to distance myself to keep you all safe. I didn't trust myself."

Out of everyone, Alex understood probably the best. None of this was about self-preservation. It was about keeping loved ones from harm. Clearly, Natalia thought distancing herself would keep the attacks focused on her and away from everyone. But the world didn't work like that. People cared. People involved themselves to protect the ones they cared for.

"As angry and as guilty as he feels," Alex said slowly, "he misses you most of all."

"I'll speak to him."

Those four words ended the conversation. There was no promise of when or how, but Natalia was promising that she would at least say something to Jasper eventually. Even though she wasn't all Fairy, so maybe she *could* lie, Alex didn't think she was. Her tone sounded genuine. Her heart thumped steadily. No physical indication called out to a lie.

Alex lifted herself off the bed. "Get some rest," she advised. "The Gods would say you need it and so would my mum."

Natalia smiled weakly. "I'll try."

That sounded like a lie. Her voice was too wobbly, too close to breaking. But Alex could do nothing about it.

Alex slipped out of the window, legs first. Warm, summer air caressed her face. She retied her hair so it would keep off her skin.

"Alex?" Natalia called just as she'd reached the edge of the balcony.

Alex turned. "Yes?"

"Can you tell Jasper to not fight anymore? Or sit on him so he doesn't?"

Alex smiled and jumped towards the garden below. Mid-air, she shifted. Because of the clothes, her fur was short. Natalia's gasp filled her ears and she smiled wider, looking up at the girl as her paws touched the grass.

She gave Natalia a nod, hoping she'd done the right thing by coming here tonight and that it would be enough. She hoped Natalia would stick to her promise.

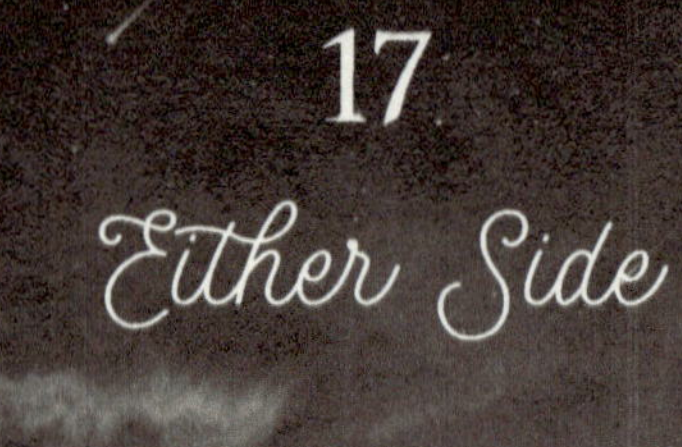

17

Either Side

THE DOOR SLAMMED SHUT.

Natalia didn't look back at it. She ran upstairs with wobbling knees and threw herself onto her bed, flopping face down.

Her time with Noah had gone about as well as she'd expected. They'd started with a film and some popcorn, but it had descended quickly. They'd spoken about her going to Russia. Noah had been enthusiastic about Natalia getting tickets to see a famous ballet and how fast approaching the opportunity was coming around. But she couldn't match him. The whole thing was a sore subject now.

Groaning in anguish, she slipped off the bed to the floor.

Eventually she got up, showered - spending easily half an hour moping and scrubbing her body like she could weather away her "bad" - and dressed in holey trousers and an even more beaten up t-shirt.

By the time Katherine had come home, Natalia had made dinner. Plates and cutlery were at the table, a space just big enough for three. Food steamed on the counter. The cooking had been a way to keep her mind and body busy.

"Natalia!" Katherine cheered. She touched Natalia's pale face as if they hadn't seen each other in weeks rather than mere hours. Katherine's eager, pink-lined eyes surveyed the food. "You made dinner!"

Natalia laughed once. "Don't sound *too* surprised."

"I'm not surprised at the act. It's the amount I'm shocked at."

A golden chicken with herbed potatoes and sliced red onion had been arranged on a serving platter. Vegetables - broccoli, sliced carrots, and steamed cabbage - sat in another large glass dish. Gravy was piping hot in a little boat. There was even a small dish of peas for the more adult adults - Natalia didn't like them much.

"I smell something good!" Natalia's dad's voice sang. The front door closed a moment later. He stalked into the kitchen with more grey hair than brown, and took in the sight. "Natalia? You cooked?"

Natalia scowled. "Why is everyone so shocked by that today?"

Katherine and her dad shared a look.

"Let's stop ogling the food, shall we?" her father suggested. "I want to shove my face into all of it."

Natalia laughed. "Don't ruin it for the rest of us."

Laughing, they picked up their plates and piled them with food. Natalia sat at her familiar spot in the corner. Katherine collected three glasses of water before joining.

"I have some news," Natalia's dad blurted after they were done.

"Rather ominous," Natalia commented, pushing some remaining carrots around with a fork. "Are you going to cut the tension and tell us?"

"No need for a drumroll," he said. "I got a promotion!"

Katherine shrieked with delight. Natalia managed to twist her face into a somewhat genuine smile and clapped. It *was* good news after all. Her dad was becoming a stock supervisor. Better pay, better hours, and more responsibility.

"That calls for a celebration!" Katherine cried. She jumped from her seat and grabbed her handbag.

Natalia's dad stood too. "Where are we going?"

"Out for dessert!"

Natalia glared at the countertops. While it had hardly been much effort, so much food sat around. There was even an apple pie slowly warming in the oven that Katherine had sent her home from the café with that morning. Now it would go to waste.

She didn't move an inch.

"Natalia?" Katherine asked, bending to look at her face. Natalia turned her head.

"Something wrong, Nat?" her dad pressed.

Natalia didn't know exactly what came over her but she threw her cutlery down. "Go out," she sniped. "Go out and celebrate but I'm not going with you."

"Natalia," Katherine looked between her and her dad, "we want you to—"

Natalia pushed past them silently, turning off the oven, and pounded up the stairs. Back in her room, she laid on her bed, face up to the ceiling. The issue wasn't Katherine, or her dad, or even over apple pie.

A week had passed since Alex's visit, since Natalia had agreed to consider talking to the Darby's again. To talk to *Jasper* again. But still she couldn't find the words to say, couldn't find a way to make what she did or what she hadn't right. She didn't deserve to be forgiven and they didn't deserve to be put in the position of trying to forgive her.

She was a Monster and there was no excusing that.

Yet she wanted, with every damned breath, to talk to them. She wanted to hug Peri and see the baby whenever it came. She wanted to train with Alex and study with Archie. She wanted to feel cared for by Sarah and James. She wanted to feel loved by Jasper.

Morpheus and Alex had told her to explain exactly what she'd been thinking, what she'd been feeling, and they'd understand. They'd hear her words and see that she'd been trying to protect them from having to make several hard choices. But would they? She was doubtful. By staying away, as much as it killed pieces of her at a time, she was protecting them still.

But did being a Monster make her one? She'd thought a lot about it. A terrible *thing* wouldn't try to protect others. That was a good thing to do and Monsters didn't do good things. But then, those spider-types had. They'd let Natalia go.

Groaning again when another door in the house shut, she rolled onto her belly, pushed her head into her pillow, and sucked in hollow breaths to her shaky lungs.

Jasper accepted his plate of bright coloured food and sat. Peri joined him and they dug in.

Archie was currently out running errands, but Peri had invited Jasper over anyway. It was always oddly suspicious when she did anything like that; it either meant she wanted a favour or wished to talk about something, and though Jasper was aware of the tricks the food was too mouth-watering to deny her.

Once they were done, Jasper cleared the plates and rinsed them in the sink. Peri toddled on, leaning up against the new blue and sparkly countertop, rubbing her *very* pronounced belly. Jasper turned towards her, noting how flushed her cheeks were. He also that the blue dye she'd used in her hair to announce the gender of their baby had fully rinsed out now.

"That was lovely," he told her, putting the plates on the rack to dry. "Archie—"

"Will be sorry he missed out," she said.

He raised an eyebrow. "Where even is he?"

Peri shrugged. "Said he wanted to run an errand, and I was too tired to question him about it. He can just have a cold tea when he comes home, can't he. I'm not his babysitter."

"Whoa. I never said you were."

Peri grinned. "If anything, you'll be ours."

"You really want to take that risk and let me watch your kid, alone?"

"Obviously not right away! We'll wait a little while. Archie and I both want plenty of cuddle time with our baby before we have our own cuddle time."

"Ew, stop," Jasper said it in the most dry way he could.

She swatted for him and he sidestepped easily. "You'll be an Uncle though, so I expect you to do Uncle duties at some point."

"Uncle duties?"

"Like looking after the baby for a few hours here and there. To begin with, anyway. We'll build up to full afternoons."

"Oh yeah? I hope you're roping Alex in for Auntie duties."

Peri laughed. "Eventually. You're just less of a flight risk."

"Need I remind you of all the stupid shit I've done?"

"I'm pretty sure your brother has it journaled somewhere. If I ever want a reason to *not* let you look after little fish, I'll do some reading. But I have faith you'll be fine."

Jasper leant up against the adjacent counter. "Why did you ask me here?" He held his hands up before she could speak. "Dinner was great, and this conversation is positively invigorating, but I know you by now, so let's not diminish my perfectly reasonable-on-a-good-day intelligence."

Peri shifted. "Perfectly reasonable you say?"

"Those words did just leave my mouth, yes."

"If that's the case, why are you doing the things you're doing?"

Jasper hoped she didn't see him flinch. "I don't quite know what you mean."

"I know you by now so let's not diminish my above average, especially compared to yours, intelligence," she mocked, tone and all.

He averted her gaze, hiding his face and the new scar forming below his right eye. None of his injuries hurt, not really – not the outside ones.

Ever since he'd started using that magic book, he knew he'd been wrong. Then he'd actively searched for Monsters to fight. Even *after* Alex had asked him to stop. He'd ignored everything though, continuing to harbour spells that might help and perform magic that had left pin-prick scars to his skin. And continuing to fight Monsters he found. Because if there were no Monsters, if he pulled them in first, maybe they would leave his family alone. At least for a while.

He just thought he was being clever. He had wanted to control *something*.

"I actually wanted to talk to you about some of the stupid shit you're currently doing." Jasper turned back to Peri, her expression made of stone. "If I wasn't pregnant, I would whip your arse with my trident for being such a little *cagna*! I know what you've been doing. You may want to hurt yourself, but you're also making other people worry about you. And in your tirade against yourself, have you stopped to notice that you're doing *exactly* what Nat is?"

Jasper blinked. "What?"

Peri huffed, rolling her eyes. "You're *both* distancing yourselves from the people you care about and who care about you. *You* are doing it because you're mad and upset, which came from her in the first place. But do you know why *she's* doing this?" Peri didn't give him a chance to reply. "Because she's angry at herself. And scared! She's something we seek to put an end to but she's not hiding for her. She's hiding so we don't have to face that fact!"

He gawked, eyes stinging. "How do you know that?"

She smiled sadly and rubbed her belly. "I'm learning slowly, but I already know you do what it takes to save the ones you truly care for."

"That can't–"

"And you forget, Natalia didn't see us, see *me*, for about a month after I lost my arm." She wriggled her shoulder's stump. "She thought it was her fault, as if I'd had no choice in being there in that fight. But Natalia thought she'd hurt me. She barely forgave herself then, so she'd *never* forgive herself if anyone got hurt or killed now because she is 'a Monster'," Peri air-quoted. "She determined to stop whoever wants her, but doesn't want us in the crossfire. She doesn't want us to see her as a Monster. And she doesn't want to hurt us if something goes awry with her powers or if *they* somehow get her and she's forced into doing what *they* want."

"But we could *help her!*" He nearly yelled. "I would *never ever* see her as a Monster! She may share some traits, some skill, maybe even blood but she would *never* be a Monster."

Peri stared, hard. "*I* don't need convincing of that."

"Natalia." Her name slipped from his mouth in a soft whisper.

"I wish I could smack her upside the head too," Peri announced. "We all have a Purpose. We're linked through it. But we also have something *higher* tying us together, something more powerful."

Peri had never stopped fighting.

The thought knocked Jasper hard enough he actually shivered. Even now, Peri was still fighting. She always fought for those she loved, in one form or another, whether against Monsters or within their own battles. And he could see that she would *always* fight for them. Her Purpose dictated she should fight and then her love made sure she did.

All souls need protecting and all lives deserve to live.

All the anger and frustration he had drained away. Fists unclenched, he looked up from the floor, green eyes shining once again. His heart sang out for Natalia. His insides and thoughts shifted, and he wanted desperately to go to her and prove that she was anything but a Monster.

Natalia was no more a Monster than any of them were.

Cascading hues of emeralds, jades, and turquoises twirled and twisted in the sky. They swooped together in a fog-like state towards the tiny black hole that was stuck open between two lampposts.

Archie contorted his magic, never letting go of his control even as sweat beaded against his forehead. When he'd been playing with his forgotten spells, Jasper had opened a tunnel in the world – there were supposed to be none except in cracks of the Veil. This didn't seem to lead anywhere *else*, but it had allowed him to bring forth Monsters already on Earth. Archie wasn't the best with verbal spells – those types of magic were hardly used anymore – but he did have years of practise of cleaning up Jasper's messes.

Fighting *actual* Monsters was good. Forcing them to come here via a tunnel that potentially did untold damage was not.

Thankfully, the yawning hole began to shrink.

His magic swirled and constricted like vines. It wrapped itself around the empty gap in this world and pulled until it tightened up. Finally, with a *pop*, it vanished into nothing. Archie sagged with relief.

"Not bad."

Archie moved his head to see who'd spoken. Aero, the Vampire boy and Gold's little apprentice, stood with his hands tucked into his trouser pockets. His hair was plastered to his head and the faintest of shimmers glimmered against his lips.

"Not bad?" Archie questioned.

Aero held up a hand defensively. "I do not mean to offend," he said. "I only meant that I am glad I did not have to intervene. You see, the Council tasked me with tracking Monster activity, too. When this arose, I sought it, prepared to snuff it out. A giant hole in the middle of a hardly used pathway was not what I'd been expecting."

Archie should've responded in aid of his brother, except something else Aero had said had caught his attention. "Monster activity?"

"Yes. I have orders to catalogue every detail that happens."

"Log every detail?" Archie's suspicions grew. "Is something going on?"

Aero wiped his mouth on the back of his hand. "I cannot say. All I am allowed to share is that you are to keep following your Purpose, as we all are, and report what happens. *I* am under stricter guidance to note *everything*. From me, no small thing can be left out."

He rarely got wound up, especially when compared to his siblings, but after the night he'd already had Archie was finding his fuse abnormally short. He stepped towards Aero who was marginally smaller than his broad size and towering height. Though he knew Vampires could be trickier. His fancy words and cryptic Council messages are *exactly* what pressed Archie's buttons wrong.

"What's going on?" Archie demanded. "I won't hurt you, so don't fear that I will, but I don't like things being kept from me. I have a family to protect." He winced, then scowled, at his own words and how hypocritical they sounded. "I will protect them however I can and I need all the information to do that. Understand?"

"I do," Aero nodded.

"So, *spill*."

When Aero spoke, he dropped his voice to the smallest whisper he could. "I have an enchantment placed on me that doesn't allow me to lie or hide any information if asked for it," he said. "So I will tell you what I know."

"Will the Council know I've asked this of you?"

Aero's head twitched side to side. "No. Not unless they ask. But I can work around it if they don't ask specific enough questions on the matter."

"So as long as they don't ask about us meeting, or what was specifically shared, you don't have to tell them?"

Aero nodded. "As for the matter here, you may have realised there has been a sudden *lack* of Monster activity. Well, the Council has noticed, too. The Council are concerned the Monsters are waiting for something."

Was the Council right? Were the Monsters retreating and waiting? But why? What were they waiting *for*?

Archie grimaced. *Natalia.* Of course she was the obvious answer. It wasn't that the Monsters wanted her but some of them worked for the *thing* that did. Was it so far out there to think the Monsters were waiting for orders to steal Natalia for whatever *they* wanted?

If that was the case, when would the attack come? What were they specifically waiting for? And how were they being coordinated?

"What do the Council know?" Archie pressed.

"That, I cannot tell you only as I do not know myself."

A firework exploded in Archie's brain. "That's why they closed Atlantis."

Shutting down Atlantis was a strategic move if the Council genuinely thought there might be attacks suddenly. They were protecting their own to the biggest extent they could.

Which also meant they didn't know about Natalia or how she was a target.

Archie and Aero shared a look. Aero's eyes were haunted, his expression withdrawn.

In that moment Archie knew Aero would keep Natalia's secret, but that meant they were completely on their own.

"Is this a private session?"

Zoe stopped dead on the stairs basement. Alex might've held a sword to the girl's throat, but her eyes weren't focused on it. Scowling, Alex tracked Zoe's line of sight - and fear.

The second wolf transitioned with several loud cracks. Alex turned back as Zoe's face screwed up. Alex forced her laugh down;

she was still mad at having their training disrupted.

Alex pulled back and flattened herself against the wall but Zoe stayed where she was.

Kiva's shape emerged from the mass of fur. Her wolf form was smaller than Alex's but equally as nimble and agile, if not faster. Alex was broader, wilder, *stronger*.

"You're welcome to join us," Kiva said. She extended a hand politely to Zoe. "I'm Kiva." Alex snorted and Kiva looked at her questioningly. "Did I do something wrong?"

"Unless you want to act suspiciously Human, don't shake hands," Alex advised.

Zoe folded her arms defiantly. "Are you saying Humans are suspicious?"

Alex snorted again. "Sometimes. But I meant that trying to over-act as one gets you into more trouble than barely bothering."

"Personal experience?"

Alex raised an eyebrow and noted that her nonverbal communication said enough.

"Is there anything we can help you with?" Kiva asked pleasantly.

"Sorry." Zoe's voice was pinched, Alex noted. "But, who are you?"

Kiva literally took to the centre of the floor to explain. She didn't leave out a single of detail; from the moment Natalia helped her out of her cell to when she'd come to reside in this house for the foreseeable future. Carefully, Alex watched Zoe out the corner of the eye, unable to stop herself though she didn't know why. Zoe nodded with every word, encouraging the young pup on, as her fingers wound around the ends of her hair.

Kiva finished with a sigh. "So, that's me," she said. "Sorry if I rambled."

"No!" Zoe jumped instantly. "Rambling is fine. I basically asked you to ramble, so ramble away." She paused. "And now I've said ramble a lot." She scowled and Alex heard her heart do a nervous stutter. "But it's interesting. I feel like I know you better now. All of you." Her eyes met Alex's.

Alex glared back. "Know us, huh?"

"Well, bits and pieces here of you."

Alex raised an eyebrow. "So you know my parents couldn't care for me and gave me up? Not so I'd have a better life, but so they didn't have to waste money on me instead of a good fucking drink? That *I* provoked the guy who turned me and then I went back and attacked him? How about the fact that my recent girlfriend dumped me because I wouldn't go along with her every whim, not that I was that interested in her. What about that I was adopted by this family and *I* wanted to change my name to theirs? That this is my family, that Archie and Jasper are my idiot brothers and I'm going to be an aunt within the next month?"

Zoe swallowed. "Now I do."

Something inside Alex snapped and she laughed, a deep, guttural sound escaping her that caused her chest to tighten. It usually took her months, if not years, to open up. Even Sarah had struggled to get much out of Alex until she'd decided to change her name. Trust wasn't something Alex did with ease. If anything, trusting people was the hardest thing she ever had to do. Yet here she was, spilling her secrets for both Kiva and Zoe to hear.

When she was done, Kiva gave her a beaming smile. Zoe also awarded a smile, but hers was softer, kinder, more disarming.

Alex blinked. It was *her*. Something about Zoe rattled her bones. Alex was unsure if it was a good feeling or not. Truthfully, it *scared* her. She forced her face into a neutral position in case she accidently gave her stuttering feelings away.

Kiva inched closer and stepped between them, looking at them both in turn. "Now do you want to get back to practising?" She was so young and several times in the past few days Alex had been reminded of just how young Kiva actually was. "Alex was teaching me how to shift with a weapon."

Zoe raised her eyebrows, intrigued. "That would explain the sword," she said, pointing to the weapon Alex had pressed against her throat.

Alex scowled. "It's not a—"

"You shift with it in your mouth!" Kiva interrupted.

"Interesting," Zoe said. "Though maybe another time? I'm not cut out for shifting."

"Because you're Human? Maybe," Kiva agreed. "But you could still learn to use a weapon?"

"I'm not fighting," Zoe said, right as Alex said, "She's not fighting."

They glared at each other intensely. Both of them knew Zoe wasn't fighting because she was Human, not because she wasn't capable. However she could still learn to defend herself, she just hadn't accepted the offer.

Kiva walked away and made short work of looking at the other weapons neatly laid out on a nearby table.

Zoe continued on. "I actually came to find Aero."

"The Vampire boy?" Alex scoffed. A tiny twist knifed her chest. She must've been more dulled out from her practise than she thought. "Haven't seen him."

"And you can't sense him?"

"That's Peri's department. If you're asking if I can hear or smell him, then still no."

"Oh, well. Thanks anyway."

Alex began to move away but a hand clutched her wrist. Normally, she would've barked or lashed out. Instead, she turned back to Zoe calmly.

"I am sorry about your family," Zoe whispered.

"Why are you sorry? You had nothing to do with their fucked

up issues."

"I'm also glad they left you."

Alex raised her eyebrows. "Talking of fucked up."

Zoe shook her head like Alex was missing some point. "I'm glad because it's allowed you to become better than them. You've become something incredible in yourself."

"I suppose so, though I wouldn't exactly call myself grateful."

She laughed and let go of Alex's wrist. Alex was confused as to why her skin prickled at the absence of the girl's touch, almost like she missed the contact. She stared.

"And I will *definitely* take you up on that training session sometime soon though," Zoe added.

Alex's mouth curved before she could think to stop it. "I'll be waiting."

Zoe waved past Alex. "See you Kiva!" She flashed Alex one more smile and ran up the stairs.

Blinking several times, Alex had to wait before she could begin to even think, let alone start to process that whole interaction or the touch. To stop the processing, mostly because she didn't want to know what it was all about, she turned back to Kiva who grinned like a wolf.

Alex threw her weapon and in one bound, Kiva caught it between her teeth. She began to shift. As she did, Alex took one last look up the stairs before moving away and crouching, relishing in the squeezing and pinching of her own shift.

The shape of Jasper nearly crippled Natalia.

But she knew it wasn't him, so she put her back to him, walking past as if he were a ghost she could not see haunting her.

"Do my shapes no longer amuse you?" came a voice so unlike Jasper's.

"*Would you prefer another form?*"

The body came up ahead of Natalia and moved from male to female. The distinct black hair, the petit height, even the painted blue lips was right. However, one thing disrupted the image.

"No bump," she said aloud, pushing past again.

Morpheus humph'd and shifted for the third time. The shape remained female, but with long thin blonde hair and wild hazel eyes. She was covered with a long drape of coral cloth which clung to her neck and arms by golden bands.

"You know you'll have to face them again, don't you," they said. "You can shut people out all you like but it will hurt them and it'll hurt you even more. They need you and you need them, Natalia."

Natalia picked up her pace. She did feel like she needed her friends, now more than ever, but trapped in a dreamland, she could do nothing. She was already torn about seeing them again, but she wanted to properly figure out what to say first. She wanted to have all the answers. That meant staying exactly where she was right now.

"Where are we going?" Morpheus asked, catching up.

Natalia scrunched her hands into fists, agitation levels rising. "How am I to know?"

"This is your dream. You're supposed to be the compass to my boat."

She stopped. "What?"

Morpheus held up their hands. "What? I've explained it plenty of times now. I can take you to the destination but you need to know where you're headed. So, what's your heading?"

Natalia focused on flexing her hands. Even here she could feel the sting of her T-shaped scar. "How did I become what I am?" she asked. "How is it even possible for me to exist? Am I wanted because of what I am?"

A swirling white tunnel, like a single stream of light, appeared ahead of them. Natalia looked at Morpheus carefully, and they gave her a nod.

Morpheus was right. Her questions were her direction and he'd opened the new pathway to her answers. Sighing, she strode through, Morpheus on her heels.

They walked into some sort of doctor's office. The area had been cleaned thoroughly, the smell of chemicals burning Natalia's nostrils. Shelves were stocked and the white and blue theme gave the room an extra haunting appearance.

A woman sat on a medical bench. Shopping bags rested on the floor beneath where her head was laid. A doctor perched on a wheelable chair beside her, probing at her small, exposed stomach.

Natalia turned to Morpheus who had propped themselves up against the wall casually. "Who is she?" she whispered, not that anyone could hear.

Morpheus flicked their head. "Look."

The doctor stood and pressed his stethoscope to the woman's chest, listened, then moved it to her belly. He drew up her sleeve next and started taking her blood pressure. Natalia watched each step, creeping around the room to get closer with every movement.

"I just need to take some bloods, ok?" the doctor said. His voice had an English accent and something in Natalia stirred in recognition. "Especially after your last visit. Mother and baby both need to be healthy and happy."

"That's fine," the woman agreed. Natalia blinked. Who was this woman and why did she also sound familiar? "I was kind of expecting it."

"Just close your eyes if you're nervous. It'll be over quickly."

The woman did close her eyes and the doctor waved a hand in front of them. When he was satisfied she couldn't see, he nodded and picked up a syringe and needle.

Another pathway opened beside Natalia. This one she didn't have to step through, it sucked her right in. But, not before she saw something going in to the woman before blood was extracted.

That same woman from before was now slouched in bed, her skin deathly pale. Cradled in her arms was a bundle that kept making tiny, whiny noises.

"Oh, my sweet Fairy," the woman cooed.

Her voice, *Natalia thought. Where do I know it from?*

"*You will be safe,*" the woman continued, "*and you will be loved. You will have a good life, a safe life. I love you, my little flower. My little Natalia.*"

Natalia made a noise of her own, something between a choke and a hiccup. She rounded on Morpheus who put their hands up defensively.

"*That's my mother,*" *she whispered harshly, not in fear of being heard, but in fear of her own voice.* "*That's me. That's my mother!*"

"*I am, dear.*"

Natalia choked again and whirled round. The woman on her bed had slouched further, her dressing gown slipped off her shoulders, and her greasy hair had fallen in her face. Her eyes were half-closed but Natalia could tell they were focused directly on her.

Natalia swallowed the rising bile. "*Mum?*" *she whispered again.*

"*Natalia, my sweet,*" *she whispered.* "*How you've grown.*"

"*Your friend, he is mine too. He's using a lot of his magic to let us have this moment.*"

Natalia looked for Morpheus but they'd vanished. Natalia and her mum were alone. How was Morpheus even doing this? She knew Morpheus could manipulate and open pre-existing portals of dreams, but she never knew they could allow her to become active in them.

She wanted to hug them so hard.

"*Now,*" *her mother said, gaining back her attention,* "*do not linger. It will not do you good to see what the end is.*"

"*But–*"

"*No buts, Natalia.*" *It was almost funny being scolded by a woman who was her mother by birth but not in life. Natalia smiled sadly and her mother smiled back, like she too saw the irony.* "*Mo is doing this so I can wave to you properly. I know this you,*" *she wiggled the small bundle by her which let out a little noise,* "*I will never say a meaningful goodbye to. Not until you come to me here. And by being here, I can only assume, if you're with Mo, it's for something important. Whatever it is, I have faith you will get through it. I am always on your side and I do love you Natalia. I will love you with my last* breath of life and the first one I take in death."

I believe you, Natalia wanted to say but her tongue was stuck. Tears sprang to her eyes and she sniffed.

"Do not cry, my flower, even though I know it's hard," her mother said. "I know I am dying. I have already made peace with that. There is never a good way to let go and I refuse when it comes to you."

"Mum–"

"And now you must go. The magic is fading. Tell your father he did a wonderful job, because I see how strong you are. I hope both you and him are happy. That's all I want." Natalia tried to touch her mother's hand, but they slipped through one another's. Natalia peered into her mother's eyes and saw a blackness infesting the white. "You must go, flower," her mother's voice was fading. "Just remember one thing, please?"

"I'll try," Natalia said, making no outright promises.

Her mother peeked down at baby Natalia. "Remember that you are so very loved."

As Natalia's heart shattered and reformed in a single moment as her body was yanked sideways.

When she landed, Morpheus stared down. The look they wore was nothing she'd seen before. He hovered like a bird watching a rainy puddle form.

Morpheus sat beside her and she tucked herself into them, looping her arms over their shoulders and turning her face into their neck. Tears fell freely. Morpheus seemed a little stunned but quickly recovered, looping their own arms around Natalia's back, and stroking in gentle circles as she cried.

Eventually, Natalia pulled back and wiped her nose. "Thank you," she muttered. "Thank you for that moment with my mum."

"Of course," was all they said on the matter. They changed quickly to a new topic as if to distract her. "You must wake now. I feel your night has dragged on a little long. I will see you again soon, I'm sure."

Natalia gave them one last hug, smiling against them, and closed her eyes.

Tony closed the front door and popped the bags on the counter. The clock read eleven. He wondered if Natalia was out, then heard the floorboards upstairs groan. Either there was a noisy burglar or Natalia was moving about.

As he was putting the shopping away, Natalia appeared in the kitchen. Her hair was ragged and her clothes were askew. He raised an eyebrow at her. Clearly she'd just gotten up. He went to ask what was wrong when her arms surrounded him. He hugged her back, his chest hitching.

"Natalia?"

She pulled back without completely letting go. He noticed the bronze lining her eyes as she spoke. "I saw her."

He blinked. "Saw who?"

"You know how Morpheus, Gold's friend," her face screwed up slightly, as if her words weren't right, "had been helping me try to find my answers?"

"I think so. Not that you've told me a single thing yet."

It was her turn to blink. "I haven't, but—"

"But what?" He wanted to make sure she was ok, that nothing was wrong.

"Has no one said anything to you?"

"Why would they have?"

Natalia cast her eyes down. "Because they know."

"Whatever your secret is, it's yours. No one would tell it if they knew. It's up to you to share what you want with whomever you want, not someone else. Under this roof, we respect that. So, is there something you wish to tell me?"

"Dad," she said breathlessly. She raised her eyes and he could see alarm. "I'm a Monster. Don't," she stopped his reply with a hand, "I'm *actually* part Monster. Remember Kei? The Geminis girl? Remember how I was cut," Tony cast his attention to Natalia's scarred arm, "how she could control shards and split pieces of things like glass or metal?"

"I'm not likely to forget the incident," he answered honestly.

"Somehow, and I'm trying to figure out how, I'm *both*. I'm both part Fairy *and* Geminis. That's why I'm diving into dreams. I'm trying to find out how I became like this. I want to know why someone wants *me* and what they want me for. And I think I'm starting to figure it out."

Tony didn't know what to say. Natalia was Natalia. Maybe she was a little less Fairy. So what? She was still his daughter, still one of the names etched into his soul. He would travel to the ends of the Earth and beyond the Veils for her. That would *never* change, whether she was Human, Monster, or Creature.

"So." Tony straightened himself up. "Now, we know that, tell me who you met."

Her mouth gaped, probably in astonishment at his lack of reaction, but she recovered and closed it. "I met mum."

He gawked like a fish for several moments. "You met your mother?" he questioned. Surely not. Was that possible? "Lavender Whitebell?"

"I asked to be shown how I became what I am and Morpheus showed mum at a doctor's appointment, and then in bed with baby me," she said, words tumbling freely. "It was so weird! I didn't even recognise her at first and then it made sense." Her bronze-lined eyes welled. "She knew she was dying, dad. She didn't want me to see it. But she said that she hopes you're happy, and that I am too. She also told me to say that you'd done a fantastic job raising me, and called me strong."

"Lavender," he sighed, grief striking his heart with the precision of a sharpened spear.

"She wanted me to know I'm loved."

"Oh, Natalia!" Tony folded his daughter back into him. "Of *course* you're loved! I love you every single day. Your mother loved you with every one of hers too."

She laughed meagrely against him. "I know, dad."

He planted a kiss on her head and pulled back. "I don't know how that magic works or how you found your mother, but I'm happy that you did."

"I'm not sure exactly how either. I just know Morpheus had something to do with it."

"Then you need to thank him."

"Trust me, I did."

Tony could only imagine how precious of a moment that must've been. He'd spent so many years trying to give Natalia the love of two people and had spent plenty of nights wondering what life would've been like if Lavender had never died. But he'd come to understand that time couldn't reverse or change. He was happy now, and happier still that somehow Natalia been able to meet her caring and kind mother.

"Thank him again," he said, "for me."

She nodded and stepped away completely.

They conversation naturally drifted, letting them settle down to put the shopping away and brew some tea. As the kettle boiled, Natalia changed and they both began to fix up some lunch.

A weird sort of sensation crawled over him as he prepared to pour the hot water. It felt like a fog crawling up his body. He turned to Natalia, wondering what she was doing, and saw how wide her eyes were. His heart lurched into his throat.

"Do you—"

A voice leached into the kitchen, as soft as a whisper, as light as air. "Did you forget about me?" it cooed. "I haven't forgotten about you, Natalia." Tony searched his daughter's face, and noticed the bronze on her skin had begun to glow. "I have not abandoned you. I am coming."

18

A Red Carnation

NATALIA SWATTED AT THE AIR like she could force away the voice with just her hands. Luckily, the voice dissipated but she knew it had nothing to do with her efforts.

"What the hell was that?" her father whispered.

Natalia stood in silence, unwilling to share her thoughts. She knew that voice. The last few months, it'd whispered in her ear nonstop. The familiarity here wasn't a comfort but a burden. The twang to the voice, the accent, Natalia couldn't identify, but she was *certain* she'd heard directly before, she just couldn't remember where.

The voice had been a mere warning, yet Natalia shivered like she'd been dropped in a pond of ice.

I am coming.

She broke free of her trance and stumbled against the counter. Her arm latched onto the side for stability. Her dad twitched, but when he saw she was ok he stayed put.

I have not abandoned you.

More shivers. Natalia's whole spine vibrated, her bones jolting like chimes. She wondered if her teeth clattered but couldn't hear around the pulsing in her head. She could smell smoke but nothing was alight.

"Where's the fire?" Katherine yelled as she ran through to the kitchen, arms wide.

Water burst from the pipes in the sink. Natalia gulped, the yelled in surprise as water crashed over her head directly. Her clothes clung to her in seconds, her skin chilling. Katherine stopped the pipes with one motion of her hand.

Natalia swiped the nearest mug onto the floor and lifted her gaze. She felt the tingle that came before her bronze dust rose. Her shoulder blades itched too, her wings begging to be free.

"Natalia?" her dad called.

Katherine inched forwards. "Nat? You have to know it was an accident. I'm sorry! I thought something was on fire."

Natalia's response was non-verbal. The shattered piece of bowl drifted upwards, as did the few paint chippings from the walls and the splintered pieces of cupboard that had come away over the past day. They began to swirl around Natalia in rings, orbiting her at the centre of their universe.

She didn't know what she was doing exactly, only that it felt *right*. Like control was hers.

Throwing her arms out, the rings surrounded Katherine. Where they'd been pleasant around Natalia, now they were threatening, *dangerous*. The rings had become a jagged cage.

"Natalia!" Katherine cried. She sucked in a breath as a ring tightened closer, forcing her back straight. "You need to stop this."

Natalia stared at her. "I don't need to do anything," she said. "You tried to drown me."

"She didn't!" her dad cried.

Katherine whimpered. "Nat, I don't know what's happening—"

The materials capturing Katherine tightened further, cutting her off as Natalia drew nearer. There still appeared to be enough room to breathe so Natalia wasn't overly worried. But then a few pieces slipped out of their circular movements. How much control did she really have here?

The question made Natalia realise one thing. *Katherine's life is now in my hands.*

Natalia had never actively used this power before. She didn't know what she was doing, or even how. The power seemed to have taken over on its own.

Slowly, she dragged her attention back to Katherine. "I don't know what I'm doing," she admitted quietly. "And I'm fed up feeling that way. I'm done with being lost, being the one who doesn't know what's going on. I'm done with being the one things happen to! I'm *sick* of everything."

Her dad crept up beside her, like she was some animal likely to spook. "I get it," he said. "You don't want to be dealing with this anymore. And we can fix that. But you need to get Katherine out."

The shards continued to circle Katherine, and Natalia grimaced. "I don't know if I can."

"You got her in, so you can get her out."

"And what if I can't?" Her voice was meagre, small.

He placed a hand on her shoulder, a calming touch. "You will."

Inside her barricade, Katherine blinked. Natalia nodded at her and watched the woman stand taller.

Pieces began to break away under control. Natalia grabbed at them, pulling a bit of bowl away here, snatching up some wood there. However, it didn't seem to make much difference. She'd forged the shards into rings but now they seemed stuck in a perpetual loop without her guidance.

The rage subdued and made way for fear again. Natalia's breaths grew shallower. Out the corner of her eyes, she saw her dad nod to Katherine. When he nodded a second time, the sink exploded again. Natalia shrieked.

The magic broke, the pieces of the loops dropped to the ground, and Katherine stepped free of the trap.

"Now," her father said, turning to her. "Tell me what the *fuck* that was about."

Natalia avoided his gaze, looking at her feet. "I don't know," she whispered. "I didn't know anything but fear. Then anger mixed in and I sort gave way to it. The voice startled me and then Katherine rushing in to quench a non-existent fire—"

"Smelt like one to me," Katherine cut in.

"It was all too much." Natalia looked up, her eyes once again fully brown. "My body just reacted."

Her dad glared. "That's one *hell* of a reaction, Nat."

"What else can I say? I don't know what happened!"

"Clearly some part of you knew what it was doing. You controlled those things. You acted like a..." he trailed off.

Natalia's face hardened. "Like a Monster."

Katherine jumped between them. "No, he didn't mean—"

"Is he wrong?" she snapped. "Part of me *is* a Monster."

Her dad's face softened with guilt. "You need to learn to control it. We can't have incidents every time you get sprayed with water or when someone jumps out from behind a bin."

"You want me to control a part of myself that I don't *want*? And how do you propose I do that exactly? Shall I just ring up the Council and ask if I can have a specific trainer?"

"Enough!" Her dad yelled. Natalia flinched; he'd hardly ever raised his voice to her. "I get this isn't easy, but when will you see that you have some incredible people in your life that can help you through it? You not being trained as a Creature was my fault, and Lavender's." He hung his head for a few moments. "But now you're choosing not to train at being anything. It's not easy. We're *all* new to this. You could at least try!"

"I *am* trying," she argued back.

"There are those of us willing to learn with you. You've just given up."

"Can you blame me?" A rogue piece of bowl floated off the

ground and sped towards Natalia. Katherine yelped but Natalia plucked it out of the air effortlessly. "I don't know what to do. No one can know about me. I put the people around me in danger. If I fight, I lose. If I don't fight, I still lose." She put the chip down on the counter, sighing. "I might know what I am now, but I still don't know *why* and I don't know how to stop it."

There was no blame, only tiredness. A tiredness because of how the world and fate had treated her. She was lost in a world made around her.

With dry eyes and a heavy heart, Natalia turned on her heels, shoved on some shoes, and left the house.

The café was bustling.

Alex had changed the calendar over before opening. It was officially September first.

She knew that was the reason so many kids were here today. They'd be back at school tomorrow, so this was their last full day of freedom, their last chance to cram in some cold coffees and ice-creams and ocean swims.

While Venderly was small, and there were fewer kids here compared to Atlantis, there had been enough of them to keep Alex and Noah busy all morning. It took until nearly noon for them to catch a break. Alex snuck out back with a glass of water and a plain flapjack as a reward.

"Haven't seen it that busy in weeks," Noah commented as he followed her.

"Not since my starter week," she agreed.

Noah hopped onto the little stool by the counter. "You used to it here yet?"

"To be honest, I never thought I'd get used to doing anything outside my Purpose. I never thought I *could*."

"Why? From what I've seen, you're good at it."

"Good at what?"

"Defusing situations, being direct, but also being happy and agreeable."

Alex tilted her head, and a sliver of hair fell over her eyes. She stuffed her flapjack in her mouth, undid the band holding her hair, and retied it. "Are they supposed to be compliments?" she asked through her mouthful.

Noah grimaced. "Did they not sound like it?"

"Not really, no." She laughed at his muddled face.

"What I meant is that you can calm people, that they don't overrun you, that you can keep a queue in order without riots."

Alex sorted and chewed the rest of her snack. Usually, it was *her* that started trouble. But maybe that was also why she could help control situations.

Noah left when the lunchtime gaggle began to trickle in. Alex watched him go, taking her break seriously - Katherine always made sure she did - and part of Alex expected her head to pop round a corner at any moment. She ate her food and sipped her drink until every minute was used. Once done, she went out to swap with Noah, taking the orders while he filled them. They'd become accustomed to working like that in the past months.

Alex had always thought she'd been a solitary wolf, when, really, she'd had a pack all along. And she was trying to be better because of that. She was using her anger and rage for something else - not completely, but enough of it.

For probably only the second time in her life, change was positive.

"Get down off my counter!"

Jasper swayed his feet. "Make me, sea bitch."

Peri flicked out her trident. "I swear to all the Seven Gods that if you don't get your arse off my *clean counter*, I will make you legless!"

Peri waggled a finger to reinforce her motion and he grinned, but jumped down.

Jasper had come over to his brother and soon-to-be sister-in-law's house to simply have a chat with someone that wasn't himself. Every waking moment he was searching through either the books of magic he had or the ones Aero had brought. And every time he came away with more questions and less answers.

He felt like he was going mad.

Peri sighed and wobbled to the counter, flopping against it and leaning on it for support. She threw her trident on the counter, within arm's reach. Jasper eyed it cautiously. He'd been pricked by the damn thing before and it *hurt*.

"Now," she said, drawing his attention back to her. "Will you *sensibly* tell me what's going on?"

"Well, first of all, I'm hungry," he replied.

Peri's glare was devoid of humour. "Then get yourself something to eat."

"So you're going to let me run amok in your nice, *new* kitchen?"

Peri burst upright. "On second thought..." She started fiddling with the fridge, pulling out peppers and mushrooms and cheese. Eggs came out of the cupboard and Jasper's mouth watered. She was going to make one of her brilliant omelettes. "Go on then," she said as she worked. "What else?"

Jasper's grimaced as he tried to explain.

Jasper didn't know where he was.

A beautiful woman slid off a four-poster bed. Jasper tip-toed slowly, watching the woman as her burning red hair swayed in the wind that pressed against his cheeks. Her long white dress dragged around her ankles and sucked in at her curves.

She got to him first and placed a hand on his cheek, gliding her long fingers down with the lightness of a feather. The smell of roses washed off her skin. He somehow knew she was trying to be enticing, but he felt nothing but indifference towards her.

The woman leaned forwards, pressing her light pink lips to his ear. "Don't you want to kiss me?" she whispered. "Don't you wish to hold me, to take me?"

Jasper tugged himself free of the grip. "No."

She blinked. "No?"

"No," he reaffirmed.

"Don't you find me beautiful?"

"I do," he said. "But I don't find you desirable. So if you don't mind, and it's actually tough if you do, I'm leaving." He walked away, the smell of her fading fast.

A rougher voice echoed from behind him. "Are you looking for someone?"

Jasper whirled round and in the place of the woman was another. Hair in golden ringlets fell past small shoulders, and a silver band on intricately woven vines twisted around their forehead. They rubbed their bare arms and chest with tanned hands. A white cloth covered their middle.

"Shifter," Jasper murmured.

"Not quite," the person smiled. "If you wish to refer to me, I prefer neutral pronouns, please. And I am a Morph, well, I am the Morph. Morpheus himself."

"Then it's you I'm looking for."

Morpheus folded their arms. "And why is that?"

Jasper willed his voice to be calm. "I'm trying to find Natalia."

"Ah." Morpheus' smile indicated they'd just figured something out and

Jasper found it unnerving. "That would be why you did not find me desirable, and still do not. You seek a connection before a primal desire comes. And Natalia is all of that for you."

"Can you help me find her?"

Morpheus didn't draw attention to how Jasper had dodged their question. "Unfortunately, I cannot seek her out for you. You must wish to find her and I can open a pathway. Though, I must warn you, I have not physically seen her for some time. She has not come to see me, she is blocking me with a wall."

You're not the only one, *Jasper thought.*

"But I can show you what she dreamed of last?" Morpheus continued. They raised their arms towards the sky.

"One thing first," Jasper said, halting Morpheus mid-movement. "How did I get here? It took Natalia Crystals and a spell to get to you."

"I can draw people to me if I feel them wandering, lost in their minds as they sleep. I bring them here to guide them back where they belong. I work through dreams and you were searching in yours."

"So you drew me to you?"

"I felt you in the space between your world and this one, not quite in the land of dreams but not close to the world of the awake."

Jasper nodded, which was clearly enough for Morpheus because they changed the scenery.

Banners and dazzling colours swayed. Laughter bubbled in the air. While the rest of the vision was blurry, like he was peering at it through tear-filled eyes, Jasper could make out two shapes at the centre of it all.

Dancing together was himself and Natalia.

Jasper stepped back, breathless. This was the Flower Parade. They'd danced together in Atlantis, just before Alex had come along and mentioned Lemonspark – a Fairy drink that could intoxicate nearly anyone. He could remember how bringing that drink up had broken his and Natalia's spell. But that hadn't been the end.

What he also remembered was that this was one of the first times Jasper had really looked at Natalia, that this was the first moment he noticed his heart stir viciously in his chest because of her.

"It's beautiful," Morpheus said. They pulled a tissue from somewhere and blew their nose into it, then dabbed under their eyes.

"Are you always this dramatic or am I just receiving special treatment?" Jasper asked.

"If we're to talk in truths..." Morpheus tucked the tissue away and folded the image around them until they stood in a red, sandy area. "I will tell you one. Your Natalia feels sad, like she has failed. You two must reconnect and she must explain. And you can encourage her to return here. The rest of what she seeks is here. I think she knows that yet refuses to find it. Her sadness blinds her. She is strong, she is, and while she is a whole person on her own, you give her that missing piece that makes her extra special."

"Are you saying—"

"I am saying nothing." They plucked a red flower from within their jacket and handed it to Jasper. "This is from her."

Jasper accepted the flower. "From Natalia?"

"She is a Fairy and they tell stories with flowers," Morpheus explained. "She wondered if you'd come wandering and told me to pass this gift on to you if I ever found you."

"Thank you."

"Do not thank me, for it was not my gift." Jasper turned away but a hand clutched his shoulder, forcing him to stop. "I hate for our parting words to be these, but I must warn you. Hell has been awfully quiet recently and silence from Monsters is never good."

"They said Hell was quiet?" Peri questioned once Jasper had recounted his dream to her. "That doesn't sound good."

Jasper's brows furrowed. "No, it doesn't."

Peri served up the omelette she'd cooked for him, folded and dribbled with hot sauce. "I suggest you eat up and go and find

Natalia. It's time you two bash your heads together, once and for all. This idiocy can't continue any longer."

For once, Jasper didn't argue.

Well that date was horrendous, Zoe thought as she stomped away. Sure, the girl had been nice enough – cute name, cuter smile – but she had a boring personality.

Recently Zoe had been craving adventure, something to make her heart race. This had made it flat-line without being fatal. Somewhere during the date, Zoe had started counting the number of tiles beneath her feet, the forks she could see, and every sigh she made.

Rounding a corner, she bumped into something. Whatever it was, it snarled.

Zoe lifted her chin. A brown haired, beady eyed, *thing* peered down at her. She wanted to scream but before she could make a sound it dissolved in on itself. Aero appeared as the ash fell. His fangs were bared and his sword was drawn.

Her tongue flicked around the inside of her suddenly dry mouth. She looked to Aero for guidance but he turned away. She blinked, thinking he was ignoring her. But then something rushed up to both of them and he cut it down before it could fully reach them.

"What the *fuck!*" she yelled in surprise.

Aero glanced over his shoulder at her and blinked. "What the *what?*" he asked, turning to join her side.

"'ave you never heard a girl swear before?"

"I have. Just never quite so crudely or proclaimed so boldly."

"You'd be bold in your shock too if some bloody thing came for you and was then killed by a Vampire *with a sword!*"

Aero slipped the sword into its sheath. "I'm sorry?" He posed it like a question.

"Are you apologising or do you not understand?"

"Maybe both?"

She laughed. "I appreciate being saved, but don't get too distracted by the language I use. I've barely had one Monster lesson and I'm still wholly unprepared for everythin'."

Aero nodded fiercely. "I have noted it."

She smiled and a thought occurred. "I never properly thanked you."

His face contorted. "You just did?"

"No, not for that. You've now saved me twice—"

The ground erupted. A Monster with six legs and a floppy tail appeared. Then another Monster appeared. And another four. *Kifflegger*, her mind pieced together, remembering the description from Noah's scrambled notes.

Aero had transformed into a blur by the time Zoe blinked. He dashed in circles around the Monsters, speeding and slicing at them like he was a main character in some action film. The Monsters all fell to ash, disappearing into tiny cracks in the ground.

Gawking, Zoe partly forgot about the loose ground the Monsters had exploded out of. She tripped trying to get to Aero. But, before she hit the floor, she was caught. She cursed herself for falling into another Monster but when she dared look up, Aero's face stared down, smiling. He was sweaty yet utterly beautiful; the fangs kind of heated the *thing* he had going on.

Zoe felt like she was in some movie. With her heart all out of rhythm, she reached up, but stopped at the last moment. Aero's gaze dipped to her lips. That was all Zoe needed.

The kiss was delicate and sweet, and Zoe wanted to deepen it. She didn't want it to end. There was too much tension crashing around them, pulling them together.

They broke apart. His eyes burned into hers, a heat resonating from his hands. A smile sprung to her lips. Aero's face twisted between confusion, stunned awe, and then boyish shyness. The fangs were gone, however, and she had to admit she missed them.

He pulled her upright. "That was—"

"For saving me *three* times," she cut in.

Aero laughed and slowly removed his hands, though not entirely, holding one of her hands. He watched their joined hands. "I was going to say that was a Gods blessed moment."

Zoe gasped dramatically. "Are you saying I'm heavenly?"

He laughed. "I'm saying I was blessed by the Heavens to have had that moment with you."

She kissed the side of his mouth and heard him sigh. Her grin broke her face and she kissed him properly.

And then Aero, and the rest of the world, disappeared.

Natalia had wandered town for a little while but the anger and frustration hadn't been stomped out. Eventually she settled on going to the café. She wasn't on the rota to work but a muffin full of sugar sounded good, like self-care.

The door's bell tinged as she went in and she strolled up to the desk Alex was manning. She smiled brightly. Natalia's gut pinched, her shoulder blades ached. She couldn't help thinking how *she* should've been behind that desk instead.

Stop, she scolded herself. *Alex is your friend, you turd.*

There was no reason to be jealous or upset. It was just displaced anger and she knew it. Alex deserved none of it.

"And what can I get you lovely lady?" Alex teased. Her wild hair was fully tucked up today, showing off her facial piercings clearly.

Natalia perused the cake case already knowing *exactly* what she wanted. "Can I have a—"

"Princess?"

She just had enough time to steal a glance at her best friend before he blipped out of existence two seconds before she followed.

Cups and a giant tea-pot sat in the middle of a round table. Natalia's brain rattled inside her skull and her stomach swam in her abdomen; she'd forgotten magic travel was a thing, and had forgotten how much she hated it.

"Natalia, my dear?"

She took a deep breath. One minute she'd been in the café and now she was in a white room. Noah sat at her right, looking sickly, and Zoe sat at her left positively beaming. Opposite them was Gold, his monocle suspiciously absent. Evangeline sipped from one of the delicate floral tea-cups already.

Natalia blanched at the last person at the table. "Kiva?"

"Ah," Gold wistfully said.

"Hello," Kiva said at the same time, waving enthusiastically.

Silence fell.

"Tea, anyone?" Evangeline offered.

"Oh yes!" Zoe cheered. "Fill me up!" She snatched her own cup too eagerly.

"Please," Noah nodded.

Natalia glared at them all. "Can we slow down for a minute here?" She fixed her sights on Gold as Evangeline went about filling up everyone's cups. "Why are we here? Where even *is* here?" She was determined to touch nothing, believe nothing.

Gold pulled out his pocket-watch. "We're in my little escape room," he said. "Though it's a place to escape to, not from."

"So, a panic room?" Zoe commented.

"Precisely!" Gold flicked his watch closed and tucked it away. He looked over at Natalia and she noticed how dull his gold eye appeared without the monocle outlining it. "I had it built for me years ago. Before the black plague, if I remember rightly. Some would call it a white void, a magical space with breathable air. I use it as an extension of my house and I love it." Evangeline unsubtly rolled her eyes at him.

"That explains the where," Natalia said. "But why are we here? Why *all* of us?" She indicated to the table, to Kiva the most – she was the youngest here – who was helping herself to a strawberry topped cupcake from the centre stand that hadn't been there moments before.

"Kiva was an accident, I will admit."

Zoe spat out some tea. "Way to be blunt, damn."

Gold wiped himself though he had not been sprayed. "What I meant is that she was trying to speak to you and entered the café behind you when Evangeline cast her magic to bring you all here."

Natalia turned to Kiva. "I didn't see you?"

Kiva bit into the cake, cream oozing down the left side of her mouth. "I was behind you," she mumbled. "But not that close. Noah spotted me."

Natalia looked at her best friend. "Is that what you were trying to indicate too?" Noah nodded as Evangeline picked her cup up silently.

"So I *meant*," Gold shot a purposeful glare at Zoe, "that she was caught up by accident."

"I don't mind," Kiva said, shrugging. "As long as the tea's hot and the cupcakes keep coming, I'll be fine."

Gold sat back in his chair. "You're here, all of you, because we need to talk about someone's honesty."

Natalia's cheeks flamed as everyone's attention shifted to her. "What? I never lied about anything."

"You did not. I quite agree on *that* fact," Evangeline reaffirmed, finally speaking. "However, you still kept the truth, and it's tearing away at your friends who are both here and not."

"I couldn't bring everyone." Gold shrugged. "This room and

this table simply aren't big enough."

Evangeline ignored. "And it's tearing at *you*. It's time you finally corrected that, for Hell has been silent, and that only means trouble is coming."

You'll need each other, Natalia's mind decoded, hearing the words that hadn't been spoken. Evangeline gave her a pointed look like she knew exactly what had just puzzle pieces had just clicked inside Natalia's head.

Natalia averted her gaze and spied Gold pulling a flower from his jacket. He held it out towards her.

A *red carnation*, she recognised. The flower spun as she took it and twirled it between her finger and thumb. Some part of her brain, some ingrained Fairy guidebook part of her brain, recognised it. *My heart aches for you.*

Her attention snapped to Gold. "Now, go," he ordered before she could speak.

Natalia's breath caught as everything vanished.

The second his brother had turned up at the door, Archie had known he needed to get away. He loved his brother, of course he did, but Archie was already silently stressing about little fish's due date and wanted just a few moments of peace to try and get himself prepared for being a father – not that there was any way he could prepare for something so life-changing.

Shopping had been his runaway excuse.

Returning home, he expected to see the walls alight given his brother's recent misuse of magic. Surprisingly, there was nothing. The hallway was empty, besides building and decorating tools, and his girlfriend and brother were in the kitchen.

While Peri was washing dishes, Jasper had sprawled himself face-down on the floor. So it appeared everything wasn't all well and good, but it was better than Archie's low expectations, which was nice.

"He's not dead," Peri explained to Archie as he dropped the groceries on the counter.

Archie watched Jasper's back rising and falling. "I wasn't worried."

The doorbell rang and Peri asked Jasper to get it. Jasper mumbled "yes mum" and disappeared from the room, crawling along the floor.

Peri threw the sponge in the bubbly sink. "I swear," she whispered. "If he doesn't sort himself out, I will make him eat seaweed for every meal for a week."

Archie laughed and kissed the top of her head. "What's he done?"

Peri looked over his shoulder and sighed. "Nothing, and that's the problem. I told him he needed to sort things out with Natalia and he agreed, but once he'd eaten he sank on the floor and didn't move."

"Drama Witch," Archie agreed.

"He said he didn't know what to say or do. He's worried about being too pushy and doesn't want to impose where he's not wanted. Which I get, I do. But he *is* wanted and so is she. They need to communicate and–"

Archie cut her off with a swift kiss. She melted into him and he groaned against her. She reached up, snaking her fingers through his hair, as he raked his hands down her back.

She gasped against him, but it was a different kind of sound to normal so he pulled back. Peri's eyes were wide, alarmed. She looked down towards their feet.

"*Amore?*" she asked quietly. Then her eyes grew wider again and she made a small noise that sounded like, "oh".

Kiva knocked on the Darby's front door before Natalia could stop her. Zoe happily swung her arms while Noah looked as peaky as Natalia felt. When the door swung in, all the words and curses and horrible noises Natalia wanted to make caught in her throat.

"Jasper."

His emerald eyes found her bronzed ones, making her realise she'd spoken aloud.

"Come on everyone," Zoe's voice filtered through the humming in the air. "Let's leave them alone for a minute."

Noah squeezed Natalia's hand before slipping past Jasper. The others shuffled into the house.

"You have a flower."

They weren't quite the first words she'd been expecting from him. She blinked and saw that he had the exact same flower in his hand. Daylight made the red as vibrant as pumping blood and, knowing what the flower represented, it was apt.

Jasper waved his arm as a direction and Natalia followed without question. Silently, they went all the way to his room. And when they got there, they collapsed.

His arms found her, or had she found him? It didn't matter. They surrounded themselves with the other. They tightened the grip they had on the other person as if they might just float away. It was as if they were both holding on, willing their broken parts to fuse back together, to alter and correct, to mend and become whole.

Natalia felt herself doing just that. She wasn't the same as before, how could she be? She was something else now, a body and mind of mixture. But her heart and soul were shaping back together again, becoming what they had once been.

With a gasp, her wings fluttered out. The room came alive with shimmers of colour. Even Jasper had little pebbles of purples and oranges and bronzes dancing along his skin. His hand looped its way to the top of a wing. A shudder coursed through her body. It weakened her knees and she fell against him further.

They kissed with a fire that could sear ice.

Natalia placed her hands to his chest and pushed, forcing him onto the bed. He grinned devilishly as she crawled up him and lowered herself, bringing her lips to his. He swerved past the kiss and caught the edge of her wings again, causing her to shudder into him. He laughed but stopped moving his hand against her bronze and glassy edge, but captured her face with his other hand.

This kiss was gentler but spoke loudly. It spoke of all the "*I miss you's*". It told of all the ways in which they knew each other. It yelled all the goodbyes and hellos.

In that moment Natalia understood why her heart had ached so hard.

"Thank you for my flower," he whispered, pecking at her jawline and cheeks.

"Thank you for *my* flower."

Jasper stopped and sat up, holding Natalia on his lap so she wouldn't fall. "What? I didn't send you a flower..."

Natalia blinked and looked to where the flowers were discarded in a cross by the door. "And I didn't send you a flower." She turned back to him. "Gold gave me mine, saying it was from you."

He shook his head though a smile was creeping in. "I think we've been set up."

"How'd you know that?"

"Because Morpheus gave me mine, saying you'd told them too."

"I didn't..." Then the rest of his words filtered through her brain and she became overly warm. Dust began to spin around them. She shuffled off his lap and sat before him on her knees. "You went to Morpheus? Why?"

"Because you weren't talking to any of us," he admitted. "You wouldn't even let us know if you were alright!"

She scowled, hard. "So you tracked me down?"

"I hardly tracked you. I didn't even find you. But what was I supposed to do? Wait another month for you to come back? Wait until you were in danger? Wait until you were minutes away from *death?*"

Natalia's chest began to crackle inside. "Did you not trust me to come back?"

The expression of pain Jasper wore made it worse. "You didn't trust us enough to stay."

She clenched her fists as her dust stilled mid-air. "I was trying to protect you *from* me."

"I could've helped you."

"And I could've hurt you."

"You've hurt us more by staying away. It really was like you didn't trust us enough to help. As if you didn't care if we cared or not. As if you didn't care if *I* cared or not."

"I know you care. I just wanted to keep you safe." Natalia dipped her head, unable to bear how his eyes were tearing anymore just when hers were doing the same. "I'm a Monster, Jasper."

"Stop!" he cried out. Her gaze flew to him in shock, all tears frozen. "You've *never* been a Monster, Natalia Primrose Whitebell. You may have some shared powers, maybe even on paper you are genetically partly the same, but that doesn't make you one."

"But I *am* one."

"And I love you anyway!"

Natalia's next cry lodged in her throat. The tears flooded. She tasted the salt and then she tasted Jasper.

In seconds, his t-shirt was gone and so was hers. Her hands tangled in his hair and his fumbled with her trousers. She gasped against his mouth when he tugged them away and touched the tops of her thighs. He smiled against her mouth.

Knocking came at the door and Jasper threw himself in front of Natalia as a barricade, cursing heavily when it opened.

Evangeline stood in the doorway but with her back to them as if to give them some sense of privacy despite interrupting. She never turned to peer over her shoulder, yet Natalia was still glad to be hidden by Jasper.

"When you're finished, I need your assistance, Natalia," Evangeline said.

Natalia peeped further round Jasper, her curiosity peaking. "My assistance? With what?"

"If you haven't heard, your friend is having her baby."

From somewhere downstairs, like she'd been waiting for everyone's undivided attention, Peri screamed.

"**I** WANT NATALIA!" Peri shrieked.

Evangeline shuffled Kiva, Noah, and his sister, Zoe, away. Archie was currently on the phone to his sister, dragging her home from work. That left the near immortal messy Creature with an *in labour* Mermaid.

"What do you need from me, my dear?" Gold asked, appearing at Evangeline's side. He was dressed in a red suit, something unusual, but his hands were covered with leather-looking black gloves to match his shirt.

Evangeline narrowed her eyes. "What unholy moment are you dressed for?"

Peri screamed again, crying until the glasses in the cabinets shook, drowning out Gold's response.

Evangeline ran to the girl and grabbed her hand, slipping her free arm around her body. She was already sweating. Labour could last hours, maybe even days. Evangeline knew from experience.

Her labour with her first child had taken nearly two full days to come to the end, and back then there'd been hardly any acceptable medicines. Thankfully, there *had* been Witch potions, but the pain and aches and tearing had been worth it.

Easing Peri off the floor wasn't easy. Evangeline managed to raise her but Gold had to come and help when they both got stuck. Together they led the girl through to the living room, Archie following like a startled deer.

"Get some towels and warm water," Evangeline directed. Gold rushed off immediately.

"What about the hospital?" Archie asked, slipping his phone into his pocket. His brows were furrowed, his skin taut, eyes hollow with nerves. It was easy to see how much seeing his girlfriend in pain hurt him.

"Darling, no," Evangeline said softly. "She's a *Mermaid*."

"Natalia!" Peri cried, reaching out for Archie.

Archie blinked. "Right." He still didn't understand, that was clear.

"She doesn't need a hospital," Evangeline explained. "She needs the water."

"Water?"

"Peri?"

Evangeline looked up at the new voice to see Natalia, followed by Jasper. Both looked slightly dishevelled. Evangeline hid her smile. Watching the pair of them now reminded her of herself and her Edmund. She'd been young once.

"Where the Seven Hells have you been?" Peri yelled at Natalia.

Natalia gaped a little before responding. "Why do you want me?"

"You're part of the plan!"

"What plan?"

"The one I've had scribbled in my brain for a few weeks. You're a bloody Fairy!" Her face strained and twisted for an agonising moment, then relaxed. "You're helping me get this baby out."

Natalia turned to Archie. "I'm *what?*"

Archie's smile was soft, though strained a little. "Fairies are supposedly good healers," he answered. "She wants your help."

"What about you?" Natalia questioned.

"Oh, don't worry. I'm the emotional mess and you're the professional medical support," he said kindly.

Evangeline observed them all. They were so young, but this life taught everyone how to grow up fast. "Shall we go?" she asked calmly.

"I'll stay," Jasper decided. "Keep an eye on things here."

"Don't do anything stupid," Archie told him, his level-headed demeanour returning.

Jasper winked and said, "Now, would I do something like that?"

There was a chorus of "yes's" and Jasper laughed.

Gold re-entered the room with a raised eyebrow, a bowl of water, and towels slung over his shoulder. Jasper gave him a nod as he left.

Peri's next scream came. Evangeline nodded, if only to herself, and called on her impossible magic. A hole in the room opened and it stole them all away to the beach.

Archie had never been so terrified in all his life.

Peri's body was in the sea, naked from the waist down, though respectfully covered by some of Evangeline's magic; it manifested like a cloud that moved when she did. Her hair had been scrappily tied back but strands kept falling out. Lady Gaga - Peri's favourite and part of her birthing plan to make her relax - was blasting from a speaker half-buried in the sand.

Night was drawing in. They'd been here for hours already. It wasn't cold but Archie shivered. He kept glancing from Evangeline to Natalia - who looked pale, even in the dark - for a way in which they might subtly ask him to help, or to give any sort of direction. He felt useless, like he should be doing more, and his agitation grew every time Peri cried to the sea-living things to literally bite her as it would been less painful.

So Archie did what normal, little things he could.

He stroked her shoulders when she asked. Suffered the strength of her hand when she squeezed. Gave her water to drink in sips. Dabbed her forehead with a cloth when she grew sweatier. Even kissed her head or whispered lovely things when she could listen.

It never felt *enough*.

"I want little fish out!" Peri yelled as another contraction came.

Evangeline checked beneath her cloud and said Peri was getting close now. Archie hated seeing his love in pain and considered magicking the pain away, transferring it to him. She glared at him every time he thought of it like she knew where his mind had gone and didn't agree with it. So instead he offered the potion Evangeline had provided. She'd called it an "old concoction" of magic and herbs that would aid with the pain.

"How much longer?" he asked as he stroked Peri's forehead.

Evangeline sighed. "Not much past midnight."

What does that even mean? he thought.

Then midnight came.

"Push!" Evangeline yelled.

Peri hunched forwards and screamed as she bore down. Then she was being told to relax.

The cycle kept repeating.

Every time, it was like Peri was being told to force out her very heart and soul. There was a feeling of being torn from a part of herself at her own body's wishes. But she didn't care. All she cared about was getting her baby out.

The pain was nearly unbearable. She'd read and seen enough to know it would be, but nothing had prepared her for how *bad* it could be, even with magic on their side. Being pregnant had its challenges. This was another. And she was just so *tired*. She just wanted her little fish. No more pain and no more pregnancy.

"Push!" Evangeline yelled again.

"Alright!" Peri yelled back.

"Then actually push," Natalia told her, though a little cautious. She was doing whatever Evangeline told her to do, but Peri didn't put much into understanding what.

"I bloody am and I'll stab you if you think otherwise!"

"If you can yell, you can push," Evangeline said. "On your next contraction!"

Peri *pushed*.

Pressure had built before, when she'd known her baby's head had crowned, but now it burned. Hands fumbled around her vagina as she screamed into the night. She bore down harder, following through with the pain and the pressure.

Relief followed.

She was told to push again, and a moment later she was being handed a bundle of blood and mucus. Natalia laid it on her chest and covered them both with a towel.

It took Peri a second to realise she was crying. Another to realise that Archie was beside her, crying too. Then one last one to realise she was holding her baby.

I'm holding my baby! She thought, just as the baby screamed.

"Fish," Archie whispered, tentatively reaching out and putting a single finger to their baby's cheek.

Evangeline appeared on Peri's other side. "May I?"

Peri didn't know what she meant but nodded. Evangeline quickly took the baby and rubbed it gently, then wrapped it in another, cleaner, towel. She handed the baby back. Fish's eyes were half-closed, apparently done with screaming for now.

Peri tucked her baby against her. "Seven Hells," she cursed, taking in a lungful of air. The bundle of joy in her arms wiggled. Sensing what he needed, she lifted her top and little fish latched onto her breast, beginning to suckle naturally.

"He looks healthy." Evangeline smiled. "Has he got a name?"

Archie and Peri exchanged a glance. When they'd taken the old family tree, the name had been so obvious it had basically jumped off the page.

At the same time, they smiled and said, "Yes."

"Are you going to leave us in suspense?" Natalia asked, sitting back on her knees. "How about we don't do that?"

Peri laughed and caught Evangeline's eye. "Edmund," she answered. "Edmund Mattias Darby."

A glint entered Evangeline's eye, one visible even in the dark. "Oh," she sighed. She touched a finger to the baby's nose. "Another baby Darby."

"Another baby Edmund Darby," Archie told her.

Evangeline's eyes widened, tears springing up in the corners. She sniffed and wiped at her nose with her wrist. "Bless you," she whispered. "Bless you both, and bless your child. Maybe the Gods bless them, too."

The saying was an old traditional one of Creature's. It meant good wishes, good tidings, and good health on all that was new. It was thought that there was power in words, even in the ones untouched by magic, and it has always been believed that these words would indeed bring forth what was wished.

Peri thought she saw a faint blue halo around their little fish's head, but when she blinked it was gone. Exhaustion was clearly setting in. But *damn* it was worth it. And she'd do it all over again.

Archie leant down and kissed Peri's head. "Bless us both," he whispered in her ear.

Peri transferred the kiss to their son. "Bless us all."

Natalia was still shaking.

She walked down the street, narrowly avoiding lampposts and tripping off the curb. She tried to act calm but the jitters held their own in her body.

Helping to deliver the baby, little Edmund Mattias, had given Natalia this *rush* she couldn't explain. She'd been able to see actual magic flow from Peri. Evangeline had not instructed her to do anything more than prepare to take the baby once born. Everything else she'd done, from reaching for the baby's head to delivering the placenta, had been instinct. On *Fairy* instinct.

It simply felt *good*.

Natalia remembered from her lessons that not all Fairies were good healers, but they could be if they tried. She'd been in the process of becoming a nurse anyway, so there was a possibility she could make it work.

After the birth, Evangeline had transferred them back to Archie and Peri's new house so they'd be comfortable. Peri had been taken directly upstairs by Evangeline to wash and lay-down – she needed to rest now for a few days. Archie had cleaned the baby in the sink under Evangeline's instructions once she'd come back down. Gold had watched intently, like he was about to pull out a straw and suck up the blood from the sink – he didn't, but it looked close.

Natalia had left them to it, leaving for her own house and the silence that resided there, needing rest of her own.

Noah met her outside the café a few hours later. Unexpectedly, Katherine stood there too. For a moment, dread filled Natalia. She hadn't seen Katherine since their fight – it was more of a one sided affair... Katherine shuddered when Natalia approached and she marvelled in the reaction. A second kind of rush in one day burst along her veins, like she had power.

Natalia quashed the feeling quick.

"Have fun at the Darby's," Katherine said.

Natalia studied her. "What? Am I not working today?"

Katherine licked her pink lips. "No," she smiled. "I'll watch the café. You go spend time with your friends. Both of you."

"But, who—"

"Alex is taking the shift today."

Natalia didn't know how to respond and Katherine spared her from having to. She turned away, walking inside, letting the door close behind her. Noah waved goodbye even though Katherine had already gone.

"Why would Alex pick up a shift today?" Natalia asked, still facing the café.

Noah shrugged. "Maybe she needs some time away? It's a big change in all their lives again and Alex isn't the most peace-friendly."

Natalia nodded, accepting it, and they started to walk on.

Plenty of questions spewed from Noah's mouth on the way. He asked about the birth, how Peri and the baby were, if Archie passed out, how Natalia had handled it. Natalia answered truthfully, that things had gone well. If she was honest with herself, considering she'd had no warning, it had gone better than she expected.

"Hey," he held his hands up defensively, "you were training to be a nurse."

She laughed. "Noah, training and jumping to action are two *very* different things."

"The only thing I've trained for so far is how to run away."

"Well, then you'll see how different it is when you're told to run away during a real fight."

He pulled a face and they carried on.

Ashturn Close was a far cry from Opal Street. The houses were made of red brick and slanted roofs. The gardens were smaller, but the space inside the houses made up for it. Natalia had only been here a handful of times since Peri and Archie bought the place - once earlier this morning - but she knew what house was theirs because it had a door painted like an ocean wave.

Archie answered Noah's knocking. His face was beaming, green eyes wild though a little tired.

"They're in the living room," Archie said, stepping aside so they could come in.

"I brought you these," Noah announced. Natalia hadn't seen the bunch of flowers he carried until he handed them out. "Congratulations."

Archie smiled, taking the flowers and hugging Noah in appreciation. "Thank you," he beamed. "I'll follow behind you and Peri will be down in a minute."

"Isn't she supposed to be resting?" Natalia asked.

Archie scoffed. "She slept a little but you know she can't be forced to stay still for long." He waved a hand outwardly to let them walk through.

Noah led the way confidently and Natalia trailed after, curious as to *whom* was in the living room if it wasn't Peri.

The space was barely furnished. A green sofa was pushed against the back wall, a glass coffee table in front of it, with two oversized chairs on either side of the sofa. The only other thing in the room was a picture of Peri and Archie at the beach, framed in gold, which hung beside the door.

"He's sleeping." Jasper huddled in one of the oversized chairs with Edmund curled against his chest, cradled into his neck.

"You both look adorable," Natalia whispered as her heart twinged.

"You do," Noah agreed, taking the other chair.

Jasper's laugh was silent. "Thanks, but I'm not ready for my own yet."

"Neither am I," Natalia blurted. Her cheeks heated when she realised the implications of what she'd said.

"Noah?" Jasper asked, patting Edmund's back as he stirred.

Noah nodded and Jasper carefully got up. He slowly passed over the swaddled baby. Noah welcomed tiny Edmund, who shifted to pop one arm out of his swaddle but carried on sleeping.

Jasper nodded towards the back door and Natalia understood that they needed to talk. Careful to tip-toe and close the door gently, they moved together.

Once outside, Jasper opened his mouth first. "When you are ready for kids, let me know. I'll consider passing on my pure genetics. But marriage? *You* can definitely propose to me and I want nothing half-arsed. I deserve better than that." He smirked.

"Rose petals, doves, that kind of thing?"

"Oh, at the very *least*. I'm envisioning a horse-drawn carriage to sweep me away too."

Natalia gave a mocking bow. "Your wish is my command." She crept closer to him until they were inches apart. "But, that's a few years off in my future. I'm only eighteen."

Jasper grinned. "And your wish is *my* command. Everything is in your hands."

"You're giving me the power? That's dangerous."

Laughing, he closed the gap between them and pressed his forehead to hers. "I forgive you, Nat. I'd forgiven you a long time ago. I was just mad at myself for not seeing you were hurting, for not seeing you were trying to keep us safe yet needed us at the same time"

Tears threatened to overflow and she sniffed. "I was pushing you away to keep you safe." She sniffed again. "I thought that if I kept you away, you wouldn't get hurt. Peri had already lost an arm and could've lost a baby. I know you all have a choice in this, and I should've let it be your decision on what you wanted to do, but selfishly I couldn't watch those things happen again. I couldn't watch any of you lose your life." She dropped her head but he caught her chin with a finger, forcing her gaze back to his.

"Nat—"

"I should've trusted you to help, should've trusted that you could keep yourselves safe. You train for your entire *lives* for this sort of thing."

His green eyes watered. "Not quite *this*," he said, smiling weakly. "We haven't trained on how to keep some evil hooded figure from grabbing another Creature because somehow she's actually a Creature *and* a Monster. I think that goes outside anyone's normal training."

"I can't imagine the Council giving everyone notes on those kinds of things."

"Exactly. But yes, you should've trusted us."

Natalia's heart pounded. "I know."

There had been no sign of storm-clouds brewing but suddenly the sky opened on them both.

"We can protect ourselves and we could've protected you," Jasper continued, unbothered by the rain, even as it ran down his face. "We're on your side, Natalia. I promise that whatever is happening, we're always going to be on your side. We're willing to fight for you and we will. *I'm* willing to fight for you."

Natalia clasped his t-shirt in her fists and pulled him down to her.

Jasper broke away first and Natalia couldn't help feeling a little disappointed. He glanced away from her, looking up a window in the house, and signalled to whoever he could see there that she couldn't.

Natalia tried looking. "What's going on?"

He held her tighter. "Hold on."

"Jasper—"

"Trust me."

"I do."

He pecked her lips, just as the floor fell away.

Noah held onto baby Edmund with all the care and love in the world.

Briefly, he watched as the baby opened his eyes, squirmed, then went to sleep again. Noah smiled. He didn't remember Zoe being born, but he remembered the love that had surrounded her.

"How is he?"

Peri staggered into the room, holding her stomach. She wore a long dress that swished at her ankles, which she hiked up when she sat down awkwardly. Noah grimaced when she winced.

"Sleeping," Noah answered.

"Just like his father. So content in sleep." Peri laughed and then let out a little hiss.

"Still in pain?" Archie asked as he came through. The flowers Noah had brought over were in a little vase and Archie popped them onto the table.

"You would be too if you pushed out something like a seven pound baby from your vagina," Peri told him plainly.

"Remind me to never do that." Archie kissed the top of her head. "Do you need anything for the pain? Do you want anything for yourself?"

She tilted her head from side to side. "A peanut butter sandwich wouldn't hurt. I haven't eaten since yesterday."

"One sandwich coming right up." Archie kissed her head again and dashed off.

She smiled and shook her head as he went. Her smile remained as said, "Thank you for the flowers, Noah. You didn't have to but I appreciate it."

Edmund fussed in Noah's arms and he tried to move him carefully to the other shoulder. When he wouldn't settle, Peri reached out her arm.

"I think he needs feeding again," she decided.

They shuffled and moved until the baby was back in his mother's arms. Noah flexed his hand, a little in relief at being able to move again.

Peri shifted herself and slipped off the arm of her dress. She took out her breast and moved Edmund to it, where he latched on after a little squirming. She looked back up at Noah, and blinked like she'd forgotten he was there. "Oh," she said. "I didn't think to cover up, I—"

"No," Noah blurted. He shook his head at her raised eyebrow. "While I'm uncomfortable with nudity in general, I do think that no one should have to cover themselves up when they're doing something as natural as feeding their baby. We don't hide under blankets when we eat, so why hide a child?"

Archie strolled back into the room, plated sandwich in hand. Peri pointed between him and Noah. "I like him a lot," she announced. "Can we keep him?"

"Me?" Noah laughed.

Archie kissed her head. "Of course."

Peri's attention honed in on the food and she smiled. "Ooh."

Noah rubbed his palms on his trousers awkwardly. "I'll take that as my cue to leave," he said, not unkindly.

"I can get you home?" Archie offered.

"That sounds slightly sketchy."

Peri grinned. "You sound like Natalia. Speaking of, where is she? I thought I heard her?"

"You did," Archie agreed. "She was here. So was my brother." Peri waggled her eyebrows.

"They were talking and then they vanished," Noah said.

"Well, it's safe to assume they're fine if they're together."

Noah tried not to fidget and show off his mild concern. Jasper was powerful and so was Natalia. Recent events where they hadn't worked so well together were behind them... Jasper knew about Natalia's powers and what she was. That dust had settled. Archie was right. They were fine.

"Just take my hands and picture your house," Archie said, approaching.

"Is that how this works?" Noah asked, coming out of his mind.

"You might feel a little queasy, but a lot less compared to when you portal travelled."

Noah's stomach squeezed at the memory. To keep the rising bile down, he closed his eyes and took Archie's hands.

His body fell away and the ground came up to meet him at the same time. He coughed when he hit the floor, the motion forcing air out of his lungs, and his eyes flung open.

Magic travel, he thought sourly. *Now I understand Princess' hatred. Ugh. Good God I want to throw up.*

His insides coiled like a snake. How did Witches do that all the time? He groaned when he realised they'd only moved part of an island over, hardly any distance compared to other jumps he knew of.

Archie waved and disappeared again, leaving Noah on his kitchen floor. It was hard to tell how long he'd been lying there before a foot nudged his side. He groaned at the presence, wishing it would leave him to endure the sickness until it passed.

"You dead?" Zoe's voice asked.

Noah flipped onto his back, staring up at his sister. "I feel like I am."

"Wha'ever. You need to come and look at somethin'."

More waves crashed inside his roiling stomach. "Is it important?"

"More important than me kicking you while you're down, yeah."

Noah groaned and clambered to his feet, swallowing to keep the vomit down. Once Noah had found his legs, they walked through to the conservatory that over-looked the sea together – the bottom of the garden ended with a gate, and the sea could been seen beyond it as they lived near the edge of the Island but not right on top of the beach.

At first, Noah couldn't spot anything wrong. But as he followed

Zoe's pointing finger, he saw what she was seeing.

Seagulls, all on their backs and flattened out, beaks sloppily open littered the garden. *Dead.*

He blinked several times. Not once did the image shift. He turned to Zoe who shrugged.

Magical recoil? His brain brought the thought forward and he scowled at the birds again.

During his time with the Darby's, Noah had learnt plenty about magic. Magical recoil happened when a spell or enchantment couldn't reach its determined destination, meaning it bounced off target and was diverted elsewhere. It didn't happen much these days - Witches were skilled and chance of recoil was low; only the unskilled or unpractised had this happen to them. *Unless* the spell's intended target was protected by other magic.

It has to be, he decided. One of the seagulls closest twitched but then went still again.

He turned away, still fighting down nausea. Who was trying to spell something? Who had been the intended target? Noah gulped. A single thought latched in his brain, a spark of an idea blooming inside the depths.

"Noah?" Zoe asked cautiously.

He glanced at her. She opened her mouth and closed it several times, her eyes narrowing tighter each time. Eventually, she gave up on words and walked off briskly. Noah swallowed the lump in his throat and his heart stammered in his chest. For Zoe to be unable to form words, it was suspicious. Noah followed to try and question her.

As he passed by the hall mirror on the way upstairs, he was sure he caught the outline of his reflection shimmer. Noah threw his eyes away and hurried after Zoe with his head down.

Natalia landed somewhere familiar.

Jasper's room. We're in the Darby's house.

Hands touched her waist and guided her into Jasper's arms. His mouth came down to hers and she kisses him back. As much as magic travel sent her stomach spinning, this time she felt queasy with nerves. If things were going the way she thought they were ...

"Wait," she whispered. He stopped immediately, watching her. "Are... I haven't..."

He sucked in a breath and pulled back slightly. "We don't have to! Seven Gods *no*! I won't force you to do anything you don't want or don't feel comfortable with."

Bronze flushed her cheeks. "I *do* want to," she admitted, earning a glint from his eyes. "And I don't want *you* to do anything you're not comfortable with."

"With you," he pecked her lips, "I want it all."

She laughed. "What I *meant* was I haven't done this before." She face grew hotter. "I don't know..."

Jasper leaned in, whispering into her ear. "You don't need to explain anything. We'll dance together, if you want to?"

Her answer wasn't with words. She moved to kiss under his jaw, up his neck, along his cheek, up to his mouth. His grip on her sides tightened and a little noise came out of his mouth as her hands teased under his t-shirt.

In a switch, Jasper clutched her neck and tilted her head back to tower over her. His mouth slid from hers and down her throat. The heat she felt intensified as it spread to her entire body.

Not to be outdone, she wrapped her fingers into his t-shirt and thrust it upwards. He laughed and dragged it off the rest of the way himself. Hers was next. If she'd have known this was happening, she might've gotten Peri's opinion on what to wear, and it probably wouldn't have been the yellow set she'd chosen that morning.

Jasper didn't seem to mind at all. He eased her bra straps from her shoulders as slowly as he could, sending goose-bumps along her skin. She fumbled with his button and zipper, and pushed his trousers away with impatience. In between kisses, she caught him smiling, just as she was.

"Wait!" Jasper rushed to the door and locked it. She laughed. He reached for her again, speaking with a husky voice. "The only way I'll stop this time is if you asked me to."

"I'm pretty sure I won't."

He picked her up and carried her over to the bed. His hands glided along her body, feathering down her sides and halting at her inner thighs. His gaze left hers to settle on her body. She rose to kiss his neck, drawing out unexpected groan.

That only spurred her on.

She shuffled backwards and Jasper froze. However, when her bra came away in her hands, her chest rising and falling with fast movements, his eyes grew wide.

"Seven Gods damn me," Jasper mumbled.

Jasper pressed his lips to hers and then trailed down her body. This time, no clothes obstructed his path. His hands never strayed from her thighs, his grip only tightening.

A gasp escaped her when his hand moved up her leg to the centre of her heat. Jasper was gentle and wound himself around her more. She held onto him in return, kissing what she could, touching whatever else there was.

As he drew up her again, he clicked his fingers to make a pink cloud appear. Natalia went to ask him what was wrong when he pulled a small packet in front of them.

"I didn't want to presume," he whispered, kissing the corner of her mouth.

She smiled up at him. "I am on the pill, but it's better to be safe than sorry."

He lent closer, the heat of his body pooling over her skin. "Do you still want this? Want *me?*"

To answer his question, she captured his face with her hands and pulled him onto her. He laughed as they kissed, only drawing back to open the packet he held before coming back to her. His mouth touched over her light, running along her skin down to her breasts where he gently captured a nipple between his teeth. At the same time, his fingers continued to circle her centre, tease however he could. There was one moment where he slid two inside of her and she groaned against him. He did it again and again and again.

Jasper's eyes flashed to hers when a whimper left her lips. He slid up her body then, though his hand stayed in place. She didn't dare take her eyes off him as she took a hold of him, building him up as he was her. Their mouths crashed down on one another's again; his tongue asked for entrance, and she let him in.

She guided him closer to her and he moved as she wanted. Just as she positioned him at her centre, he slowly slid into her. He was careful, and made sure to move gradually. The whole time he peppered her with kisses and she stroked her nails up his back. When she caught his mouth again, she smiled against it to let him know it was alright, that she was fine and still wanted this.

Gradually, he built them up together. Pressure built low in Natalia's stomach, a pleasure she'd never experienced before. At one whispered word Jasper began to shift stronger above her. Natalia's eyes began to drift closed.

Flames engulfed their bodies. It was like one thousand moments had carried them here.

Jasper was fighting for her and Natalia was fighting for him. They would work together to find out what wanted her and they would stop them. They would, from this tender moment onwards, trust each other completely with it all.

His hand raked down her body to near where they were joined, teasing her as he had done before. Moans escaped her mouth and he tried to drag more from her as he kissed her throat.

Natalia crashed like a crescent wave and Jasper followed a few moments later.

With sweet kisses, they came down from their high, lying on top of screwed up covers facing each other, both flushed and unashamed. Jasper held onto Natalia's hand and she grinned back, stroking the stars on his face.

At some point, Natalia had fallen asleep. The covers had been pulled up over her body, though the fire from Jasper kept her warm enough.

The rain hammered against the window, flashes of lightning casting the room in pale yet wondrous glittering light.

Natalia's eyes strayed from the storm and looked to Jasper. He appeared peaceful with his eyes closed. She knew he wasn't asleep anymore, because his hand traced lazy shapes along her skin.

She smiled and burrowed her head into his chest. "Jasper?" she whispered, like his name was secret.

"Mm?" was his response.

Searing pain blinded her, cutting off her next words. She shot up, whimpering. It felt like there were claws inside her brain, slowly scratching away at the edges of her skull.

"Nat?" Jasper burst upright too, the covers falling from him. "What's going on?"

Oh, Natalia.

The voice wasn't hers. Jasper threw his arms wide like a barrier, like he meant to protect her against whatever was happening, but she was certain he couldn't hear what she could and swallowed when the pain dragged itself away.

"There's a voice," she told him, scared to be too loud.

Jasper touched her forehead with three fingers and began to

chant. Pink light shot from his hands, into her face but it rebounded. Jasper went flying across the room, crashing near the door.

Natalia, my sweet, the voice called to her.

"What did you do to him?" she whispered, more to the voice than Jasper. When there was no response, she crawled to the edge of the bed to see for herself. "Jasper?"

Jasper groaned and sat up, still obviously naked but that was far from their main concern right now. "What's it saying? Are you alright?"

"Are *you* alright?" she cried, jumping out of bed. She held his face.

"Kiss me, Fairy, and I will be," he joked.

"Witch," she mumbled back.

But she did kiss him, and she began to feel better herself, even if her heart was in her throat and her stomach was down by her feet.

Tut tut Natalia, the voice scoffed.

She pulled back and stared at Jasper in terror. His hands came up to her ribcage, holding her protectively. She smiled weakly at him.

What do you want? she asked.

You are safe, protected. You have surrounded yourself with those who serve you and those who wish you well. They even love you. But soon I will have you, and I will love you too.

"No," she said aloud. Jasper's grip tightened. "No!"

You will come to me, my Queen. I promise you that.

20

Whispers in the Shadows

KIVA TENTATIVELY PEERED DOWN AT THE BABY SHE CRADLED. Peri watched her, trying to keep from laughing.

"He won't bite," Peri promised her. "Nor is he going to grow a second head."

Kiva grimaced. "Things can bite without teeth," she said. "My cousin bit me once when she didn't have teeth. That still hurt like..." She trailed off as the baby shuffled.

"A duck could bite." Peri scooped her baby back into her arm, welcoming him home against her. Kiva sighed with relief. "Alex was bitten by one once. Archie told me it happened the week the family adopted her. He *also* told me she bit the duck back." She shrugged and started rocking back and forth to ensure Edmund was adequately jiggled. "So, how's the training coming along? And speaking of Alex, is she behaving?"

The girl's eyebrows twisted inwards. "Shouldn't you be concerned about whether *I'm* behaving?"

Peri laughed. "No."

"She's actually a good teacher."

"I have no doubt she'd be good at anything if she thought about applying herself. When she gets rid of her anger, it's like she's someone different entirely."

Kiva's face morphed as if she knew what being with and without anger was like. Peri knew it too. She'd trained many hours with her trident, wielding it as an extension of herself, stabbing at nothing until her anger leaked out of it.

Turning anger into action was the easy part. Stilling it after or before was harder. Breathing practises and numerous counts to ten to soften the heart that wanted nothing more than to tear others' out helped control, but even that was slow acceptance.

"I know Noah still trains," Peri continued, still bouncing. "What about Zoe? Has she even started?"

"Not always," Kiva admitted. "Noah's obviously more interested in the books—"

"Which has been my department for the past few months."

Kiva nodded. "Zoe turns up or she doesn't. She never does anything besides watch."

"She hasn't tried?"

"Not yet. She says she still has school to worry about and can't turn up with a black eye."

"Shouldn't *you* have school to worry about, dear?" Sarah asked as she came into the room. A kind smile was clearly visible with her hair tied back from her face.

Kiva had been living in the Darby's house for a few weeks now, and though it wasn't entirely hers, Peri could tell she was settling in. Archie's old room belonged to her now and she'd filled the space with all her things - clothes, a desk, a tall mirror, even plenty of pop-star posters. She was part of the family now really, in some ways.

Peri stopped bouncing when baby Edmund made a cute whiny noise. She peered down at his sleeping form. His little nose scrunched up, and his little thumb rested on his bottom lip. He had an adorable pair of bright orange socks on and his tiny ankles were crossed.

Peri had brought little fish over to Opal House to be examined by Sarah and Evangeline, who was also visiting. The two women had deemed baby Edmund was healthy. Peri's body was also recovering nicely.

Archie sauntered into the room with a wide grin and peered into Peri's arm. "How's my little guppy?" He kissed his son's head.

"Guppy?" Kiva questioned.

"He's taken to giving our little fish an *actual type*," Peri explained.

"I didn't even catch that you'd called your baby a little fish."

Archie laughed quietly. "It started as a joke but it kind of stuck."

Kiva pointed between Peri and Archie. "You're a Mermaid, and you're a Witch. So—"

"What's the baby?" Peri pursed her lips. "It's still too early to tell. He could be either. He could have traits from one but be the other."

"Sounds like a headache."

"We just have to be patient and wait to see what he does," Archie said. Peri raised an eyebrow and he scoffed. "Fine, *I'll* be the patient one for both of us."

Sarah smiled warmly and turned back to Kiva. "To turn this back to schooling, you do need it as much as Zoe," she said gently. "I can offer to home-school you with a tutor, or I can apply to send you to a public school."

"I get a choice?" Kiva asked.

Sarah nodded and Kiva's mouth dropped wide. It was like the poor girl had never been given two options before. Peri didn't know how she'd become a werewolf, but by the looks of things it certainly didn't seem to be her fault.

"School," Kiva meagrely answered.

Nodding, Sarah's voice went into "mother mode" when she said, "I'll start the paperwork and get on the phone." She turned and left promptly.

"Good choice," Archie winked.

"Own your choices," Peri advised. She handed baby Edmund over to Archie, who wriggled for a moment before settling. "That's the one lesson I can give," she said, returning back to Kiva. "Whatever you do, own it."

Kiva nodded but Peri's attention had already gone back to her boyfriend and baby. She smiled at them both. They were her choices and she owned them with all her heart.

Noah sank into his bed and groaned at the comfort.

It'd been a long day. His sister had been a non-stop pest, leaning over his shoulder while he'd been trying to read at home, so he'd gone over to the Darby's for a few hours. But Zoe had followed.

To ignore his sister more, he had given over a few hours to finally physically train with Alex. She'd thrown things at him repeatedly, asking him to dodge or catch whatever the object was. The whole idea was to learn defence, with just enough skill for him to run.

When he'd finally mastered the catching, Alex had thrown *herself*. She was faster at moving her entire body than a tiny object that'd been shot like a bullet. He hadn't stood a chance. Things got worse when Zoe joined, though her efforts had been half-arsed, which had surprised him. She'd said she was ok when Noah had asked. But he had caught how Zoe looked to Alex as she'd been instructing.

Groaning, he rolled over on his bed and got stuck half-way. An ache burrowed into his bones, and a tiredness fogged his brain.

He yawned and closed his eyes. But that was his mistake. Because tired people were vulnerable, yet he gave way to the voice that sounded like honey.

"*Noah,*" it whispered into his ear. "*I know you hear me.*"

"I do," he said, or had he thought the words?

The voice grew softer somehow. "*I want you to rest. You will need your strength in the morning.*"

Noah tightened his eyes. As his breathing slowed and he slipped into sleep, the last thing he felt was something akin to a giant spider crawling up his body and securing him in its web.

The world was almost quiet. Seagulls still ducked and weaved overhead. There was the rush of water. Stacks of crates and containers knocked in a breeze. But nothing else moved.

Then Natalia saw through the magical mess.

She almost choked.

Morpheus had to loop their hands under her armpits to keep her upright. Her forehead broke out into a sweat, her knees weakened, and her heart threatened to stop. Her bronze dust even drew itself to the surface, sensing the need for its use.

"Be still," Morpheus whispered. "These are only memories. They cannot hurt you."

She swallowed and nodded, and Morpheus dropped their arms after a moment, unsure.

Natalia took an awkward step as if she was a new animal learning to walk. After a breath, she peered around. Something in the distance caught her attention and she zeroed in.

"That's them," she seethed, pointing at what she'd just spotted.

Kei stood before them, exactly as Natalia remembered. Even from a distance, the smell of vanilla wafted towards Natalia, and Kei's hair distinctly hung around her face. Natalia's scar twinged at seeing the Monster, like it recognised it's maker, and she hissed in pain. Morpheus eyed her but she waved them off.

Alarm bells rang in Natalia's mind when she spotted who stood beside Kei.

The hooded figure with a clock threaded with symbols.

Natalia edged closer to them, her shoulder-blades burning.

"I want you to take the girl," the figure said. Like before, their voice was

soothing and familiar, just unplaceable. "Do not harm her any more than you need to. I want her alive and I want her now. So go." Their fingers stroked down Kei's face suddenly, almost affectionately. "Bring my Fairy home to me."

Natalia's dust rose off her body. "Your Fairy my arse!"

Another window seemed to open at her anger and pushed warm air onto her face. It wasn't the stifling heat of summer but it a swell of heat nonetheless.

Natalia marched over to Morpheus, grabbed their arm, and dragged them through to the image of Atlantis.

Bunting hung from house to house. Flowers were dotted everywhere; Natalia managed the symbol she'd chosen for the event, a daisy, growing wildly by a house's wall.

The ground shook and Morpheus stumbled into Natalia. It was her turn to catch them and set them right. They gave her a gracious smile but she turned before they could respond.

The heat Natalia had felt before crossing into this memory should've been a clue as to what she was walking into. An enormous Calefaction stood before her; its teeth black and eyes redder than the fires it could spew.

"Beast!"

The Calefaction moved to reveal the hooded figure again. Natalia blinked. She'd known the hooded figure from the last vision because she'd met them there moments after that memory. But here? She'd never encountered them before.

Natalia knew she'd been thinking of the figure before crossing here and that's why she'd been led to them. But the shock upon seeing the evil that wanted her in a place she hadn't known they'd been was like a punch to the gut.

If this figure could get into Atlantis, a place only Creatures could be – though the Calefaction did defy that rule on its own – then what were they?

"Beast," the figure called again. The Calefaction still looked towards Natalia as if it could see her, and she shivered. "Beast!" It turned compliantly then, bowing its head in submission. "That's better," the figure said, and Natalia could almost picture a grin on the face beneath the hood. "I need you to create a distraction while I go and search for what I need from this place. It's one thing from a long list. So I need you to do what you do best. You need to destroy."

The Calefaction reared up and roared. Natalia shuddered at the memory.

"This is not good," Morpheus said as they reached her side.

Morpheus had changed into a black suit and shirt to match. Long black hair was slicked backwards and tied with a black ribbon at the nape of the neck. They extended a hand to Natalia, which she took.

"What's happening?" Natalia asked.

"This figure is more dangerous than even I thought."

Natalia blinked up at them. "You know who they are?"

Morpheus only stared back. Natalia thought about how much they knew, about life and love and loss, about everyone and everything. Surely they could see and find all they liked with their power.

Natalia nodded once, to herself. Morpheus' silence was their answer. They'd seen this person before, they knew of them.

Morpheus looked off into the distance. "I can say this, you will meet him."

She gaped. "Him?"

"At that time, I will break my golden rule."

Natalia was confused and scared all at once. "Golden rule? But–"

They stared down at her, eyes blacker than the skies of night, silencing her completely.

The next dream portal opened beside them, and it was dimmer compared to the last. Natalia could smell the chemicals on the other side before her feet touched the over-polished tiled floor.

"Natalia," Morpheus whispered harshly.

Natalia ignored them.

A bed sat off to one side, tucked against a blue wall. A woman so *familiar, so slight yet with a growing belly, was sprawled across the top. Natalia had to reach her.*

"Mum," Natalia gently called out.

Of course, her mum didn't react.

"You will feel a sharp scratch," the doctor said. He wore white and a stethoscope around his neck, a small pager on the pocket of his coat.

The doctor raised a clear needle and the woman sucked in air before turning her head away and shutting her eyes as the tip pressed into her skin. Blood slowly came out. Natalia wanted to yell, to scream a warning, but it was not good. The doctor raised a second syringe, using the pressure of the first as a distraction.

The needles were switched out quickly; red blood came out with the first and black something went in.

Natalia stumbled back and Morpheus' arms encircled her. She openly wept at how her mother noticed nothing amiss and how the doctor's face morphed with a light of strange fascination.

"What's he doing?" she asked through tears.

When Morpheus didn't respond, Natalia twisted from the scene. Morpheus looked equally stunned, mouth stuck open without sound. But then their face changed, almost to a mask of understanding.

The appointment finished and the woman was aided out of the room by a nurse. A boy replaced her on the bed, holding a stuffed dinosaur and swinging it around and making tiny roaring sounds of his own. He couldn't have been older than four.

"Mayer?" called a voice. The doctor strolled through the door, having left at some point. He sighed. "You know you shouldn't be on the bed."

"Daddy," the boy said, jumping off. "I want home."

"I have one more patient to see," the doctor said. "Then we can go home."

"Will Pop be there?"

"Your dog? Why wouldn't she be there?"

"I don't like leaving her," the boy sulked.

"*Unfortunately, you have to when you go to school, bud.*" *The doctor rubbed his son's head and peered around the room, his gaze settling on the closed door like he was either waiting for someone to come in or hoping they wouldn't. When no one came, he crouched in front of his son and dropped his voice. "Mayer, you know I love you, right?"*

"*Yes dad,*" *the boy nodded. "And me and Pop and Duck love you too.*" *He wiggled the dinosaur.*

The doctor suddenly looked impatient. "Your mother didn't love you, or me," *he said bluntly. "But remember how I said we would pay her back? That the world will love you and so will the next one over?"*

"*And Duck?*"

"*Mayer!*" *he half-shouted. Mayer threw his gaze down. "You need to keep this close, as close as anything I've told you.*" *The doctor glanced suspiciously at the door again. "These Creatures are heartless, and your mother is one of them. But I've found a way in which the world will love you, son. They'll love you, I promise. You'll have your power and revenge. You'll rule over them like a King.*"

Natalia burst out of Morpheus' arms and tried to reach for the little boy just as he vanished.

Mayer, *her mind repeated the name, ticking like a clock.* Mayer. Mayer. Mayer. Mayer. Mayer.

Natalia trudged into work scowling, an aching heart pounding in her chest. Her sleep had been fitful once she'd been pulled from Morpheus, and she'd not been able to discuss what she'd seen to anyone yet. Her dad had been called into work, Katherine was asleep, and everyone else wasn't immediately nearby. She could've texted, but this felt like an in-person kind of conversation.

Mayer.

The café door swung open as a customer blundered out. Natalia slipped in before it slammed shut. She passed Noah at the desk and ducked out back, dropped her bag, and strung on an apron.

Mayer.

She set about working on some muffins, baking the mixture and pouring it into purple cases. Just as she was putting them in the oven, Alex came out back carrying dirty mugs.

"Hey!" Alex cheered. "The Fairy returns."

Natalia smiled, then changed it to a concerned grimace when she spotted Alex's under-eye bruise. "How did you hurt yourself?"

"Got into a fight," Alex answered bluntly, dropping the mugs off in the sink.

"With who?"

"Myself."

Natalia managed to turn her laugh into a cough quickly. "Yourself?"

"During practise yesterday a knife rebounded off the target and smacked me straight in the face, butt end first." She sighed. "Could've been worse. Could've been blade first." She set about washing the mugs as the door upfront dinged its bell. "How are you? You look dead."

Mayer. Mayer. Mayer.

"Charming. But I'm fine," she lied, stomach twisting. Even her shoulder blades itched like they sensed danger but she refused to give them room to sprout.

"Well hello Wolf and Fairy."

Both girls looked up at Noah, who leaned casually in the doorway, his hands on the frame as if to obstruct the view beyond him.

"Wolf?" Alex challenged, shaking out her soapy hands. "Who are you calling a Wolf, *Human?*"

Noah overlooked her for Natalia. "Pretty Fairy," he cooed.

"Noah?" Natalia shifted towards Alex. "Have you taken

something?"

His face shifted from calm to blank, like the light inside him went out. His dark eyes then rolled to the back of his head. Natalia went to catch him but he never fell. Instead, his arms outstretched like he was suddenly playing the part of a zombie.

"You're an idiot," Alex huffed, stepping in front of him.

Noah reached out and latched onto Alex's shoulders. In one, swift movement, Noah somehow overpowered Alex and threw her to the ground. Natalia gasped and backed up, but ran out of space to move.

"Sweet Natalia," Noah spoke with a tone and pitch she'd never heard from him before.

Natalia didn't know what was happening.

Noah stepped closer but Alex had crawled forwards. She latched onto his hand and dragged him backwards. Natalia hated seeing her friend hurt, yet she couldn't see this person as her friend, as if all of Noah had been scooped out and another soul owned his body.

Mayer.

Red coloured Natalia's vision when the imposter Noah hauled Alex up and flipped her over his shoulder, before opening the back door and throwing her out. The door slammed in her face. Natalia took the diversion to draw her dust around her.

Noah picked up a knife.

Dust barrelled towards him in a blizzard at Natalia's command. He thrashed and spun inside of it, and she edged closer to him. When she raised her hand, the dust dropped and slithered back to her.

He made for her again and, with all the effort of a dancer running on adrenaline, she raised onto one leg. With enough time for a half rotation, her foot connected with the side of his face with surprising power – it wouldn't make any martial arts expert proud but she was. His body stumbled back and landed on the floor, eyes rolling to the back of his skull.

Alex stumbled through the front door; clearly she'd rushed round the building. Her gaze roamed over Noah's stumbled form, and she kicked his outstretched arm for good measure. He didn't budge.

"I'm impressed," she mused.

Natalia's stomach scrunched into knots. "He's my friend."

Concern washed over Alex's features. "He was trying to kill us."

Mayer.

Natalia turned away. "We need to close up for the day. We can't carry on like this," she said. "And then we need to get him some help. I'm convinced that wasn't Noah."

"Oh really? What was your first clue?"

"Alex," Natalia sighed.

She barrelled on. "At what point did that thought occur to you? When he wielded a knife or when he threw me to the floor?"

"Alex!" Natalia cried. Her friend blinked, a little startled.

Natalia dug out her phone and rang the first person she knew who would help. Alex worked around her in silence, dragging Noah into the storage area, out of view of the shop, and then went to clear the customers from the shop. She used the excuse of a small fire and no one questioned her, taking their things and leaving.

Mayer.

Natalia's mind rattled. Was he somehow behind this? Looking at Noah, she felt so lost, more than ever before. What had Mayer's father done with those two syringes? What had the black substance been? What had he meant about getting revenge, power, and having the world love them?

How did Natalia fit into that?

Mayer. Mayer. Mayer.

The stone weighing down her heart told her she'd get her answer to that question, whether she wanted it or not, very soon.

Zoe had never peddled faster on her bike. She tore away, legs burning, without a goodbye to her fellow sixth-form mates. Most of them didn't care anyway. They never asked about what she did on the weekends or what she did at nights if it didn't involve them.

They're not real friends then, her mind scoffed.

She shook her head. This wasn't the time for that argument.

At the bottom of Opal House's small hill, Zoe jumped off and threw her bike down. Her brother had attacked his best friend. There was some spooky shit going on and she didn't like it.

The front door swung open before she could touch the handle. Alex's golden face appeared, basked in streams of sunlight. Guilt wormed inside of her gut.

Zoe blinked briskly to knock herself out of it. She didn't want to think of the kiss she'd shared with Aero, how it made her feel good but like a traitor, and she certainly didn't want it to tumble from her lips to the other one her mind was partially latched onto. She diverted her attention so Alex couldn't read her face.

Zoe pushed past Alex without a word and she let her go.

She skipped up the stairs and threw herself through the open bedroom door. Her heart lurched.

Her brother was laid out on the bed, arms at his sides, eyelids closed, chest barely moving. Natalia was curled on the floor beside a woman – Zoe thought her name was Evangeline? – wearing a rich purple dress. Jasper was there, gently holding a hand to Natalia's shoulder, and Peri was at the end of the bed with her eyebrows knitted.

"Kiwi green," Peri muttered.

"Kiwi *what?*" Zoe pushed closer to the bed. "What does that mean?"

"It refers to undisturbed unconsciousness."

"He's unconscious? And how the bloody hell does it have a colour?"

Peri looked up and smiled sadly. "All emotions have colour and Mermaids can see them."

"You said he's undisturbed?" asked the unknown woman on the floor. Peri nodded and Zoe waited with held breath. "I am not sensing anything inside either."

A cold breath of air moved behind Zoe. She turned to see what had caused it and nearly fell on top of her brother in shock. The Vampire, Gold, stood with fangs bared and red running from the corners of his lips. He had never looked more like death, with pale skin and a white shirt and trousers, no monocle and no fancy jacket.

"He may be deep," Gold said. "I feel a pulse and he is breathing, but it's minimal. His spirit is hiding, and someone must go find it before it's lost."

"I will!" Zoe volunteered immediately.

The woman on the floor peered up at her with a grim expression. "I'm afraid not, child."

"That's my *brother*. I bloody well will help him and you can't stop me!"

Gold stepped closer to her and Zoe felt her body involuntarily relax as a cool heat radiated from him. "If we let you go in, your soul could also become lost. A Creature must go in. Magic was used to take him over so only magic can pull him out."

"Nat?" Zoe stared at her. "*You* go in."

She swallowed. "I can go in, right?"

Peri looked at her curiously. "Are you sure you want too?"

"He's my best friend."

"There's no shame in letting someone else do this."

"I have experience travelling through spaces," she argued. Zoe nodded solidly.

Gold raised a finger. "There may be no shame, true, and yet

there must be enough of a connection to pull him out."

Jasper stood and sighed. "There goes my plan to go in and kiss him to get him out with shock," he joked.

While Zoe appreciated the light moment, she swatted his arm anyway. He winked at her, knowing what she really meant by her hit and she glanced away.

"Dear girl," Gold said, addressing Natalia again. "You may want to lie next to your friend."

Natalia gulped visibly, but slipped off her shoes and crawled onto the bed. She rested her head on a pillow and took one of Noah's hands. Out of everyone, Zoe would've chosen her at any point to do anything if she couldn't do it herself.

The woman stood and leant over Natalia. "I don't have any Crystals to ease this, so you may feel some pinching," she warned. "But this will be similar to how it was with Morpheus, ok? There will be a slight difference in spell so you can reach Noah's spirit."

Zoe never heard the reply. Instead she focused on a dreadful hissing coming from the doorway, where Alex barred her teeth in wolf form. Normally, Zoe would've been scared. But she was already beyond scared; she had nothing left to give the emotion to feed it.

The wolf inclined its head. Zoe peered back at the bed. Natalia was taking care of the situation, Zoe couldn't do any more. She ground her teeth and turned away, praying to whatever Gods these Creatures believed in that this distraction would be a bloody good one.

Alex - back in Human form - clasped a hand around Zoe's neck once the door closed to her room. Their breaths matched pace. Zoe leant forwards first, her lips sweet and smooth, and Alex kissed her back.

Walking backwards to the bed, Alex flipped them so she fell

first. Alex smiled and pulled Zoe's body down onto hers, their lips crashing rough and rapid.

Alex had pulled Zoe away to keep her distracted. She always preferred to keep her mind occupied while something was happening she couldn't control. She also knew other people appreciated it, even if they didn't make the first move or admit to it out loud.

She wasn't upset by the progression at all. She just hoped Zoe knew what she was doing, that she would not regret it later.

Hooking one leg under Alex's, Zoe tried to shift them over. Alex laughed against Zoe's mouth at her weak attempt. She took over, grabbing the girl's hip, earning a delicate gasp, and rolled them. Zoe giggled until Alex licked her neck.

"Do you want me to stop?" Alex whispered into her ear.

"No," Zoe said breathlessly.

"The second you change your mind," Alex nipped her ear, "tell me."

"I started this because I wanted it."

Zoe leant up and kissed Alex again so she couldn't reply.

Alex ran her hand up under Zoe's top while spreading her legs with her own. Zoe moaned as Alex touched her bare skin gently. Zoe arched into it so Alex dragged her nails along her ribs.

Apparently Zoe was growing impatient because her hands wound up Alex's back until her t-shirt came over her head. Alex pulled it the rest of the way off and then removed Zoe's. While Alex had a sport-bra on, Zoe was bare. Her skin was smooth and inviting. Alex had scars running all along hers.

Zoe's fingers traced some. "The Werewolf that turned you?"

Alex nodded. "*After* he'd turned me."

"After?"

"I went back to him for what he'd done. I wanted blood and I got it. I just happened to spill some of my own in the process."

Zoe shuffled to kiss one of the scars along Alex's chest. "I like them," she said, and her eyes went darker as they met Alex's. "I don't like how you got them, but they also made you who you are. And I happen to be quite interested in that person."

Alex dragged a finger down Zoe's face, right down to her breasts. Zoe gasped as Alex firmly grabbed one, and Alex smiled. "You sound so sure," she said.

"About?" Zoe asked, sounding like she was struggling to breathe.

"My scars," Alex said, grinning. "This moment. Me."

Zoe wrapped her hands around Alex's bra and snapped it off, then fumbled with her trousers, sliding them down. "Do I really have to explain myself more?"

Alex kissed Zoe and they became infinitely more tangled and desperately more breathless.

Evangeline had said this spell would feel similar to when Natalia had first met Morpheus. Natalia had not expected it to feel exactly *the same.*

Except, when the world came up to greet her, it was stark white and blank.

"You are protected where you are."

Natalia swung round in the whiteness, unable to spot anything. She could turn this way and that, and nothing changed.

"I cannot reach you up there," came that distinct voice, the one that haunted her every moment. "You are protected in the outside world and I must say, I'm impressed by that."

"Are you?" she challenged, still unsure if she was speaking to empty air or not.

"I'm also impressed by you, Natalia. I like how you've been trying to figure out who you are and how you came to be."

Natalia's spine straightened. She tried to call to her dust but none came.

The voice persevered. "A Geminis who smells like burning yet has only one skin, that of a Human. A Fairy who has wings yet they are the glass a Geminis commands. A Human who was really a Fairy." There was a soft laugh. "It's all terribly confusing."

She tightened her hands into fists. "You have no idea."

"Oh, I'm sure I don't."

"What do you want?" she seethed.

"I cannot hurt you here, my love."

"I am not your love."

The voice ignored her. "Nor can I appear to you. I have managed to catch you in the space between your souls' realm and where your friends' lies, the one you're looking for? I will release you and send you to him, don't fret."

"How are you doing this?" Natalia sounded weak and felt it too.

"We share a connection, an important one."

"Does it have anything to do with me being part Geminis?"

"Not entirely," the voice answered. At that moment, Natalia could almost form a face from the voice but the image floated away too soon.

"Let me go."

"I could always keep you here with your friend. I would have you then." There was a small pause. "But I will release your spirit, Natalia, only because I want the full and real you. I am coming for you and you will come with me."

"Like Hell," she fired.

She thought she heard a snort. "Oh, you will. Our connection is strong and you will want it."

"I will not!"

"Natalia?" She blinked as Noah's form materialising in front of her, and a park beyond him. "Who are you screaming at?" He twisted his head this way and that. "Where even are we?"

Natalia reached out. "We need to get out of here," she stressed.

She was thankful she'd found Noah, relief flooded her in droves, but she didn't want to stay here one second longer.

The sound of a school-bell ricocheted through the area, forcing Natalia to close her eyes in a wince. A rush like running water cascaded over her and *she hoped Noah would hold her tight until they woke, and hopefully he would return without that other voice and person attached. A voice, she realised, that could be the very boy she'd seen before but grown now, the one after power and vengeance and her.*

Natalia dragged in a breath and Jasper lurched forwards to catch her in case she fell off the bed. He reached her side as she gasped again and Noah bolted upright. Peri grabbed for Noah, holding onto him until he'd settled. The friends looked to one another and Jasper sighed heavily when Natalia lifted her best friend's hand to her mouth to kiss.

But the beauty faded.

Natalia explained what happened. She looked to those still in the room, eyes wide and fearful. "There was only this disembodied voice," she said. "It was all around me. It called me their *love* for fuck sake!"

"Language, dear," Gold chastised. "It's not fitting for a young lady."

"Screw those rules," Peri mumbled.

Jasper held Natalia a little tighter as she continued. "It said it was coming, just like it always does. But I recognised it though. I just don't know where from."

"You did?" Jasper pressed.

"And I'm sure that it belongs to a person called Mayer."

"Mayer? I hope that's a last name."

She shook her head and launched into the story of last night's walk with Morpheus. Jasper's stomach sank when Natalia mentioned needles and a man injecting some substance into her mum, and how a young boy called Mayer had come into the same medical room flashes later. It was like Jasper could sense the impending doom. That doom-level increased when Natalia explained what the doctor had said to Mayer, about the people loving him and how he would rule over them.

"They've *got* to be the same person," Peri surmised. "Right? It can't be a coincidence."

"I agree," Gold concluded.

"Speaking of people." Noah rubbed his forehead, wiping away the layer of sweat that had formed. "Where's my sister? I thought she'd be here?"

Jasper watched Gold wiggled his eyebrows. "She's... talking a walk," he said. "I'm sure she'll come and see you soon. She knows you're in good company."

"But he must rest," Evangeline urged gently. "Everyone out!"

Jasper helped Natalia up and walked out alongside her. While everyone went downstairs, they remained behind in the hallway. Jasper felt her shaking like a leaf in a storm.

"Mayer can't hurt you," he promised.

"Funny," Natalia whispered, voice devoid of humour. "That's what he said."

"I don't mean it the same way he does. This Mayer cannot hurt you because we won't let him. And he's pathetic and needs to get over himself, honestly. So much drama."

That inspired a small laugh, but it turned sour quickly. "I might know his name," she said, "but I still don't know what he wants."

"Sure you do."

"Do I?"

"Power, women, to rule the world, a nice crown. You know, the everyday stuff."

She snorted. "That's not helpful."

He smiled and kissed the top of her head. "It's helpful to me."

"How?"

"It's calming my nerves."

Natalia tucked in closer and the questions flooded out of her like a dam bursting. "But what was the doctor injecting into my mum? Is that was killed her? Is that how I was made? If it did make me, it had to be Monster-y, right? Did she know something was wrong? And how does this affect Mayer? How do we link? What revenge does he want exactly? How is he going to do it, like what's his plan? How do I *fit*?"

I don't know, Jasper thought but did not say.

The best thing he could think of was to keep her in his arms as if that would protect her like a barrier. He had no answers otherwise. His stomach dropped at the thought as she burrowed her head into his chest. He felt like he could only hold her this close for so long because, though Natalia had said this Mayer person was *maybe* coming, Jasper didn't want to admit to feeling that that time may be creeping closer than they thought and it was more than just a small possibility.

He squeezed her even tighter.

21

Ash and Dust

"I NEED A BREAK!"

Peri shoved the towel into her face and scrubbed. Her entire face burned, and her body was drenched in sweat. This was a welcome reprieve from what she had been doing, which was a whole lot of nothing.

They focused on basic hits and kicks in the middle of the living room. Peri hadn't even brought her trident. She needed her necessary fighting skills and fitness back first. Tricks would come naturally in time, though she'd be lying if she didn't admit to being excited about doing them again.

Archie stepped towards her. "We're supposed to be taking it easy anyway," he reminded her. "You're the one that keeps pushing."

She flung the towel at him but he plucked it out of the air with ease. "Don't you love me for it?"

"I do," he admitted. "But I don't want you to get hurt."

"I've done everything your mum or Evangeline has advised. But I can't keep running for five minutes every day and nothing else. I need something *more* to my life sooner rather than later or I'll go crazy."

Archie pressed his lips to the corner of her mouth, and then turned to check on Edmund who was cradled in a self-rocking basket.

Edmund was nearly a month old now. Peri couldn't believe how fast the time was flying or how big he was getting. His blue eyes were shifted daily, and Peri and Archie had a bet going on what colour they'd become. Archie voted green but Peri bet they'd be light brown. Both could agree on how delicate his lashes were.

Evangeline and Sarah had advised she still do minor activities because, like Humans, the healing process after birth took close to six weeks – though it could be different from person to person. But with Edmund growing, now was the perfect time to begin getting back into shape.

As long as she didn't take on any big Monsters too early, Peri thought she'd been sat still long enough. A war was coming after all, dragging closer to their shore with each dawn. Peri *had* to be ready to protect her family. The incident with Noah last week, how he'd been spiritually overpowered, had forced her hand even more.

The faintest giggles erupted from the other side of the room. Peri looked over to see Archie lifting their son.

Then Edmund was gone.

A new giggle came down at Peri's feet. She would've screamed if the shock wasn't so paralysing. Edmund was by her and then gone again. He reappeared on the green sofa.

Archie and Peri chased their baby around for several minutes until he appeared in Peri's grasp, laughing so fully. She pressed her cheek to his head, capturing Archie's eye.

"Did I just imagine all that?" Archie asked as he approached.

"If you did, so did I," Peri said.

"So he definitely jumped around the room?"

Edmund yawned in Peri's arm but didn't close his eyes. "He did."

Up until now, they'd had no indication what Creature type Edmund would fall under. With mixed parents, the children didn't fully grow into who and what they were until the age of two. So while

Edmund could hop around a room, it didn't make him a Witch. Because mixed parents sometimes transferred a power, the kid could be one type of Creature but with a capability of the other. Those extra gifts could fade out or stay.

There was a year and eleven months left to fully determine Edmund's gifts.

Archie stroked the side of Edmund's cheek when he turned towards him. If Peri wasn't so shaken, she would've completely melted. Tears sprang to her eyes, however. Archie saw them and moved his hand to cup her face.

"Little guppy is going to be a little terror," Archie mused. "Taking after his mother early." His smile was beautiful and Peri loved it.

"I'd be disappointed otherwise." Peri leaned over, holding Edmund awkwardly, and kissed Archie. "I'm teasing," she said. "I want him to be exactly like he is. A perfect combination of us both. A terror *and* a sweetheart."

"You think I'm a sweetheart?"

"Oh shut it, you know I do!"

Archie's gaze slipped to her lips. "I think we did a pretty good job in making him, if I do say so myself. And we'll do a good job raising him too, I know it."

She raised her eyebrows. "I don't want another one right now, thank you. So pop those googly eyes *back* in your head."

He laughed softly. "But, eventually?" he asked, almost shyly.

Peri looked at Edmund, then Archie. "Eventually," she nodded. "If you do."

"With you?" He pecked her lips. "Anything."

Peri dropped her voice to barely a mumble. "Doesn't mean we can't do other things."

"Put them googly eyes back in your head yourself, you little siren!"

She laughed so heartily it gave Archie the chance to steal Edmund and start swaying him around the room. Peri watched on with her heart exposed in front of her. These two boys were her everything and nothing compared. A man who was her equal. A son who would become all they wanted and more.

Calming, Peri pulled off the strapping from her arm and went to the kitchen for a drink. She poured the water and chugged it back in four gulps, sighing once done.

With Edmund's new-found jumping power, if the Seven Hells came, he might just be able to escape to somewhere safe on his own.

She ran her fingers over her face. Because she loved her boys, she wanted to protect them. She would do whatever it took. No one would stop her. And pity anyone who tried to cross her.

As she looked out, watching her family, she also thought about what she'd lost last time. Her shoulder ached, her missing fingers twinging. So while she would do whatever it took to protect what she had, that also meant putting in other precautions too. Just in case the worse came.

Taking a deep breath, she went out to talk to Archie about what she'd been thinking.

Tony opened the door to the drizzle and Jasper.

"Happy birthday, Jasper," Tony said, shaking the young man's hand.

"It's not the big one-eight or the big two-one," Jasper shrugged, "but the one-nine will do for now."

Tony shook his head, laughing, and stepped aside. He closed the door and turned as his daughter came bounding down the stairs.

Natalia looked stunning, and more like a Fairy and her mother than ever. She had on simple white shoes and a lovely flowing purple skirt and white blouse. There was a silver headband pinning back her long hair. Her star earrings shone as if a piece of the night-sky had floated down to Earth.

"You look beautiful," Tony told her honestly.

She came and kissed his beard, aiming for his cheek. "Thanks, dad."

They still hadn't talked about their fight from the other week. The air had settled between them easily as if it had never happened. Tony knew it wasn't healthy to ignore, but just this once he let this small thing slide. Natalia had bigger things to worry about right now.

"Decent enough," Jasper teased, propping himself against the wall. "I *suppose* I can be seen with you today."

Natalia scoffed and pulled a present from behind her back. "It's a shame," she said. "If you'd been nice, I would've given you this. But clearly you're not interested."

Tony watched as they squabbled for a few minutes. Eventually, Jasper won the present by magically stunning Natalia. Her bronze dust rose around her, breaking the charm, and then flicked him in the face by becoming a hand with fingers to do so.

"I'll have you know, it's my birthday," Jasper declared despite everyone already knowing. "Fifteenth of September. There shall be no flicking the birthday boy today."

"Do you really think that will stop me?" Natalia quipped back.

"I'm surprised you can even do that with your dust."

Jasper sounded genuine but Tony agreed with him. He thought Fairy dust could break some spells and enchantments from Creatures and Monsters, and made a trail behind each Fairy. But creating a physical hand was new.

Tony could tell things were going to change and shuffled down the hallway to give the two young ones space.

Jasper kissed Natalia's cheek. "Thank you for my present."

She laughed. "You haven't even opened it yet."

Jasper tore into the brown paper and Tony laughed when he

pulled out a box of four delicately decorated cupcakes and a black framed black-and-what photo picture of himself and Natalia.

Jasper stared at the picture. "Where did you get this from?"

"A camera?" Natalia asked, knowing she was being cheeky.

Dramatically rolling his eyes, Jasper asked, "I mean, where was it taken? Who even took it?"

"I did," Tony acknowledged. Natalia smiled at him and Jasper raised his eyebrows. "It's from the campfire evening at yours, when Natalia first came back."

"I didn't even realise you had a camera then."

Tony shrugged. "It was just my phone."

Tony could see the picture in his mind. Natalia was leaning on Jasper's shoulder with his head on hers. They watched the fire before them. Tony had taken the shot just before the uproar about Natalia's wings, before life had become real again.

It was a beautiful photo, a story of peace and connection and love.

And it was clear to Tony that his daughter loved this boy – it had been clear even back then. They annoyed each other and were sweet together. In the end, they would protect and care for each other. Tony could see it. That was why Tony had taken the picture for Natalia.

"Now go!" Tony clapped his hands. "You have a date."

"Date?" Jasper wiggled his eyebrows at Natalia.

Tony briefly thought about wiping that smirk off his face because he knew what it meant. He sighed instead. He'd had the sex talk with Natalia when she'd gotten her first period at fourteen. It hadn't gone too badly, he thought. Certain things they hadn't covered, because it hadn't been important or really that relevant at the time, but Natalia had had friends she could talk to. Of course he'd been, and always would be, there if she wanted and needed his guidance too.

"It's a *breakfast* date," Natalia told Jasper. "Food and food and more food."

"But it's still a date," Jasper teased.

"You'll be late." Tony cut in, shooing them out the door so he didn't have to hear more. "Out, out!"

"Bye dad," Natalia said, kissing him again.

"I'll see you later?" he asked. She simply nodded.

"Thanks for the photo," Jasper grinned.

"You're very welcome. Have a wonderful breakfast and birthday."

"I'll definitely try."

Tony watched as they stepped into the rain and reached for each other's hands at the same time. Tony hoped the rain would let up for them.

Natalia gave herself a mental high-five at the astonishment on Jasper's face.

The rooftop bar was just as Natalia remembered it, a contrast of natural greens and concrete. Today, the open sky was hidden by a pull-out roof because of the rain, but fairy lights were strung along the poles in dazzling multi-colour. In the centre, two tables were pushed together, decorated with a white tablecloth and a golden runner, and balloons tied to the backs of the chairs.

"Was this all you?" he asked, eyes carefully taking it in.

Natalia's face heated and she felt the dust rise to the surface. "Yes."

"Oh you wonderful *Fairy!*" He kissed her smoothly.

She took his hand, squeezing it, and Jasper kissed her again.

Hand in hand they walked over to meet Peri, Archie, baby Edmund who was bouncing in little bursts on the table, and Alex. Natalia felt comfortable here, surrounded by the people who showed her respect and love. They didn't care about what she could do and didn't wish her harm or to steal her away because of it. Not like *him*.

Jasper squeezed her hand as if knew where her thoughts had gone. But she couldn't help it. Last night, she'd dreamed of *him*.

Mayer.

He'd been older in this dream, about fifteen, and alone. Darkness hung around his sad eyes. He'd looked even more familiar though still shapeless and blurred. Natalia reckoned that if he'd spoken, she would've finally been able to put pieces together. But he hadn't spoken.

In frustration, she'd thrown herself from the dream on purpose.

"Happy birthday, Kifflegger," Alex chimed as they reached the table. Jasper dropped Natalia's hand to take the pink papered present his sister offered. He shook it and Alex huffed. "Here's a suggestion? *Open it.*"

Natalia went to up the bar to order drinks as Jasper opened the present. He pulled out a lush silver watch. Alex swatted at him when he kissed her cheek but her smile didn't fade.

"What do you think?" Jasper asked, flashing his newly decorated wrist when Natalia returned. "All Creatures get a watch for their nineteenth from their family."

"Oh?" she asked, handing over the drinks.

"It's a respect thing," Peri explained.

"There's more to it than that," Archie said. "It's respectful to get one and then to wear it at a funeral, birth, or celebration. Its so the Creature can respect every moment they have."

Natalia grimaced. "A tad morbid."

"It is," Peri agreed, pursing her blue lips.

"But it also teaches us to celebrate each moment we have," Jasper concluded. He kissed Natalia's temple lightly just as her wineglass touched her lips.

"It's from mum and dad too," Alex told him.

Jasper smiled. "I'll give them my thanks, don't worry."

"Us next!" Peri chimed, handing over two presents.

Jasper tore into them while Natalia looked around impatiently. Her brain was unsettled, like she shouldn't be here. But everything was *right*. Nothing was out of place or missing or *wrong*.

Jasper's booming laugh drew back her attention. The first present was a mauve coloured shirt. The second was an oversized pillow with a "J" stamped on the front in black velvet. Peri told him the cushion was for whenever he bought his own home. Jasper thanked them both, kissing Peri's cheek and hugging his brother. He gave the biggest thanks to Edmund, giving him several quick pecks all over his face that made him giggle.

Natalia tried to smile, letting the sour taste of her wine coat her tongue. It did little to settle the unease. As she lowered her glass, she noticed Peri had raised her eyebrows in her direction and she grimaced. Could Peri see how on edge she was? How crossed were her strings, what colour were they?

"Have you noticed," Alex started, putting her glass of white wine down, "how much Natalia looks like a Fairy? She's all skirts and headbands now. It's sickening."

"I *know*," Peri laughed. "Next it'll be flowers in her hair and bows on her wrists."

Natalia shot them both a look, which only prompted them to giggle into their drinks. She groaned. "Can we change the subject?"

"Fine," Peri dragged out, still kind of laughing. "I've started training again." Edmund reached out to her so she took his hand and wiggled it as he clenched one finger.

"That's awesome!" Natalia cheered.

Peri let go of her son and pulled out her retractable trident from her nearby bag. She twirled it around her fingers. "I'm even allowed to carry this again."

"You only weren't because of the temptation," Archie said.

"You said—"

"It wasn't me that made you put it down."

"That would be *me*," Alex declared like she was searching for praise. "You're too bloody-thirsty. You needed the obstacle of temptation taken away. You were too likely to dive into a fight or training, and that could've been damaging to you both. Now that baby is *out*," she poked Edmund, who capture her finger with grabbing hands, "there's no harm."

Peri's lips made a tight line, and she peered at Archie. "Speaking of..."

Archie grimaced. "Edmund, it seems, can jump."

A chorus of "what" echoed.

Archie explained but Natalia only half listened. Her mind slipped away. She couldn't help but drift and think of Noah, who should've been here with them. Then, her mind went dark.

Mayer.

"Nat?" Alex's voice called her back. Her face popped in front of Natalia's. "Are you alright? We're not going to have to pick you up off the floor or anything are we?"

"I'm just worried about Noah," she admitted. It was the truth, at least, just not all of it. Jasper took her hand and squeezed.

Archie gave her a worried glance. "I wanted to talk to you about that?" His words shot through Natalia's heart, spiking it. Jasper squeezed her fingers again. "Have you considered that whoever is behind all this was using Noah?"

"Using him?" Her voice cracked.

"Somehow, yes. To get to you."

This was nothing Natalia hadn't thought of herself already, yet the words were like a blast of lightning striking her directly. A buzzing hummed in her ears. Her lips were dry, her throat drier.

Natalia knew that the Mayer boy and the person searching for her were one in the same. He was coming for her, and was becoming more brazen in the attempts. There was no care for anyone or anything in his way.

How much time do I have left?

Natalia went to speak when Peri's face paled suddenly. She threw Edmund into Archie's arms and dived for her trident, and threw it across the table.

Gasping, Natalia leapt aside. The trident, still in miniature form, had punctured a small Scorpio that had been creeping up behind her, stinger extended. It snapped one pincer and tumbled into ash.

Peri rounded on Archie. "How's *that* for taking it easy, *caro?*"

He shook his head, smiling slightly. "Delightful."

Jasper glanced over his shoulder curiously. "Not a great time for an "I told you so" moment, even if I do love them," he said. "Where the fuck did that come from anyway?"

"I don't want to ask it," Alex said. "Do you?"

"Not exactly. Not that I can now, anyway."

"And I think that concludes this pleasant portion of our day."

They stood, paid the bills, and left hastily.

No one on the streets seemed to notice, the same way no one upstairs had noticed, that this group had just killed a Monster that had been among them. Natalia surveyed the streets as they walked, waiting for something else to try and get the drop on them. They rounded a corner into a quieter road. They hadn't seen a Monster in a while. Why now? What had changed?

Out of the darkest shadow cast by a nearby car, a Shadow swooped up. Natalia dodged it perfectly, though she wished for a weapon.

"I will let you hit me," it said. "I must deliver a message first."

Archie stepped up and wrapped the Shadow in green magic, but it outmanoeuvred him. The Monster grabbed onto Natalia's arm, and she threw her other one up to halt her friends. Alex growled unhappily, and dared to step closer but did nothing more. Peri had moved away with Edmund in her arm, shielding his head against her chest. Jasper's hands glowed pink.

Natalia shook the Monster's hands off. "I must speak," it urged before she could tell it where to stuff its words.

"Then speak," she seethed through gritted teeth.

The Shadow grinned, wild and wicked. "I see through these creatures. I cannot see you for myself. But I will soon. This is my final message. I am coming, sweet Fairy of mine."

Crying out, Natalia dove for it. Before she could tear its head off, pink magic tied a rope at its throat and yanked until it burst apart. An arm covered Natalia's head. When she peered up nervously, she saw Archie. Protective Archie, hiding her against him the best he could.

"We're getting you home," he said strongly.

Luck seemed to be on their side as the local tram pulled up near them. They shared one look before hopping on. It only stopped a few times before Natalia's house, where they all got off. They stormed inside, the door slamming behind whoever came in last. There was only time to stop and breathe in the living room.

Jasper moved in front of Natalia and said, "Nothing can get you here."

"So everyone keeps saying," she said, her eyes darting to the clock, the mirror, and the window. "But no one will explain *why*, just like everything else in my life!" She took a deep breath and sighed. She hadn't realised how agitated she was and regret filled her instantly. "Sorry. I didn't mean to shout."

He reached out to caress her face with his thumb. "Because, after you got that scar," he pointed to the T-shape on her skin, "and before you went back to work, I put a protective spell around your house."

She blinked harshly despite the soft lighting. "You did *what?*"

Jasper looked suddenly nervous. "I know you care about your dad and I care about you. So I spelled your house. Like a force field of sorts, but the magical kind. Nothing Monster related can get in."

"A force-field," she mumbled.

"It was an old spell. I had to search through dad's records and everything. He had a few spells written down, and I remembered him saying at one point that he used to ace defensive spells. They were his thing." Jasper shrugged. "I took a chance and it paid off."

"Better than some of your other exploits," Alex mumbled gruffly.

Natalia ignored Alex as her mind twisted back in time to remember the Shadow in her bedroom. Her shoulder-blades itched. It was one more thing she'd never shared and decided not to mention it now. But there had definitely been one in her room before. If there was a shield spell here, how had the Monster gotten in?

But now that she thought about it, she did feel more comforted whenever she was at home, as if a blanket was permanently draped over her shoulders.

"Thank you," she said, barely above a whisper.

Jasper smiled sadly at her. "There's no need to thank me, not for this."

Peri began to rock Edmund. "We're safe," she reminded them. "That's what matters."

"That *is* what matters," Natalia's dad said in agreement as he came in to the room.

Natalia smiled at him. Jasper hadn't just protected her. He'd also been keeping her dad and Katherine safe. People she could never find herself living without.

"Where's Katherine?" Natalia asked, noticing her absence and panicking.

"At the shops," her dad answered, and she sighed with relief.

Alex fell to the floor and when Archie went to help her she shifted. Everyone's eyes flew wide in confusion but soon understood when the ground shook.

Archie and Peri seemed to have a silent discussion before Peri nodded, clutching the baby tighter as Archie kissed his head. Natalia's dad nodded at Jasper, and Natalia didn't understand why until Jasper slipped his hand into hers and tugged. She followed him out of the room after a guilty look back at her dad.

They stopped in the kitchen. "You'll need this," Jasper said, unfolding a large piece of cloth from his pocket.

Natalia stared down. Her Fairy blade lay inside, all new and pieced back together. "You—"

"I collected the pieces. I couldn't let them melt away and I hated seeing you without it. It's *your* weapon." He pressed it into her palm. "Add your dust and it'll be wholly yours again."

"You fixed it."

Jasper pressed a kiss to her temple. "For you."

Natalia gazed in wonder. She thought the blade was lost for good. How Jasper had mended it, she didn't know, only that it was back in her hands and as comfortable there as ever. She smiled, and immediately dust rose on her cheeks. She touched her fingers to it and dropped some under the gemstones, just like last time. The blade began to hum in her touch.

She rose up on tip-toes to kiss him, to thank him, to do *something* as a way of showing her appreciation.

But the moment was broken before she could do anything when the ground rumbled again.

They both looked up to see a *beast* Monster climbing over the cliffside towards her garden.

Don't face it, my sweet.

Natalia stopped short. Jasper turned in concern, but his face and the scene became blurry.

Come with me, this other voice inside her head said. *Come the other way. I await you, blood of my heart.*

Natalia's feet moved on their own as she let go of Jasper and moved. For a second, part of her considered going away from the fight. But she fought it. That wasn't her.

In a rush, the spell that had wrapped her up broke apart. She even tripped forwards from the force of the eruption. Jasper caught her before she could fall, bringing her upright with two very raised eyebrows.

"Are you—"

"Don't, please," she begged him. Her gaze searched the sky. "He's here."

"Natalia? How do you know? Are you *sure*?"

She nodded weakly once. "I heard him." She lowered her head and his face was screwed up. "It's the first time I've heard him outside of a dream or Monster possession."

"And what did he say?"

"He wanted me to go to him."

Jasper looked over his shoulder, at the progressing Monster that still wasn't too close, but nor was it too far. "This is a distraction," he mumbled. "Shit." She nodded again. "That's not good. If he's controlling the Monsters... *Fuck*."

"I definitely agree with the—"

A terrifying scream called away Natalia's attention.

The oncoming Monster had crossed the gap. Archie and Alex flew at the beast as it tore at the wood on the fence. However, it stopped short. When Jasper smiled, Natalia realised that there was indeed a force-field around her house and it was *working*. The Darby siblings continued to take it on, easily darting around the stunned thing.

Natalia swallowed thickly and touched her earrings for comfort. "His voice was the same," she answered finally. "But I broke out of it somehow."

Jasper rubbed his hands down his face. "He's strong if he can make his magic work inside this field enough to control you, even for a split second."

"That's not a helpful thing to say. I already know that!"

"I know you know."

"Part of me wanted to go, Jasper. An actual part of *me*. It didn't feel like a control or command that I was blindly following. It was like there was this connection. A string between that voice and me."

"You're stronger than that kind of connection. You broke it on your own. But a magical connection is bad news." He leaned forward and pressed his forehead to hers. "I might be able to protect you with magic here, but something's breaking through and I don't want to see what happens when it does."

She wanted to argue that it wouldn't happen but couldn't form the words. Instead, she said nothing.

What would've happened if she hadn't been strong enough to break from the trance? She side-eyed Jasper but he was looking ahead at his siblings. She didn't want to even think about how deep the connection *did* run, if the dreams and words were true – it unsettled her, right to her core.

Taking in a deep breath, she stole Jasper's hand and nodded when he looked at her. His mouth slipped into an easy grin. She loved it.

With all the energy she had left, she headed away from the Monster, but not because the voice had told her to go.

Noah shielded his face with a hand against the blinding light of the room. But soon that hand was pulled away. He wanted to complain but stopped himself when he saw Sarah Darby's motherly face above him. She helped him shift into a sitting position without a word, then handed him a tall glass of water which he drank in three gulps.

She sighed. "You should've sipped that."

Noah laughed awkwardly and handed back the glass. "Could I have some more? Please?"

"In a minute," she agreed. "I want to talk to you first."

Noah had been in and out of sleep for the last few days. The

Darby's had let him stay at their home for easy observation. His parents thought he was at Natalia's and they were having a massive movie marathon – even Tony had validated the false story.

"What about?" he asked, pushing past the itching throat.

"Let's start with how you feel," she suggested, taking a seat on the bed beside him.

Like my brain's been taken from my skull and beaten with a stick.

"Not bad," he said.

"Have you had any dreams?"

"Not ones I remember when I'm awake."

Sarah's face relaxed, which was promising. "And what do you remember of what happened before you went to sleep?"

Noah pushed his bruised brain to think. "I remember being tired," he said. "I'd been reading all day, yeah!" He perked up. "I'd read all day and was so tired, but there was this voice. It just told me to go to sleep."

Her face morphed to a stoic state. "Then what?"

"I saw Natalia in this white room and then I woke up."

"And you don't remember anything in between?"

A shiver stroked his spine like cold fingers would. He *could* remember feeling like his mind had been in chains, locked away from his body. It was a weird dissonance between two things that made him whole and it was hard to explain.

He shook his head. "No."

Sarah nodded and stood. She tapped the back of her hand against Noah's forehead. He could feel himself burning but didn't know if it was from keeping a secret or being ill. No one had actually explained what'd happened on their end; why he'd seen Natalia in the white room, or why he'd woken to a room full of people.

"Do you still want that water?" she asked, removing her hand.

Noah?

He cautiously moved his eyes around the room and tilted his

head at the same time to make it look like he was stretching. "Yes please," he said.

"Anything else? What about something to eat?"

"Maybe a piece of toast?"

Sarah smiled. "Sure. I'll bring it up." She left with the empty glass.

Noah.

He slid the covers aside and stared at the doorway. Nothing obvious was there. He rubbed the side of his head, sighing. When he pulled back, there was a black ashy layer covering his palms. He sprung from the bed, barely breathing, and found the sheet covered with the same ash.

In the mirror, Noah.

Instantly his eyes went to the long mirror. He didn't know what he expected, but what he found wasn't what he wanted.

His face was gone. The reflection showed someone else's, a face with light olive skin and blue eyes. The face smiled, frowned, and even stuck out its tongue when Noah did. It was him. And it *wasn't.* Not to mention the black ash coating him in patches, usually the sign of a dead Monster. But this was not a dead Monster. He worried for a moment that Sarah had seen it, but she'd said nothing.

"What's happening?" he whispered to himself.

The face in the mirror tilted its head when Noah didn't and smiled. *Hello Noah.*

22
Starfall

"YOU LOOK LOVELY, DARLING."

Evangeline purposely shoved her blade – a knife with a hooked end – into her belt with force. "You could help," she said roughly. "Comments won't be much good out there."

Gold swished his glass, the red blood swirling. "I'm surprised you're taking up arms."

She scoffed. "No you're not."

"You are right, of course. I am not surprised and I won't lie about it."

Evangeline pushed her other matching hooked knife into the other side of her belt and wiggled the handles with her palms to make sure they were secure. "They're my family."

"Weeks ago, you wanted nothing to do with them."

She whirled on him, all fury and brilliance. A light inside of her seemed to flicker on, one that had blinked out many years ago. It brightened her face and Gold marvelled at it. He smirked deviously.

"What did you expect?" she asked. "What did you expect me to do when you pushed me towards them? Even in the few moments I have been with them, I have come to love them like family. They *are* family, God damn the Heavens!"

Gold smirked into his glass as he drank. "Language, young Eva."

"To the Seven *Hells* with your language, Goliath Damder."

He put his glass down with a soft click and stood. His hands reached Evangeline before she could shy away from him. To hear his real name again, after all these years, a name so few knew anymore, made him feel both alive and more cursed than ever. The last time it was used, he was condemned to servitude at the Council's discretion for a love he could not control nor give up. After that moment, his name and life had meant nothing.

But if Evangeline could light again, why shouldn't he?

"You *pushed me*," she continued. "Of course I would love them! They are my own blood and life. Even if I have spent my years teaching, I never lost *that* urge or the need to care."

Gold knew. He'd visited Eva during the years she'd locked herself away. She had left the fight behind, thinking herself too old and having nothing left to fight for once her children had passed. That wasn't the Creature way, they should fight until their last moments. But the Council, for once, had given leniency for all Evangeline had done. She had become a shell of herself, a blank piece of wet cloth compared to what she'd once been. But something had changed now, something was bringing back her original form and fire.

Love, Gold thought. *Love could bring back what was lost.*

"So now what?" he asked, feeling his own undead heart rise from the depths it'd fallen to.

"So now I find the will to bring myself into battle. I go to their side and I will stay where I can protect them, and fight when the time comes. I have lived beyond my years and then some. They have not. I may have vowed to leave the ash and danger to the younger generations," she tilted her jaw upwards, eyes wet and shiny, "but now, I break that vow."

Gold nodded and allowed his hands to extend. His next words would end him yet he didn't care. "And now I break mine."

Mo groaned impatiently at Natalia's side and she kind of agreed.

For the past few weeks she'd been taken to the same damned vision every time she slept. It was the one at the docks. The hooded figure – which she assumed was Mayer – was tormenting a past version before being thrown into the sea. Each time, Natalia witnessed the same minutes like clockwork.

"I'm still not seeing anything new," Morpheus complained. "So why are we here, again?"

Natalia shook her head. "I feel like I'm missing something."

"From the first twenty times we've seen it? I would say no, you're not."

"Then will you help?" Natalia grimaced. "I'm sorry." She hated how her temper spiked. These days, it seemed like she was always bubbling, like an old fashioned kettle beginning to scream. There was no joy in this, not that there had been to begin with.

Morpheus turned to Natalia. She wanted their long red hair to stop tickling her face. When they didn't even speak, she huffed loudly. She hadn't thought she'd missed their voice until it was absent.

"What?" she questioned, unable to keep up the staring contest.

They held onto her shoulders like they were the one needing support. "You can find the truth in all this, you need only reach out and take it. Believe in what you can do and who you are. Because you are strong enough to find what you need and strong enough to fight for it all afterwards, but we need the truth to at last start the end."

Natalia closed her eyes and thought of what she'd been through.

Originally she'd thought of herself as Human, only to be told she was a Fairy – a Creature with a lifelong Purpose to destroy Monsters. The Council, who were meant to be made of her own people, had criticised her and thrown away the key to the cell they'd locked her in until she'd come to their aid. When her wings had finally appeared, they'd been bronze and glass. The reason was because she wasn't a full Creature. Instead, she was part Monster, part Geminis – a Monster type that could burn, yet she had no red body, only smelt of smoke, with the power to move broken objects. Now she was on the hunt to find her would-be kidnapper to discover the truth; why was she made and why was she wanted?

She'd already been through so much. But she'd survived. She would continue on, she just had to believe in herself that she could. If she believed herself to be a Creature, and then part Monster, she could indeed believe herself strong enough to find the truth.

Opening her eyes again, Morpheus smiled down upon her like the sun. They nodded as a portal came into existence beside them. Twisting, Morpheus spun them towards it and together stepped through.

The other side looked no different to the first.

The docks, cargo, and seagulls were still there. If Natalia only blinked, she would've seen nothing new. Except she did blink. And the differences smacked her in the face.

Mayer, face covered by the hood up – assuming it was him under there – bent over on the ground, wheezing. His body convulsed, and a spray of ash flung from his mouth followed by several drops of blood. Natalia gagged right as the figure fell to their knees.

"Magic that is not your own is not meant to be used light-heartedly or so flippantly," Morpheus told her when she gagged again.

"What?" she squeezed out.

"Your friend here uses magic that is not born from them." Morpheus nodded at the figure who had begun to groan. "Magic knows when it's used by someone else than the one who made it. Do not ask me how for I do not know. Only the Gods hold that answer and we cannot speak to them. But as a price for its use, black ash is left behind. Some magic will leave a residue that's painless and harmless. Other times..." they drifted off, pointing at the perfect example before them.

"So the magic isn't his?"

"That is what the ash is telling us."

"Can some of it be his?"

"It might."

"Then where did the rest come from?"

"Gold has borrowed magic before," Morpheus said instead of answering.

"I've never seen these kinds of effects before. Why? Is Gold getting better consequences?" She didn't know why her next question popped into her mind, but she asked it, sensing that it was somehow important. "Does it matter if the magic is given to another to use or not? Because I know Gold's was gifted. What if it was stolen instead?"

Morpheus remained silent and Natalia had no real conclusion to draw on her own. She simply continued to watch as the hooded figure pitched forwards and spewed some more. She grimaced and touched her earrings while willing herself not to feel sympathy.

Had any of the magic that'd been used on me been his? If not, where did it come from?

The figure heaved more black ash and tipped onto their back. Somehow, the hood continued to cover their face. With all the other horrible things done, Natalia didn't want to know how they'd come by magic that potentially wasn't their own.

"I will come for you," the figure said suddenly. Natalia's heart stopped and restarted with a heavy thump. But the figure never once turned to her.

Of course he wouldn't, she chastised herself. To him, right now, I'm not here. I don't exist. I'm just a ghost.

"I will," the figure continued. "I will take more magic, all of it, if I must. You are important." He grunted and sat up, coughing. "Not just to me. But for what you can do to and for the worlds."

The scene vanished upon Natalia's gasp.

She whirled on Morpheus. They were back in their space, the white bed floating on a sea of crimson. Morpheus' red hair was fading, iridescence taking its place – something Natalia hadn't seen on them since they first met.

"Worlds," she hissed.

They scowled. "Now it's my turn to ask. What?"

"Worlds," she repeated. Morpheus' eyebrows quirked. "The figure, he said worlds. He said he will have me for what I can do to and for the worlds.

It was pluralised."

"Pluralised," Morpheus nodded. "Indeed it was." They said it in a way that suggested they'd just heard it for themselves.

Natalia started pacing. She dug her fingers into her hair, tugging slightly. What was Mayer planning? She was certain his word choice hadn't been a mistake. Nothing he did ever seemed like a mistake. So what did he mean? How could Natalia contribute to his plans? What worlds was he even talking about?

"I don't like this," she stressed.

"I can understand that," Morpheus agreed. A whirling portal full of darkness formed in front of them then. Morpheus motioned to it. "Here we are. One last one."

"The last one?" Natalia blinked in surprised. She thought these trips would never end, and she felt like there were still so many questions that needed answering.

"Sometimes a journey ends without a full conclusion and the rest waits on the other side of that ending." Morpheus took Natalia's hand and wrapped it through their arm. "You always knew this path would lead somewhere."

And yet she'd never expected it to actually come.

"We are wasting precious seconds dallying and time waits for nothing," they continued. "Be strong."

Time waits for nothing, Natalia thought. Letting go of her hair, she touched her star earrings instead. And be strong? She had this faint feeling that Morpheus wasn't just talking about the here and now anymore. The paths here were meant to stop, but now the end seemed to have rushed up to meet them.

Had they run out of time here because she had now run out of time in life?

Mayer.

If he was growing in power, and obsession, how close was he? Is that what Morpheus meant? Mayer himself had promised that he was coming, was he here now?

The end was upon them. The fight was coming.

Her brain snapped into focus when screams sounded from the other side of the portal. Had Morpheus been distracting her or had she done that to herself? Either way, it was too late. Her feet crossed the threshold.

Archie stroked his son's soft cheek, and stepped into Tony's house behind Peri. They were led through to the cosy living room. Archie stared at it. He wanted a house like this. Maybe not one that was so tired and unchanged, but one that felt homely.

"How can I help?" Tony asked, taking a seat.

Peri sat beside him, perching on the arm of the sofa. "We wanted to ask you something."

Edmund yawned and Archie tucked him against his chest. "Something important."

"It's about Edmund," Peri added.

Archie glanced down at Edmund. Little guppy's tiny fist had wrapped around Archie's t-shirt, holding him close. He smelt of baby powder and clean laundry. He was precious and small and just the best. And Archie loved him, probably more than he loved Peri, and he knew she felt the same.

"Is he ok?" Tony asked. Archie caught him frowning in concern.

"He's fine," Archie promised, smiling.

"Then how can I help?"

Archie glanced at Peri who took over. "You know how our lives work," she said plainly. "They aren't easy and there are definitely no guarantees in regards to our safety."

Tony gulped. "I do know that, yes."

"Then you also know people sometimes get left behind." Archie watched as Peri's eyes watered, but she didn't ask for him to take over. She persevered. "We don't know what's going to happen with this coming war," she said. "But we don't want our baby to be left alone in this world. We want him to be cared for and loved no matter what."

Tony blinked. "Wait. You're both going to be fighting?"

"We are," Archie answered, hugging Edmund closer. "To protect the world and him."

"So, you're—"

"We're asking if you'd be Edmund's godparent."

The words came out of Archie and Peri's mouth together. They looked to one another. Edmund wiggled in Archie's arms and he patted his back protectively.

Tony shifted. "What about your parents?"

"Mine are out of the question," Peri answered adamantly, looking back at Tony again.

Archie began to rock. "My parents will be fighting with us. It's our duty, to the end."

"We know Edmund would be safe with you," Peri told Tony. She took his hand in her own. "We know you'd love him and raise him well. Just like you did for Natalia. We trust you enough to care for him no matter what happens. You'd give him a great life, a Human *and* Creature life."

Archie carefully stood and walked over to Tony, whose mouth gaped wide. He passed baby Edmund over, and he instantly curled into Tony's chest as he had done with Archie.

"*He* trusts you already," Archie said, smiling. "And, like we said, we do too."

"What about you? Why doesn't one of you stay with him?"

"We're fighting *for* our son."

A tear slipped down Tony's cheek. "Is this really what you want?"

Peri nodded. "It is."

"You already love him like your own," Archie told him, knowing the truth of that. He'd watched the few times Edmund had been passed to Tony, and how they'd interacted. It had been endearing and sweet every time.

"I do," Tony agreed. "If this is what you want, then it would be my honour."

Peri leaned and kissed his cheek. "We *knew* you'd say yes." Tony laughed. "We know kindness and love when we see it."

Tony's face shifted and he pointed with his free hand. "Don't you go getting yourselves hurt on purpose now though," he warned. "This isn't a get out of jail free card."

Archie raised his hands in surrender. "Yes sir!"

"But you'll still look after him on the weekends and have him for sleepovers, yeah?" Peri joked, all signs of tears gone.

Tony smiled. "It would be my honour."

Archie kissed the top of Peri's head and they settled into a gentle, jovial, conversation about nothing specific.

A weight lifted off Archie's shoulders. He hadn't wanted to hear Peri's idea at first, but he realised how much it made sense – their lives really were unpredictable at the best of times and this was something *new*. It was a worst case plan, but at least one was in place, because Peri was right. They didn't know what this war was going to bring.

But whatever was coming, the worst would *not* happen because, no matter what, Edmund would be safe.

Jasper watched his father instead of the door, evaluating the lack of surprise on his face and what it meant. He'd been back from Atlantis since baby Edmund had been born, though still had business to keep up with and so had mostly kept to himself in his office.

Evangeline came into view once the gap was wide enough. Jasper had only ever seen her in dresses before, but today she was in all black with knives at her hips.

"Welcome," his father said, stepping away.

"I may not be *all* Vampire, there is Witch blood in me too," she tipped forwards on her toes, "but I do still like to be asked inside. For politeness."

"Enter!" Jasper declared with a sweeping bow.

Evangeline laughed as she stepped in, offering her own head bow. "Thank you."

Jasper's father shut the door slowly. "Jasper, why are you in the hall?" he asked.

Jasper shrugged. "I heard the door and came to see who it was. You just happened to beat me here."

Cutting off Jasper's father before he could reply, Evangeline said, "I have come to help."

"Help?" Jasper's father questioned.

Jasper raised an eyebrow. "Are we expecting trouble?"

"Some," she nodded. "Gold told me to prepare, said he saw it in a Crystal." Her eyes shuttered a shade darker. "We have known trouble to be on the horizon for some time. It was only a matter of waiting. But it seems the wait is coming to an end. *Very* soon."

"Is Gold coming to help?" Jasper searched around. If Gold had seen trouble, as much as they all suspected but never said, then surely it was to be all hands on deck.

"He will," she assured "He must do something first."

"Did Gold see how far out this fight was?" his father asked, taking control of the conversation again as he looked down at his suit. Jasper scoffed- a suit wouldn't fare well in a fight.

"It's coming to our shores," she told him cryptically.

"Yes, but when? I need to gather everyone, to make sure they're either ready or hidden." He turned but stopped half-way. "This is about Natalia, isn't it?"

Jasper's heart jumped into his throat. Static filled the air with a hazy fuzz. His palms grew sweaty and there was an itchiness to the bottom of his feet suddenly.

He wanted Evangeline to deny it, but she nodded. "The one who wants her promised he would come," she said. "And he is. That is who Gold saw. The next storm on the horizon will be him. I would say we have days at best."

Jasper's father blanched. "*Days?*"

"That's fucking it?" Jasper cried, looking between his father and his distant descendant.

"I can't prepare everyone in days!" Jasper had never heard his father shriek that way before.

Evangeline drew closer. "And I have come to help with that too," she said. "I will protect you and fight alongside you." She withdrew to look at them both. "We Darby's are one of the few oldest Creature families. We've been fighting against Monsters since the start and we want to be following our Purpose to the bitter end. All of us know, or have known, love. And that's what we desire to protect most of all. I may not know you, but you are my blood, my life. My *family.* So I wish to protect you all and to see you live."

Jasper's heart swelled. Here was this woman, so boldly declaring her life to secure what was hers long ago and wanting it to be again. Jasper smiled at her, hoping that said enough.

But he couldn't help thinking about her words. *Days.* That was all they had now. There were only hours left for them to tie up whatever ends they could. There were only minutes left to prepare. There were only seconds left until Hell arrived for them all, but it was falling specifically for Natalia.

The handprint made of blood was drying on the Atlantis barrier.

Natalia sneered at it, disgust bubbling in her stomach, as she remembered the first time she'd seen it – in Jasper's arms as they moved through the nearby streets. Her eyes had been mostly shut then, exhaustion wearing her thin, but she'd caught sight of the blood. Before, she thought maybe she'd dreamt it. Now, she could see the bold redness.

The streets whizzing by demanded Natalia's attention. She turned to Morpheus, who sashayed away with their new-found black skirt and skimpy top tucked inside the waist. Natalia huffed and followed.

They started walking through the scenario as it played out.

Just like before, the ground shook and people screamed. The first time this happened, Natalia had been locked away, hidden underground like some heinous Government secret. In truth, she was, only they didn't know it.

A roaring Calefaction bounded round the corner. It skidded along the smooth floor as its large legs fumbled the manoeuvre through the narrow space. Natalia's first instinct was to duck and hide. Her second was to fight.

Morpheus gripped onto her arm with enough force to stop her from doing either.

"We are not here to chase pests," Morpheus said, though a hint of mischief had entered their hazel eyes. "They can wait a few more days."

The Calefaction skipped away, rounding another corner.

"They can," she agreed loosely. "But what are we here to see?"

Morpheus lifted Natalia's arm and pointed with it, hinting at a nearby building of white and gold. Natalia wiggled free and walked right to it.

The building looked like a temple. Natalia scowled at it. She couldn't remember seeing it before. There was no memory of phoenix statues, of the golden leaf design that crawled up the side of the building instead of green vines, or even the five steps that led up to any of that.

"What is this place?" she asked quietly.

"Atlantis," Morpheus answered. "The true extent of it." They flung their arms wide.

From where they stood, they could see look down upon Atlantis. Natalia hadn't even realised she stood on a hill. But as she looked, the temple on her right, she spotted the long centre road that trailed right through the city and out towards the distant horizon. Mini roads broke from the main one, splintering towards houses and shops and other buildings that looked similar.

Natalia even spied the Council building down below – she'd only been there once and never wanted to go again.

Turning her head, she caught the waves of the endless sea she'd been warned about, the one that was trapped here as much as the land. Atlantis existed in a realm of its own, outside of everywhere else, but inside the same Veil as Earth, along with the homelands of Fairies. Merfolk, however, could use that sea to travel in, like a portal, to other bodies of water this side of the Veil.

"You will never have the piece!"

Eight hooded figures stepped out of the temple. Seven wore white. Natalia recognised the Council instantly. But the final figure was in black, gold markings lining their cloak.

"Why gold markings?" she whispered to Morpheus, stepping to their side again.

Morpheus shushed her and she rolled her eyes.

"It's one of the few things I need!" The black-cloaked figure cried. "And I will have it."

"Need we say again?" One of the white figures said snootily. "You will not have it. Not now, not ever. Never in our lifetime."

Natalia wanted to scream at the Council for that, despite the deep running hatred she had. How could they not see what would come next?

As the black-cloaked figure raised their hands, sleeves slipping down arms to reveal thin, pale wrists and bony fingers, an almighty cracking sound came from the ground. The figure jolted before taking off in a sprint. Natalia jumped to action, following the figure immediately.

The black and gold figure leaped over the side of the hill without fear. Natalia gasped and leaned over the edge carefully. The figure landed as if they'd simply walked down a single step. Near them, the ground yawned open.

And she saw herself crawl out.

She was so close to herself, and the hooded figure, in that moment, had been a breath away too. However, the figure rushed by as if they didn't even know who Natalia was.

Natalia watched as her past self pulled Kiva out of the hole she remembered creating with her Fairy dust. They'd been trapped beneath the Council building, in cells made of stone and immobilized by magic, for being supposed criminals. Natalia had barely thought in the moment, but could see how close the roof had been to collapsing in on them.

Fires began to burn in the distance and Natalia could remember the heat of it.

She gulped and backed away from the edge of the hill. Morpheus studied the figures in white. They were useless, silently turning in circles with their arms outstretched. No wonder Natalia had shouted at them when they'd finally arrived to help the citizens. She wanted to do it again. They'd just lost a criminal and weren't bothering to chase them, nor did they seemed entirely stressed that their city was alight.

Eventually, one broke the cycle and moved, and the rest fell in line. But Natalia was no longer interested in their idiocy.

Morpheus hummed and Natalia looked at them but the scene shifted to one without anything but faintest of light.

A Shadow sprang up in front of Natalia.

She yelped and dived backwards. Morpheus caught her with a smirk, so she pulled herself away. The Shadow, as she should've known by now, paid her no mind and went through her like she was made of air.

"My Pet," came that all too familiar, tip-of-the-tongue voice. It sounded even clearer here and a face was beginning to form yet she couldn't quite form an image.

The Shadow bowed, but it didn't look like respect.

"I need you to keep watch," that voice said. The body that accompanied it stepped up from the darkest part of the shadows. "I need you to follow her. Do not attack. I will know if you do," they warned gruffly. "There will be a time when we can enter the fray. The magic will be broken around her and she will be the one to break it."

Natalia's gaze shot to Morpheus, but she only found empty air as her body lifted from the dream.

Natalia groaned, lifting her head off the pillow. She rubbed at her eyes and tried to adjust herself. As she did, she sensed something was *wrong.*

Suddenly, a hand clamped over her mouth. Her eyes rushed around the room in search of help. But she was alone and without any aid. Or, at least, she *should've* been alone.

Her unwanted bedroom mate definitely wasn't Jasper. She knew it wasn't even any of the others either.

"Will you keep quiet?" the person asked. "I promise I'll explain."

Natalia nodded, only because they had their hand tightly over her mouth.

The person slipped their hand away, trusting her to not cry out or try to bite them. She wasn't sure if it was the look in their eyes or their eyes themselves – they were grey – that made her feel that she'd made the right decision in not tricking them.

In fact, the more she looked at them, the more they seemed familiar.

Their hair was sharp, short, and black, with a white stripe in the only curl they wore against their forehead. Their skin was pale but their lips were ruby, and their cheekbones were sharp as was the jaw. Even the suit – white shirt and navy trousers – appeared crisp.

"Do you see who I am yet?" they asked. "I always told you to look carefully with your eyes, Natalia. Look with them now. Look beyond the surface."

Looking at their eyes again, she realised they weren't just grey, but iridescent. It snapped together in her mind. "Morpheus." She whispered their name like it was a secret.

"In the flesh," they announced, opening their arms to show themselves off.

There were no layers, no fake skins to wear. This was Morpheus, in the flesh, all real and no manipulation.

Morpheus backed away, grinning from ear to ear, rather pleased. They backed up from her, sitting gracefully on the edge of the bed, one leg folded over the other with hands tucked on top of the knee. They didn't fit in with the rest of the room; both too old and too new for Natalia's personal areas, too pristine and otherworldly for a place so *Human* and messy.

"How are you here?" was her most pressing question. Then, "*why* are you here?"

"I need to be here," Morpheus said. Their voice was softer outside the realms of dreams, like silk over silk.

"Need to be? Isn't that a little strong?"

"No," they argued. "With Hell bringing itself, I came for you and another."

Natalia felt small despite all the room she had. "Why me?"

"Because *he* is more dangerous than we ever thought. You saw him in many states. Tell me you didn't sense danger. Lie to me about it."

She glanced down at her bare legs. "I can't."

"He is doing nothing good and wants to break the walls for himself."

"Break the walls? What do you mean? Morpheus, are you feeling ok?"

They went on, ignoring her questions. "There have been whisperings, between Monsters. I hear them and I can sense what they do. Bad tidings are coming."

Thankfully, Natalia was freed from Morpheus' ramblings when the doorbell rang.

She threw on some clothes and ran down the stairs to catch it, but as she grabbed the handle, Morpheus' hand came down on hers. "Natalia," they whispered. "You need to be careful."

At that, she could agree. If Morpheus was here, things were bad.

And although his ramblings sounded like just that, he'd mentioned something about bad tidings...

"I know," she said. "I will be."

Morpheus shook their head. "I will wait for you in my realm and will return here when you do."

They retreated and she opened the door. Jasper's beaming smile met her and she gaped, having completely forgotten that it was already nearly the middle of October.

Aero spied his drink suspiciously. "Bubble tea?"

Zoe couldn't help the laugh that slipped out. "It's sweet," she promised. "Just make sure you chew!"

"There should be no chewing tea." He grimaced and tried anyway. He remembered to chew, at least, and then swallowed almost a little dramatically. "Not bad," he decided. "I'd still prefer normal tea."

Zoe laughed again and sipped her drink. They walked along the beach front, winds blowing at them. Summer seemed to have lasted an age on Venderly this year, so it was hard to see the Island change into autumn. As they aimlessly wandered, Zoe grew curious and wondered if Aero would be staying to change into winter. He'd told her that the Council had said he could stay as long as he was needed. But what did that mean?

She smiled when he glanced over at her. Was there a way to make his time here last longer? She enjoyed his company, enjoyed *him*. She abruptly turned her gaze away, self-conscious. What if he didn't enjoy her company?

"Oh!" Zoe squeaked, spotting another seaside stall. "You need to try these too! I bet you don't have them back in Atlantis."

Zoe rushed up to the next stand, leaving Aero with their teas, and returned to him a few moments later. The white bag in her hand held some of the best treats, arguably the best doughnuts *ever*, in her opinion. She always used to beg her brother to get some so they could share every time they passed this stall.

"What did you procure?" Aero asked, looking at her and not the bag.

"Procure?" she mocked. "You need t' get a new dictionary."

"Acquire?" he tried again.

She scoffed. "Not much better, but it'll do." She lifted the bag to his nose and heard him take in a deep breath. "Welcome to the sweet world of fresh donuts, made by Baba herself. It's batter and sugar and warmth tenderly made."

He squinted at the bag. "Do they have healing properties?"

"The power to heal your soul."

She offered the bag and he took one, pinching it between his forefinger and thumb like it was a bug. He carefully took a nibble. When it didn't bite back, he took an actual bite. Zoe took out her own doughnut and bit into the sugary goodness. She almost groaned. Her mum had always been the one to say these treats had a soul-healing ability and Zoe couldn't disagree. Every time she ate one, it was like a whole year had been added to her life.

Out of the six she bought, she ate two. Mainly because Aero couldn't get enough after the first. She envied him. Two was normally her limit before she felt queasy.

They continued down the path, minding their own business compared to the onlookers and other walkers. As they went, Zoe could almost think of Aero as Human. He appeared like one, no super-speed or fangs in sight.

Aero licked his lips to clear them of sugar and she had to look away, aware of how intensely she was watching, of how the action reminded her of their kiss.

Weeks had passed since. Neither of them had mentioned it

but they both kept meeting up, mostly by accident; Zoe kept finding Aero just wandering the streets and they ended up doing something because of it. Since that first kiss, they'd shared a few more, nothing too *forward* – he was brought up in a different time with different rules, which Zoe respected – but still, there were brief moments.

Nothing more had happened with Alex since that one *very intimate* moment they'd shared. Zoe didn't know where they stood. They'd had sex, for goodness sake. It had been a spur of the moment thing, a desperate need in her to feel something other than hurt, but she did also have other feelings. Maybe Alex simply didn't. Maybe that was that.

Zoe craved a connection with someone, a rich feeling with another person. She thought she was getting that with Alex. But Aero also appeared in her mind when she thought about it. Was it possible to like more than one person at a time?

She groaned inwardly. They just *both* happened to be Creatures, to make things more difficult.

Zoe had a sneaking suspicion, one that had been growing from a quiet whisper, that her life wouldn't be going back to where it had been before.

Natalia wiped the tears from her eyes. Jasper held her other gloved hand strongly in his.

Light and fluffy snowflakes fell upon the streets of Russia. Jasper swung her around inside the snow at one point, only stopping when her heeled boots slipped and she nearly fell.

Back in their hotel room, a traditional log fire brewed in the corner. Natalia removed her gloves, shrugged out of her coat, and bent to warm her hands. Thankfully she didn't feel too cold. Probably because Jasper had placed a protection spell over her for this trip, and it trailed her skin like a bubble of soft heat.

The ballet had been everything she thought it would be. It had been better than a dream. The lead had danced like she was made for the part, a beautiful chemistry between art and artist. The music had bellowed around the stadium. And, best of all, she hadn't once had to elbow Jasper to wake up.

Tonight, she'd been given the single best gift; to be able to ignore the world crashing around her.

Jasper's body pressed up behind hers, his hands snaking around her waist. She straightened up at his touch, flattening against him. "Do you miss it?" he asked.

"The ballet? Sometimes," she admitted. "I miss the high of executing a twirl or lift that looks effortless to everyone else but took years of training. I miss performing. I miss being part of a group." She sighed heavily. "But I don't miss the brutal competition between dancers or the damaged feet and ankles, or even the long rehearsal hours and barely having anything to eat."

"So, you're not thinking about going back?"

Natalia shifted round in his arms, putting her hands to his chest. "I think I'll stick to Monster fighting, until I find something more exciting."

"Oh?" The firelight cast his smirk red and gold. "What're you thinking you'll do?"

"Cow wrangling."

That earned a laugh. "Cow wrangling? Interesting."

"I've wrangled a Calefaction. How hard could a cow be?" She pushed herself onto tip-toes, inching her face closer to his. "Thank you for tonight."

"You're more than welcome, you know that." He kissed the tip of her nose.

Pressing her lips to his, she could feel the cold still on him. His hands rubbed against her sides, wrinkling her purple dress – the one that had meant to be for their first date.

Abruptly, she turned from hum and laughed when his hands went still. She moved aside her hair to show the long zip at the back, one the one she'd struggled to do up – a coat-hanger had been involved. Jasper's hands pulled on the zipper slowly. At halfway, he kissed the back of her neck, drawing out a surprised gasp. He then continued, his mouth following his hands down her spine until both stopped together.

The dress fell away and Natalia shivered. Jasper brought her back to him, touching her waist and then her chest, his lips leaving goosebumps along her shoulders.

In a sudden burst, her wings flew free.

Jasper had jumped away at the obstruction; she knew because of the lack of contact, and she began to miss it. She started to turn and face him, and went to tuck her wings away again, but Jasper stopped her, placing his hands on her hips.

"Don't," he whispered from behind her, somehow managing to lean into her despite the barrier. "You see all of me all the time. I want to see all of you."

Just like that, Natalia relaxed. His hands stroked the glass of her wings, careful in case they broke though Natalia knew they wouldn't. She shivered or sighed as he caressed her. When he somehow kissed right between her shoulder blades, she groaned unexpectedly.

Not wanting him to feel left out, she forced her wings back inside of her and spun round. She pushed him onto the small loveseat at the end of their bed and sat on his lap. She ran her hands from his arms to his chest to his neck. Her fingers ended up in his hair as they kissed, pulling through it with need. His hands gripped onto her thighs, clawing at the bare skin.

Somewhere between kisses, Natalia undid his trousers and Jasper undid her bra, throwing it aside. His hands touched and pulled and gripped every way she wanted. She ran one hand down his stomach, passing under herself, and inside his trousers. When he gasped against her mouth, she kissed him more fiercely and kept on moving against him.

"Natalia," he breathed against her neck in between slow pecks.

"I love you," she told him, announcing each word with her whole heart. She was no longer scared to admit it. She'd known for a long time. Her heart was hers to give away, and she wanted Jasper to have it.

Without words, he hoisted her up and walked round to the bed, laying her down. He kicked off his trousers and boxers, and pulled her legs apart. He climbed over her, coming to cradle her head in one hand and drew circles into her hip with the other, drawing closer and closer to her centre with each repetition.

"Do you want this?" he whispered, nipping at her ear.

"Did you bring protection?" she asked back.

He waved a small packet in front of her face and tore the corner off with his teeth, spitting the tiny piece somewhere they'd find later. He had to pull away from her and sit up to cover himself. When he was done, she met him halfway. She grabbed the back of his neck with one hand and pulled him down, kissing him fully and deeply, touching him again with her free hand, which earned a heavy moan.

"Say it again. Tell me you love me," he pleaded between breaths. "Because I love you, Natalia."

She smiled up at him, staring past the freckles to see that *he*, in his entirety, was the real constellation and the only one she ever wanted to look at again. "I love you, Jasper Darby."

His smile burned as he brought his mouth back to hers.

That night, fire in the corner continued to blaze, but it didn't match how bright they shone.

23
Two Paths Ahead

"You'll miss the film!"

Natalia bounded down the stairs. Her slippers slid around on her feet so much she had to be careful to not accidently fling one at Jasper who waited at the bottom. She watched him shake his head at the sight of her bright yellow onesie.

"Dressing as a Minion for the occasion, are we?" he teased.

"At least I dress up," she said, pointing to his boring black tracksuit bottoms and grey t-shirt. "And this isn't a fashion contest."

Jasper grinned. "Everything's a contest."

Katherine poked her head out from the living room. Her hair was bundled up somehow and her make-up was missing, making her look entirely different. "The opening credits are already rolling," she told them. "So get your arses in here!"

"Milady," Jasper mocked, bowing and holding out his hand.

Natalia swatted it and led on, looking back with a winning smile.

Over the past week, Natalia and her dad had spent time beginning the transformation of the living room. They both knew it was about time to start refurbishing it.

The peeled wallpaper was gone, replaced with simple dark orange paint on two walls with the others white. A golden mirror hung on one of the white walls, and three white floating shelves decorated an orange. A rather large potted plant rested in the corner of the room while a large light grey corner sofa sat opposite the TV. The fluffiest white rug outlined the carpet and a light grey bean-bag was snuggled in a corner.

For the last two Fridays, everyone had come together to watch a film. This week was Noah's choice, so of course it was something Marvel – Natalia knew it was the new Avengers: Endgame.

She slid onto the floor beside her best friend, propping her back against the sofa. Her dad and Katherine were squished together on the sofa, with Sarah and James beside them. Archie, Alex, and Peri all occupied the other half of the sofa. Baby Edmund had his own personal crib here – her dad said it had been hers once – and he was asleep inside it peacefully. Kiva was sprawled out on the floor on her stomach, legs twisting in the air.

Jasper dropped into the beanbag on the other side of Noah. Natalia half-climbed over Noah to kick the beanbag, trying to kick Jasper out, and he stuck his middle finger up at her with a grin when she didn't succeed. Noah laughed.

"I've got popcorn!" Zoe cried, coming into the room. She had managed to carry through three large bowls of the stuff and passed them out. It smelt *amazing*, so sweet and buttery.

The film rolled through without anyone getting up. No one dared. Natalia founding herself gawping with each new scene, unable to assess what she was seeing.

When the credits began rolling, the screen suddenly went blank. Noah was the first to jump and run to it. He looked helpless, but when the rumble of thunder came everyone sighed. It was just another Island storm, one that was washing out the night.

"Are you all camping here tonight?" Natalia's dad asked, standing. He flicked on a nearby battery powered wall light – they were planning on installing a few over the house for exactly this reason.

"I am!" Noah announced immediately.

"Same," came Zoe and Jasper.

"Three," added Alex.

"Six," Peri said.

"Seven!" Kiva half-yelled.

"I think we might make our way home," James answered politely.

"I don't blame you," Natalia's dad said. "You'll be the ones with a silent house for a change."

Sarah sighed blissfully. "I could take a bath in peace."

"And in complete darkness," Jasper said, shoving popcorn into his mouth.

Sarah bent forwards and pinched the back of his neck. "*Peace and quiet*," she emphasised. "We might even go wild and change the locks."

"Those idiots have *magic* to get back in with," Alex pointed out, indicating to her brothers.

"Oh, we'd barricade the house."

"Are you sure you'll manage without us?" Archie asked. "You won't suffer?"

James nodded. "I'm sure we'll be fine."

Sarah's smile was motherly, sweet and daring. "You're more than welcome to come home with us if you're concerned about our welfare."

Peri pointed to her sleeping baby. "He's already asleep. We wouldn't want to disturb him."

James looked at Natalia's dad. "Are you alright with them all staying?"

"They'll be no trouble," he promised.

"Just perfect," Archie said, fluttering his eyelids.

"No devils to be found," Peri said.

"Little Angels," Jasper agreed.

Sarah raised her eyebrows. "Little Angels?" she questioned, and then shook her head. "Just remember. If *any* of you get scared of the dark, you can't ring us and we won't answer if you can."

The group laughed and the adults all walked out.

Another rumble of thunder from above had everyone twitch. Natalia felt the hairs on her body stand to attention. Strangely, she remembered her eighteenth birthday and how the thunder then had really been a Scorpio. Now she thought she could tell the difference. This thunder was real. But there was still something in the air, a tangible tension.

"Who's sleeping where then, mini-adults?" Natalia's dad asked as he returned moments later.

All it took was one look and Natalia could answer. "We'll sleep here."

In minutes they had pillows, blankets, and make-shift light from their phones or battery lights. Peri had given Edmund a baby giraffe toy when he'd woken at the commotion, and it'd settled him right back down. Archie and Peri took the sofa, Kiva huddling at the end. Alex stole the space by the door, saying it was easier for her to sleep there, especially if she was a wolf; she shifted and started snoring in minutes, her back to the room. Noah collapsed next to Natalia, Zoe on her other side. Jasper stuck to being on the other side of Noah.

Natalia relaxed. She listened for each thunder crash, wondering what the sea was like tonight. She could imagine white foam and scrambled sand.

Eventually, she closed her eyes and couldn't remember falling asleep.

Natalia appeared at the docks, and frowned in confusion.

How long had she been asleep beforehand? She thought she wasn't supposed to have any more portal and dream journeys, yet here she was despite what Morpheus had said. Not only that, but she'd built a wall in her mind to make sure it wouldn't happen.

She walked beside the metal containers, stroking the side of one. At least, she attempted to. Her hand went through it.

Clanging metal made her pause.

Natalia turned her head in the direction of the noise. Her heart leapt. The hooded figure was hunched over like they'd been kicked in the stomach. But when they moved, Natalia could see they were bent over someone. Kei huddled on the ground before them.

"Yes, sir," she breathed out, sounding winded.

Natalia moved to see why the Monster sounded almost pained and saw that the figure was kneeling on Kei's chest. They were pressing her into the ground further each time she wiggled.

"My name is not to be spoken," the figure spat. "It is not a name that belongs in your mouth."

"Yes, Sir."

"I am to be nameless until I announce otherwise. From that moment it will be spoken by all of your kind, including you, and the generations after. When I am King."

"NO!" Natalia yelled to empty air.

The figure climbed off Kei and helped her to her feet. Natalia watched, blinking harshly, as the two embraced. When they pulled back, they seemed like nothing could come between them, like that moment had just been a small lesson and nothing more. But Natalia knew this arrangement had an end. Kei's end. And it was designed by the figure themselves.

The figure stepped away. "My Natalia will break you free," the figure said. "She can set you all free."

Nausea rose through Natalia and she wondered if she could be sick, even in this dream-land.

Kei dipped her head. "Yes, Sir."

"You must bring her to us so she can."

"Yes, Sir."

"She is one of you, after all."

Kei's glare shot to him and Natalia shivered. "She is?" Kei asked.

"She is. She is half Creature, half Monster. Fairy and Geminis in one body. But the soul does not fight itself. She is balanced." Natalia sucked in a breath. "That is how she will set you free, set us all free, under my reign."

"Of course, Sir, yes."

"Go and get her, Geminis. Go and bring our long lost love home."

A silent scream left Natalia's lips.

When she found the effort to stop, it was all gone. The scene had vanished. In its place was a bloody handprint looming over her like a letter written and signed from Hell itself. Only, it looked fresh.

She crept towards it, the urge to scream still close inside her lungs.

The handprint was red ruby and still dripping. Beside it, Natalia could see the actual disturbance it'd caused. She felt stupid. The handprint itself wasn't what they should've looked at. It was the shield around Atlantis itself.

Because the shield shimmered under the strain of losing a sizeable chunk.

That's how the Calefaction got in, she realised. The handprint was the how. It must've been some sort of spell, or spell-breaker if it ruined the barrier. The Calefaction would've forced its way through the hole made by the print.

Did that mean the handprint was his blood? How much more magic had he taken to pull this off? And for what?

If that was what his blood could do mixed with magic, what about hers?

She shuddered and stepped up. She didn't want to know what her blood could do with its combined abilities. Plus, she didn't have magic – her own or stolen from a Witch. It would probably do nothing. She hoped it would do nothing. But, she was wanted for something...

NO! She didn't want to think those thoughts. There was nothing in her blood and she would not be setting anyone free.

The ground began to shake beneath her feet. She rocked, her entire body jostling. Shouting erupted nearby, so close it sounded like someone was yelling into her ear personally.

"Natalia?"

"Natalia?"

She rubbed her groggy eyes at the sound of her name. Her brain slowly orientated.

The ground was shaking here, too.

She launched upright and found the room in chaos.

Alex, in wolf-form, was crouched at the end of the room, growling. Zoe was tucked behind Alex, but had her own knife drawn – did she carry a knife now or had she stolen it from the kitchen? Kiva looked like she was mid-shift, her skin changing to fur. Noah was in the far corner with Peri, using his body as if to shield her. Archie stood before them both. Jasper was in the centre of the room, eyes cast towards the ceiling.

Natalia stood, feeling ridiculous for being the last one to wake. Her cheeks flushed. "What's going on?" she asked.

"Shh," Zoe snapped.

"They might be able to hear," Archie explained nicely in a whisper.

"They?" Natalia whispered.

"I think you might have an infestation," Jasper said.

"I thought you said this house was protected?"

"It is. But it's like a layer over the house to protect what's inside. Think of cling-film."

"Which means," Archie continued when Jasper didn't, "that things can walk on the roof."

Natalia smoothed out her onesie as if that'd help the situation. "But nothing could even get into the garden last time."

Jasper turned his head to her, regret bare on his face. "I had to pull the spell back," he admitted. "It was starting to drain me. I had to pull back, keep some energy. That opened the garden up."

"We wouldn't be safe at all if you hadn't pulled back," she told him. If he had let the spell consume him, the protection would've snapped, breaking entirely.

"I need to get Edmund out of here," Peri whispered from behind Archie and Noah. "I *can't* have him near danger."

Archie turned to face her. "You need to go with him."

Natalia glanced away and caught everyone else doing the same. Somehow, Natalia understood their predicament. Even if all three of them went, they'd be leaving people behind. But Archie wasn't about to leave his siblings, and Peri wasn't about to leave him. And neither of them wanted to leave Edmund.

Natalia knew they'd asked her dad to be Edmund's godfather and he'd told her the reasons. It made sense. If anything happened, he would raise Edmund the same way he'd raised her, and she had to say that she turned out mostly alright - complicated internal things aside. Her dad could go with Edmund, that was what the whole arrangement was made for.

Thinking of her dad, she wondered where he was. Had he not heard the disturbance? What about Katherine?

Suddenly, Alex barked and sprinted from the room. Zoe cried out and stupidly followed. Natalia's attention flicked to Jasper and without another thought she set off after them. He caught her up at the back doors, his expression calm like he'd expected her to follow. They gave each other a lousy smile.

"There's no barrier out there," he reminded her.

"I know," she nodded. "I haven't forgotten."

"But have you considered what that means?"

"I'll be in trouble."

"More than the rest of us."

She slipped her hand into his. "I know."

"Natalia—"

Natalia grabbed his hand, cutting off his reply. This was her fight, as much as it had ever been. The Monsters were on the roof of her house. Nothing about this felt similar to the last attack, where the Monster had been ashed at the bottom of the garden. She knew one hundred percent, this time, they were here for her.

Jasper squeezed her fingers and they stepped out from the safety of the house together.

Outside was foggier than Natalia had ever seen it. It rolled across the land like thick arms with grabbing hands. Everywhere felt cold and as Natalia stepped into it, she realised how dense it was. She could barely see the grass.

Natalia grasped her blade and crept slowly though her garden. At her side, Jasper was blowing at the air, trying to clear it. Tiny sparks of pink burst from his fingers. The fog began to twist and shrink, lowering to rest against the ground at knee height. Things could still hide underneath if they were sneaky, but at least she could see ahead of her.

She wished she couldn't, almost opening her mouth to ask Jasper to raise the fog to cover her eyes.

Tens of Monsters were crawling or growling or dragging themselves around the garden. Natalia spun round. Five were littered along her roof and balcony by her bedroom. Her heart sank.

While they could now see the Monsters, the Monsters could also now see them.

Natalia tightened her grip on her blade's hilt, holding it out in warning. The Monsters around began to creep towards her, like her movement allowed theirs.

"I fear if you stop, they won't."

Natalia whirled and nearly stabbed Morpheus, just managing to reign in her instincts in time. They eyed the blade and pushed her hand away. Behind them was Gold, fangs elongated, and Evangeline, who rubbed her hands together.

A tiny Scorpio leapt from the fence. Evangeline caught it mid-air, trapping it in her white magic, and then slammed it into the ground until all it could do was twitch.

Apparently that was some sort of signal to the other Monsters because they started advancing.

"Leave, Natalia," Morpheus told her as they moved in front of her. "Get where it's safe and stay there."

Three different Monsters attacked at once. A Scorpio, larger than the last, swung its tail out so Morpheus and Natalia had to duck together. A Mitter erupted from the ground; Natalia would've fallen if Morpheus hadn't caught her. And a Chiksaaz floated along with its rows of yellow teeth exposed from within its flower-like head.

Morpheus gasped, clearly surprised, when Natalia dove round them. She thrusted her blade into the Scorpio, and it squealed before simmering to ash.

The Chiksaaz tilted its head, seemingly looking Natalia up and down. She remembered from the last time she met one that Chiksaaz only retaliated an attack and never instigated. If that was the case for the Monster type, why was this one even here?

The Monster chortled and flung its head to the side. Natalia followed its direction to see Morpheus somehow magically stretching out the Mitter's neck. It seemed Morpheus' powers, in this plane of existence, were different. Instead of *them* being able to shape-shift, they could instead make other things shift.

She faced the Chiksaaz again. "If you leave me," she whispered, "I'll leave you." The Monster closed its mouth a little. "I know you don't attack unless provoked. Neither do I."

The Chiksaaz laughed, fully shutting away its teeth. Natalia sighed when the Monster shuffled off like a leaf in the wind, rounding the house and disappearing.

Natalia's attention went back to the fog as she tried to steady her breathing. Her eyes roamed the chaos, and found Gold just as he sank his fangs into the side of a Monster she'd never seen before. In a single motion, Gold tore and the Monster's small head came away with one tug. Natalia had forgotten how strong and vicious Vampires could be and this was an ice-cold reminder.

Gold's mismatched glare snapped to her and she sucked in air. Black blood fell from his lips and down his chin, pooling somewhere within the endless fog below. Natalia gulped and backed up. This wasn't the Gold she knew. This wasn't some demure Creature. This was a Vampire that knew how to hunt and had an age of fighting behind them.

She took another step and crumbled, falling into the fog. Below the line, it was thicker than it appeared above. It threatened to choke her.

A tap on her shoulders forced her to inhale, the shock jolting her into action. She rolled to face an immense grin but the saddest icy-blue eyes she'd ever seen. The Monster tilted its head. It didn't reach out, and it didn't try to hurt her. It only watched.

"What are you?" she whispered. Within the fog, all other noise seemed to be washed away.

The Monster moved its jaw but it crunched half-way and became stuck. Natalia gasped and reached out, realising it was hurt. She pressed her hand to the bottom half of the jaw so the Monster wouldn't try and move it further, and cause itself more pain. The Monster's eyes lit up but not in a way that said it was going to attack. It was more like a look of appreciation. Mutual respect passed between them.

"Can you move?" she asked it.

"No," it managed to say sloppily.

She blinked, a little astonished. "You speak English."

"Some," it agreed.

"Am I hurting you?" she asked, her eyes flicking to where her hands cupped the Monster's jaw. "Do I need to move?"

"No."

She dared to look at its eyes, right as a droplet leaked from the left one. The Monster was *crying*. "Are you in pain?"

"Yes," it replied, hissing slightly.

"Is there anything I can do?"

"No."

Natalia's own eyes began to well. "I'm sorry."

"Not you," it said. "You didn't... Not you."

It tried to move its hand but seemingly couldn't, so Natalia shuffled closer to hold it with her free one instead. "Still, I'm sorry."

Natalia looked at the Monster, knowing it wouldn't attack her. Its hands were blue, as was its face, but its entire body was white fur. On top of the head was a single navy horn. From the left corner of the mouth, hanging from the gums, a tusk protruded.

Leaning closer, Natalia could see that it should've had two horns and two tusks, but it looked like one of each had been ripped out. How? What'd happened? Her eyes welled. This Monster seemed *gentle*. She didn't think it to be some trick. She didn't know why but she truly believed that this Monster would be gentle no matter what.

"Do you have a name?" she asked, peering into its cold eyes.

"No," it slurred. "We are Maddner."

"Your species type is a Maddner?"

"Yes. Your name?"

"Natalia. I'm Natalia, a Fairy and Geminis."

"Nata—"

Its jaw slackened in Natalia's hand. Desperately, she tried to hold it firmer as black blood began to trickle out the corner of its mouth. More tears threatened to drown her.

The Monster folded into blue ash.

Natalia wiped her eyes and sniffed before she clambered to her feet.

Hands touched down on her shoulders, and she startled. She peered up to watch Archie's eyes scan over her fiercely, zipping from side to side, checking over for any problems. Cautiously, he reached out and touched her cheek, wiping away her last tear with his thumb. She smiled weakly.

From behind him, a hoard of flying Monsters charged. Archie swung round, hands sparking with green magic. He twisted his magic into a sort of whip, knocking one Monster after the next out of the air.

Natalia turned in circles as Archie slashed. She could see Jasper working back to back with Morpheus like they were old friends. Gold shielded Zoe, though she stabbed the air wildly with her knife. Alex was somewhere beneath the fog, her small barks echoing every-so-often. Peri, the baby, and Noah were all thankfully absent. Natalia went to ask about them when Archie cut down three flyers at once. She threw her blade in response, slashing at one's centre as it crawled back onto its hind legs.

A heart-stopping scream from inside the house cut through the commotion.

Natalia looked to Archie but he was dealing with more flyers. Everyone else was busy. In fact, it looked like no one else had heard anything outside what they were dealing with. But Natalia had. So she picked up her blade and cautiously picked her way back to the house.

The house should've been secure. There was magic still, she could feel it like a hug. But why did she also have the feeling something had encroached, turning the warmth to ice?

Quietly, Natalia tip-toed inside. Her heart beat so fast she could hear the blood rush around in her ears. Her shoulder blades itched as her wings wished to be come out, but she wouldn't let them, not now.

"I can hear you, Natalia." The voice sounded unlike anyone she'd heard before, but is also overlapped with another. "Why don't you come out?"

Knowing her anonymity was gone, though still prepared to

attack, Natalia rounded into the living room. The baby was gone, leaving Peri free to hold her trident directly towards Noah.

Natalia scowled. "What's going on? Did you hear that—"

"Voice?" Noah answered. Only, it wasn't completely his voice speaking.

"How are you—"

"Doing that?" He finished again. "Well, Natalia. You see, I needed to find a way to you."

Natalia blinked. And all at once she knew that wasn't her best friend. "Get out of him!" she cried.

"I'm afraid I will not for now. This is the only way I can survive."

"I *will* hurt you," Peri warned.

Noah's body turned and stared with eyes that didn't entirely belong to him. "And risk hurting the innocent here? I don't think you will." Not caring that someone had a weapon to them, he turned back to Natalia. "See, with this magic here, I couldn't get close, but I needed to talk to you."

Mayer.

"Say my name," the voice hissed.

Natalia stiffened. "So it is you."

Noah's body spread its arms. "I am here," it said. "And I am here for you."

"I'm not going anywhere with you! Now get out of my friend!"

The head shook and then Noah's real voice came through. "Natalia?" She gasped but then the recognition of a friend slipped away. "Natalia," called the other voice, *Mayer's* voice.

"How are you controlling him?" Peri asked. She held onto her trident so tight, her knuckles were turning white.

"Magic, of course," he said, like it was obvious. "I needed a level of magic to combat yours. So I took over his body. His innocent soul and body allow us to pass through your wards, hiding mine inside."

Peri held her trident inches away from his back. "I thought we got rid of you?”

“Oh no. I just let you think that.”

“Princess!” Noah’s real voice called out.

“Please.” Natalia dared to move closer, holding out a hand. “Get out of him. Leave him alone. As you said, he’s an innocent. A Human.”

He raised his eyebrows. “So you’ll come with me?”

Natalia reached for her blade with her other hand. “Never.”

“Never say never, and be careful what you threaten.” Noah’s hand grabbed his own throat. “I may not be able to touch you, but I can still *hurt* you.”

Natalia showed both her hands in surrender. “Why are you here?” she asked as she desperately searched for a way through to Mayer without hurting Noah in the process.

“It is time.”

Peri scowled. “Time? Time for what?”

He ignored her. “It’s time you came with me, Natalia. Time you came and discovered what you were made for.”

Natalia blinked. *What I’m made for?* For months she’d been searching for that answer and it was the only one that kept evading her. She knew who she was now, just not why. But this couldn’t be the way she found out.

She shook her head. “I’m not going with you,” she said.

“Natalia!” Noah yelled.

“Shame,” the other voice replied. “I was hoping you’d make this easy.”

In one swift motion, Noah pulled out a knife from under his t-shirt and thrusted it into the space between his collarbones.

No one could stop him.

The body fell to the floor, gurgling and coughing. It was Noah’s eyes that searched the room, betrayal and sorrow written into the depths. Natalia’s vision blurred as Noah’s eyes rolled to the back of his head, one eye-lid drooping.

Natalia staggered a gasp.

All at once, the TV screen cracked and the new mirror shattered. The glass rose in the air. Peri took tiny steps away from the window as it began to bow. She made it to Natalia's shaking side as the glass blew in, scattering along the blood-soaked carpet. But those shards too entered the swirling mass that was forming. She stared at her best friend as her whirlwind built.

Noah was *gone*.

No, Natalia thought. *He's not just gone. He's dead.*

Dead.

The word was so final, so devastating. His life was gone. It's come to end at his own hands but not under his control. The weight of it crushed her more than any stone. Her knees buckled and Peri caught her before she landed.

She looked at his paling body hopelessly, waiting in vain to see his chest rise and fall. But it didn't. It never would again.

Noah, her best friend, was dead. He was never coming back.

And it was her fault.

Tears freely fell as red hot anger burned throughout her body. She ground her teeth. Her nostrils flared. The swirling mass she was creating grew even bigger with every new piece that broke away from the house at her command. Even her dust began to pick up and spiral, adding a bronze delicacy to the storm.

This was her life. Danger clung to her, and it fired back at any of those close by.

"Noah," she whispered.

Never again would she hear his laugh, listened as he called her "Princess". They'd never watch films together, share secrets, or have special birthdays. All they'd done, all they'd become, had been wiped from the board of life. His soul was forever lost.

The last thing he'd yelled had been her name and she'd done

nothing.

Her heart broke, and she knew the piece that came away would not be repairable.

The storm she'd made exploded, shattering and falling everywhere at once.

"And, just like that, the spell is broken."

Peri stiffened at Natalia's side. Through blurry eyes, she looked up to find why. A figure stood by the open window. Natalia tried to make a distinction, but both the light and her eyes couldn't reach beneath the hood they *still* wore. The mass of sharp shards passed by behind them, and they didn't seem too troubled by the sight of it.

"You allowed me in, Natalia," they said.

"Get out." She bared her teeth.

"Do you know what you've done? You broke the magic protecting you inside here."

The broken pieces she'd commanded rose once more, hanging like twinkling crystals of a chandelier. She realised all at once that, by letting her storm crash, she'd broken Jasper's spell on the house.

The figure took her silence as a chance to move closer and Peri shifted, but *their* hand touched Natalia's shoulder before she could be forced away. The hand moved up to the side of her face and then down to her neck, the thumb drawing one full circle on the skin. Natalia expected pressure, either of magic or pain, but surprisingly there wasn't any.

The figure held onto her, despite her obvious shaking. "Do you know who I am yet?"

"I don't *care* you are," she spat. "You just killed—"

"No one important."

"He was fucking important to me!"

In blind hatred, Natalia slashed out with her knife. Because the figure hadn't been expecting it, she managed to catch the side of their face. Red had been heavily drawn into the skin. But, from beneath the hood, Natalia could see a smirk.

And then they were running.

"Nat!" Peri gasped, dodging out of the way.

Natalia shook her head at her friend before taking off after the attacker.

If they were to be believed, and the spell around the house really was broken, that meant Monsters could come in. But she'd just let possibly the biggest Monster in herself.

"Natalia?" Jasper caught her arm as she flew out the door and spun her half back round with the momentum. Peri stepped silently out of the house behind them, face grim, trident high. "The spell—"

"Is broken," she finished. Jasper grimaced and that was all the confirmation Natalia needed to know it really was true. "It was me. He used me. He used *Noah*."

"What?"

"He never left Noah. He'd climbed inside his body, rooted himself there, and then killed him. He *killed him*, Jasper!"

"Noah's..."

"He's not coming back." More tears slid down her face and her head began to ache. "I need to get the bastard that did this. I need to *get him*." Jasper nodded, understanding.

Together they faced the oncoming swarm of Monsters. Natalia squeaked in surprise. Everyone was in some way cornered. The Monsters numbers were overwhelming. This didn't actually looking like a fight they could win.

Yelping suddenly, Evangeline pitched forwards.

Natalia slashed through a few Monsters to get to Evangeline, but still they kept coming like an endless wave. She managed to force a few back and in the seconds she had, blew out her cheeks, felt for her dust, and cast a shield around them.

Gold pulled Evangeline onto his lap. His fangs were still dripping but neither of them cared.

Evangeline touched Gold's face. Her hands stroked his cheek as if Gold was the one injured when really it was Evangeline who had a hole through her abdomen - black marks charred her dress and blood was pooling through. Natalia watched the wound, waited for it to close, but saw it wasn't healing.

"I'm glad you were my friend," Evangeline whispered, her voice quiet but calm.

"Evangeline the brave." Gold smiled weakly.

"I get to see—"

Evangeline took one shuddering gasp before collapsing, her head flopping backwards. For the first time, Natalia spotted two little black puncture marks on the woman's pale neck.

A strangled noise drew out from the back of Natalia's throat. In the span of minutes, she'd lost one Monster, then her best friend, and now another friend. They were all lost to a realm she couldn't follow them to. Her eyes burned again.

"She was brave," Gold muttered. He looked up at Natalia just as her tears began to fall. "You remind me of her, you know. You would both do anything for family. Your love for them has no end."

Natalia didn't know what to say.

Gold sighed and stood, wiping off his trousers. "Come," he said. "We have a fight to win."

How exactly they were going to win, she didn't know, but she released her shield all the same.

And that was when she spotted *him*. By the corner of her house, partially covered by the thick fog that was once again rising, stood the killer of innocents.

Like a bullet fired from a gun Natalia shot towards him.

When in range, she thrusted out her blade and pointing it at his neck.

"That cannot hurt me," he told her.

"It did before," she spat.

"I correct myself then. I should say that it will not hurt me *now*." He reached up, grasped the edge of the damned hood he hid beneath, and finally withdrew it. "Do you know who I am?"

Clarity smacked Natalia in the face.

This was Mayer, and he was exactly the same as the last time she'd seen him.

The dots in her mind connected. From the blue eyes to the light olive skin to the English accent. While he didn't wear a black suit or a purple iris anymore, she knew why he'd seemed familiar all those times.

This was the man she'd run into at the Flower Parade all those months ago in Atlantis. She'd even been thrown through his damned front window. But she'd also seen the hooded figure at the same time. So *Mayer* had never "just returned home from a trip". He'd been there the whole time, releasing a Calefaction into the city so he could go and steal something from the Council. The suit and flower, and story, had just been a back-up escape plan.

"I crashed into your house," she whispered.

He nodded. "And I believe you *do* know my name now, too."

Her face contorted. "I refuse to *ever* say it." Like it was nothing, he shrugged. But she cared. "You're a *snake*," she hissed.

He raised his eyebrows, and she could see how young he was really, no more than a few years older than her. "You need to make a choice."

"Like fucking Hell!"

"More will *die!*" he threw back.

Mayer waved his hands and Natalia followed to where he pointed, and she grimaced.

Jasper and Archie were double-teaming quite a few Monsters but were only just managing to stay on their feet. Morpheus was with Kiva and Gold, but they'd sustained wounds that were bleeding through their shirt and down their forehead. Peri was alongside

Katherine, double water trouble. Aero and Alex tried to shield Zoe who attempted to creep away unnoticed. James and Sarah were criss-crossing their magic, interlocking it, though it was barely making headway through the Monster hoard.

Noah's already dead.

Where's my dad? she thought suddenly. *Did he take Edmund and hide?*

"Make it stop," Natalia breathed, watching as Kiva was pushed to the ground by six Monsters, howling in pain.

He shook his head in her peripheral. "Only you can do that."

"I don't have that power!"

"You do."

"How exactly do I possess it then?"

"All you have to do is choose."

"Choose?" she asked, almost choking on the word.

"You can come with me willingly or you can stay and watch your loved ones die, and *then* we'll take you by force."

She gripped the hand of her blade like a lifeline. "That's not much of a choice."

"Ah, but it still is one."

"*Fuck,*" she murmured.

"I have been watching you, you forget," he said, soothingly so. "You seek answers about how you came to be and why. I have those answers. You have some now but I have the rest."

Natalia's heart quaked in her chest. There wasn't a war-drum beat to it, but a soft thumping of despair.

I have those answers.

Her feet moved automatically.

Monsters moved out of her path. She hoped they didn't suddenly come to their own minds and aim again, and also didn't she want to think about why they'd stopped in the first place.

She grasped Jasper's wrist, making him turn to her. Several long cuts and bruises ran along his arms and face, but nothing appeared broken or beyond repair. He'd heal. He just might need a few candles and some space. But the same could not be said for her.

"Jasper," she whispered. "Do you trust me?"

"Yes." He surveyed the Monsters, then looked at her. "Natalia, what's going on?"

She gulped back the rising acid in her throat. "I need you to keep trusting me."

He couldn't reply as she kissed him. It was brief and she ached inside, wondering if he did too. Before he could hold her, before she changed her mind, she ran away.

Shouting rose up behind her as she reached Mayer. The shitty grin on his face was highlighted by the red stain of the scar she'd given him. Hopefully he wouldn't ever heal.

"Princess," he acknowledged. Oddly, it didn't sound mocking.

She shivered and her shoulder blades itched. "You promise to not hurt my friends and give me my answers? You'll call the Monsters off?"

"You could call them off."

"Promise me you will!"

Mayer tipped his head in a bow. "I promise to give you all you were meant to have and more."

A black convulsing portal that smelt of toffee apples whirled to life behind him. He indicated to it but she stole his hand, gripping it like a vice. She didn't trust him and wanted to keep him close, meaning they'd go together. He seemed more than happy by the gesture despite her nails digging in.

Her left foot stepped and then her right. Her weeping eyes caught on Jasper as he struggled to fight past the Monsters that had moved to block any path to Mayer and Natalia.

I love you, she thought, hoping he could hear though knowing he couldn't. *Please, trust me.*

The portal sucked her in, pulling her chest first while leaving her entire heart behind.

THE END OF BOOK TWO

Acknowledgements

Hannah. You are honestly my rock and were by my side for every step of this process, from the start to the end. Not once did you shy away from telling me I was being a twat or that I needed to change something because it didn't work or typed aggressively when I shuffled things around, but you also said when things were going right. You made this story alongside me, really. You are the kindest, least selfish, and generally funny fucking person ever. There is no escape, I'm sorry! Have the emotions! I love you and I couldn't ask for a better bestie. Cheers and here's to more chaotic messages mid-afternoon, mushrooms, and adventures – and Tony time.

Kirsten. Thank you for answering any stupid question I ever have, for helping me every step along the indie author path, for being so wonderful and supportive, and for being genuinely all over kind and lovely. Your support means everything and I'm so glad I found you, and that we've become friends. And yes, you may still have Jasper.

Alexandria. You are a damn star. Everything about you is just so *good*. Your support means everything, and all the little messages we share really cheer me up or make me laugh. You have been there for me through this journey – and through future ones too, I know it, I feel it. (just as I will always be there for you!) – and I'm glad we connected to be good friends.

Sydney. Once again, every word in this book belongs to you. You helped shape this story, gave it all the care and attention you could, and made the very best out of every spelling mistake or nonsense sentence there was. I wouldn't have gotten anywhere without your support either. Oh, and your comments are just top class, always. Thank you 333 pages over.

My mum and sister. The support you've given me has been incredible. The true wonders I've shared with you, and that you've shared back, has been great to have. It's made me feel like this really isn't a dream, that it's all real.

To the designers of this book. The beauty to be found in these pages is all because of you. You helped bring the magic to life, stole the stars from the heavens, and twirled the impossible into the possible.

Bookstagram friends. Thank you for everything you have become to me. Thank you for sharing my posts, writing reviews, messaging me, just all the wholesome goodness. I consider you all friends, very much so, and I can't wait to share more worlds with you all.

To Joe. A lot of the magic in this book is because of *you*. The kindness behind characters actions, the strength, the love and devotion, that all comes from you. You inspired that. Thank you for being who you are, for always joining my crazy train, for laughing and thinking I'm sometimes dumb but in a smart way, and loving my brain and just me in general. You are the best thing in my life. My brightest star.

To all. This isn't the end. There is one more book left in the STARLIGHT trilogy. This isn't a dream. It's happening, and it's coming. It's a world of stars out there and they're falling to you.

About the Author

LAUREN JADE is a writer from a seaside town in England. She loves writing and reading fantasy, but also sci-fi, dystopia, and occasionally crime/mystery. When she isn't writing, she can be found reading or talking on face-time with her best friend about future projects. Either that or she's watching Doctor Who, a Marvel/ Disney film, something fantastical with her mother, or something ghostly with her sister.

STARLIGHT is her debut novel and the first in a trilogy, and STARFALL is the sequel.